ALSO BY R E LEWIN

THE CHILDREN OF PISCES SERIES:

THE TWO PENDANTS

THE CRYSTAL EARRINGS

COMING SOON:

THE RETURN OF THALEN

"The start of the story is brilliant and really grabs you right from the get-go: it's pacy, dramatic and startling! If you like books that set in the normal world, but with a slight twist (like Phillip Pullman's Northern Lights trilogy), then this is the story for you. And there are more on the way!"

"My daughter read this book and literally couldn't put it down! In her words, 'This is better than Harry Potter!'"

Dream big, live bigger...

R E Lewin

THE CHILDREN
OF PISCES

THE CRYSTAL CUBE

THE CHILDREN OF PISCES

THE CRYSTAL CUBE

PART 3

R E Lewin

R E Lewin Publishing
Wallingford Road
Near Reading
RG8 0JD
Email: info@rachaelruthholistic.co.uk
Web: www.rachaelruthholistic.co.uk/mywriting
Twitter: @rachaelruthh
Tiktok: @relewin
Youtube: @rachaelruth

Paperback ISBN: 978-1-7394262-7-9
Hardback ISBN: 978-1-7394262-8-6

British Library Cataloguing in Publication Data.
A catalogue record for this book is available from the British Library.
Typeset in 11pt Minion Pro.

I dedicate this book to my children, Thomas and Olivia. For your brilliant imaginations, feedback and support. I love you more than words can say. And to Gracie.

To all the teenagers brave enough to be different.

*Hydrogen is a light, odourless gas, which,
given enough time, turns into people.*

– Edward Harrison

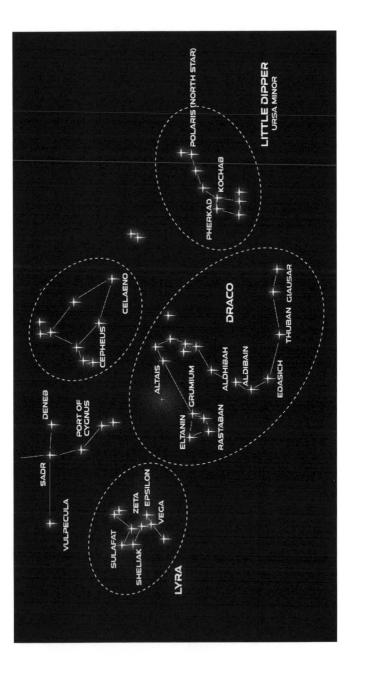

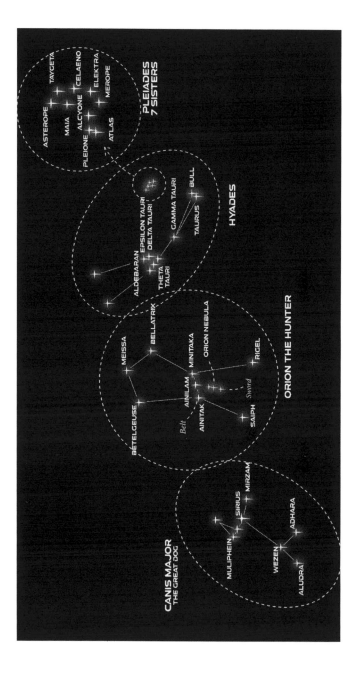

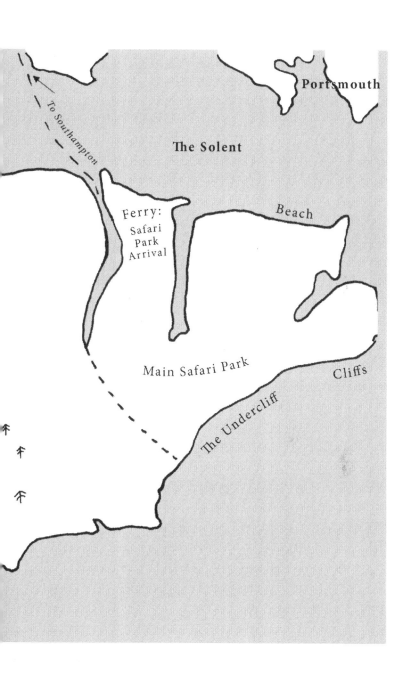

PROLOGUE

A MOTHER'S PROTECTION

WINTER 2057-2058, LONDON

Sarah stood on the bridge overlooking the river. She looked at her baby, awake now, quietly gazing up at her. His beautiful eyes so wise and powerful. She smiled down at him and felt his inner power. He was going to be an almighty warrior, that was for sure. A terrifying weapon in the wrong hands. He must be surrounded by good people. Sarah looked up at the sky, blinking as the rain fell onto her face, washing away the dirt and the tears. The morning sunshine wiped away, yet again, by the rain. It had done nothing but pour down the last week, as far as she was concerned. So much for a mild winter. It would have been nice to have sun for her last few days. At least her mood matched the weather – miserable and dreary. She couldn't remember what it felt like to be dry. Her body hurt so much, all over, that she could barely do anything.

She was standing on London Bridge, looking down at

the Thames River and the small boat that awaited her. It was busy; people were marching past, going about their daily lives, oblivious to the young woman cradling her baby. She knew the aliens could see her. She was in such a public place, but there was no way they could come after her here, at this time of day. They would catch up with her later.

Sarah bought a hot dog from a stand on the bridge; she loved London hot dogs and wolfed it down, having never before been this hungry. She hurriedly ordered a second and looked around her as she ate that one too. No one paid her any attention. They never did in London. She looked wet and dirty, almost like a bag lady, but still no one noticed her. That was both the love and the hate of London. You loved it when it served you and you loathed it when it left you too alone.

She stuffed the last of the hot dog into her mouth, barely chewing it before gulping it down and heading off. She made her way to the river's edge and climbed aboard her small, electric-powered canoe. It would churn the water behind her and take her along the river until she reached her destination. This was the final part of her trip but it would be the worst. She clung onto Diego, still asleep in the carrier on her chest, and climbed into the boat. She removed him from the carrier, laid him gently onto the floor of the canoe, inserted the key and was off along the river.

Slowly but surely, she made her way towards Gloucestershire where, at the Thames Head, she would leave her fourth baby. Her eyes grew heavy, desperately wanting to close, and her head kept dropping to her chest. Somehow, she managed to stay awake. She knew that if she closed her eyes that would be it. It would all be over. The river seemed to drag on forever.

Suddenly, from the corner of her eye, she caught a glimpse of red and black behind the trees on the riverbank. Her sluggish and tired body suddenly became very alert and she paid full attention to her surroundings. The hot dogs had fuelled her body and she had been on the river for over an hour, which was the most rest she was likely to get. With narrowed eyes, she squinted at the trees and then sighed. It was time to take them out.

Pretending not to have noticed the aliens, she continued for a further twenty minutes and then turned the canoe towards the bank. She could feel energy surging through her and knew he was helping her. The father of her children was sending his life source to her. She would be temporarily charged with borrowed energy. It saddened her because she knew that while it extended her life, it also shortened his. And yet as parents, they just wanted to protect their children. She closed her eyes, breathed in slowly through her nose, accepted his energy, then released a long sigh. Then, she opened her eyes. She was once again a warrior with the strength of ten men. For now. It would not last long. She secured the canoe and carried Diego onto the grass. She had hoped to have enough time to lay him safely under a tree somewhere, but that was not to be. As soon as she stepped out of the canoe, they surrounded her.

Two of them wore the red and black soldier outfits, whilst four were dressed all in black, ninja style. It was their favourite attire, covering them fully and being comfortable for fighting. Only the bulging black eyes were visible, glaring at her. Sarah had deliberately picked an isolated spot along the river. She had to face them now or else she would lead them straight to where she intended to leave Diego.

'That's a little unfair isn't it?' she said, trying to sound nonchalant. 'Six to one and me still holding the baby.'

'Hand him over to us and that is one of your problems resolved,' said one of the aliens, in a deep husky voice.

'If you're suicidal come at me. I dare you,' she said.

From somewhere deep inside, Sarah felt the anger swell and rise. She was dying. She had been running from these creatures for years, trying to stay one step ahead of them. They would do anything to have her special babies. Soon she would be gone and their fate would be in their own hands. Despite how frail her body was, the borrowed energy she now held gave her the strength she needed. She held her baby in her left arm, cradled into her chest, and prepared to fight with her right. The alien who had spoken stepped forward first. As he reached for the baby, she turned away, spun around and returned to face him with a hard punch to his face. He stumbled back. Sarah dropped to the floor, dragged her leg along the ground, and tripped him over. He fell backwards just as she pounced to her feet.

She kicked another alien backwards, sending him into the body of the third and they fell away from her. This gave her enough space and time to place her baby under a tree, safely out of their reach, before turning to face them again, taking her combat stance – legs apart and fists raised. They knew not to mock her, they knew how good a fighter she was, and they hesitated as they stared into her narrowed eyes.

All six of them were on their feet and coming towards her. Sarah's face was a mask. No one could read her true feelings and thoughts at that moment; her head tilted slightly to the side, attentive, watching to see what they did next, her fists held ready to attack. She preferred the boxer's approach. She punched like a man. In fact, being an expert kickboxer, she punched better than a man.

The aliens found this out rapidly. As they approached Sarah, she punched, kicked, punched and kicked, threw them around or used the body of one to take out the body of another. They fell, got to their feet again and fell once more. One ninja refused to fall as Sarah landed punch after punch speedily on his head as it bounced side to side, like some sort of comedy sketch. Sarah appeared to be unstoppable; a tired, dishevelled-looking woman wiping the floor with six large contenders. Then her strength waned, and the tables turned.

Four aliens still faced her: a little bruised, but far from tired. Sarah had knocked out the other two, who lay on the grass, face down. Two approached her at the same time, one on each side, but it was the third that did the damage. She hit one, ducked out of the way of the arm of another, and as she went to come upright again, the third caught her. It happened so quickly and unexpectedly, and she was lying back on the grass, looking up at the sky, before she knew it. He had hit her with the butt of his heavy laser gun. She was stunned.

From the corner of her eye, she saw one of them heading towards her baby. She was suddenly angry. How dare they! If she had all her strength they would never have gotten this far; she would have finished them off by now. She grunted and tried to stand up. She couldn't quite make it all the way so charged, bent over, into the alien closest to her baby. She hit him like a bull charging into his gut and sent him reeling back into the water. Then she felt the laser, hot and painful, deep in her stomach.

For a moment, no one moved. They expected her to fall, finished. The fight, at last, won and over. Out of respect, they gave her that moment to fall gracefully and in her own time. They waited as she stood, holding her stomach and looking up at them. She looked down at her wound, a large burn mark showing through her t-shirt, above her jeans, too burnt to bleed for now. It was a fatal shot, she knew that much, deep enough to finish anyone off. However, Sarah wasn't just anyone. The shot was not enough to take her out just yet. She reached into her pocket, took out a tablet, and promptly swallowed it. Thalen had given it to her as a last resort. It was the equivalent to injecting adrenaline directly into her heart and would keep her alive for several hours longer. The pain was excruciating and her face could no longer hide the agony that she was in. She spat out some blood and wobbled side to side as she looked at them.

'You cowards, you shot me! Well, is that the best you've got?'

The aliens looked at each other, amazed and confused, unable to answer.

'You're going to have to do a lot better than that!' she yelled.

She turned to the one who had shot her, jumping in the air, landing a sidekick on his throat and sending him to the ground. As he fell, she took the laser and used it on him. She turned and fired repeatedly at the others who were unable to move quickly enough to disarm her now. One by one, they dropped to the ground. It was over.

She fell, exhausted, to her knees, and dropped the laser.

Then, she ripped some material from one of the alien's outfits and tied it tightly around her waist, to stop the bleeding that was now starting, and hold her together for a while longer. She crawled over to her baby, gripping her stomach, then carried him back to the canoe. She placed him on the floor and fell in after him. Gasping with the difficulty of moving, she started to move up the river again. She never looked back, focused on the way forward, and was breathless with the effort of every move. Then, suddenly, a wave of peace washed over her as she realised, with wide startled eyes, that the pain was lifting.

'Thank you, Thalen,' she whispered, smiling up to the sky, wondering if he could see her on the spaceship screens. Perhaps he was too far away. At least he could energetically feel her and knew what she was going through. He was with her – he would never leave her alone. 'I will miss you, Thalen. I will make this final part of my journey!'

It seemed longer than the two hours it took to reach Thames Head, where she secured the canoe and got out. Stumbling weakly, she made her way along the riverbank, carrying the baby. She fell several times, sometimes unable to get up straightaway. She felt no pain, despite the gaping hole in her abdomen and being very weak. Thalen had done all he could by ensuring her last moments were pain free. She had to find strength for just a little while longer. She wanted the struggle to be over. She wanted the peace that death would bring to her broken body.

'Not until he is safe,' she told herself.

She hid from anyone who might see her – people in boats on the river, anyone looking out of their windows along the bank. She needn't have bothered; the weather was bad and had kept most people uninterested in the outdoors tucked up in their warm homes. She envied them their plain, simple and normal lives. How she would have liked to live with their ignorance and be oblivious to what was really going on in the world. She was able to make her way to the cottage, uninterrupted. It had a sign up saying it was available to be rented, and Sarah shook her head.

'He's moving again!' she muttered, weakly, under her breath. Then, as an afterthought, added to the baby, 'You'd better get used to that, my love.'

She put Diego on the step, losing her balance as she did so, placing the envelope beside him. There was a very small bag attached to the belt on her jeans, which she now unzipped. Inside the bag was a very strange quartz crystal cube, about the size of a duck egg, with strange shapes and images moving within. She tucked this under the blanket wrapped around him, kissing him, one last time, on his little forehead. Then she went to ring the bell but realised that she wouldn't get away in time.

It was still raining and she couldn't leave the baby there for long. She looked down and found a large stone from the path. Picking it up, she walked away and hid behind a nearby tree. Once hidden, she took the rock and threw it, with accuracy, at the window. It made a loud noise and cracked the glass. As the door opened, she hid further behind the tree, again holding her stomach.

Charles opened the door, angrily, looking for who had thrown something at his window. He looked scruffy, like a man who hadn't slept nor shaven in a while, his addictive lifestyle worn heavily on his face and body. He did not expect to find the baby at his feet and stared at it in horror.

The rain had started to soak the envelope on the floor, which he picked up. On the cover, it read: *Diego, born 26th February 2058.* Charles stared at the letter, then at the baby, then again at the letter. He opened and read it.

For a moment, he looked as if he would leave the baby and shut the door, his face showing his disbelief as he finished reading. He looked out at the fields and trees, narrowing his eyes, trying to find signs of whoever had brought the baby.

'It wasn't that big a favour!' he shouted. 'I am no good with children, whatever was she thinking? Come and take this thing back!'

Sarah giggled. He had always been grumpy like this. She had loved him once; he wasn't this bad at all. With obvious reluctance, he bent down and picked the baby up, noticing a bump in the blanket. He pulled out the crystal cube and stared at it in wonder. Then he shook his head and sighed. He held the baby awkwardly, almost terrified of it, trying to decide the best way of holding it.

'It just wasn't that big a favour!' he repeated, loudly, but to no one in particular.

Taking the baby and crystal, he awkwardly turned and entered the cottage, kicking the door shut behind him.

Sarah sighed yet couldn't help the smile that crept upon her lips. That was almost exactly as she had expected him to react. The loss of her babies now weighed heavily upon her as she turned and walked numbly back towards the canoe. She felt nothing except the life running out of her. She untied the canoe and fell into it. The rain had stopped briefly and she lay on her back, staring up at the gloomy sky. She wished she could see the stars one last time. It was over. She had done it. She had succeeded in hiding each of her four babies. She leaned back with the relief that washed over her. There was still no pain and she could just relax and let go. She could feel the tide getting stronger. Thalen would be doing that, making the boat travel faster so that when the aliens next located her it would be far away from where she had left Diego. She felt him close to her. She could see his face looking down at her, smiling.

'I will never get over losing you,' he whispered, tenderly. 'You know I'd have given my last breath to save you.'

'I know, my love. We discussed this. The children will need you and I cannot give them what you can. You must protect them now.'

'I promise you do not need to worry about them.' Thalen kissed her gently and stroked her cheek. 'I hate to see you like this.'

'You are wasting your energy being with me like this,' Sarah whispered.

'It's my energy to do with as I please. I will be with you to the end.'

Sarah smiled up at him. His large, green, alien eyes twinkled brightly. He was the most beautiful soul. Their time together had been fleeting. They drifted along the river as the tide pulled them far away from Diego.

'I will find you in the next life,' Thalen told her, squeezing her hand and watching her life fade away.

Sarah nodded, smiling, at peace. Then, she let out one long, slow breath and looked up at him for one last time.

'I've left them safe for you, my love, and now it's your turn,' she whispered, as she released her final breath.

Thalen dropped his head in sorrow. The only woman he

had ever loved, so brave and strong, was now gone. Only his promise to her, to protect their powerful children, would give him the strength to keep going. He disappeared, leaving her to drift along the river as her watch started to beep. It was imperative that the aliens didn't get hold of her DNA to experiment with. Her watch had been programmed to detonate when her pulse stopped. It was not a loud noise, just a whoosh and puff, and she was alight. The flames subtle but effective. No one could use her DNA now which meant her babies were even more important. They were the only four that carried this special bloodline in the entire universe. They were worth more than all the precious metals in the world and this put them in great danger.

ONE

THE HUNT

PERU, 12 YEARS LATER

The sudden loud bang, followed by the deafening roar, snap and crack of thunder, echoed through the dark sky. Silver laces of lightning flickered and cackled like the end of a wizard's whip before vanishing into the darkness. The trees shook to their roots; the ground rumbled. Diego couldn't believe it was still daytime, it was so dark. He had never seen a storm like this before. The rain fell fast and heavy, forcing the tree canopies to sag under the weight. He stared at his hand as it rested on the trunk of a tree, conscious of the vibrations passing through it, and marvelling at the force. Peru had the most amazing storms and he loved them. His pale white skin and golden hair were soaked, as was the only piece of clothing he wore – a black loincloth made from alpaca wool. The fierceness of the storm made him feel alive.

'Diego, he's heading right towards you. What are you doing? Wake up! He's all yours.'

Diego looked away from the tree to see who had shouted at him. It was Manco, the Inca Prince. Diego turned to where he was pointing and saw the boar heading straight towards him. Diego gulped – the boar was enormous. Conscious that Manco and the other Inca boys were now staring at him intently, he stepped into the path of the boar, held his spear high and took aim. Diego's legs trembled and his arm shook violently, making it difficult to hold the spear steady. The boar seemed bigger the nearer it got. Diego gulped again.

'Now, Diego!' Manco yelled.

Diego froze. He could hear the rapid breathing of the beast and stared in fear at the grizzled grey hair and sharp tusks protruding from its large ugly head. He had never seen one this close before, preferring to linger at the back of the hunting trip, out of the way of the actual hunt. Now he was forced to face the beast head-on, and all eyes were on him. Diego felt the sick rising in his stomach as he realised the moment had passed, and he had left it far too late.

The boar charged into Diego, sending him up into the air then hurtling to the ground. He lay, stunned and breathless, the rain falling on his face, as the boar disappeared from sight. He shook his head in order to regain his senses, and then wished he hadn't. His long hair sent mud all over his face and now he could hear the Inca boys even above the thunder. They were all laughing at him.

He cursed his uncle and his ridiculous decision to move to Peru and embrace traditional ways. Of course hunting with the other children would be great for his confidence! Like heck it was. Diego felt what was left of his self-esteem fizzle away into nothing as he slowly stood up. His pale white skin was now covered in mud and leaves from the ground, making his golden hair stand out even more.

'Oh, Diego, you are such a dreamer, off in your own world all the time. If you weren't so entertaining, you'd just be completely useless,' Manco said, holding his stomach as he laughed.

The boys ran off after the boar, leaving Diego behind. It was humiliating and he almost headed back towards the village, ashamed and defeated. How could his uncle Charles have thought this would be good for them, living in a village of primitive Incas, hunting like cavemen? He didn't fit in, and he certainly didn't feel good about himself. The other boys didn't look up to him. Sluggishly, and head bent, he trudged after the others. They had yet again turned the boar around and it was coming back for him. Manco was deliberately doing it for the sole purpose of having a good laugh at his expense.

His uncle Charles had decided Peru would be a good place to hide and keep a low profile for a while, considering what had happened in England. He and the king had been good friends at Oxford university and, seemingly, he owed Charles a favour. The king had honoured the favour by reluctantly letting them stay on the condition that they worked as part of the tribe. For Diego, this meant he had to go out hunting with the boys; good practice for becoming a man – apparently!

No one liked Diego; they thought he was strange, with his unusual looks, wavy golden hair and city attitude. At school his nickname had been 'Cupid'. The girls adored him, the boys despised him. These Inca boys had never been out of the forest, unlike the king, who was well travelled. It was a complete change of culture and Charles had convinced Diego that it would be good for him, that it would give him a chance to build his self-confidence and control his anger. Not that he had any other options. Diego sighed and shook his head. Charles was very wrong. His self-esteem was being crippled by the day. He felt even more awkward and useless, and even more of an outsider, than he had at home. 'Diego, quick, get ready! You have another chance,' Manco shouted, a large smile spread across his face.

Diego felt a sense of impending doom and stared at the sodden ground, unwilling to look up and acknowledge what was inevitable. He heard the boar's rapid breathing and stamping on the ground as he grew nearer. Reluctantly, Diego raised his eyes. Both he and the boar had dark eyes, intense and fearful of each other. Their eyes locked. They glared at each other, both full of dread and anger and yet determined to avoid confrontation. The anger grew in Diego as he felt it bubbling up inside of him, heat soaring through his veins. This just didn't happen in England.

It was ridiculous. Who faced animals like this? Until he came here, Diego had only ever seen the occasional dog in his whole life. Animals didn't make sense to him. He really didn't want to do this and didn't even bother raising the spear this time. He would not be played or bullied into killing an animal. Instead, he jumped out of the path of the boar, lost his balance and rolled backwards down a ditch in the trees. He landed in a pool of muddy water and was barely recognisable when the boys reached him. Manco howled with laughter, barely able to stand under the pressure, and pointed at Diego as the others joined in.

Diego stood up and turned his face up to the sky, letting

the heavy rain wash away the dirt. It didn't take long. He cringed at the shame and embarrassment but then, from somewhere deep inside him, he felt an even greater surge of anger. The really bad sort. So dark, only evil could come of it. Well, they had pushed him too far. It was their own fault, after all, he decided. It bubbled in his gut and slowly started to rise until his ears burned. He opened his eyes and glared up at the boys as they roared with laughter. His unnatural dark eyes glimmered with golden specks, like fire, and expressed an evil they hadn't seen before. It silenced them. Then he was gone.

He raced after the boar, jumping over debris, ducking under branches, pushing his way through the trees with such speed that the Incas had a hard time keeping up with him. They were very serious now, chasing him without laughter. Something had changed and his look had chilled them to the bone. He found the boar, and pulled level with it, keeping pace. The boar was exhausted but Diego was exhilarated by his anger, the thunder, and determination. They looked into each other's eyes as they ran side by side. Now Diego wanted to hunt. In his own way.

Diego touched the crystal cube held fast on a strap around his wrist. It started to change colour and sent a tingling sensation up his arm. He looked up at the storm and gritted his teeth. He pushed himself harder, picking up speed, until he overtook the boar. Then he raised his eyes to the sky, saw a bolt of lightning and raised his wrist. The lightning reached through the sky and found the crystal cube, just as Diego opened his hand and directed the voltage towards the boar. Instantly, the boar fell. Dead.

The Inca boys, who were close behind, were blasted up

into the air, landing hard on the forest floor with the force of the lightning strike. The entire area, where the boar lay, had been struck down. Several trees were burnt and when Diego saw the boys, he noticed their faces covered in shock and dirt. He smiled. They now looked far worse than he had. There was a stunned silence as they got up and walked on shocked, unsteady legs to view the carcass of the boar, no longer able to laugh at him.

'You think that is funny?' Manco said, brushing himself down. 'Wait until we tell the king that you cheated! You use magic because you're not brave enough to tackle the beast like a man.'

'In case you hadn't realised, none of us are men, Manco. We're boys. Just twelve years old. You're not a man. Besides, isn't this supposed to be fun?'

'Fun? Yes, we can enjoy a hunt, yet this is also our food. What will the women say!'

'They have a whole boar for dinner. How can the women possibly moan? We got them what we set out to get. I got them the boar. You are just upset that I did it on my own,' Diego snapped.

'Then you can carry it on your own,' Manco said.

Diego watched as they walked away, leaving him alone with the burnt forest and the dead boar. He sighed in annoyance as he looked at how large the beast was. They were far away from the village and it usually took a few of them to comfortably carry a boar.

'You have to be kidding me,' he muttered.

He moped his way over to the boar and tried to lift it up. Not only was it big but it was heavy, far too heavy for him to carry all the way back to the village. The village rested at the top of a steep mountain, and he had struggled with acclimatising to it let alone lugging a dead carcass all the way up. How could he possibly do this alone? He tried a couple more times to lift the boar and then dropped to the floor next to it. He couldn't be bothered with all this. Diego sat and sulked over the ordeal that lay ahead of him. He knew, somehow, that he had to get this boar up the mountain to the villagers, otherwise, he would be completely shamed. The Incas were having a celebration next week and needed to hang the boar in preparation before it could be cooked. If he didn't succeed, they would have no boar for the festival. Eventually, Diego used some vines, found a couple of pieces of wood and tied them all together to make an ugly yet effective stretcher. That would have to do.

He could feel the pain of the ordeal already. He had been pushing weights for months, trying to add some bulk to his tall, skinny frame, and knew he was far stronger than a normal boy. Charles had helped him create a few weights he could use in the Inca village to continue his workout. He would hang off trees and do weight building push ups and chest presses. He could do this. He just had to build up the motivation. He had to draw in some energy and he had plenty of trees to pull it from. So what if a few were burned? Peru was rich in trees. Diego was so deep in thought he didn't notice the Andean Cock-of-the-rock bird, the national bird of Peru, land directly in front of him. The bird paced back and forth, watching him, for a long time before Diego realised it was there.

'What do you want?' he asked.

He was used to seeing them; they were abundant in this part of Peru, and were constantly trying to eat the fruit grown in the village. This one was a male, which was obvious even to Diego, by the strange, bright orange head and disk-like crest protruding from its head. The bird was pretty, with a black body and bright orange legs, but this one was acting oddly. It was definitely interested in Diego even though it was obvious there was no food around for it. They were not normally this curious about a person. The way it was watching him was eerie and unnatural.

'Stop staring at me like that, what's your problem? Get lost,' he said, and threw some dirt at it.

The bird flew away, but not far, landing on the branch of a nearby tree. With a huff, Diego crouched next to the boar and rolled it with all his might onto the stretcher. It must have weighed over 300kg, since the king forbade any hunting until a boar was fully grown and had lived several years of a good life. He already felt his legs buckle under the pressure. He had too much pride not to get it back to the village so he resigned himself to the task. He let out a long breath, braced himself, grabbed the sides of the stretcher and stood up. Gritting his teeth, he started to walk and drag the heavy carcass behind him. He felt his leg wobble as he took a step and barely caught his balance before taking another step. His arms ached already with the immense weight. He was going to have to do this step by step and not think about the distance.

*

Diego dropped the boar and sank to the ground when he reached the mountain. He was soaked in sweat and rain, filthy and exhausted. He breathed heavily, trying to catch his breath. He looked up at the mountain and felt all hope drain out of him. It was so steep. The village sat right at the very top. Diego felt like he was their unwanted enemy. An outcast from the start. He found more vine to tie the boar to the stretcher and hoped it would hold as he climbed up the mountain.

No matter what he thought, he would never give Manco the satisfaction of winning. He would get this boar back to the village alone. He would look the hero and show Manco and the king that he didn't need anyone else. He felt his strength returning, fuelled by anger and determination.

As he heaved the stretcher back up into the air, he looked up and saw the Andean Cock-of-the-rock bird again, this time sitting in a tree facing him. Could it be the same bird? He frowned and then assumed he was being ridiculous. How could it possibly be the same one? They all looked alike anyway and there were loads of them around. He gritted his teeth and started up the mountain.

TWO

TEAMWORK

PERU

Diego struggled with all his might to carry the carcass of the boar to the top of the mountain and when he saw the village, he almost cried with delight. He was exhausted. He was drenched from the rain, covered in mud and blood, and every muscle in his body was agony. The village had never looked more beautiful to him than it did right now. The top of the mountain had been cleverly engineered to work as a farm and village. Terraces along the mountainside were built to ensure good drainage and soil fertility while also protecting the mountain itself from erosion and landslide. The Urubamba river was the source of water, when needed, which wasn't often due to Peru's heavy rainfall. The irrigation system was brilliant and they had fresh spring water in abundance.

Diego loved it in the early mornings when the mist from the river would creep up the mountain, and he would sit with Quilla (pronounced *kiya*), Manco's sister, his only friend. Then they would take the slide to the river, wash, and race each other back up the mountain for breakfast. The Incas worshipped the moon for all the benefits it bestowed on the Earth. The moon was used to calculate the passage of time, as a calendar, and festivals and sacrifices were based on the lunar calendar. The moon also moderated the planet's wobble on its axis, leading to a relatively stable climate. It also created tides, a rhythm that has guided humans for thousands of years, influencing their moods. Diego knew the word 'lunatic' was derived from the lunar cycle because mankind often lost their minds prior to a full and new moon. He and Quilla would sit for hours talking under the moon.

Manco and the other children had created a very steep water slide along the mountain and into the river. It was the best part of the entire village. Diego could go the fastest, being so tall, and Manco was the only one who could almost match his speed. Quilla was slow so she always sat in front of Diego so that his weight helped her go faster. They loved it. The lads had made it from wood, bamboo, vines, mud and clay and meticulously shaped it into a smooth slide. Part of the irrigation system on the top would pour water out for approximately twenty minutes before it switched off. Diego had to admit that they had done a brilliant job. If only he could get along with the lads like he did Quilla.

The houses in the village were made of stone blocks, carved so that they fitted perfectly and had no need for cement, and adobe – the clay-like material they used on the slide. The houses were rectangular with wooden beams and a thatched roof. This was a tradition the king retained. Alpaca wool was used for the doorway curtains; there were no thieves in Inca villages so no need for locked doors. There were no windows due to the rainfall.

Guinea pigs pitter-pattered around their feet and in and out of their huts, never running away despite being a stable source of food, much to Diego's surprise when they first arrived. They seemed very similar to rats in London. Nicer looking, but strange little critters all the same. They tasted bearable.

Children played in everyone's huts, welcomed by every family. This always amazed Diego; so different from in the city. Many people still avoided children and considered them virus carriers. Yet here they were cherished. The children adored Diego and his unusual golden hair.

The villagers had gathered in the centre of the village, talking loudly, unhappily noting the lack of food they had for the evening. The women had expected to have the boar early morning and the whole day to prepare it for the festival, and it was late. They were furious about the approaching darkness and the king was trying to calm them down. Diego smiled as he watched them all, thinking how proud and relieved they would be when they saw him with the boar they thought was not going to appear.

His knees started to buckle at last, as he walked the final steps to where they were gathered, and he saw Manco standing smugly next to his father, the king. Manco wanted Diego to be sent away. It was Manco who saw him first and his mouth opened in astonishment as he saw Diego dragging the boar behind him. He had obviously not expected him to do it. Diego smiled. Then, when he saw the shocked looks everyone else gave him, he smiled even more. They had expected him to fail and he hadn't. He had made it. He felt like he could die from exhaustion, but nevertheless, he had achieved the impossible and unexpected. He had actually made it all the way alone with this big, fat ugly boar.

Diego put the very last bit of energy he had into walking with strength and dignity into the centre of the circle, then he dropped the boar onto the ground. He didn't want them to know how out of breath and exhausted he really was so he gasped for air as quietly as he could. In fact, he couldn't have spoken if he tried; he had no breath left in him. Everyone was silent as they stared at Diego then at the sizzled body of the boar lying at his feet. The smile slowly left Diego's face as he realised they were not impressed.

Then it started. The women hovered over the carcass, poking and prodding it in disgust, and started complaining and moaning at the state of it. They were in an uproar, even worse than when they were moaning about not having meat at all. Now they were complaining over what they had to work with. Diego walked away from them, towards the king, feeling weak and fed up. He vowed never to get married. Women were impossible to please. Although Quilla was different. He had never met anyone quite like her. She was two years older than him and wiser than most adults and yet he felt so connected to her. As if they were in their own private world somehow.

Diego listened to their comments as he walked and noticed, with a heavy sigh, the smug and knowing smile on Manco's face as he stood watching, arms folded. He couldn't win no matter what he did. Manco had seen to that.

'Está quemado hasta quedar crujiente,' said one woman, saying: *It's burnt to a crisp* in Spanish.

'No puedo cocinar eso, se ve terrible, nos va a envenenar

a todos,' said another, which translated to: *I can't cook that, it looks terrible, it will give us all poisoning.*

'¿Cómo podemos preparar una comida con eso? ¡No estoy trabajando con eso! Tengo estándares, ¿sabes?' The first woman said again, meaning: *How can we possibly prepare a meal with that? I am not working with that! I have standards, you know.*

Quilla had taught Diego some Spanish and he had learned fast. She and her family spoke perfect English too. Charles had started teaching Diego Spanish early on since his contingency plan was to live with the Inca king. Diego heard the women loud and clear.

He sighed, and he thought the hard part was carrying it up the mountain! He felt angry with these people; nothing he did worked, and nothing he tried was good enough. He just didn't get them at all. The irony was that he had felt like a complete outsider in England, and yet, he hadn't realised what the word outsider actually meant until he had arrived here. The king stood tall and proud, in his cloth tunic and jaguar skin cloak, as Diego approached. The jaguar had been his pet once and had lived a long time. The king had cherished it. Diego felt a knot in his stomach and couldn't quite decide whether it was fear or anger.

'Diego, what is this you bring to us?' the king asked.

'Everyone left me to carry this thing alone, and I did, because I know that today is prepare the boar day. You wanted a boar – I got the boar. Why are you not happy?' Diego replied.

'Why? Do you not hear the same as I from the women?'

'I don't understand their problem, it's a whole boar, and it's what they wanted. It's going to be cooked anyway so what is wrong with it being a bit charred? I cannot win no matter what I do!' Diego said with frustration, trying to remain respectful to the king.

Charles, Diego's uncle, approached. He was wearing a similar tunic to the rest of the men in the village. He looked comfortable and as if he fitted in, like he belonged here. He looked very disappointed with Diego. Diego sighed. Here we go again, he thought.

'No, Diego, they wanted a freshly killed boar that they could prepare and cook for us all day long. You bring us a carcass that looks as if it's been to hell and back just when they are getting ready to go to bed. They have babies and children to get up early with.'

'So, it's a little burnt, I even part cooked it for them.' Diego smiled cockily. 'I made their job easier.' He saw Charles cringe and he knew he had made a mistake and shouldn't have said that.

'You have been here for a month now and still you fail to grasp our ways,' said the king. 'Throughout history, we have been a strong tribe and have always been admired for our strength. This strength came from working together, as a team, in harmony with nature. The one moment we Incas failed to work as a team, the Spanish invaded and defeated us. We learned a big lesson from that and have since valued teamwork. Why can you not see the value of working together – as a team? You are old enough to know better.'

Diego looked at the king, not knowing what to answer. How could he work as a team when everyone laughed at him? He couldn't start telling the king what a rotten son he had who made his life hell each day. He shrugged, then immediately regretted the shrug when he saw it annoyed the king even more. Respect was a big issue here and something Diego struggled with.

'You have no regard for our traditions and ways, Diego. I have tried so hard with you and yet you consistently fail to understand the wisdom of our ways. Your uncle told me that you were an outsider in England. Do you not see that you will always remain this way unless you learn to work with the community you are in?' The king sighed.

Diego stared at the ground, desperately wanting to sit down and rest his aching legs. He would have done anything for a bath. A hot bubble bath.

'But I don't understand, all I did was kill the boar. Does it really matter what I killed it with?'

'Yes, it does matter and this is the most important thing. If you use the hunting skills then you are working as a team and looking out for each other. You protect each other. When you used the lightning, you didn't just kill the boar, you killed the trees and anything else that lived in that area. Goodness knows how much you destroyed. You also endangered the life of the boys around you. You thought you had control over the lightning but, in fact, you only used it and it killed and threatened much more than the boar. That is the problem.'

'So, a few trees got hurt...' Diego began.

'And if you did that each time you went hunting, what then? Before long, the whole forest would be on fire or ruined. These trees take centuries to grow and cannot be replaced as quickly as they can be destroyed. We worship what grows around us, it keeps us hidden, keeps us safe. Isn't that why you are here?'

'Yes, but–'

'But nothing! Our law dictates that you honour nature and respect what grows around you. We must work together to keep each other safe. Part of becoming a man is to see the value in working as a team, not seeking the glory in trying to be something special alone. If you want to remain here with us then you must learn to value your fellow man. If you persist in working alone, in a way that is damaging to the nature that grows around us, then I will have no choice but to banish you from this village.' The king glared meaningfully at Diego.

'You are giving him another chance?' Manco gasped with disappointment.

'Work as a team? Where was the teamwork when I had to carry this thing up the mountain on my own?' Diego said angrily, glaring at Manco.

'Do you not see that you dishonoured my son, and that by persisting in this lonely venture of yours, you must face the consequences alone too? There is a pattern to your life, dear boy, that you must come to face. Wherever you go, you are an outcast. You refuse to fit in and work with the social structure of that environment. If you do not learn from your mistakes, you will only continue to make the same ones. I will not carry you if you fail to learn, do you understand? Even my own son must follow these laws and learn our ways. If you continue to shame my son and put our people in danger then you are, and will always be, alone. Can you not understand this?'

Diego must have looked so exhausted at this point that the king knew talk was of no further use. He dismissed Diego, told him to go and get some rest and indicated that Charles should join him. As Diego turned to miserably slump off to their house, he saw the glare that his uncle sent him. Charles was a tall, slim man and he looked depressed and miserable to the core, with slumped shoulders and head bent so low his chin was almost touching his chest. Diego sighed. He was ashamed and frustrated. It pained him to see how Charles looked so defeated and beaten. He knew that this was truly the last place on Earth Charles could think of bringing Diego, and if this didn't work out, he didn't know where else they could go. Right now, it looked like this wouldn't work out.

Diego pushed the door curtain aside and walked into the bare stone house he and Charles shared. His bed lay to the left, a pile of dried grass woven into a mat on the floor – basic but surprisingly comfortable. Despite the actual comfort, Diego felt sad at the thought of not having a proper duvet, pillow and raised bed. Oh, how he longed for such basics right now. Moreover, to have a hot bath to relax in and soothe his aching muscles! Diego flopped onto his grass bed and released a long sigh. He felt so tired. How could he bear to be here even one more day?

THREE

VIRACOCHA

PERU

'Well here lies the resting place of Prince Diego, the boy who died in a bed of self-pity,' said a voice from the doorway.

Diego raised himself up onto one elbow and peered at the girl standing there. Princess Quilla, Manco's sister and the king's daughter. No matter how hard Diego tried to pretend that she didn't faze him, the butterflies flew around his stomach every time she spoke to him. He tried to look nonchalant. She had straight, long, black, shiny hair, golden sugar coloured skin and a smile that melted his inner core. Diego thought that she was the most angelic and beautiful person he had ever seen. She seemed more than human somehow.

Her silky hair was pinned up in a piece of red cloth, dyed by the blood of the sacred beetle. She wore an ankle length skirt of red cloth with a matching brassiere and small shoes, for her tiny feet, made of grass. Most of the Incas now wore shoes of leather – they lasted longer – but Quilla preferred the basic and traditional ways. Being a princess, she sometimes wore clothes made of cloth instead of llama and alpaca wool. She had once told him that she even had a silk dress made especially for her. She enjoyed her privilege rarely, mostly living simply like everyone else. He liked that about her.

'Princess Quilla, can I help you? Please don't ask me to get up!' Diego groaned. He ignored the palpitations in his chest, the ones only she made happen, the ones that didn't exist before or after her presence.

'Usted bebé pobre, siempre tan solamente,' she murmured, as she entered the house. *You poor baby, always so alone.*

He loved her accent and the way the words fell like warm toffee dripping from her red lips. She loved henna tattoos and had loads over her cheeks, arms and hands. Quilla had spent time in India learning about traditional herbal remedies and had learned how to do henna tattoos on herself. It looked stunning. When she was around him, he felt lost, weak, and even a little scared, but he also adored her company. He had never had a close friend before and they could talk for hours. He was just conscious of the way the king and Manco scowled at him if they saw them talking.

'Quilla, when your father dismisses my uncle he will come here and find us talking. Or worse, if your brother or father finds out you are talking to me again...' Diego warned, shaking his head and releasing a heavy sigh.

She smiled – such an elegant and graceful smile. She was very petite and her eyes, those bright brown translucent eyes that stared so delightfully at him, knew so much and told so little. Her eyes were both fascinating and intimidating – they knew or found out too much. He knew she could look at him and know everything he was thinking and feeling. He ignored his beating heart and his suddenly sweaty hands.

'Listen to the stranger telling me how to behave when I'm told not to do something. My sweet, rebellious, Diego.' She laughed. 'I do not let men control me. Not you, my brother or my father. I control the men.'

'You shouldn't be here, Quilla, I'm a lost soul.' Diego sighed, fell back onto his back and covered his forehead with the back of his hand.

'Oh, Diego!' she said, moving fully into the house and coming to sit alongside his bed. She was barely fifteen and yet, somehow, she seemed so much older. Diego felt out of his depth around her.

Quilla knew that Diego was far older than his years. She knew sixteen year olds who seemed younger than Diego. He was older in body and in mind.

'Quilla, your father and your brother hate me, it's not a good idea to be seen with me,' Diego said.

This was not the complete truth since he wouldn't normally care whether he was accepted or not by anyone. However, he had harmed enough people; especially those he meant to look after and care for. Many innocent people had been injured and now, he was scared of killing Quilla, Manco, or any other child in the village. He didn't want to hurt anyone. Especially someone he really liked. He couldn't live with himself if he killed her.

If Diego had the physical energy, he would have got

up and left the room there and then. Nevertheless, he was exhausted and couldn't move his legs. They had seized up completely now that he was lying down.

Quilla realised this and knew he couldn't get away this time. They could talk about anything for hours, but as soon as she tried to talk about serious matters he would get up and walk away. She was enjoying this moment; he was trapped and all hers.

'I saw how tired you looked and made you a drink with special herbs. It will give you back your energy – drink.' She took a bowl and bottle from the bag hanging from her shoulder. It was made of wood and animal skin, and he watched as she popped the top off and poured the purple liquid into the bowl.

'I will drink it later. Right now, I just want to lie still,' he said, trying to hide his look of disgust at the strange-looking drink.

'No, drink it now, you need it. It's a very powerful herbal juice,' she said. 'And here is some more of that essential oil solution to rub into your skin, which we will do after your surprise.'

'Surprise?'

'I will tell you when the time is right.' she smiled and knelt beside him, pushing the drink towards him.

'What is the oil for anyway? It's oily. Why do you insist I cover myself in it each morning?' Diego asked, sitting up and taking the drink.

'It will stop the black bullet ants stinging you. It's a great deterrent. Trust me, they are awful. You don't want them on you.'

Quilla watched him reluctantly sip the drink. She urged

him to keep drinking until it was all gone. 'I have never told you about who I am named after have I?'

Diego shook his head and lay back down, giving in to the tiredness he felt.

'My ancestor, Mama Quilla, which means *Mother Moon*, was the goddess of the moon, the third power. Protector of all women. She was superseded only by her brother and husband Inti, the sun God – the first power, and Illpapa, God of thunderstorms – the second power.' She smiled, sweetly.

'Thunderstorms are more powerful and also worshipped here? Then why is the king…?'

'For your sake, Diego, he doesn't brag about the God of thunderstorms. He knows you worship him, without realising it, but he doesn't think you should. Anyway, we were talking about me! I am named after the goddess of the moon who oversees marriage and is the protector of all women. This is my job now. I have a very important role in the village, you know. My concern is to protect women so I follow my brother and father's advice only so far. I put the women first and what I think is best for them. I'm told what to do in my dreams.'

Diego looked at her and frowned. He was unsure why she was telling him this but he liked listening to her voice.

'Tell me more about Mama Quilla,' he said. He knew bits of this from Charles but enjoyed hearing her tell her stories.

'She was worshipped for her beauty and because the moon affects so much of the year in different ways – such as the calendar and people's moods, especially women's. The sun and the moon obviously have a great effect on farming and times of the year. They say that the silver tears of Mama Quilla is why Peru is so rich in silver – she cries when being attacked by an animal, perhaps a mountain lion or a serpent. The lunar eclipse is when this animal is attacking her. This scares people because if the animal wins during the attack, then the Earth would be left in darkness. My ancestors would scream and yell and make as much noise as possible during the eclipses to scare away the attacking animal. We still do.'

'So, Quilla, do you cry tears of silver?' Diego smiled as he watched her blush.

'No, only the goddess does that, but I do believe in reincarnation. Perhaps I am she reincarnated? Then maybe I have already cried tears of silver?'

'I wouldn't put it past you.' He smiled.

'Do you know what causes the dark spots you can see on the moon?' she asked.

'No, what?'

'A fox fell in love with Mama Quilla, because of her beauty, but when he rose up into the sky, she squeezed him tightly against her and produced the patches on the moon.'

'Oh, that's not very nice,' Diego replied.

'Do you not think it shows her love and passion for the fox by how tight she squeezed him? Diego, there is not much in Inca history that has a nice ending.' Quilla smiled.

'What do you mean?'

'We sacrificed the young when we worshipped. Girls like me were made sun virgins and raised to be sacrificed at my age.' She shuddered. 'It was considered an honour.'

'An honour? At such a young age? I hardly think so. Well, I'm glad you don't do that sort of thing anymore.

Do you?' His furrowed brows letting Quilla know he was worried.

'No, not anymore, except on rare occasion. Perhaps with you? Maybe my father will decide to sacrifice you to the sun God in order to make up for the damage you did in the forest today, huh?' Quilla teased with the tongue-in-cheek humour that Diego had come to adore.

'Perhaps he has brought you up as a sun virgin sacrifice but hasn't actually told you yet.' Diego smiled sweetly.

'Hey!' She hit his arm and laughed.

'Well, what strange things to do.' He chuckled.

'We all have our ancient ways and we are all different now. I have heard a lot of bad things about the English throughout history.'

'Yes, you're right, we all have things that were better stopped. So, tell me about your sun God, because you're the same as the Egyptians in the way you build and worship aren't you?'

'We are not the same but there are big similarities, yes. As farmers, my people were governed by the sun and the moon and anything else that greatly affected the calendar – the tides and the days and, hence, fishing and farming needs. Inti was the first biggest power, the sun God, the creator of civilisation. Legend has it that Inti sent his two sons and a daughter down to Earth for the sake of the people. He wanted them to stop living like animals. Therefore, his children would rule and protect the people by being their kings.'

'So, your father is the son of a God, I suppose?'

'Yes, he has descended from that line. Inti said he would travel around the world each day to ensure he always knew what the people wanted and each day he would bring light and warmth, making crops grow and cattle breed. That is how men stopped behaving like animals and the civilisation of man began. You have to admire all the Gods and understand how they all work together. Diego, you only know and understand the God of thunderstorms, you must know more.'

'Well, I guess I'm beginning to, aren't I?'

'Our supreme creator God is called Con-Tici Viracocha; he is a synthesis of the sun God and the storm God, and ultimately powerful.'

'I thought the sun God was the first power?'

'He is, but Viracocha is everything, a mixture of the two most powerful Gods. Mama Quilla is the daughter of Viracocha and Mama Cocha, goddess of the sea. She is the wife and sister of the sun God, Inti. My father is a descendant of the sun God. Do you see what I'm telling you? You look more powerful than my father to the people of this village. You are sun and storm, Diego. My people and I appreciate sorcery and you seem like, what do they call it in English? You seem like a wizard to us. That could make you very accepted here. But my father must trust you and know that you are working for us and not against us. That is all you have to prove to my father and my brother.'

'Why are you telling me all this?' Diego asked.

'Because you need to understand, Diego, that I have seen the future and I can see how great you will be. You must make the effort to make my father and brother like you and trust you.'

'You have seen the future?'

'Yes, I am not without powers of my own, you know.'

She smiled sweetly.

'How can you do that?'

'I don't know, I just get visions and see bits of information. My father and grandmother could see things too. I have not yet told my father, so he doesn't know I can do this, but Manco knows. He doesn't believe me all the time, though.'

'Why?'

'It depends what I tell him. The other day I told him that you and he will be great friends soon.'

Diego laughed.

'Yes, Manco laughed at me too.' She sighed.

'Well, we hate each other!'

'No, you don't. You're just both insecure.'

'I am not!'

'He said that too.'

'Quilla, tell me more about your Gods. I prefer to talk about them!' Diego huffed moodily.

'If you take the second drink I brought you,' she replied.

Diego watched her take another bottle from her bag and top up his bowl. He looked at the bowl in his hand. It was hard to tell what colour the liquid was, but it was all the unknown green things floating in it that bothered him most. The other drink had been hard enough. He wasn't too happy about all her herbal knowledge if truth be known. He sat up and braced himself for the foul taste. The first tentative sip let him know it was disgusting.

'How can someone so beautiful make something so horrible looking?' he asked, as he wiped his lips with the back of his hand. And then he blushed as he realised what he had said.

Quilla laughed. 'Drink up.'

Diego huffed and then gulped down the drink. At the end he gagged and dry retched as his stomach resisted and threatened to return the drink pronto. Unwilling to vomit in front of Quilla, he battled with the situation for a moment, putting a fist in front of his mouth and willed the drink to stay put. It worked. Quilla bit her lip to stop the smile she felt tugging at the corners of her mouth.

'Viracocha was also Inti's father and he walked about with a golden head and thunderbolts of lightning coming from his hands. Not unlike you, Diego. One day, he walked the Earth and looked at all the creatures he had created and the sight broke his heart. We were not good people. He travelled the Earth and cried tears of pain at the evil he saw. His tears created the great flood and cleansed the planet.'

'I thought that was why Noah built the boat?'

'Perhaps. I believe there is only one God but he is known by many different names and in many different forms. Perhaps God is Viracocha; Viracocha is God? Perhaps he asked Noah to save any good people from the flood?'

'Well, if that is so, then your God's had a much better deal than my God's son,' Diego said.

'Meaning what?'

'Well, Jesus didn't have a great life and he was crucified on a cross, but Inti and his sons became kings and lived to rule with respect. Now, you tell me who had a better bargain?'

They laughed and then fell silent as their eyes met.

'You really should go, Quilla,' Diego whispered.

'You cannot hurt me, Diego,' she whispered back.

'What? Why do you say that?' Diego was shocked.

'I know you,' she said.

'You really do have visions, don't you?'

'Yes, and I see who you are; your fears, the constant worry you have of hurting those around you. It will not always be that way for you, Diego, your worry will go one day.'

'How do you know all this?'

'I just know.' She shrugged.

'I've hurt people before, I killed someone...'

'Shush, I know, and you will kill again before you die. A lot! It's something you will come to live with and you'll learn to control your powers. I know, I have seen it, and you are unable to hurt me. Let that be one worry from your mind so we can enjoy these conversations from now on?'

Diego was suspicious that she was only saying this to stop him running away from her every time she got serious. He knew she liked him. Was it really true, that he couldn't hurt her, even by accident? He smiled at her, and from that moment on, he accepted it as truth. He trusted her completely, that much was for sure. They could now talk together whenever they liked. He didn't care if Manco stared at him from now until the day he died. It was worth the price.

'It is time for your surprise,' Quilla said, standing up and clapping her hands.

'What surprise?' Diego asked.

'Come, get up.' She took his hand and pulled him up to stand next to her. She barely reached his shoulders. He was far stronger and taller than her brother. Quilla knew he was going to be like Hercules when he was fully grown. She led him to the back of the hut where she had put up a curtain

in the corner of the room. Diego hadn't noticed. She now pulled the curtain back and revealed an iron bath full of hot soapy water. She giggled as she watched Diego's eyes light up.

'A bath!' he said, beaming brightly. 'You are amazing!'

'I asked some girls to help me earlier. We have been filling it up and keeping it hot so you can soak in it. We were spying on you. Taking it in turns to see how close to the mountain you were so it would be ready. This will help those aching muscles and then I will rub some oil in for you. Keep the bullet ant oil for the mornings but tonight I have some special essential oils that will ease the muscle pain away.'

'Wow. I don't know what to say. I never even noticed anyone spying on me.'

'That is because we women are better than the boys. We practice fighting and hunting in secret. Don't tell anyone. You are the only man who knows. When we go off to gather herbs and fruits, it is not all that we do. We will not sit around waiting for men to save us or protect us. We are strong. And we are sneaky. We spy on everything, and no one ever knows.' She threw her head back and laughed.

'You're incredible.' Diego smiled.

As she looked down and blushed, she saw some paper sticking out from under his bed mat and pulled it out.

'What is this?' she asked, looking at it in surprise. She didn't realise he was an artist. He had drawn strange shapes that looked a little like elephant trunks in space with stars and clouds around them. 'It is beautiful.'

'That is of a strange dream I keep having,' Diego replied. 'I keep seeing this and somehow I know it's important and holds some significance to me. It is like I know this place somehow. I've always had strange dreams, even more so since I arrived here.'

'Hmm, this is very interesting. I will ask my father if he recognises this from his studies. What else is significant about your dreams?'

Diego blushed and looked away. 'I don't want to tell you.'

'I can't help you if you don't tell me,' she replied softly.

Awkwardly, he huffed and shook his head. 'You'll think I'm weird.'

'Well, I already do so nothing will change there.' She giggled. 'Come on, spill the beans.'

'Since I arrived here I keep getting visits from a rather strange creature that talks to me and keeps telling me things.'

'What sort of strange creature?'

'It's like a talking otter with a moustache, would you believe it? He seems very real, but obviously he is not. It's just my imagination. And yet...'

'And yet what?' Quilla gently pushed.

'Sometimes I'm sure I see him watching me, even when I am awake, as if he is really here. This strange otter is not much higher than my knees – less than three foot in height. It's been bothering me because he keeps trying to speak with me but I won't talk back. It's weird, right?'

'No, it's not weird. Many spirit guides are in animal form. Next time, Diego, talk back. See what is said and keep a note of it. I'll help you to understand these dreams.'

'OK, I will. Thank you, Quilla. Again.'

'Now, get in the water, before it goes cold. I will wait out here.'

Diego didn't need telling twice. He got in the bath and

sunk under the water. He released a long slow sigh of relief and closed his eyes. 'I can't thank you enough, Quilla. I will do anything for you after this.'

Quilla squeezed her fists together and pumped them in the air in glee. She must help Diego find his place here. She could not lose him.

FOUR

PISCES

VIVACITY ISLAND

Breakfast was suddenly a massive, busy event and took all morning to make and serve then clean up afterwards. Making pancakes and scrambled eggs, wolfed down eagerly by all the children, exhausted Jude and Lei. Ed snuck off and ate his in quiet in the library with Stephen, the noise of over thirty children too much for them after so little sleep.

Lei looked over at Jude.

'We need a better system.'

'Don't we just!'

'I'm feeling overwhelmed if I'm honest. How are we going to handle this?' Lei asked.

'I was thinking that. We can't just hire help with hybrids. Let us sit and plan this afternoon with a nice cup of tea. We can do a rota and the children will just have to help. They're old enough to learn and chip in. They can make breakfast and sandwiches. Teach a few how to do some basic cooking and then they teach some others, and so on. A rota with chefs and washer-uppers will spread the load. We shall have to get them contributing or we won't maintain this. That is how the Scouts and Brownies used to do it. Very independent. I was a Brown Owl,' said Jude.

'What's that?'

'A leader for a Brownie guide pack. I can teach them to cook outdoors over fires safely. Soups and vegetable kebabs that they can assemble themselves and cook. We can turn such things into fun events that keep them all busy rather than long chores for us adults. Right now, they've been too frightened or weak to help much and I just wanted to get some nutrition into them. They look at death's door. We will do it.' Jude smiled positively. Her mind was already halfway through the rota.

Lei approached Mina.

'Would you like to join Crane and I in his laboratory?' she asked.

'What for?'

'We were going to examine those pills you brought and see what's in them.'

'Yes, please, just give me a minute to say bye to the children.'

'Sure.'

Mina almost collided with number three, who was standing right behind her as she turned to go, with his hands tucked into his pockets and his head lowered and partially hidden under a baseball cap.

'Number three? Are you all right?' she asked.

'What do you think?' He smiled and looked up at her.

Mina gasped. His skin looked clear and unblemished,

with no sign of any holes, scars or marks.

'What happened?' She grabbed him and pulled him into a tight hug.

'Jax did some surgery on my face and then Tammy and Mikie stayed up all night moving around us as we slept, and healed us. They said they will keep doing it every night until we are all completely cured. We already look better!'

'You look a-a-amazing,' Mina stuttered, trying not to cry.

'Can I come with you?' he asked.

Mina looked at Lei, who nodded in approval.

'Shall we take the Jeep?' Lei asked.

'Can I drive?' Mina asked. 'Not like last time, I promise.'

Lei nodded and smiled.

*

'So, number three, how about we pick a proper name for you?' Mina asked as they drove towards the safari park.

'Jude has already done that. Last night, she read us a bedtime story and explained how people have names and not numbers. Then she ran through loads of girl and boy names and we had to tell her the ones we liked then decide on our final choices during breakfast this morning. She asked me to translate everything, even the story, to the other children. It was such good fun,' he said with glee.

'What a brilliant idea,' Mina smiled at him.

'What sort of names are we looking at here, normal ones or space alien type?' Lei asked.

'Well, Ed said he would do names from all around the world. Number twelve and twenty-three both wanted John, so twelve chose Johnny, spelled with an H. Twenty-three got Jon without the H. Jude said that was a smart way to do it. See? We also have Claire, Carlos, Gabriel. I can't remember them all yet.'

'And you chose?' Mina asked.

'Pedro.' He beamed. 'I am Pedro. Nice to meet you, ladies.'

'I love it,' Mina said, putting her hand on her heart and smiling at him.

'It's Spanish.' He added.

'It suits you,' Mina replied and bent down to hug him with all her might.

'How are you the only one who speaks such good English?' Lei asked.

'My mother spoke it. I was the only Draconian, so they allowed her to stay with me for several years. She was taken away about two years ago. She taught me both languages.' He went quiet after talking about his mother.

Lei put her hand on his shoulder from her seat in the back. 'I'm so sorry.'

'Pedro, just you wait until you see all these animals. I think you will particularly love the reptile house,' Mina told him.

Lei looked at Mina, confident and kind and driving like an adult. Pedro had been a very positive influence on her.

*

Crane was in his laboratory, expecting them. He smiled when they arrived and waved for them to join him.

'This is Pedro. Pedro, this is Crane – he's a vet,' Lei said.

'Hello, Pedro, nice to meet you,' Crane said.

'What is a vet?' Pedro asked.

'It's an animal doctor. I look after animals. Come over here, guys. I have everything ready.'

'Do you think you'll be able to find out what is in the pills?' Lei asked.

'If my machines can't, then I can send off the results and get an answer soon enough,' he said.

'Careful what info you send to the mainland,' Lei warned.

'Duly noted and already considered,' Crane said, nodding. 'Why don't you all gather round here, out of the way, so you can see, and let's see what you have.'

Mina tipped the pills out onto the table, lining them up according to colour. Pedro gasped and stepped back.

'It's okay, Pedro, we want to see what they were giving you,' Mina said. 'You'll never have to take one again.'

He grabbed Mina's hand and stood stiffly at her side. 'They are painful and hurt everything.'

Crane sighed and started with the first pill, a blue one. He pulled on a pair of gloves, covered his mouth and nose with a surgical mask and told them all to do the same. He cut the pill in half, putting a small piece into a test tube. He added water, waited for it to dissolve, then placed the test tube into a small machine on one side of the table and pressed a button. A whirring noise filled the room as it spun into action, analysing the contents of the test tube. Moments later, a few words and symbols appeared on a virtual screen just above the machine.

'Hmm,' Crane said, as he read the data.

'What is it?' Lei asked, leaning over his shoulder to get

a closer look.

'It seems familiar, but I can't tell what it is, can you?'

'No, I don't recognise those ingredients at all, what now?'

'We send it off to the mainland and start on the next pill,' he said.

Crane worked his way through the pills, and it became apparent that the results were very similar, indicating only a couple of differences between the contents of each pill.

'Just the white ones to go,' Crane said.

They waited for the machine to finish and then analysed the results. Crane shrugged, seeing nothing unusual, and moved over for Lei to look. She glanced at the results and suddenly froze.

'Something wrong?' Crane asked.

'I recognise this,' she said.

'What is it?' Mina and Crane both asked simultaneously.

'It's the code for the Pisces vaccine! A little altered somehow but I'm sure it's that.'

'Why would they be giving the vaccine to the children?' Crane frowned.

'If the white pills counteract the effects of the coloured ones...' Mina started.

'Then that means...' Lei paused and stared at Crane.

'The coloured pills probably contain different mutations of the Pisces virus. Dear God, we need to isolate the room now! Jenny, Jenny!' Crane shouted for his nurse, who came running in, and they rushed around using clear tape to seal the edges of the windows and doors in order to lock down the room.

'Oh my God, I didn't even suspect they might be

viruses.' Lei held her forehead heavily and tried to calm her breathing. 'What if we've spread it on the island already?'

'It isn't contagious, don't worry,' Pedro said.

'How do you know?' Lei asked.

'Because they don't want us to be cross-contaminated when they make us take it. They want us to experience totally different viruses. I could have told you they were viruses if you'd asked. We stood next to each other all the time taking different viruses yet never sharing the same strand,' Pedro explained.

'But why?' asked Mina.

'I don't know, let me send these results off and we'll see what comes back,' Crane said. 'Jenny, let's do a quarantine clean to be safe and spray each other down too. Change clothes here and burn the lot. Alert all staff that we will be doing daily virus testing across the park – people and animals – just to be sure and stop anything before it has chance to spread. We will start with the hybrids and all of us. Anyone positive will need to be isolated.'

Jenny, white as a sheet, nodded.

'Tammy has already been to the park with all the animals,' Mina said.

'We'll just have to isolate and test as best we can now.' Crane sighed.

'You can only get it if you drink it. That is how the aliens stayed safe,' Pedro told them.

'I am grateful to hear that. We will still have to follow emergency procedures to be extra safe just to ensure nothing starts spreading from here. We cannot risk an outbreak on this island,' Crane said.

'All the same, I wouldn't worry or panic. As he said, they

all took different ones together in the same room and the infection didn't spread. I think the vaccine destroyed strands before contagion became an issue,' Lei said reassuringly.

Crane and Jenny nodded.

*

They waited impatiently for the responses to come back from the mainland. As they waited, Crane and Lei hunched over the results, discussing what they revealed and what they could mean. Mina took Pedro to the reptile centre and watched with adoration as he met each animal with wonder. His face was a picture. He adored lizards the most, like the iguanas and bearded dragons. He felt they were most like him and he surprised Mina by being really scared of snakes. They returned three hours later and nothing had yet come back about the pills. The computer Crane used to contact the mainland was a tiny device that was on the wall, smaller than his hand. When activated, images of people on the other end could be brought up into the air like a hologram effect. Frustratingly, no one was calling and the screen remained blank.

'Variations of Pisces – they're messing with the strand. Why would they do that, Crane?' Mina heard Lei ask as she walked in.

Crane rubbed his forehead and paced the room, deep in thought. He was shaking his head, about to say something, when the computer on the wall beeped. Lei shot over to the screen as fast as lightning.

'Crane, it's a response for the results of the white tablets. We've caused a bit of a stir on the mainland with this one because, apparently, it's an antibiotic effective against a different Pisces strand.' Lei stared at him.

'Bacterial and not viral?' Crane gasped.

'What does it mean?' Mina asked.

'Pisces was a virus. This is a bacterial infection. It's like pneumonia – the cause of that can be viral, fungal or bacterial. Same result, different cause. Therefore, it's not immediately contagious, as Pedro said. For example, with bacterial pneumonia, you aren't normally contagious after two days once the fever has gone, whereas with viral pneumonia, you are contagious all the way through. They do like their bacteria.' Lei released a long sigh.

'So, the Pisces virus was definitely a biological attack on us in the first place?' Crane said.

'Of course. However, we knew that already,' Lei replied. 'I guess I just always hoped it was a conspiracy theory,' Crane said.

'I'm afraid not. Let's review their feedback,' Lei said, and they looked at the information.

Jenny brought some tea and biscuits in and there was silence as they nibbled.

'And why call us the Children of Pisces?' Mina added.

'Who?' asked Crane.

'The aliens. They call Tammy, Mikie, Diego and me the Children of Pisces. I think they're experimenting to see if they can give these children powers like ours. Think about it.'

'Of course – the Children *of* Pisces!' Lei exclaimed. 'All the pregnancies I heard about, all the women and children that died. Yet, against the odds, Sarah had quadruplets. Not only that… babies with supreme gifts. They're trying to figure out how it happened. Why did Sarah survive as long as she did and why do her children have special gifts? They're trying to mimic you, create children with special powers for their own use. Wow!'

'So, they think the key to it all is the Pisces virus?' Crane asked.

'Yes, it makes sense now! Some alien species have gifts like telepathy. However, Sarah's children have not simply inherited existing gifts from an alien species. They have something better. How can that be? I remember that Sarah had a unique blood type. We talked about it – this gave her better tank training than I could have. I remember her and Thalen discussing it. They said something about the virus or vaccine affecting the women's pregnancies in some way. Sarah's blood was different, and she must have been able to handle the virus or vaccine differently. Perhaps her immune system was hyperactive to fight the virus, and this maintained the pregnancy. It must have kept Sarah alive when no other woman could have survived.'

'So, what happened?' Crane asked.

'I don't know, Crane. I remember Sarah had a unique blood type. We had to have the vaccines early in order to help others safely, and she only learnt afterwards that the vaccine did something to her for several months. The babies must have used the virus strand from the vaccine somehow, while in the womb. The vaccine did have a live strand in there, diluted yet still live. Marcellus must have found out somehow.'

'Do you think any other children are like this?' Mina asked.

'Thalen is a fantastic scientist. Better than Marcellus or anyone he would have on his crew. He has found a way to do something Marcellus cannot and, yes, maybe this is how he is building an army. Marcellus has clearly been experimenting with this for years and hasn't figured it out yet. They couldn't possibly know about her blood type and are focusing only on mutating the virus. Clearly, they think that getting hold of the Children of Pisces will help them piece together the gaps. The secret will be in your blood. The combination of half alien, half human and your mother's rare blood condition or type. Thalen will know because I wasn't there. They must never have you.' Lei looked at Mina, rubbing her brow.

'They tried to make me join them. They want us on their side but they would experiment on us, use our blood to create more hybrids and make their own army stronger than the greys.' Mina gasped.

'I think you're right. Whoever has even just the four of you will have a far stronger army. Imagine you all together after combat training with your father. Imagine how powerful you will be. Thank goodness they didn't take blood samples when they had the chance.' Lei bit her bottom lip. 'I'd love to take your blood, Mina, and study it. However, I'd need help off the mainland from professionals, and that would stir up unwanted attention. I already have some of Mikie's blood. I will ask Jax if he can help me. I think we can study and learn together and he can hack into systems and secretly ask questions. Can I take some of your blood?' Crane asked Mina.

'I'm out of here, this is getting creepy, and no one is touching my blood,' said Mina, turning to leave.

'Will they find us here?' Pedro asked, keeping hold of her hand.

Mina looked at him. 'No, Pedro, you're safe here with us.'

'Can we go back to the house now?' he asked.

'Yes, come on, we can share our news. You tell the hybrids so they understand what is happening. They need to trust us and feel safe,' she said with a smile.

As they drove back, Lei looked sideways at Mina. Pedro was in the back this time.

'I'm really proud of you, Mina. You've shown great strength of character and courage over the last few days,' she said.

'I almost got you killed,' Mina said flatly, staring straight ahead.

'I wasn't giving you what you needed, Mina. Forgive me. There's something I should have told you, and I never had the courage. Now is as good a time as any.'

Mina glanced at Lei, her face questioning.

'My own daughter died because I was too protective of her. I wouldn't let her make her own decisions. I overprotected her, didn't talk to her about anything and pretended everything was all good. I locked her in her room during the outbreak, thinking I was keeping her safe and giving her a happy childhood with no stress or worry.'

'You literally locked her up?' Mina gasped.

'Yes. I'm not proud of it. I just wanted to lock her away from the dangerous world outside. From her window, she started feeding birds, and if I had only told her that even small animals were spreading a nasty virus, she would have known. Instead, she was bored and made friends with a little robin redbreast. The robin died. Shortly after, so did my little girl and then her father. All I had to do was tell her and be open. I just thought she was too young and would be scared and it would ruin her childhood. Instead, I destroyed her childhood and took away her future. I didn't want her to have the fear that I had inside of me. I've always felt that I caused her death.'

'Lei, I didn't realise.' Mina took her hand in hers and gave it a gentle squeeze.

'I'm not proud of myself and can't normally think about it, let alone speak of it. When your mother sent you to me, I saw it as a second chance and promised I wouldn't make the same mistakes again, but instead I made a lot of new ones. I gave you too much freedom and not enough support and guidance. I guess I even shared too much with you far too young. I'm not very good at being a mother and I'm very sorry for that, Mina. I'm a good agent but motherhood is something I can't ever seem to figure out. I'd like to try harder. Can we start again?'

Mina threw her a charming smile. 'I can't afford to look too soft,' she said.

'One day, you *will* look too soft.' Lei smiled. 'One day!'

'Lei.'

'Yes?'

'You aren't a bad mother. Even with the freedom you gave me, I was restless. It was the best way to be for me. Otherwise, I'd have run away from home or rebelled more. I have a shadow inside of me far darker and scarier than Mikie or Tammy have. I have a monster inside and it's desperate to get out. It wants to take me over and some days it scares me that it will. This monster is real and it's part of me.' Mina took a deep breath and let it out slowly. 'You have had to deal with that monster too and I never realised before.'

'Thank you for sharing that with me, Mina. It means a lot,' Lei said softly. Then, she looked away before Mina could see the tears fall down her cheeks. She watched the countryside passing by and gulped back her sobs. She had to be strong and not let Mina know she was crying. She quickly wiped her tears away when Mina wasn't looking. She had not realised what Mina was facing each day.

'It's why I spot shadow people. I can smell, taste and see the darkness within them because it takes one to know one,' Mina added.

'Fortunately for you, I'm rather good at slaying monsters,' Lei added nonchalantly.

Mina glanced at her out of the corner of her eye, a smile twitching at her lips. 'Good answer, Lei.'

*

They were outside by the pond, watching the children run around, eating, drinking and laughing for what was probably the first time in their little lives. Some were still too traumatised and sat together in tight balls watching the others. Tammy stood with Jude and Lei. Mina and Mikie were with the hybrids. Everyone had done Tai chi in the morning, including Mina, and they were all about to head to the lodge. They needed to feed the children there since the house was too far away to keep walking back and forth for each meal. It was wasting time and energy they didn't have.

'It will take years of healing, if they ever overcome this trauma at all,' Lei said with a sigh.

'Not true,' Tammy replied.

'How so?' Lei frowned at her.

'Mikie and I work every night on healing them all. The more we heal, the more our healing powers evolve and advance. We are finding that we can actually go into each chakra and break them down and remove even the tiniest seeds of fear and trauma. Permanently.'

'In each chakra?' Lei gasped.

Tammy nodded. 'Yes, there are twelve chakras and many of them hold these seeds that can be fully removed. Organs hold them too. The Egyptians understood how important the body's organs were, retaining certain information about that person in the actual organ, and that is why they put them in jars when they died. Some organs hold fear and others hold anger and trauma and we can see it. And remove it. Most people only work with their five senses and that is all the average person thinks about. Chakras are part of our body –twelve main chakras and hundreds of minor chakras – and they are working or malfunctioning all the time.'

Lei just gaped at Tammy as she continued.

'They are powerhouses that draw in prana energy from our surroundings. A chemical reaction then takes place, and a process starts to happen with each chakra doing what it's there to do. Each chakra governs a specific part of the human body. They malfunction and cause issues when things like trauma and fear damage and block them. Disease is just dis-ease. To not be balanced. It will take us a few days but we are getting there. Then, the energy transference between them and within their chakras and systems will operate at optimum levels.'

'Tammy, wow, that is really amazing,' Jude replied.

'I can't process what you have just said. My goodness, you are something else. All of you are amazing, I'm flabbergasted. Do you think you might be able to do some of that on me when you have the chance?' Lei asked. 'I don't want to take away from the hybrids.'

'Of course. Join me and Mikie each night. We are doing mass healings so you can sit in with the children. I can see what you need me to remove. It won't take long,' Tammy said, smiling.

'Thank you, that's really kind of you. Mass healings... whatever next!' Lei shook her head, smiling.

'Tammy, how are you coping with all this?' Jude asked softly.

'I'm fine,' Tammy said.

'Really? I can imagine you see or feel some rather hard things when healing the children. That can't be easy. You know I am here to talk to at any time, right? Perhaps I can help you with what you should and shouldn't say to those you are healing,' Jude suggested kindly.

'I'd like that. It would be nice to be able to talk about it,' Tammy replied sadly. It was a burden and she hadn't thought to speak to anyone else.

'Good. I suggest we have a daily catch-up before Tai chi each morning, just us. Now, let's get back to what we are here for,' Jude said. 'Fortunately for the children, we still have the old brick bread oven around the side of the house. Otherwise, I'd never have been able to bake enough bread for sandwiches. We used it during Pisces when we had to feed the whole island. We can't move that to the camp, since it is a large permanent construct, so we need a daily rota for putting the bread on, monitoring it and taking it to the lodge. Maybe, eventually, we can build one at the camp. It's great for pastries too.'

FIVE

TLACHTLI

PERU

Charles came stomping into the house, furious, but stopped suddenly when he saw Quilla standing by the curtain.

'Oh, I'm sorry, Princess Quilla, I didn't see you there,' he said.

'Just call me Quilla, Charles, we try to be modern and this isn't the first time I've asked you to do that for me.' She smiled sweetly.

'Of course. Sorry, Quilla.'

'It's time I went. I'll leave this oil on the floor by the curtain so be sure to put it on when you get out. See you later, Diego,' she called as she left.

'Bye, Quilla, and thank you so much,' Diego shouted after her from behind the curtain. Charles frowned at the unexpected curtain, and pulled it aside to see Diego in the bath.

'Whoa, you're in my personal space man, back off,'

Diego yelled, covering his privates and glaring at Charles.

'Unbelievable. I'm fighting to keep you here while you're causing all sorts of mischief then soaking it off in a posh flipping bath. Alright for some, isn't it!' Charles moaned. He dropped the curtain, giving Diego his privacy back, and angrily paced the room. More upset that he wasn't even aware that a bath was possible in this place.

'Quilla was trying to be helpful. She gave me some essential oils to help with my pain. I'm trying my best.'

'You shouldn't have been alone with her, Diego, what if something went wrong? The king wouldn't just banish us from the village if we killed his daughter, he'd have us killed!' Exasperated, Charles ran his hands through his hair. He had become increasingly more stressed since the accident in England and now he didn't have any access to gaming – his only stress relief.

Diego knew he was addicted to that and other things. Poor Charles had struggled with addiction and Diego was a huge stress to him. The English police were still after him – both of them now – since the fire. It didn't look good back home.

'So did the king give you a hard time?' Diego asked, getting out of the bath and wrapping a thin towel around his waist. The oils and drink had worked wonders remarkably fast. They were like magic; he felt energised and barely any pain remained.

'What do you think? He chewed me up out there! Plus, he's my friend and I don't want his children hurt either physically or socially. You have to stop showing Manco up. Just being shorter than you is hard for a prince. The girls would be all over you like a rash if it wasn't for Quilla keeping them at arm's length. Think of his position here. Have some decency. Look, Diego, I don't know what else to do with you, we have nowhere else to go, and no one we can turn to. If we cannot exist here, I don't know what we will do, please try to understand. There is nowhere else.'

'I do understand and don't worry, I know what I have to do now,' Diego said. 'Quilla has helped me to understand the way they think and what they believe in. She understands me, Uncle Charles.' Diego didn't have the heart to add 'unlike you'. His uncle tried his best.

'Well, I hope so because we're running out of time. This is your final warning and we've only been here a month. We cannot afford or risk any more mistakes.' Charles paced up and down the room, anxiously, now talking more to himself than to Diego. 'What do we do if he makes us leave? We'd have to roam the world, move secretly from one place to another, live in absolute poverty, be nomadic, and never have any comfort. Oh, I just couldn't bear it! The police are still asking questions in Liverpool, after that poor boy's body was found all burned and—'

'Don't, stop talking about it,' Diego interrupted. 'I didn't mean to.'

'I know, Diego. You never mean to, but that doesn't stop it happening, does it? I left London, then Gloucester, then London again, then Devon, then Birmingham and then Liverpool because of you. We couldn't settle in Egypt, even though I thought the desert would help avoid another fire, but nope, you can certainly whip up a brilliant sand storm! Six fires in two years, Diego!'

'Eight actually.'

'Oh, please!'

'Charles, just breathe, you are too stressed. I hate seeing you like this,' Diego said, trying to soothe him.

'I can't cope with you.' Charles sighed. 'Whatever your mother thought, leaving you with me was insane. I mean, we loved each other, yes. I dated her for a year. She was the most beautiful girl in the world. But I'm not the father type. And I can't cope with your powers at all. I can't even cope with a normal life. That's why she left me, you know? I was a mess.'

'I know. But you're stronger than you think. It's all right, I know what I have to do. We won't have to leave this place. I'll fix it,' Diego said.

'It's not all right, Diego. The whole village is fuming. The king has made them prepare the boar, refusing to waste it, and they're not happy about it. Manco wants you gone. The women have to stay up late preparing the boar under candle light, which is hardly acceptable. And the men have to get up early with the children so that the women can sleep.' Charles, starting to have a panic attack, was struggling to breathe.

'The men here are hands-on dads anyway and often take turns getting up with the children. They won't be angry for ever, it's not that bad. Sit down and put your head between your knees and just breathe,' Diego soothed and helped him, rubbing his back.

'The whole village now hates us; these people work hard and can't afford to waste food. I haven't had sex in six years!'

'Oh, TMI! Look, I promise I'll fix it. I'm going out for some fresh air. Don't wait up for me, I'll be a while. Get in the bath and relax while it's still hot.' Diego sighed heavily, straightening up.

'But it's late, it's too dark…'

'You know I'll be fine.'

'A bath would be nice,' Charles murmured.

Diego stepped outside and saw how bright and full the moon was that evening. He smiled as he thought of the goddess Mama Quilla, *Mother Moon*. It was a clear night, the stars were all out and he could see well, despite the darkness.

'A perfect night for a hunt,' he said, stretching.

'Yes it is,' Quilla said, suddenly appearing behind him. Diego jumped, startled by her presence and then smiled at her, speechless. She pushed a spear at him and gave him the reigns to a cama as she smiled.

Over the years the Incas had bred llamas with camels to have a much stronger bone structure designed for heavy loads. The Crown Prince of Dubai first achieved this via artificial insemination in 1998, creating the first hybrid. The Incas expanded on this hybrid breed. Their spines were as capable as any camels to take the weight of a person and avoid a spine injury. They lacked a hump, so desert life would not be for them, which wasn't a problem in the rainforest, but it was a bumpy ride and only intended for short distance to help carry people or heavy objects up and down the mountains – especially the elderly. It was a cost-effective solution that worked well. However, the Incas still preferred to keep both llamas and alpacas because one of the downfalls to the cama was its unbelievable moodiness.

The moonlight shone on Quilla's hair and made her whole head sparkle; it was a while before Diego could move to take the spear. They didn't say anything else as she stood there, patiently, as he stared at her. The connection between them was intense like a magnet pulling in metal – Quilla was the magnet. Then, he turned and left. Quilla watched Diego disappear down the mountain with the cama.

*

The villagers were barely up by the time Diego returned. He marched boldly up the hill, next to the cama with a huge amount of fresh fish hanging over the saddle. Enormous wild rainbow trout glimmered in the sun. The Incas loved fish and since the men had to start hunting late today, giving the women chance to sleep, Diego had done the fishing for them. The villagers noticed and then started talking excitedly in Spanish, waking up those who had not yet left their huts. He had been up all night hunting, with only the spear, in the traditional way, and after many failed attempts, he had succeeded. Thanks to Quilla's training the week before, when neither of them knew he would need to know how to fish. Or perhaps she did and that's why she taught him in secret. Diego now suspected she had known. She was far better at spear fishing than any of the men and none of them knew it – except Diego. She had entrusted her secret to him alone and made him promise never to tell anyone. It had made him feel special.

Quilla looked out of her house then shouted for her father and Manco to come and see. Nobody could understand what was going on. How crazy was this young boy, going out into a dangerous forest in the middle of the night, all alone? It meant the men got the day off. It was, to say the very least, a most exciting start to the day. For everyone except Diego. As he reached the villagers and heard their excitement, he felt the normal fear and insecurity return. His legs buckled beneath him for a moment before he regained his balance and tried to act confident as he approached. He thought it was strange how he could go out into the forest, where he faced cats and snakes large enough to have him for breakfast, with no fear for himself at all. Yet, as soon as he was in the middle of a group of people, he felt petrified beyond belief.

He saw the king and Manco staring at him in wonder and Quilla beside them, smiling reassuringly at him. Diego awkwardly walked up to them. Charles came out of his hut then, to see what all the commotion was, and sighed when he saw Diego. Charles headed towards the king too, feeling miserable and worried that Diego had been out all night up to no good. What had he done now?

'Forgive me,' Diego said, catching his breath. 'I understand what I've done wrong and wish to make amends. This morning I prove to you that I can hunt following your ways and will do so with the other boys from this day forth. I will improve my skills to work as a team and show you that I mean well. I have a lot to learn, this I now understand, but with your guidance I shall become a good student.'

Manco folded his arms across his chest and shook his head in disbelief. The king said nothing for a moment. He looked at the gathered crowd and their excitement at the abundance of fish.

'Hunting a boar is not an easy thing to do and is not our traditional way. It is something we do on a rare occasion and it is supposed to be an exciting group event. My son requested no older men this time to help you young men bond, and it was not a successful event,' the king explained.

Diego forced himself to maintain eye contact with the king and not throw Manco a knowing look. He knew he had been set up. Yet he was starting to realise what a threat he was to Manco. He didn't want to undermine or belittle him. He could not alienate himself with Quilla's brother – for her sake.

The king continued, 'I appreciate your gesture, Diego, of wanting to make amends for yesterday, but it was dangerous to go out alone. You put yourself in harm's way, which is both brave and risky at the same time. Let this be the last time you do such a thing. I do not wish to see you harmed while in my care. I take your gesture as a good meaning and we thank you for this effort. I'm sure the men will appreciate an easy day.'

Charles looked at the king, with surprise, and then back at Diego. He nodded his approval of the situation.

'That must be the most abundant fishing trip this village has ever seen,' Quilla said, clapping her hands together excitedly. She glanced at the bandage on his thigh and knew his wound needed treatment.

'It is indeed,' replied the king. 'You must be exhausted and I'm impressed you did so well for your first time. You have a lot of strength in you, for such a young boy. You have great potential.'

Diego breathed a sigh of relief; it had worked, the king was happy. For once, he was getting praise instead of a scolding and he had to admit it felt good.

'Tonight, we have an extra feast before our big celebration,' he told the villagers.

They cheered and came to look at the trout with keen interest. It was an unusually lucky fishing outcome and they

wondered what luck Diego might have. The king went back inside his house. Manco didn't look happy and stared coldly over his shoulder as he followed his father. He suspected Diego had used power to get so many large trout all alone. Surely, it was not possible.

'Remember, he will be your friend soon,' Quilla said to Diego.

'I know,' he said. 'Thank you for the training.'

'Like I said, we women hunt better than the men. They just don't want to know it.' She playfully winked at him. She and some friends had fished in secret, hidden from him, and when his back had turned, she had added their catch to his. She knew Diego suspected. Her team of warrior women were trustworthy and they all trusted Diego and knew that a boy this powerful would soon become a man that could trample his enemies. They wanted him on their team. It had been a fun fishing game.

'That was risky but clever,' Charles told him. 'Well done.'

'I said it would be OK, didn't I?' Diego smiled with a confidence he didn't feel.

'Yes, you did.' Charles smiled back and smacked him affectionately on his shoulder before walking back to the hut.

'You stink of fish. Let's go for a swim and wash it away,' Quilla said, taking his hand in hers.

Diego nodded. 'Let's take the slide, I'm exhausted.'

'I'm not sure I want to be near you on the slide with how smelly you are,' she replied, tilting her head and smiling up at him.

'Well, it certainly put an end to the wonderful essential oils you gave me.'

'I will give you more after our swim. It will be nice. Ones that will take away the fishy smell.' She giggled.

They took the slide down to the waterfall, a place Quilla loved to swim, and slowly waded into the water. Quilla swam over to him.

'You were successful and very brave,' she said.

He smiled, shyly.

'Diego, I noticed your wound and it's starting to bleed more. I know that the bandage you have so poorly put on your thigh is not covering a minor wound, is it?'

'No, it's pretty deep,' he replied.

'Does it hurt?'

'I think I have gone past feeling the pain.'

'Let me take a look at it?'

He showed her his leg. There was a large gash at the top and it was deep and still bleeding. He winced when she touched it.

'Come, take the bandage off, let the water clean it and then sit on the side so I can have a look. What happened?' she asked.

'I slipped and then fell on the spear. I didn't want you to know. I had a piece of cloth I intended to use as a towel so used that to tie it up.' He blushed.

'Come, I shall fix it for you.' She smiled kindly.

He gritted his teeth in agony as he pulled himself out of the water and sat on the side of the bank. She bathed the wound and took out a tube of superglue from her first aid kit; a waterproof belt-bag she carried with her at all times. She often stopped to help injured animals in the wild as well as people in the village. She rubbed an ointment on the wound and then glued it together. She was impressed with his brave face and knew it must be hurting, but he never showed a sign of it.

'My father is right, you do have the potential to be a great man, but you need to work on your fear of people,' she told him.

'You have done this before,' Diego said, raising his eyebrows with surprise at what a good job she had done.

'Of course, I have fixed many of the men's wounds. Some of them even cry.' She laughed.

'I don't think I have ever cried,' he replied.

'That is not a good sign. I have never cried, either.'

'Really? Perhaps because of all those years you cried silver tears on an eclipse?'

'Perhaps.' She smiled. 'And perhaps we both need a good cry.'

'I'll remember that when Manco next invites me on a hunt.' Diego sighed.

They heard Manco and some boys in the distance; they too would often swim by the waterfall. Diego looked uncomfortable for a moment. Quilla took his hand and held it, softly, and reassuringly. He relaxed a little. They heard the boys laughing and talking and Diego looked up and saw Manco in the distance; he was heading for the top part of the river, above the waterfall. No one spotted Quilla and Diego.

'Let's go under the waterfall now the glue has dried,' she said.

'It dried fast.'

'Yes, when I work on animals in the wild I need it to be fast. I worked with my father to create a new type of superglue for this reason. My father is a very intelligent man and with my herbal knowledge we created a glue with herbs for the ultimate healing solution.'

'Wow, you should sell it,' Diego said.

'Maybe one day I will,' she replied.

They swam back into the water and headed to where the water fell 300 metres over a series of steep drops cascading down into the rocky area where they were. The water fell in three distinct falls; the one in the middle was the most thunderous and heavy, but the two either side of it were thinner and smaller and made it possible to stand under them to shower. The middle fall was deadly, roaring with speed, and was where most of the water from the top channelled down. They had to scramble over the rocks to get there. It was also refreshingly cold. They laughed at each other whenever one of them slipped and fell into the water. They splashed each other until Diego dived under the water and swam away. Quilla followed, watching the fish swim between them and smiling at each other under water. They surfaced close to eachother and Quilla, not for the first time, marvelled at how Diego was so much older than his years.

'We are lucky to be able to swim here with such a variety of fish,' Quilla explained. 'This was home to loads of piranha before the Pisces infection took them out. Father decided not to reintroduce them here afterwards so we can swim. It is the only place I know of that is safe to swim so never enter the water anywhere else, Diego. Promise me.'

'OK.' He smiled.

They could see Manco and the other boys from where they were and Diego realised, with disappointment, that they could now see him too. Manco looked furious to see his sister swimming alongside Diego. He scowled at them.

'Ignore him,' Quilla said.

'What are they doing up there?' Diego asked.

'That is where they play tlachtli.'

'What's that?'

'It's a ball game; they use a rubber ball and have to hit it into the air using hips, thighs, and upper arms. The object of the game is to score as many points as you can by getting the ball through the stone ring that they have hung from a tree up there.'

'Sounds easy enough,' Diego said, trying to see what they were doing.

'It's not that easy. You have to work in pairs and the rubber ball is as hard as rock so you can be really badly bruised by playing it, that's why I never play anymore. We have a clearing on the other side of the river where we play volleyball instead. But Manco likes it, he always wins, and he never seems to get too bruised.'

Diego made a visor with his hands and peered up at them as they played. He wanted to join in but knew none of them would want him. Manco wasn't paying the game too much attention; he was too busy glaring at Quilla and Diego in between shots. They saw the ball hurtling towards Manco but no one had time to warn him. The hard ball slammed into Manco's shoulder, knocking him off balance, and sending him plunging into the water.

'Manco!' Quilla screamed.

Diego watched as Manco struggled in the water, caught immediately in the current as the rapids dragged him towards the edge of the waterfall. The other boys panicked and shouted in fear. There was nothing they could do for the rapids were fierce at the crest of the waterfall. Anyone who jumped in would topple over the falls with him, and he was far from reach even with the branches they found and tried to hand to him. None were long enough. They could barely make out Manco's head as he was pulled, helplessly, under the water and towards the edge, right in the middle of the cascading falls.

'He will not be able to fight the current, Diego, he will be swept over and land on these rocks and surely die. Do something, please,' Quilla said, unnaturally calm. She had foreseen everything and knew exactly how this was to play out.

For a moment, Diego felt the panic rising in him too but almost as soon as the feeling started, he took one look at Quilla and something changed. She nodded at him. He suddenly felt protective and with a sudden sense of calm. He looked around, wondering what he could do. Manco would be over the waterfall before he had gotten out of the water so there was no chance of reaching him. He couldn't catch him and it was too dangerous to be near the bottom of the middle waterfall. The sky was perfectly clear – no thunderstorm or lightning today – and there was no electricity out here, which was one of the main reasons Charles had selected this place. There was only one thing he could think of trying.

Diego had always used what was around him but never before had he tried to make it happen. This time, since there was no other choice, he activated his crystal cube and tried to make lightning appear. He held his wrist, and the cube, high into the air, closed his eyes and tried to imagine a cloud coming, carrying a storm, and a bolt of lightning for his use. Diego was more surprised than anyone else when he opened his eyes and saw the cloud forming suddenly, darkening the sky. He could hear the low rumbling of the thunder and called upon it. Then lightning came, struck the cube, and sent the bolt directly to the tree Diego was aiming at. The tree hovered over the edge of the water, at the top of the waterfall, and came crashing down as the lightning broke it in half. It fell across the water and wedged itself tightly in between some rocks. Just in time.

Manco banged heavily into the tree by the force of the current and held onto it, looking down over the waterfall with large, terrified eyes. Then, he looked at Diego and something passed between them. It had been a close call. Manco climbed onto the tree as a couple of his friends raced to help him out. He stood, on shaking legs, and looked from the fallen tree to Diego. He was not the only one who was shocked by what had happened. The cloud disappeared as swiftly as it had come and the sun shone brightly again in the clear blue sky.

'Wow, Diego, you just created a storm from nothing.' Quilla gasped.

'Yeah, you saw that too?' Diego smiled widely, cockily. 'Scares the hell out of me.'

'I bet. How old were you when things like this first started to happen?'

'Before my earliest memory, I think. The first fire I started – by accident of course – I was six. I remember that. The worst was when I electrocuted Charles and his girlfriend in hospital. I didn't mean to. He was hooked up to machines following an accident that I had caused and I got cross with her yelling at me and, well, it just happened. I was seven then. He was OK. She left and never spoke to us again. I don't think Charles ever recovered after that. He's scared of me, you know. Are you?'

'No, not at all. I feel terrible for you being so young and having to handle such powers. That's terrible. I'm not scared of you one bit, Diego, and I never will be.'

Diego and Quilla were climbing out of the water as Manco and the boys headed towards them. Manco stopped in front of Diego and everyone fell silent. Quilla threw her arms around her brother with relief. He hugged her back. Quilla looked at Manco and Diego, both the same age and yet Diego seemed much older, more her age. It was strange to see.

Eventually, Manco spoke, 'You saved my life.'

'I destroyed another tree though,' Diego replied.

'I think that under the circumstances, that is all right.' Manco smiled.

Diego smiled back and felt the relief run through him when Manco put his arm around his shoulder.

'We must be friends and put our issues behind us,' he told Diego, and the other boys.

They looked at Quilla as they realised that what she had said had just come true and a strange feeling of apprehension went through them. She really could predict the future.

'I knew you wouldn't die,' Quilla said.

'I didn't!' Manco tutted. 'You could have given a warning about *how* we would become friends, Sis. A heads up would have been nice!'

'Yes, I agree with that,' Diego added.

'I can't see the details like that. I'll try to see better in future.' Quilla smiled. It was a lie. She had been guided not to share details because that often changed the outcome.

'Come along, everyone, let us go home and tell my father,' Manco said.

As they walked into the forest, Diego noticed the Andean Cock-of-the-rock bird sitting on the branch of a tree and watching them. He frowned, wondering for a moment if it really was the same bird. After all, they all looked alike – right?

'Pretty, isn't he?' Quilla said, following his gaze.

'Yes, he is pretty but I keep thinking that he's following me,' Diego replied.

'Don't be silly,' Manco said, cheerfully. 'They all look the same.'

'Yes, I guess they do,' Diego agreed, but his answer didn't convince Quilla that he believed that. She looked over at the bird and frowned.

'I have seen that bird watching you, Diego,' she said. 'They don't normally behave like that. Nor for so long.'

'That's what I was thinking,' Diego said. 'It's weird, right?'

'Yes,' she said, looking at it one last time before they continued back to the village.

*

The king and Charles both looked at each other as they listened to Manco tell them what had happened. The king's face changed from shock and then to relief. He was not, at first, sure how to react.

'You have saved my son's life and for this I am grateful,' he said. 'You showed control over your power by only damaging the tree which was required to save his life. I thank you, Diego, and am in your debt. For this, I shall make a promise here and now that I will never turn you away from my village. You have shown that you have a golden heart. You and your uncle will always be welcome.'

'Thank you,' Diego said, noticing the relief spread over Charles' face. It annoyed him a little; he felt as if Charles was relinquishing his responsibility by making Diego the king's problem. He felt abandoned and yet perhaps it was for the best – Charles was not looking well. The king had taken over parenting Diego.

'You have proven to me that although you have a God's power to command storms, you try to use it for good and not, as I initially suspected, for destruction. You have greatly improved and we shall all share in the boar you caught and use the annual festival to formally initiate you into our tribe,' the king continued.

'Thank you,' Charles said.

Diego was speechless and felt proud for the first time in his life. He looked at the happy faces of Quilla and Manco and knew he had good friends in them both. He felt the relief inside him as the village cheered and called out his name. When he looked at his uncle, he was surprised to see the tears of relief in his eyes, and Diego tried not to be disappointed in him. Charles had tried his best. He really couldn't blame him.

SIX

BOOT CAMP

VIVACITY ISLAND

The hybrids had devoured over a hundred croissants and boiled eggs for breakfast, along with a tremendous amount of apple juice. Jude was doing maths on a regular basis all of a sudden.

'My poor chickens haven't been under such pressure to lay in years! I'll have to hatch more. Fast. Or rather, I think I just need to get a load from the mainland, and you'll have to build another coup especially for your camp,' she said to Lei. 'We need more apple trees, that's for sure. They grow apples quickly, so we can take cuttings and establish more. At least we have plenty of land.'

'We can do that,' Lei said.

'I'm already out of lemons, eggs, fruit and vegetables. You'll need to establish your own fruit and vegetable farm because mine is done within three days with this lot. The children are old enough to be self-sufficient and help, because it will be a lot of work, and we cannot have humans see them. My goodness, they aren't even teenagers yet. They will undoubtably need huge amounts of food then. This is nothing compared to what it will be like,' Jude said with a sigh.

'The primates and elephants can help with building things and farming. I can oversee that,' Tammy said.

'What a brilliant idea. I hadn't considered that,' Jude remarked.

'We need to get a shopping list and pull things in from the mainland. My team of agents can be trusted to help and they know about aliens so we can safely use them. I contacted them last night with the urgent supplies list you and I agreed on. They'll be here today,' Lei said.

'That is good news,' Jude said, smiling.

'Yes, I have also asked them to bring bikes with waterproof pannier bags and trailers for the hybrids to move about on, as well as collect food and bread supplies,' Lei added.

'What a brilliant idea. Well done, Lei.' Jude nodded, pleased, as everything was coming together.

They were distracted by a noise and turned to see Pedro on the other side of the pond, speaking to Mina. The other children were gathering around, getting really excited.

'I wonder what that is all about,' Lei pondered.

'Oh, I have to go,' Tammy said, and started off at a run towards Mina.

In no time at all, the children had gathered in a large, excited circle around Mina, Tammy and Mikie. Everyone else – Stephen, Lei, Ed, Jude and Jax – walked over and stood behind the children. Pedro stood up in front of the group and, feeling very important, made the announcements in both languages.

'Ladies and gentlemen, please be quiet as we gather here today to witness an extraordinary show of power. For one day only, please let me introduce you to the one and only Children of Pisces,' Pedro said, repeating it in Galidian, then bowing smartly.

Everyone clapped as Mina, Tammy and Mikie took a theatrical bow and began a fun demonstration of their powers for the children's benefit. The children watched, enthralled. Tammy made the water dance and Mikie made some children get up and dance too, or act like a chicken clucking in circles. It made the others laugh and he was careful to keep it fun and not embarrassing.

Mina went invisible, snuck up on Stephen and lifted him up to make him fly in the air. Mikie then made him act like a gorilla, thumping his chest and picking imaginary lice from his hair and eating it, and everyone laughed again. Mina made plates and glasses move in circles and fly close to their heads, making them duck and scream and laugh in turn. It was like a magic act. Everyone was smiling and having fun. It seemed that nothing could spoil their happiness.

*

The camp was an hour's walk away. It was hidden on the island, surrounded by trees, with a lot of cleared yet overgrown land around the wooden lodge. The lodge was larger than Lei had expected and was indeed needing a lot of repair. Doors were falling off or completely gone, there were holes in the roof due to numerous planks of wood lifting off and, in some cases, rotted through. However, it was not half as bad as Jude remembered and they could turn it around in no time. Jax shared his secret treehouse with them all, which he had built several years ago with Ed. He told them he would extend it and maybe even build another one opposite so they could have base camps.

'Do you remember making that for Jax?' Jude said with a smile, looking up at Ed.

'I do indeed.' Ed nodded. 'Those were the days. Looks as good as new, too.'

'Yes, it does. I remember watching you boys do that. Such lovely summers we have had. Tammy suggested using the animals to help, like the primates and elephants.'

'Makes sense,' said Ed.

'Not sure I'd be happy to see a silverback gorilla with a nail gun in his hands,' Stephen said as he approached.

'In your capable hands, I'm sure it'll be fine.' Lei laughed. 'Oh, I have an incoming call.' She activated her watch and walked away to take the call.

'Equally, it may be the last thing I see before I die a tragic death with large nails sticking out of my head. Anyway, I'm impressed with this lodge and it doesn't need that much doing to it,' Stephen said as Lei walked away, speaking to a holographic image of Crane on her watch.

'Yeah, we could fix this up pretty quickly,' Dave added.

'I just got off the phone with Crane,' Lei told everyone a moment later. 'He's at the ferry port greeting my team and the huge vans full of stuff they've arrived with. We have tons of food and drink, blankets, clothes, bikes, sleeping bags, pillows, towels, slippers, shoes, toiletries, hairbrushes, books for fun, and books and audio tapes on school subjects to teach them with. What else? Oh yes, established fruit,

vegetables and trees, so we can get self-sufficient faster. Not to mention a vanload of ducks, chickens, rabbits, six kittens, and a couple of donkeys and carts, apparently.' Lei let out a long breath and smiled at everyone.

'And a partridge in a pear tree.' Stephen chuckled.

'Why the kittens?' Jude asked.

'One of the women on my team rescued a stray cat that she loves and wants to keep. However, soon after taking her in, she learnt that she was pregnant and now she's had kittens. She basically blackmailed me – said she would help if I rehomed the entire litter on this island. She wanted them to have loads of space and be together. I figured you wouldn't mind or notice, and they'd make cute pets for the children and keep rats away from our supplies,' Lei explained.

'Very clever. Not sure how the dogs will take to them. Nonetheless, it is what it is,' Jude said, nodding.

'No doubt the hybrids will give them a loving home,' Lei added, smiling.

'I can't believe you have done all that in a day, including delivery.' Ed shook his head in amazement.

'My agents can be changing a baby's nappy one minute and then setting up bombs and surrounding a factory full of drugs or terrorists within six hours. I run a woman heavy team, most of whom are single mums, and trust me, they work hard and fast. Shopping for thirty children is easy in comparison to the missions we normally do. We do shifts and have our own viral-isolation bubble, so those off shift does childcare for those on shift, whether they need to isolate or not,' Lei said proudly.

'I never underestimate a woman.' Ed laughed. 'Thank you so much, Lei.'

'I'm all for equality, it just turned out this way over the last few years because more women survived than men. Used to be mostly male agents,' said Lei.

'That is true, and yet London has eleven women to every man and I have found that hard to complain against.' Stephen smirked.

'Oh, trust you!' Jude exclaimed as she clocked Lei rolling her eyes.

'Well, I can't lie! What's the plan regarding Diego? Mikie said they were lying about having him,' Stephen said.

'Yes, good point. I'm even more worried for him now that we have taken the hybrids, as they'll be full throttle after him,' Lei said with a sigh.

'Well, we chatted about this earlier with the children and decided to stay for a couple more days so that they can carry on their urgent healings on the hybrids. Not to mention Mikie's leg. We all still need more rest. Tammy and Mikie have barely slept, working on the children every night. Then, we'll go back to where we were heading – Peru,' Ed said.

'I hope he's still safe,' said Mikie, approaching with Jax, Tammy and Mina.

'We cannot afford any further delays. The good news is that from what you all saw and heard on the spaceship, it's unlikely they have any idea that Diego is in Peru, so we should get there first,' Ed said.

'We only need two more nights here,' said Tammy, 'to complete the healing of the children.'

'Can I help? I saw what you did. Perhaps I can help strengthen the energy somehow,' Mina suggested.

'Of course you can.' Tammy smiled. 'In fact, if you did

that, we could leave sooner, since they'll heal faster with your help too. Plus, we can always do distant healing, as we are learning that now.'

'Well, you can finish that and then try to contact Diego. Let him know the danger he's in. You guys be extra careful and convince him to tell us where he is exactly. Maybe if he knows about the hybrids, he will be more helpful. Jude, I'll leave you in charge of the camp and island again,' Ed said.

'I'm already dying to get stuck in,' she said, smiling and rubbing her hands excitedly together and looking around the lodge.

'You never could turn away from a good project, could you?' Ed laughed.

'Well, to be honest, I think Stephen, Lei and her team will have it all in hand. It won't take long. We need wood to secure the walls and put together some new doors,' she said.

'I can do that,' said Stephen. 'Carpentry is my favourite hobby. I made all my own kitchen cupboards and my dining table and chairs.'

'He did, actually, really nice ones too,' Mikie said.

'Perfect. You'll need more land to expand the camp so you can take these trees and use them,' Ed said, gesturing around him. 'Save the bottom of the trunks for little seats.'

'What a good idea. Tree-stump chairs.' Stephen smiled.

'And me,' Lei added. 'I'm good at DIY.'

'I'm not so bad either. This will be fun,' Ben said.

'The children will also enjoy helping us. We can teach them,' Stephen added.

'It will be very therapeutic,' said Lei.

'We can sleep out under the stars on good nights and under the roof on the floor until we have made enough bedrooms,' Stephen said cheerily. 'I'll get started fixing that roof for when the rain comes.'

'Wonderful! We need to add the extension here, to create something like an outside school, for when it rains. The weather is terrible here in winter, so we need fireplaces in every room.' Jude moved her arms about, imagining the schoolroom extending from the main building.

'Well, it's a good-sized cabin and I can do an extension. Some of it may be open air, which will be nice on warm days. Other separate buildings too, so they can move from school classes and break up the teachings. And we must have a gym. Leave it with me,' Stephen said with a nod, his mind already planning how he would do it.

'I can make bunk beds with you,' Mina said.

'This is wonderful! I can sort out the mattresses to go on the bunk beds. We can just use straw for the time being and get the rooms ready for autumn with proper mattresses. It will be super fun sleeping under the stars for now, and the children can help with the bales of straw,' Jude said.

'With the donkeys and carts! This is so much fun.' Lei squealed.

'We can create a boy and girl section, especially for bathroom purposes. There is a small kitchen. However, we will need to modernise and extend it. We don't have a laundry area, though. Never mind, I can do the laundry at the house,' Jude muttered quietly.

'You can't do that,' Pedro added.

'Do what, Pedro?' Jude asked.

'You can't have boy and girl toilets. Some of us don't categorise ourselves by gender. We are nonbinary,' he said. 'We had this problem on the spaceships.'

Jude frowned, puzzled. 'I hadn't thought of that. How did you handle it on the spaceships?'

'We were told to pick which one we were most comfortable with and use that. Most are males. There aren't many females on the ship. It wasn't nice.'

'What would *you* suggest as a solution?' Jude asked, smiling at Pedro and kneeling in front of him.

Pedro thought about it for a moment and then beamed brightly. 'No distinguishing whatsoever. Create individual cubicles alongside each other that one person at a time can use.'

'Unisex?' Lei questioned.

'Yes,' Pedro replied.

'That could work. We can do some all-in-ones, like shower, sink and loo combined, some single loo and sinks only, and some showers only. It could work.' Stephen nodded.

'I love that idea.' Jude clapped her hands and stood up. 'Well done, Pedro! All to be disabled friendly too, naturally. I think we have everything covered.'

'I'll help you with that kitchen. My dad was a carpenter,' Ben offered.

'Perfect!' Jude nodded.

'I'll get the elephants to help with carrying tree trunks and wood supplies,' Dave said.

Ed and Tammy smiled as they listened to Jude organise the tasks required and different people to take over certain areas. She, Lei and Stephen were in their element. Jude more so. She had just become the world's busiest mother. Ed was feeling rather emotional as he watched her.

'She's going to love doing this, isn't she, Ed?' Tammy

whispered to him.

'Yes, she is, and it's great that she'll have something to keep her so busy while we're off getting Diego. This is a good thing. I've never seen her so happy. She always wanted to be a mum.'

'I'm coming with you, aren't I?' Jax asked. 'I can fight well now and I'm not standing for being left out yet again.'

'I'm not sure your cockiness with your newfound fighting abilities is such a good thing. It will probably get you killed,' Ed replied.

'Well, there's no way I'm staying here and making quilts! The only way I am helping with this base camp is if they let me set up a tech room,' Jax declared, arms folded.

'I am fully aware that I couldn't get rid of you if I tried. Besides, after what I have seen you do, I don't think we can manage without you.' Ed laughed and ruffled Jax's hair.

'I'm not a child, you know!' Jax complained, as he ran his hands through his now tousled wavy hair.

Ed watched him and couldn't believe this was his little Jax. Now he saw a strong man. It took him by surprise. In the blink of an eye, his boy had vanished. Ed realised that his features had changed a lot just in the last year. His jaw was squarer, his nose sharper, his cheekbones higher. The dimples in his cheeks were more obvious. And despite his hair being dishevelled and untidy, it somehow managed to enhance his strong jawline and make him look like a male surfer model. Ed watched Jax blush as he glanced towards Tammy. Ed smiled. They clearly liked each other. Normally he would worry that Jax was maybe a little too old for Tammy, at least at this age. However, he had discussed it with Jude and she had decided that Tammy was no ordinary twelve year old. She was years more advanced than girls that age. Jude felt this was the alien side to her and Ed was inclined to agree. He could see them both taking over Vivacity Island when he and Jude were too old.

'Yes, I guess you've grown up quite quickly this year.' Ed looked at him with pride. 'I just realised how I've lost the little boy I helped raise. Now you are a man. I'm proud of you, Jax. I'm just sad too. I will miss that little boy.'

'I will miss the childish things we can no longer do as well. I loved making that treehouse with you,' Jax agreed sadly.

'Now we just make different kinds of memories together, Jax.' Ed looked at Jude. 'Jude, do you want me to get anything for dinner tonight?'

'Tonight? Oh dear, Ed, I didn't think about that. I've just noted down a tech room for their school – good idea, Jax. The children will need computer skills. I need you to compile a shopping list of everything we need to get in for this tech room and you can set it up later. You know, for this many people, we're going to need a full-time cook. I can't do all that as well.'

'It's okay, I got my team to bring a ginormous paella pan so we will be cooking outside, like you suggested, Jude. We can put it on the fire and make soups, curries, stews, paellas and all sorts.' Lei beamed.

Dave chipped in, 'I'm sure I can feed you all until we have a system and the children are trained. This lot will probably appreciate anything I cook, no matter how badly, judging by how skinny they are. So, I volunteer to be the chef. My mum ran a restaurant, so I'm pretty good at cooking for large numbers. I can build a pizza oven, do some breads in it, and the children can make their own pizzas and whack them in. I'll have my own little staff.'

'I can help you build that pizza oven super-fast,' Mina volunteered.

'That's amazing, thank you.' Jude smiled warmly at them all.

Ed smiled gratefully too. 'In that case, do you want me to get anything for you, Dave?'

'No, thanks, Ed, you have enough to do. I know what to do. I did most of this with Jude when we shut off from the world last time. I made the bread oven. We even have our own mill still functioning here on the island. Might need to build on our farmland.'

'Sounds good. I know I can leave you to it, as always.' Ed patted him on the shoulder.

'I want to be impressed tonight then,' Crane added, cheekily.

'Listen, Crane, didn't anyone ever tell you not to taunt people who can mess with what you eat? One thing you learn when you work in a restaurant – never be a disgruntled customer and return your food,' said Dave, winking.

'Why?' Mikie asked.

'The chef will always spit on what you get served next,' Dave said.

'That's disgusting,' Mina said, grimacing.

'True, all the same,' Dave replied.

'I can cook too,' Stephen said.

'So, you can cook as well? Is there no end to your talents?' Lei asked.

'Of course, and if you don't mind me saying so, a few extra pounds would look great on you.' Stephen nudged her cheekily.

'Good lord, I've found myself a feeder! Not on your life.' She giggled.

'Oh, get a room!' Mikie chided.

'Good job you can cook, Stephen, 'cause her food can kill you.' Mina smiled teasingly at Lei, who thumped her.

'Ouch!' Mina laughed, rubbing her arm.

SEVEN

DETECTED

VIVACITY ISLAND AND SPACESHIP

Later that day, everyone was busy with their task lists and the hybrids were being encouraged into smaller groups, working with each grown-up. They were now coming out of their shells and interacting more. Stephen asked for children to join him on woodwork and was a bit disappointed when only two volunteered.

'I didn't expect everyone to want to do this but I thought more of the children would step up. Only two volunteers – what's going on?' He sighed.

'I suspect that has something to do with it.' Lei smiled, pointing to Dave.

'Oh, I see how it is,' Stephen said, nodding. Dave was building the pizza oven and everyone was fascinated with what it was and what type of food a pizza was. Mina was making the bricks move in the air. Pedro was translating Dave's descriptions of pizza and the hybrids were hanging off every word. Dave's group was like *Charlie and the Chocolate Factory* – the place every child wanted to be.

'Well, I guess I can't blame them, just ironic that two little girls have volunteered with me,' Stephen said with a chuckle.

'They aren't tarnished with our outdated gender rules of what is a girl's or boy's job. Don't you think it's nice that they're just making up their own minds without society intruding? They're following their hearts.' Lei sighed dreamily.

'As always, Lei, you're right. Although there is a huge food bias and it is deeply unfair,' Stephen said loudly to Dave, who laughed back.

'You have enough helpers for now,' Lei said with a smile.

'How will I explain things to them?'

'You show them, they'll pick it up quickly,' she replied.

'Pedro, don't you want to help me?'

'No, he doesn't, he is my translator. Don't you dare try to steal him!' Dave interrupted, before Pedro could say anything.

'He may be feeding these children, but it's my blood and sweat that will give them a table to eat off and beds to sleep on,' Stephen muttered, pretending to be put out.

'It's nice to be appreciated for your own talents, isn't it?' Mina laughed and nudged Pedro.

'Wait a minute... Mikie, get on over here and do that teaching thing. Give me that language,' Stephen said.

Mikie walked on over to Pedro, explained what he was going to do then took his head between his hands and used his telepathy to learn the language to share with Stephen. After a few minutes, Mikie let go and did the same on his uncle's head. When he had finished, Stephen smiled and started singing in Galidian. They all laughed. Four more hybrids ran over to help him, leaving Dave. Stephen punched the air and started flossing – a silly dance move he had learnt as a child – as he smiled sweetly at Dave. Two more hybrids joined Stephen and some started flossing with him. Dave tutted, shook his head and smiled, then sighed. Lei was looking at Stephen with a bright smile on her face. Mina saw this and was happy for Lei. They did, after all, make a lovely couple.

'I can already see the school in my mind's eye,' Jude said. 'Once all the hard work is out of the way and the camp is nice enough, we'll need classes and education. We obviously can't send them to school on the mainland. We can all chip in on education.'

'I believe we could handle that. What do you think, Lei? You and I could even sleep at the camp with the children. We can monitor the dormitory together. Interested?' Stephen asked.

'We can teach them martial arts, sports, maths, English, languages, all sorts. It will be great.' Lei smiled and nodded enthusiastically. 'Start and end the day with a run around the island. Our own running club. How lovely.'

'I have an idea,' Tammy said.

'What's that?' asked Jude.

'This is going to be our own orphanage. I know how horrible they can be and it's made me think of my old friend Sukie. I bet she has had a horrible time since I left. I know it's a big ask but would you consider adopting her? She would be a great help with the orphanage and be able to teach the children to write, and she's an artist so she can teach art too. Having grown up in an orphanage, she can show you the positive things, how to organise the children and what things to avoid.' Tammy hoped they'd say yes.

It took Jude and Ed a second of silent communication to decide.

'What a brilliant idea, and I think we can manage that. What is one more mouth to feed anyway?' Jude said with a smile.

Tammy beamed with joy. She couldn't wait to see Sukie again. She had thought of her often. Her only friend at the orphan school. The only person brave enough to stay her friend. Now she could make it up to her and give her a nice home too.

'She hasn't had it that bad, though,' Ed told Tammy.

'Have you seen her?' Tammy asked.

'No. However, we got that awful woman running it removed. She was investigated and it was unanimously agreed that she was not fit to work with children. She is no longer working in any orphan school,' Jude said, hugging Tammy.

'Oh, wow, thank you.' Tammy squeezed her back.

'I can teach them science,' Crane added, joining them.

'I only know reptiles but I could teach that,' Ben chipped in.

'I want to do science!' Dave said.

'You're the cook,' Ben and Crane said simultaneously, and burst out laughing.

'Funny, very funny.' Dave folded his arms and shook his head.

'We can all teach these children how to fend for themselves. Then they can have a rota in place and take turns at cooking, therefore freeing up Dave's time to help with the elephants while Tammy isn't here. Don't forget, we all still have to do our normal jobs alongside all this,' Jude explained.

'Actually, we'll never be short-staffed again.' Dave smiled.

A little hybrid girl wandered up to Stephen. She had curly golden hair and couldn't have been more than six years old. Apart from her seal-like blue eyes and tiny holes in place of a nose, she looked almost human. She tugged on Stephen's sleeve until he looked at her.

'Oh my, aren't you the sweetest little thing.' Lei sighed, looking at her tiny features.

'Hello, poppet, what can I do for you?' Stephen asked in Galidian.

'I help you. I make things with you,' she said quietly and shyly in English.

'Well, I never. I just got myself another brave adventurer!' Stephen declared, picking her up and holding her high in the air. 'What is your name then?'

'Alice,' she laughed as he spun her around.

'Well, Alice, welcome to Wonderland,' Stephen said, laughing and placing her up onto his shoulders.

'What is Wonderland?' Alice asked.

'Oh, I bagsy storytelling tonight.' Lei squealed, jumping up and down. 'Me, me, me! I want to tell this story. It's my favourite.'

'Alice, this lovely lady is going to tell you the story of *Alice in Wonderland* tonight while we all have a Mad Hatter's kind of tea party under the stars,' Stephen declared.

'Jude, they can use your library, can't they?' Tammy

suggested.

'Yes. Lei, I'm putting you in charge. What's taken out I want returned, and I'll speak with you tonight on ones that are never to be removed,' Jude said sternly.

'Don't let anyone near my historical books, and no children allowed in there directly,' Ed warned. 'We have some great things that can be brought here for your own library too.'

'No one BUT LEI enters my library – is that clear to everyone?' Jude shouted to the whole group.

Jude seemed just like her mother at this time and everyone nodded and promised not to ever venture into the library. The hybrids didn't know what a library was, so they would have to teach them all of these small things.

'Mikie, you're going to need to run around getting English into all these children's heads,' Stephen said.

Mikie nodded and got started. Tammy followed him. If it hurt anyone, she would heal them afterwards.

'I promise I will look after everything, Ed,' Lei declared.

'Lei,' Mina whispered, coming to her side.

'Yes, Mina?'

'Alice has hair. Not all the girls have hair and none of the boys do. Do all of the aliens have hair?'

'I'm not a big expert and I don't know if the experiments have made some of the female hybrids hairless, or if it is the luck of the draw or species. Why do you ask?' Lei replied.

'Alice's hair is golden like mine. I just wondered if we were half the same species. Why don't the males have hair?'

'Lots of the species do. Your father has golden hair like you and Diego. The tall white ones have a lot of hair. You will meet many different species once your father comes.

Don't forget, Mina, they have learnt to live among us in secret for many centuries. You will love the canine and feline humanoids.'

'Why?' Mina asked.

'Because they are huge cats and dogs who walk upright and talk like us,' Lei smiled.

'Oh, cool,' Mina sighed. All she could think was that a human lion could be her next best friend.

*

The aliens had been scanning the monitors for years; looking for a sign, any sign, of the childrens' locations. Thousands of the *seekers* were sent off to scan and report any facial recognition possibilities and they were reviewing photos of children in groups and alone constantly. They had technology that analysed Sarah's facial features and predicted what her offspring could look like at each age. The only other chance of spotting the children was random power surges in energy and unnatural events when they were powerful enough to create them. As each child matured, so did their powers. Time was running out.

Lieutenant Kodo had been in command of the attack on Vivacity Island that had failed miserably. His colleague had shot Tammy and they were unsure if she had survived. Marcellus was furious and speeding up his arrival. He had failed to capture Mina in the scrap yard and, as a result, he had been demoted to screening duty. Greys were the least likely alien to get promoted, being a hybrid slave. Very few rose in rank and escaped servitude. His entire future depended on these children being apprehended. He scanned the screens miserably, much preferring to be out in the field and hating the boring images that appeared in front of him.

As usual, Lieutenant Kodo sulkily flipped from one image to the next, looking at various images of Earth. He had razor sharp eyes and missed nothing. A few days ago, he had finally found Dr Peter Lloyd sitting sadly outside an igloo in the middle of Antarctica. Without Dr Lloyd knowing it, he provided the only bit of pleasure in Lieutenant Kodo's life. Each day he watched the doctor's isolation and misery with pleasure. He especially loved the look on his face at having to eat raw fish every day, and struggling to go to the toilet in the extreme cold each time. Not to mention that Dr Lloyd had reported Lieutenant Kodo for killing Colonel Ludwig at the scrapyard and lost him the promotion to Colonel. Dr Lloyd had been gunning for his power long enough. He planned to kill Dr Lloyd at the first opportunity. Unlike the greys, the General was a rare tall white. Similar in looks but paler whiter skin and a few feet taller than most greys. A different species of alien. Lieutenant Kodo had informed the General that he had found Dr Lloyd and wondered what he wanted him to do about it.

'Let him sit there and feel sorry for himself, it will teach him a good lesson,' the General had laughed. 'We know where he is if we ever need him again.'

'Yes, sir,' Lieutenant Kodo had replied.

If! The man was useless and couldn't even withstand crystal technology training, why they ever think they need him puzzled Lieutenant Kodo immensely. Diego was his focus, the only one not yet found by the Brunswick's. They knew he had left England and he also suspected that Ed had flown to South America. That was where he was focusing on the search although he could be anywhere in the 17.84 million km square vast landscape. It was 95% larger than North America. Lieutenant Kodo was meticulous and knew he must find Diego before they did; otherwise, both his career and life were at risk. He zoomed in on different parts of the rainforest and sighed as he saw nothing but the trees, one after another. Until suddenly, on this day, after so many boring uneventful days before, he got lucky and something caught his eye.

Lieutenant Kodo squinted and paused the screen, then rewound it and watched again. It was a lovely sunny day over the trees he was watching by a nearby waterfall. Then, out of nowhere, a storm cloud appeared, shot a bolt of lightning, and hit a tree. Just as suddenly as it came, the cloud disappeared again. It was not natural behaviour. He rewound the tape and zoomed in even closer, watching a group of Inca boys playing some sort of game. He watched one boy fall in the water and the fallen tree come to his rescue.

'How did it happen?' he whispered under his breath.
He searched the surrounding area until he spotted two more children swimming in the water and looked at what they were doing at the time the lightning struck. A tall blonde boy with a crystal cube on his wrist directed the lightening. Then he grinned.

'Got you!' He sneered and rubbed his hands together in glee.

He rewound the tapes and sat there, this time enthusiastically, as he watched the surrounding area over the previous days. They kept recordings for a week just in case they missed something and had to go back and look, as he was doing now. It didn't take him long to find the moment, the previous day, when a similar bolt of lightning struck the trees, again in a way that didn't seem quite natural. He zoomed in and saw the burnt patch of ground and the same golden-haired boy standing there. Then he flipped to the live feed to see if Ed had found him yet.

Ed. That awful man. Lieutenant Kodo had become increasingly bitter over the years. Suddenly billionaires like Ed Brunswick were doing all sorts of great things for humanity. He remembered the days, before Pisces, when all the billionaires were selfish and out for themselves. Draining people of everything they had. He quite liked those humans and he missed those days. During the outbreak they all hid in underground bunkers talking about what they would do with Earth when everyone else was dead. Until the contaminated sushi was discovered, they hadn't imagined fish being the source of the virus. That put an end to most billionaires almost overnight. The bunker became a hospice. Then a grave. He still missed those people. They were just as evil as he was. He lost the only humans he respected in that bunker. Dr Lloyd would have been fine if he hadn't been after his power. Neither of them were team players who could share.

But there was no sign of Ed on the live feed – Diego was alone with these unintimidating people. He used his hand to drum a beat on the tabletop and struggled to contain his excitement. This was it. This was his lucky break. His smile grew wider.

'Have you found something?' one of his supervisors asked, coming over.

Lieutenant Kodo quickly switched screens and reverted to a serious face. 'No, nothing, I just saw something funny but irrelevant,' he lied.

'Try to focus better, will you?' his supervisor growled and stomped off, irritated.

Some images on the screens were snapshots of areas, and some were rolling footage of events. Therefore, he was unable to track the boys and find out where they had gone off to. However, he now had a marking from the waterfall and their hunting ground; it would be relatively easy to find them now. He would start at the waterfall. A playground was more likely to be nearer home than a hunting ground. He was an excellent tracker. He quietly left his seat and walked out of the control room, hoping no one noticed him. He wanted this to be his moment and his alone. If anyone suspected he had discovered something they could track what he had been viewing and report it themselves. He had to get out of his boring seat; he needed to do this and go back to the field before he went insane.

'Where are you going?' His supervisor had spotted him and was heading his way.

Lieutenant Kodo was quick to conceal any emotions on his face and looked the other alien squarely in the eye. In this room, this was his commanding officer and he must show respect, but technically, he was beneath him. It was why the officer picked on him. He relished having a Lieutenant report to him as punishment. Competition was rife between the aliens; it was hard to reach the top and hardly anyone was permitted to speak with the Supreme Commander. He wanted, more than anything, to be acknowledged by the Supreme Commander – Marcellus. That was his ambition.

'I have been called to report to the General,' he lied.

'I wasn't told of this.'

'I shall tell the General that you didn't know when I see him,' Lieutenant Kodo said, boldly.

The other alien eyed him suspiciously and then, because he didn't want to look incompetent himself, nodded and said, 'No need to say anything, just be back soon.'

Lieutenant Kodo left the room and as soon as the door had shut behind him, he ran, as fast as he could, down the long white corridor. He raced along at full speed, almost knocking a few fellow aliens down as he skidded around a bend and entered the General's office. He stood in the doorway, panting. The General was sitting at a desk, alone.

'What is it?' the General growled.

Lieutenant Kodo gasped for breath and as he caught it, his eyes travelled to the dark pool of water in the corner of the room. His heart sank as he remembered his failure to hold the prisoners he and Dr Lloyd had caught, and how they had not just escaped but had taken all the valuable hybrids and the Colossal Illuminator too. That had been a massive loss for them. Now greys had to transport heavy objects around the ship and they all hated him for it. The fact that they had lost control of their underwater army would mean death when the Supreme Commander arrived. He had to impress Marcellus to avoid execution. He had to get power. The General saw what he was looking at and huffed.

'Yes, a complete waste of resources under there now, thanks to your incompetence. It will take weeks to find a new program or method to control them and years to breed the numbers back up. We have to find food for the few that are left and get nothing back; other greys are carrying boxes back and forth like slaves. Perhaps that could be your next assignment?'

'I've found him.' Lieutenant Kodo gulped.

The General stood up, paying full attention to him now. 'Where?'

'In South America. I have the coordinates, shall I show you?'

'Yes, I have a link to the control room here, show me where he is,' the General said, activating a virtual screen above his desk.

Lieutenant Kodo walked over to the screen and moved his arms, pulling the holographic screens up and around in the air, until he had the right images for the General to see. The General smiled in delight and nodded.

'Excellent, Lieutenant Kodo, you have restored some of my respect towards you,' he said.

'Please, sir, permission to take over this field trip and make up for my previous errors?'

The General sighed and looked at the screen as he debated his answer. The truth was, Lieutenant Kodo was his best field agent, and no one else would have done as good a job as him. Those children were clever, powerful and incredibly lucky. No one could have imagined they could talk to animals, be invisible and get a Colossal Illuminator off a ship without being seen. Not that he would admit that to anyone else.

'The Supreme Commander is almost here and you know what it would mean if you continue to fail me?' the General barked.

'Yes, sir.'

'This is your last chance; it will mean death should you fail.' He pointed to the slimy creatures in the black water. 'I'll feed you to them like the useless piece of meat that you are.'

'I understand, sir, of course, that's only natural. I appreciate how lenient you have already been with me.' Lieutenant Kodo nodded.

'OK then, where do you aim to go and what do you need?'

'I need one small spaceship. I just want a crew of twenty. I'll go to the waterfall; I'm certain he lives near it and I should find his tracks from there,' Lieutenant Kodo said.

'Only one ship? Why only one?'

'I wish to be discreet and with all the trees and mountains you cannot easily fly or land anywhere. I have a plan. The children know they aren't human and they must all be eager to know who their father is, if you get my meaning.' Lieutenant Kodo nodded slightly, winking.

The General smiled. 'Make it happen.'

'Yes, sir, and what about Lloyd? Shall I collect him on the way?'

'Do you need him?'

'Certainly not, sir.'

'Then leave him where he is until we do need him. He isn't going anywhere.'

'Will we ever need him again?'

'Well, I suspect he hopes very much that we will, otherwise he'll be spending the rest of his days shivering in the cold, hiding from polar bears and eating raw fish. If I remember right, he was a strict vegetarian so that must be bothersome.'

The General was still laughing as Lieutenant Kodo left the room. Poor Dr Lloyd, he thought, but he couldn't stop the satisfied smile creeping eerily across his face. He loathed humans and couldn't see the point in them. They were no more superior to a chimpanzee, except that they talked more. Lieutenant Kodo couldn't wait to get back to the control room and tell those low lives that he was out of there. His brain would explode with the lack of use if he had to stay watching those screens any longer.

EIGHT

HYBRID ORPHAN CAMP

VIVACITY ISLAND

The children were excited and couldn't wait to start helping to build their new home. Lei's team of eight female agents arrived in three large vans and the hybrids gathered around, all thrilled at what came out. It was a chaotic day as her team created a list of all the hybrids' names, ages, guessed sizes and split the shoes and clothes between them, ensuring everyone had a few items each and making a note of what else they needed to get. The kittens were a cute mix of black, black and white, calico and ginger, and much adored, along with the donkeys. The bikes created a lot of fascination. Stephen, Mina, Mikie and Jax started showing the hybrids how to ride the bikes and spent the afternoon giving lessons while Jude, Lei and her team organised the deliveries. Everyone was laughing and having fun.

Dave, along with his enthusiastic hybrid kitchen crew, made huge amounts of cake and sandwiches for the Mad

Hatter party Stephen had promised them. Lei made loads of tea. They used bales of straw as chairs and tables. Lei had a great time sitting at the end and reading *Alice in Wonderland* as they ate. The children were mesmerised. No alien had ever read them a story before. They often wandered up to have a look in and around the book, wondering where all these words were coming from. Lei stopped to show them the illustrations when they appeared, and her team also sat and enjoyed the story and the hybrids. The kittens were fast asleep in the arms of different hybrids, exhausted after having had far too much attention all afternoon.

'We need more goats,' Dave said. 'I'll make my own cheeses and yoghurts like you, Jude.'

'Bring some up from the park, we will increase the breeding programme,' Jude said.

'So, what do the aliens eat?' Ed asked.

'All sorts of things, depending on species and beliefs. Thalen is very spiritual so he is vegan,' Lei replied.

'I saw something wiggling in their bowls on the ship. Live insects,' said Mina.

'Well, they are a little like us. Some eat meat, some are vegetarian, and some are vegan. Honestly, we are very similar in so many ways. They experiment with our food. Some even eat earthworms and things we wouldn't even think of. Some consider earthworms and snails a delicacy.'

'That's disgusting. I saw them eating live snails on the ship. I puked in my mouth and had to swallow it!' Mina emphasised.

'Oh yuck.' Tammy scrunched her nose up in disgust. 'For a tomboy you certainly puke a lot.'

Mina stuck her tongue out at Tammy.

'No different to the French with their snails and frogs' legs,' Ed murmured.

'Oh, please stop.' Mina turned away.

'The French and their *escargots*. I'd quite forgotten. That's the one thing not in shortage since the pandemic. They can mass produce those in most French homes and do. I guess the aliens saw this and figured anything goes,' Lei said with a smile.

'Perhaps someone should tell them about garlic butter.' Stephen sniggered as he scratched in the soil under his feet and pulled up a worm. He let it dangle by his lips, pretending he had bitten into it, and edged closer to Mina. She screamed and pulled away at the sight of the worm but was unable to stop herself laughing with the others when she realised what he had done.

*

After dinner, Ed took his abundant supply of wood from the woodshed behind the house, loaded it onto a trailer attached to the back of the Jeep and headed off towards the camp. Ben and Crane helped him. Dave was cooking. Meanwhile, Stephen took his helpers into the woods to cut down trees and gather as much wood as they could, fit for furniture, in order to get them started. He planned to use tree trunk sections for custom natural-looking chairs and benches, being quicker and easier to build, as well as making some more comfy ones longer term. They also needed to clear more space nearer to the camp to give them more ground around where they were going to live. They needed a playground area. They would also plant more trees elsewhere. Stephen was enjoying thinking of ideas in order to set up a home for all these children.

It was getting late when they returned and piled what they had collected into another trailer behind the Jeep. Stephen drove them all to the hospital, where they could have a couple of hours' head start on making the chairs. Alice never left his side. The children squealed in delight as they bounced over the tracks. Stephen smiled and went a little faster, and the children laughed louder. Unable to resist, he swerved into a field and picked up speed, cranking the Jeep around in tight circles as the children enjoyed the thrill of speed. Alice grabbed his arm, clinging to him, screaming with delight. Stephen felt his heart soar and knew this tiny fragile girl had won his heart over. He kissed the top of her head, vowing to himself, and to her silently, that he would never leave her.

Eventually, he pulled back onto the track to continue on their way, and they had almost calmed down by the time the Jeep pulled up outside the animal hospital. Crane had given them a room to use. His helpers were keen and hardworking, eager to please Stephen as they helped him tidy the hospital and clear an area where they could work. They watched attentively as he showed them what to do, and he was impressed with how easily they picked things up. Stephen smiled, realising that it was going to be nice, building things with these hybrids. He didn't think about his old life at all. It no longer mattered.

*

Later that evening, back at the house, Ed was looking for

Tammy. He found Jax in the kitchen, trying to find a snack. All the cupboards were bare.

Ed laughed at the disappointed expression. 'Jax, I know exactly how you are feeling right now. Do you know where Tammy is?'

'Yes, she went with Mikie and Mina to the treehouse. They said they were going to contact Diego,' he replied. 'I'm starving.'

'Brilliant, I'll go and see how they're doing then. If you're quick, you might find something hidden inside Jude's old slow cooker.'

Jax smiled as he looked and found some jam, spreadable and a loaf of bread that Ed had hidden.

'That's just between you and I, understood?' Ed said with a wink.

'Understood! I'll catch you up,' Jax said as he started making a quick jam sandwich.

*

Mina, Mikie and Tammy sat in the treehouse and began to meditate. Away from the chaos and noise of all the hybrid children, they entered a trance and searched for their final sibling. It didn't take long with the combined power of three of them. Mikie looked at Diego, who stared at him from afar, his face painted red. They were having some sort of a celebration and dancing around a fire. He wasn't happy they were trying to contact him again and told them so.

'Just leave me alone, all of you,' he shouted. 'I don't care if you're my brother and sisters. I want absolutely nothing to do with you. Now get lost. I'm fine here alone.'

'Just talk with us for–' Mikie began.

'Stop contacting me. Leave me alone! I am better off without you,' Diego said sternly.

'No, you're not. They're coming for you, Diego. You need to hide well and help us to find you before they do. Please help us,' Mikie begged.

'No. I don't need you. Go away!' Diego said angrily.

'But, Diego…' Mikie started. However, it was too late. Diego disappeared.

'He blocked us again,' Mina said.

'Yes.' Mikie sighed.

'I'm sure he'll come around eventually,' Mina said, releasing their hands and standing up. 'We still have no idea where he is.'

'Well, that's not strictly true,' Tammy said, smiling brightly.

'What did you get?' Mikie asked.

'A little birdie told me,' Tammy replied. 'I know the Andean Cock-of-the-rock that has been watching him for me. I had all the animals watching out for me.'

'Animal spies, I love it!' Mina smiled.

'And the bird flew around for me and gave me a bird's-eye view of the area and I saw a waterfall,' Tammy boasted.

'We can look at maps in Ed's library and figure out the location,' Mikie said, smiling. 'And the painted face… that's going to mean something, we just got a little bit closer.'

*

Mikie, Tammy and Mina were on their way back to the house when they bumped into Ed and Jax as they walked with the dogs.

'Any luck?' Ed asked.

'Tammy has great news despite the fact that Diego won't listen to what we have to say. He keeps blocking us,' Mikie said.

'He doesn't want anything to do with us and doesn't want us to find him,' Mina added.

'Why?' asked Ed.

'We don't know,' Mikie said with a shrug. 'However, Tammy saw something and knows where he is.'

'That's incredible. What did you see, Tammy?' Ed asked. 'The animals have been searching and a few days ago a bird – the Andean Cock-of-the-rock – located him for me. There is only one place that bird lives,' Tammy said, smiling.

'As we suspected – Peru,' Ed said.

'The bird was telling me there are Incas there, and I got a bird's-eye view of their home. It is high on the top of a mountain within more dense green mountains and a forest with a nearby waterfall. I can recognise it if you show me pictures.'

'No need; there is only one place that they can be. This is brilliant news. I'll show you a picture of the same waterfall, I'm positive which one it is. However, we cannot fly all the way there – there's too much mountain and forest – so we will need to travel on foot,' Ed said, frowning.

'That is where Jet is from. He will get to see his home. That's why I remember everything so clearly about this area. Peru is big and it is something else too.'

'What?' Mina asked.

'Absolutely full of animals, just like Africa,' Tammy stated.

'And?' Mina frowned.

'And they can all get us safely to where he is.' Tammy opened her hands as if to ask if they were getting it yet. 'Really, it's easy.'

'You think the animals can guide us there?' Ed asked.

'Of course.'

'Well.' Mina sighed. 'I'm happy to believe that if it's what you think. I just don't fancy hiking for days through the rainforest with snakes and predators,' she moaned.

'I'm with you on this one, Mina, although you forgot about getting hot and sticky. It's not going to be pleasant, that's for sure,' Ed agreed.

Mikie and Jax exchanged a smile at the thought of Mina in a rainforest. She may come across like a hardy tomboy but she liked her luxuries.

'I'll record all her moments and make a short movie called Mina's Misery,' Mikie silently told Jax. They walked away to hide their smiles.

*

The following morning was the final time they would all be able to do Tai chi as a big group. Everyone joined in. Stephen and Lei chatted and laughed as they moved alongside Pedro and Alice, who were now always with them, oblivious to the approaching war and all the danger they were in. They didn't notice the long look Mina gave them either. She still wasn't fully decided on them being together and what it meant to her. When the class ended, Mikie and Tammy approached Mina, sensing her mood.

'You know, Stephen has often talked about settling

down. I've never seen him like this. I think he's definitely in love,' Mikie said.

'And Lei is so gorgeous,' Tammy added. 'I can see why he has fallen for her.'

'She knows she's gorgeous and plays games with men all the time. She is far too pretty to want to settle down with just one man. She'll dump him when she's bored, she always does. I like our uncle but he'll get hurt just like the others,' Mina said, and walked off moodily.

'Wait, Mina, why is it such a bad thing?' Tammy asked, running after her.

'You don't understand, leave me alone!'

Tammy and Mikie looked at each other in surprise as Mina stomped away.

'For a moment there, I thought she was starting to be all right,' Tammy said.

'She's coming round, give her time.'

'Tammy, can we go for a walk? I need to talk to you,' Jax asked, coming to her side.

'Sure. Are you joining us, Mikie?'

'No, thanks, got to do something.' Mikie smiled and winked at Jax, knowing from their talk earlier that Jax aimed to tell Tammy how he felt about her. Mikie still couldn't believe that Tammy had no idea how much Jax liked her.

They set off into the woods. Jax turned as he heard a neigh and saw Sirocco, the dogs and Jet bounding up behind them.

'I thought we could walk alone, just the two of us,' he suggested.

'We are alone, Jax. I can't very well tell them to leave. What's the matter?'

'Nothing.' He shrugged, sighing.

'We can walk for a while and then go for a ride. How about that?' Tammy offered.

Jax stopped and looked at her intensely.

'Tammy...'

'Yes?' Tammy asked.

'Well, er, I...' He blushed and stumbled, wiping his suddenly sweaty hands on the sides of his jeans and looking about awkwardly. He blew a big puff of air out of his cheeks and immediately felt stupid.

'Jax?'

'I was just–'

'Jax, you look sick. Are you all right?' Tammy frowned.

'I'm fine, Tammy. I just wanted to say that Ed has arranged for me to sit the exams early to qualify as a vet. I won't be going back to the mainland for any education. Ed has asked me to stay here.' Jax could feel Mikie eavesdropping telepathically and couldn't say what he meant to say.

'That is brilliant!' Tammy declared.

'Yes, I'm happy. I'm needed here. Tell me about Clarissa again, and what happened on the spaceship. Don't leave anything out.'

'Well, did I tell you about the time I first met her? It was incredible, Jax. She lit up the water for me. Like she did when we set her free, although on a much smaller scale. It was dazzling. That scared all the creepy black things away that had gathered around. She looked so beautiful.'

Jax listened as she gushed with excitement and silently kicked himself for being such a wimp. From afar, he felt Mikie poke his nose into his business and heard the words, *'Pathetic, Jax. So lame!'* Jax reminded himself to thump

Mikie when he was next within arm's reach and warn him not to eavesdrop next time.

*

Close by, Mina watched as Tammy and Jax strolled through the woods, listening into snatches of their conversation. It was so obvious that Jax was besotted; why didn't he say something? She knew he was afraid of rejection, she had seen it regularly enough with Lei's boyfriends. Yet, how could he not realise that Tammy adored him too?

'Wimp,' she muttered, with a long sigh.

Her earrings were activated, and she wandered absentmindedly between the trees, thinking about Diego. Why was he so reluctant to speak with them? She had felt some sort of a connection, something similar that she recognised and couldn't quite put her finger on. What was it? It wasn't the monster. Not a dark shadow. Why had she been keen to be found and yet he wasn't? Perhaps Diego had lots of friends in the Inca tribe. She tried to picture what it would be like and could imagine Diego running wild in the jungle, hunting with spears. Or perhaps he used his crystal and impressed the other boys with his powers. Her mind drifted as she wondered what he might be doing right now, what he would think when they found him again. Would they find him?

She heard a noise and dived behind a tree, then remembered she was invisible anyway. There was another noise up ahead and soon she saw Lei and Stephen walking towards her, holding hands. She watched as they walked past and then they stopped, Stephen pulling Lei towards him and kissing her, tenderly and slowly. Mina lowered her eyes and crept away. She couldn't help admitting that what she had said earlier was a lie. It had come out before she had even thought about it. She had never seen Lei behave like this and knew she had fallen in love with Stephen. It was written all over their faces.

She felt the tears start to well up and sniffed, cleared her throat and walked on. She wouldn't cry; she never cried! Even with the hybrids being here, especially Pedro, she felt wrong inside. The monster was restless. She had suppressed it for far too long while she indulged her nicer emotions and had been besotted with the hybrids. Now the monster was stirring and waking up. It wanted out. She was losing control over suppressing the shadow within. She again started to think about what the greys had said, about her being one of them, and how she felt a bond with them. She had the choice to join the aliens.

*

Mikie watched the children help Jude, the joy evident on her face. One of the older girls, a nine-year-old who had lost the ability to speak, was called Jen. She had become Jude's shadow after showing Jude her chopped-off tongue. Jude couldn't believe they had tortured her and cut her tongue out. Mikie had read Jen's mind and told Jude that Jen had tried to escape once and they had made an example of her. She followed Jude everywhere, helping her and her alone. Jude looked happy and they had been learning some sign language together. All the children were looking healthy; their pain had gone and the wounds too. It had surprised

Mikie how strong the energy was when Mina and Tammy worked with him. He wondered how much stronger it could be with Diego.

He saw Stephen and Lei returning to the house. It made him happy to see them together, so much in love. He understood Mina's resentment towards the relationship; he knew she was jealous of both Tammy and Lei. What surprised him, though, was that she had nothing to be jealous of, because when she didn't act horribly, she was lovely to be around. If only she could get rid of that chip on her shoulder, she would see that she did fit in after all. Mikie was starting to understand her inner battle with the monster more and was worried that she wouldn't slay it. Lei and Pedro were helping her, but was it enough?

Somehow, in his heart, Mikie suspected Mina would not be all right. She was trouble. He hadn't told the others because he was still desperately hoping he was wrong. He remembered how interested she had been when the aliens had tried to convince her to join them, that day in the scrapyard. And he knew how big the monster was getting and that she thought of the aliens often. He saw her dark side, and Mina knew it. His only hope was that Diego might be able to help in some way. He knew Mina was watching him and turned to look at the spot where she stood, still invisible.

'You know I'm here?' she asked in surprise.

'Yes, I knew all along.'

Mina smiled, deactivated her earrings and joined him. They walked back to the house; it was time to pack. They were overtaken by Jax and Tammy racing past on Sirocco. Mina was pleased to see Jet fall into step at her side rather than following Tammy.

'He likes you,' Mikie noted.

'I guess he does,' she said, smiling.

'I think you both have the same wild side. Race you to the house?'

He started off before she could respond and she chose instead to continue to walk.

'There's nothing to rush back for, is there?' she muttered to Jet. She had loved the rescue on the ship and getting everyone off. Now life was boring again. Mina just wanted constant action. She didn't want or value a normal life in any way.

Dinner was to be at Brunswick House on their last night, and most of the staff, the hybrids, plus all of Lei's team, were there for dinner. Over fifty people to be catered for. The house was in chaos. Jude told Tammy and Mina to occupy the hybrids. The dogs and kittens needed Tammy to help them socialise and be friends faster than they normally would. They spent hours giving the hybrids turns to ride Sirocco or – their favourite treat – to canter, with Tammy holding them on. Tammy left the hybrids adoring the kittens, dogs, Sirocco and Jet and joined Jax in the kitchen. They were sitting with a group of hybrids when they saw Ed trying to fight his way into the kitchen, trying to get a share of the pasta bake Dave had made. Every time he got close, more hybrids would cut him up and push him further behind. Ed was struggling with all of the noise. They laughed.

'Are you looking for this?'

He turned to see Jude standing behind him, holding a plate with a large serving of the pasta and a big chunk of garlic bread.

'You are my angel!' he said, taking the food and giving her a grateful kiss on the cheek.

Tammy jumped up quickly and made her way over to Dave, smiling as he handed her a plate.

'It smells good,' she said.

'I hope you enjoy it.'

'I miss the elephants.'

'They miss you too,' he shouted over the heads of the hybrids.

He couldn't dish out the food and serve it fast enough, Lei and Stephen at his side going as fast as they could. Helping to organise the line and keep people in order was Pedro. He was good at ordering the children about, telling them to remain quiet and orderly and in line. They respected him now.

'You know what, Tammy? Adventure is one thing, however, before long, you realise that it's the simple things you want. It took me years to learn that and yet somehow I think you already know it. I wouldn't be able to cope if it wasn't for this lad Pedro,' said Dave.

'Yes, he's doing a great job. I know what you mean. I'd just like to live in peace with the animals. No adventures. I'm worried, Dave, about what will happen. About everything. What if something happens to Jude or Ed? Or anyone else? What if I never get to wash and feed the elephants again?'

'I know, Tammy, I know. I think we're all fighting against such thoughts at the moment. I worry if you'll make it or if we'll all die, or if another pandemic will see us all off. Crane showed me the pills Mina found. Terrifying! They created variants just to mess around with the hybrids. What else have they been doing with the virus? Does no good thinking about it though. We can worry ourselves forever, and the only thing I can tell you is that it is a waste of time.' Dave touched her cheek. 'It's easier said than done, of course.'

'I quite agree,' Jude said, joining them. 'Worrying won't fix anything or help in any way. Plus, what you focus on, even in your mind, is what you energise and create. Worry is just the devil's trick to make us create bad things. It's a clever trick indeed. We manifest our thoughts and if you keep focusing on them, you give them more power. Keep it simple. Sleep and eat well. Meditate a lot.'

'Eat your pasta and enjoy every mouthful. Then you'll feel better. Focus on the basics!' Dave told her.

Tammy smiled and took a mouthful. 'It's really nice, love all the garlic. You're right! Keep it simple.'

He laughed as she left the kitchen.

Ed caught up with her as she headed to the outside pond. 'I can't move in my own house.'

'Everyone is so excited,' Tammy said, smiling. 'It's so much noisier than it used to be.'

'Well, that's what happens when you're feeding over fifty people in one place! Oh, and everything is sorted with Sukie, by the way.'

'Really?' Tammy gasped and clapped her hands, giving a little jump of excitement to boot. 'Is she thrilled?'

'Oh yes.' Ed nodded. 'Jude asked a friend to visit her and make all the arrangements. She burst into tears of happiness, apparently. She is arriving tomorrow, once we are out of the way. Jude's friend told her that you wouldn't be here, and she said to tell you a huge thank you and she can't wait to see you when you get back.'

'Thank you so much.' Tammy kissed Ed on the cheek and they both tried not to lose their plates of pasta.

'It's my pleasure, Tammy, it was a great idea on your part. She will have a good friend join her, a Japanese girl slightly older than you. She will be here working with Jude and Lei on a solution to address the food crisis in Japan. Her family is very powerful and insists she is here to oversee everything. We are hoping they will become friends although Jude is worried about her reaction towards the hybrids. It's impossible to refuse that family anything so we have no choice but to host her. It is what it is. Now, I've been thinking about how we get off the island tomorrow. I don't want to take the spaceship. It could be tracked and is better left here. It might come in handy later. The ferry isn't safe. I don't suppose those lovely basking sharks are still around, are they?'

'Yes, they are, they'll stay here most of the summer.'

'Do you think they could help us out again?'

'Of course,' Tammy replied.

'Perfect,' Ed said with a nod. 'Probably best that we don't tell Mina until the last minute.'

NINE

THE DREAM

The spaceship landed in the water, away from the rapids and the waterfall, and close to the side of the riverbank where there was no current. Lieutenant Kodo stepped outside and walked along the riverbank. He was the only one not wearing the black and red uniform; instead, he was dressed in a glamorous white and gold kaftan. It was white, with long wide sleeves, and featured metallic golden embroidery along the centre and edges of the sleeves, as well as the skirt rim and belt. He had chosen this outfit specifically for the task ahead. It was not made of the fine linen it should be and the polyester looked cheap and tacky compared to what would normally be worn by a person of distinction. A design that merged the Egyptian pharaoh with an African tunic design, and although it was not as stunning as what Thalen chose to wear, Diego wouldn't know that. He did not need the re-breathing device the army suits offered, since he had taken the medicine that allowed

his body to adjust for several hours. He could walk about for a day and had a nose device if he started to struggle.

'This way,' he said to the other aliens. 'I want only two of you with me, out of uniform, simple tunics. The rest to remain hidden on the ship for when we return.'

He investigated the stone ring on the tree that the boys played tlachtli with, then the surrounding area, nodding as he followed the tracks. Fortunately, for him, it hadn't rained. He followed the footprints in the dirt and walked over to the fallen tree, touched the blackened wood and smelt his fingers. He could still smell the lightning and feel the life source energy from the tree fading. He searched the floor for more signs of tracks. They all headed into the forest, in the same direction. This was too easy.

It was getting dark and before long, the tracks became harder to see. The moon was full and yet the trees shaded the ground. The debris on the forest floor hid signs of footprints and the trees were so dense that finding an obvious pathway was impossible. Lieutenant Kodo raised a hand, stopping the other aliens in their tracks. He closed his eyes and listened. Perhaps he could find a mind to read or get some sort of indication as to where the village might be. His senses were heightened more than most. From a distance, he could hear music. He strained his ears and his mind and found a man that he could try to read. He got a little information but could not read much else from this distance, and because the man's brain was damaged. However, the music was there, travelling through the forest, reaching out to him. He licked his long bony finger, put it in the air to track wind direction, then listened carefully, trying to detect what direction the wind and sound were coming from. He knew the village was close. With all the high mountains around them it was crucial he went in the right direction. The echo made it challenging. He opened his eyes and pointed to a mountain in the distance.

'That way,' he told them.

The two aliens looked and couldn't see or hear anything. 'Are you sure?' one asked.

'That is why I am the best field soldier there is,' he smiled, knowingly. 'I never make a decision until I am sure. Now, you know the plan. Follow me and smile sweetly at all times.'

They looked at each other, puzzled, wondering what sweetly meant. They walked, confused and mouthing 'What?' and 'I don't know either!' as they tried to work out what a sweet smile looked like, practicing to each other and shaking their heads at the scary results. Every attempt resulted in one of them shaking his head. Lieutenant Kodo marched on, oblivious to their confusion. He could taste the thrill of the hunt and he would soon have his prey in his hands.

*

The king and Charles sat around the fire watching Diego, Manco and Quilla dance with the rest of the villagers. It was nice to see them finally getting along and having fun. Diego soon joined them, sitting next to Charles, breathing heavily with the exertion, not used to all this dancing. Manco and Quilla didn't last much longer and breathlessly plonked themselves down alongside Diego. They were all picking at pieces of fruit and boar.

'You are now officially accepted into the tribe; how does it feel?' the king asked, smiling.

'It feels good,' Diego replied.

'I'm glad. It always feels nicer to fit in and not be rejected by the society you are in.'

'Isn't that the truth!' Charles nodded.

'Why did you have boar introduced into this area? Quilla tells me it wasn't native until after the Pisces outbreak,' Diego asked.

'Ah, now there is a story—' the king began.

'Ha! A story indeed. Don't you believe it, Diego.' Charles laughed and the king smiled knowingly.

'Now, Charles, don't you dare ruin my reputation,' the king warned jokingly.

'But I must! You see, guys, your king is not the hard man he tries to make people see. He is a huge softie. At university he met the best people in his life; your mother and myself. This was before Pisces and we English adored the occasional hog roast to celebrate certain things. We had a hog roast at the May ball. Three things had never happened to your king until that May ball. One, he had never looked so gorgeous thanks to me and my tailor. Two, he had no idea what a hog roast was—'

'Nor apple sauce. Oh apple sauce, the most amazing invention!' the king mused as he remembered.

'Indeed, apple sauce. You sat and ate a whole jar! Then three, he met your mother, the queen, that night. She was also from a prestigious Inca family and they ate their first hog roast bap together. And they were hooked – with each other and the idea of a hog roast. From that day on, they always had a hog roast on their anniversary.'

'You met at the time of the sun festival?' Quilla asked her father.

'The Inti Raymi, the sun festival, is every June. I met your mother at the May ball. However, I proposed to her the following year at the sun festival and we married the year after that, also at the sun festival. So we merged the two most important things together on the same day,' the king answered.

'And that is why you asked for hogs to be introduced here and used for the festival?' Manco asked.

'Yes. It was special to your mother and I.'

'I miss her.' Quilla sighed.

'Yes, we all do. She is a great loss.' The king nodded his agreement. He had never wanted to find another wife. There was a stretch of silence for a while as they remembered her.

'I'm really sorry,' Diego said.

'We have being raised without our mothers in common,' Quilla said, taking Diego's hand in hers.

Upon seeing this, the king continued, 'I must explain my reluctance to have you here, Diego. It wasn't just because of your destructive ways, which I now understand to be of the accidental nature, it was because of things that I have seen in my dreams and it worries me. I saw dark demons falling from the sky and trouble bought upon my village. I was concerned you were the cause.'

Diego exchanged looks with Charles and then with Quilla.

'I thought you were directly responsible for this darkness and believed it would be best if you and Charles left.'

'And now?' asked Charles.

'Now I believe the trouble will come anyway. You are

linked with this but not the cause. My village will soon have trouble to deal with one way or another, I fear.' The king sighed.

'We thank you for offering us your protection,' Charles said.

'I think you are right, father, and they need our help. I think one day they will be the ones helping us.'

'They have already helped us, Manco.' The king placed a grateful hand on his son's shoulder.

'I owe Diego my life, father, and so I shall always support him,' Manco added.

'We all shall, son.'

'Come and dance with me again,' Quilla said, jumping to her feet and pulling Diego and Manco up.

Diego moaned as he was pulled to his feet, still tired yet unable to refuse Quilla anything. Manco, laughing, joined them. They raised their knees and held hands as they danced around the fire.

'Why don't you tell your father about your visions?' Diego asked Quilla.

'Not yet,' she replied.

'Why?'

'I'm not sure. I'd like to wait until they are clearer and more reliable.' She frowned.

'What's wrong?' said Diego.

'Father has dreams and they only come in his sleep, whereas my visions come at any time. I can also make them come when I go into a trance. I, too, had a vision of dark demons falling from the sky.'

'When and why didn't you tell us, Sis?' asked Manco.

'They scared me. It's not good what I saw. I saw death and

destruction and our village suffering miserably. There is a big war coming.' She stopped dancing and looked at them.

'Quilla, why did you not say?' Manco said.

'I needed time to understand my visions, they came in pieces, and I didn't want to believe them. I wanted an easy life and to go to university like father did. Not fight in a war and face all that death.'

'Does Diego cause this war? Sorry, Diego, I must ask.'

'To be honest, I kind of expected me to be the cause. I am trouble.' Diego shrugged.

'No, Diego fights with us, which is why I always knew you would be good friends; I saw you fighting side by side. And then today, after our swim, I had another vision.'

'Why aren't you dancing and showing your joy to the sun God, Inti?' the king shouted.

Quilla smiled at him, took her brother and Diego's hands, and pulled them back into a dance. They laughed.

'There is time to talk later, when it is quiet and the dance is over,' Manco said.

Diego noticed the look of concern briefly pass over Quilla's face before she dropped her eyes and quickly concealed it. Her smile was not convincing and Diego knew she was worried about something. But then, she looked up at him and smiled brightly, and he forgot everything. They spun around and around, dancing under the moonlight and the stars.

*

Lieutenant Kodo yelled at his fellow soldiers for being so slow and hurried them up the mountain. It was steep and their bodies were not made for long and difficult journeys. It was their minds they used the most, not their bodies. The altitude was playing havoc with their lungs and they couldn't catch their breath. Even Lieutenant Kodo was struggling. Yet those trained for the field should be fitter than average and he was angered that they couldn't keep up with him. He was very driven, more than them, and he had to succeed or his life would be over. Didn't they feel the pressure too? He marched up the mountain, growling at the others as he went, forcing them to pick up pace.

They zigzagged up the side of the mountain, hearing the music get louder as they went, grateful for the bright moonlight guiding their way. It took them most of the evening to get there and it was late when they finally arrived. Lieutenant Kodo was surprised when he saw the village; it was the most impressive home that the humans had ever built, as far as he was concerned. Most of the places he had seen were ugly and shabby and he couldn't wait to knock everything down and create plain white homes everywhere, linked by plain white corridors. It would be clean, minimal and fresh looking.

However, he had to admit that there was something about the village design working with nature that was warm and inviting. It appealed to him greatly. It was simple; stone houses, alpaca wool for curtains and doors, irrigation systems running through all the crops, carefully shaped into little fields around the mountaintop. Yet, it was also complicated; the fields cleverly aligned, in order to get both shelter and ample sun, the irrigation system was impressive and the houses were positioned perfectly. The animals: llamas, alpacas and guinea pigs roamed free around the village, somehow knowing where they could and could not go. Lieutenant Kodo knew he had found his own Kingdom. This is where he would lead his own life and village and raise his family when they settled on this planet. He smiled an evil and sinister smile and looked at his soldiers.

'Catch your breath; I don't want your heavy breathing attracting any attention!' he ordered. 'We rest here for a moment and then go where they are all gathered.'

Once his crew were breathing normally, he crouched behind a hut watching the fire and everyone dancing around it. He indicated with his hand that they should all get down and hide. He peered through the fire and immediately noticed a man sitting down, white with dark greying hair, contrasting with the darker and healthier looking man next to him, who was dressed far more glamorously.

Then he spotted the golden-haired boy dancing around the fire; he didn't fit in with the rest of the crowd at all and was far taller. There was no doubt about it: that boy had to be Diego, a child of Pisces. Lieutenant Kodo closed his eyes in relief, knowing that none of the others were here yet otherwise they would be sitting together with the Incas. He had done it, he had Diego all to himself, he had found him first. He took a deep breath and watched them dance, trying to focus on the strap around Diego's wrist. It flashed in the moonlight and the light from the fire seemed to catch strange colours every now and then. It was a complicated device and he marvelled at its beauty.

'The crystal cube,' he whispered.

'What is that?' asked one of his soldiers.

Lieutenant Kodo turned to face his soldiers; he had forgotten how young they were. He could spare a moment to share his vast knowledge with them before he made his move on Diego and claimed the cube for his own. He looked at them, feeling superior, and calmly rested his hand on his hip. Eagerly, they gathered around him and listened.

'You are both so young, not even in your first century yet, but I am old enough to remember our world,' he said.

Lieutenant Kodo was fortunate to have never fully died in the field. He had come close and been so severely injured his body only had moments left. However, with their technology you could transfer the mind to a fresh, newly cloned body. He had lost count as to how many times he had been reborn in this way. From near death experiences and old age. It saved training new greys when the old and experienced ones could be salvaged.

'Our planet was magnificent and held an abundance of remarkable crystals,' he began. 'We mined them for centuries and they were shared between the army and the lords of faith, headed by the senate. The army used them for weapons whilst the lords used them for peace. When our planet died, it was burnt up in its own crystal power and still burns angrily today, similar to Jupiter, a planet in this universe.'

Lieutenant Kodo paused for effect, watching their eager eyes widen with excitement, enjoying the story of their own lands.

'We built the spaceships and escaped into the sky, barely in time, before the planet turned on us,' he continued. 'We could only bring with us the crystal we had already mined and it wasn't much. Marcellus thought the lords had taken more crystal but he could never prove it. There were rumours and legends about the different crystal technologies that had been created and what they could all do. Thalen engineered one of the most powerful crystals into four of the strongest crystal weapons ever made and gave them to the Children of Pisces. This boy here has the crystal cube; you can see it on his wrist. It is one of the most powerful crystals ever mined and can summon and control electricity and storms. Rumour has it that Thalen found a way to charge it with starlight. Not just any starlight either; it contains the rare starlight from the pillars of creation.'

'Starlight?' one asked, his eyes wide and incredulous.

'Yes. A feat no one else has ever managed to achieve. Starlight from the Eagle nebula, which contained the pillars of creation. This was destroyed and nothing exists of these pillars anymore. So you see, this is a rare and unusual crystal. We have been hoping to find more. Very few can wield the power of such crystals. I have trained long and hard and must be the only grey who stands a chance. I expect that crystal to be my reward when Marcellus sees how brilliant I am. His race can handle far more crystal power than us greys and what aggravates me the most is how these children can wield it without any training or experience. That is genetics for you. Those crystals belong to us not human children!'

'I thought they were not human?' asked one of the aliens.

'They are human to me. They look human,' Lieutenant Kodo growled.

'The children of Pisces can wield the power naturally?' asked one alien. 'That has never been heard of before.'

'Yes, they can, which is why we must try to get them on our side,' Lieutenant Kodo explained.

'Look, they are leaving the fire.'

'It's time. We must strike now whilst they are still awake,' he said.

Lieutenant Kodo looked at Charles, who was beginning to stand up, and started to read his mind.

TEN

THE LAST INCA TRIBE

PERU

Stephen waited outside the front of Brunswick House with the Jeep. The sun was starting to go down as they said their farewells. As always, Jude kept a brave face as she kissed Ed and Jax goodbye.

'At least you are both in safe hands,' she said, thinking of Tammy, Mikie and Mina.

'Take care of them and bring them back to me. Don't let Ed be a hero,' Jude warned, kissing Tammy on the head.

'I will get him back to you.' Tammy nodded, trying hard to hold back her tears.

'I'll miss you, and I promise we'll go shopping when you get back, just like I said we would. You, Sukie, Lei and Mina, just us girls on a shopping trip to Paris.'

'It's a date.' Tammy tried to smile.

'I don't like the way you are asking children to look after me. It's the other way around, you know,' Ed said with a pout.

'Is it?' Jude smiled up at him sweetly.

Lei said goodbye to Tammy and Mikie, then turned to Mina, who waved awkwardly before turning away and heading for the Jeep.

'Mina?' Lei called.

Mina paused, reluctantly turning to face her.

'I'm going to have to do it, aren't I?' she said, smiling, and went over to hug her.

Lei breathed a sigh of relief as Mina squeezed her tightly in return.

'I have a present for you,' Lei said, and handed Mina a small parcel.

Mina opened it and took out a pretty bracelet made of silver and small black balls of some kind.

'It's really pretty,' Mina said.

'It's obsidian, a protective gemstone, made from volcanic glass. It kills monsters and is used for safety and grounding. This will help to keep that monster down deep until we find a way to permanently remove it.' Lei smiled lovingly at her.

'I love it, thank you,' Mina said as she slipped it onto her wrist.

She kissed Lei on the cheek then turned back towards the Jeep before anyone could tell she had tears in her eyes. Suddenly Pedro threw his arms around her legs and, unable to hold back anymore, Mina swept him up into her arms and felt the tears roll down her cheeks. Drat!

Ed, Mikie, Mina and Jet sat in the Jeep as Stephen drove them down to the shore. Jet knew Mina was sad and alone so was comforting her. Tammy and Jax rode Sirocco ahead. Everyone was silent as a feeling of foreboding passed over them and they wondered when they would next be back home. When might they next be together? Would they ever come back? No one wanted to ponder on that for long.

*

'Oh no, not again!' Mina moaned, as she saw the basking sharks waiting for them just off the beach. 'And what about Jet?' she added.

'Well, it's going to be hard for the animals. However, they both insisted on coming, so they'll have to bear it,' Tammy said.

'You're kidding, right?' Mina stared at her sister.

'Nope,' Tammy said with a smile.

'Ed?' Mina looked at him with pleading eyes.

'Mina, I had to take Sirocco and Jet to Africa, so if they want to travel to Peru and are willing to ride a basking shark to get there, who am I to judge?' Ed said with a shrug.

'We aren't riding them all the way to Peru, are we? That would take forever, we'll probably die!' Mina gasped.

'We would definitely die.' Jax chuckled.

'Relax, it's only to Southsea. We can't risk the ferry – remember last time? And we know they're watching this island very closely, however, not closely enough to see anything smaller than a boat in the water.'

'Of course, that makes more sense. Jet can ride with me if he likes.'

'I think he'll like that,' Tammy replied. 'It won't take much more than two hours.'

'Good, then we can feel awkward with out transport together,' Mina said, finally smiling.

'I have a little children's blow-up boat for Jet,' Stephen

said, getting it out of the Jeep and using a small electric pump to blow it up. He took it out to the water, lifted Jet in, and said hello to the sharks.

'Why can't I have a small boat?' Mina complained.

'Because you don't have his claws that he will need to dig in to cling on. Not kind to the sharks,' Stephen explained.

'We need to go,' Ed said.

'No problem, just wanted to get a close-up. Don't forget all your bags with supplies in them,' Stephen said, reluctantly pulling himself away from one of the sharks.

He stood, soaking wet, on the shore and watched them all wade out towards the sharks. It was getting dark now. They would be safe from any surveillance; the aliens wouldn't be expecting this.

Tammy, Mikie, Jax and Ed were soon safely on the back of a shark. They all stared at Sirocco and watched as he swam towards Tammy.

'This is going to be interesting,' Mina said, smirking.

'Yes, I'm keen to know how this goes myself,' Ed mused.

At that moment, Sirocco neighed and stopped swimming. He seemed to wobble a little and then regained his balance. Then he slowly began to rise out of the water like a magnificent statue.

'I don't believe it!' Ed gasped.

'That's my boy, always looks magnificent!' Tammy clapped.

Sirocco was balanced across two of the largest sharks and stood high above everyone else. He would be travelling sideways with his front legs on one shark and back legs on the other. They were very close together under him. He looked comfortable and at ease, as if he were standing on a pedestal.

Stephen laughed, shaking his head, and waved them goodbye as they set off to sea. Now he had seen it all. He messaged Jude to shut the part of the shield that they had opened back up. He also sent her a picture of Sirocco on the sharks.

'That's something you don't see every day,' Jude laughed when she saw the photo pop up on her watch.

Jet, obviously hating the water, stayed close to Mina in the boat and shook or licked himself as dry as he could if any water so much as touched him. The boat was just big enough for him. Mina kept one hand on his shoulder the whole time.

*

It took almost three hours to reach the coast of Southsea and they purposely stayed away from the pier and main beaches. Mikie and Jax had taken several photos on their watch of the journey, deciding to put together that short movie called Mina's misery. They had some great images of her scowling and gasping and picking seaweed off her leg in disgust. Jax, although older than Mikie and Tammy, seemed equal in age since they appeared far more mature than human children of the same age. Tammy encouraged the plankton to grow abundantly, showing her gratitude for the basking sharks' help and ensuring they were well fed. She again said goodbye to them before heading away from the beach to the houses. From there, they walked to an address Stephen had given them. They were soaking and uncomfortable. A plumber and was waiting for them in his van. He was a friend of Stephen's. They hid on the empty floor in the back of the van as he drove them to the airport.

'It's tiring riding basking sharks,' Mina stated, lying down and putting her head on Jet.

'At least the walk dried us off a bit and warmed us up,' Ed said. 'Sleep while you can.'

Jax took a sneaky picture of Mina lying on Jet and realised how soft she could look when she wasn't complaining. It was the first time he had seen her look content. The plumber snuck them into the airport and they were taken secretly around the back of the terminal by security. Ed had connections when he needed them, especially when it came to travel. The four security guards were used to Ed and his animals, yet one of them was very nervous. He was new.

'Don't worry about the cat; tame as a kitten. Just focus on us,' Ed said, shaking the child out of his petrified trance.

'Oh, s-sorry, Mr Brunswick, I waited, just like you asked. This way,' he said gesturing ahead of him.

'Thank you,' Ed replied. 'And you haven't seen anything.'

'Not a problem. I appreciate your need for privacy. Can't have the press at your heels all the time, can you?'

'What press?' Tammy whispered.

'I lied about the press being after me,' Ed whispered. 'Less terrifying for the poor chap than aliens, right?'

'Oh, definitely,' Tammy said, smiling. 'Good one.'

In no time at all, they had helped Sirocco and Jet into their own section of the hover plane and then boarded themselves. They had seats in the furthest forward part of the cabin and Ed had ensured no other passengers were seated near them. They were also travelling under fake passports that Lei had organised. The HPs were shaped like large white duck eggs and sat upon something resembling a clear plastic slide.

'We had a rather unpleasant problem with plastic waste in the past,' Ed explained for the benefit of Mikie and Mina, who had never travelled like this before. 'Plastic caused all sorts of environmental issues. No one knew what to do with it and all the greatest scientists and inventors were competing to find a solution. Basically, the HPs won. The hover plane. All the plastic, which takes centuries to decompose, was collectively used to create a road that connected all main areas of land via the oceans. Then, using a similar technology to that of the hovercraft, the HP was designed to hover above these plastic roads on a cushion of air.'

'Like slides,' Tammy added.

'Yes, steep at the beginning, like a roller coaster. It's a slow crawl up, they are mechanically pulled and then you go down the steep slope. This helps the air build up between the plastic road and the bottom of the HP and then the road evens out and away you go. Makes your stomach feel a little odd at first, then it's smooth until the very end. Travel is very restricted nowadays. It's expensive and the HPs don't run too often. Spaces are hard to find and cost a fortune for most people. I, however, travel to Africa frequently, so I bought the airport,' Ed said, laughing.

'It's designed to be aerodynamic and because of the thin exterior, it cannot hover over water, like the hovercraft, nor can it move in the air without a vast amount of fuel. It needs a smooth surface to work with, which is where the plastic came in perfectly. Two problems solved in one go. The other reason it needs the plastic beneath it is in case it breaks down for any reason – rare yet always possible. The HP would sink, unlike the hovercraft, so it has the plastic road to rest on until help arrives,' Jax added.

'We have a small shower in the back and on the back of each of your passports is a different seat number. An empty row of seats on the plane. You will each find a rucksack with fresh supplies under that seat where the life jacket should be. That way, you get the right bag. Courtesy of Lei's team,' Ed said.

'Impressive,' Jax muttered.

'It is rather, isn't it?' Ed mused.

'I hope they're fashionable,' Mina said.

'Feel lucky Lei organised it and not me. I'd put you in a potato sack,' Ed said with a smile.

Mina pouted sulkily at him.

'My underwear is still soaking wet,' Tammy moaned.

'Mine too. Just as well the seats are waterproof. Here we go,' Jax said, as the engines rumbled to life.

They buckled their seatbelts and sat back as the hover plane rose high into the air, then the engine noise rose a level and with a sudden lurch forward they were off – gliding downhill and then along the ocean slides. Mina and Mikie had never travelled this way before and couldn't believe it. They watched in astonishment.

As soon as they were mid-flight and allowed to move around, they all took it in turns finding their bags, without drawing attention to themselves, and showered and changed. They had only been finished half an hour when food and drinks were served. Small cans of juice and mini portions of fruit salad, tomato and basil pasta, cheese and biscuits and a mini muffin. They all adored the tiny food parcels. Then they slept, trying to get as much rest as they could. Ed had warned them that sleeping in the jungle would not be easy.

*

They slept a little, although not nearly enough, and they all felt groggy when the plane finally touched down in Lima, Peru. They immediately boarded a smaller plane for the flight to Cusco. Sirocco barely squeezed in, and Ed had to argue with the pilot to let him and Jet on board or be fired and he'd have someone else fly. It was funny to watch.

'How would he feel if we had Pedro with us?' Tammy wondered.

'Those hybrids may never be able to leave the island,' Jax replied.

'That's awful. We just have to educate people,' Tammy answered.

'One day, in the not-too-distant future, we will have a huge number of aliens all over this planet killing people. The hybrids won't seem so strange after that,' Mikie said seriously.

'Then, let us hope they will know freedom one day,' Mina said quietly and sadly.

From there, the plan was to acclimatise to the high altitude of the mountains. You could not just go from ground level without giving your lungs time to adjust. At least human ones, Ed admitted. He wasn't so sure about their lungs. Tammy rode Sirocco while they all sat in the open back of a farmer's truck, normally used to transport his vegetables. They bounced along the roads which got progressively steeper, and breathing became harder as the altitude changed.

The next two nights were spent hidden away in a small hotel in one of the quieter parts of Cusco, with nothing to do except concentrate on breathing. It wasn't as high as the mountains. Cusco has an altitude of 3,400 metres.

'How long before we can breathe normally?' Mikie gasped.

'A couple of days should do it for us, Mikie, and it's hard to tell with you. I've never travelled with a half alien before,' Ed said, smiling.

'Funny.' Jax laughed breathlessly from the altitude.

'We should be all right to start moving on tomorrow or the next day, we'll just have to see. This is nothing compared to Everest, where I think even the base camp is higher than this. You have to sleep in a tent in order to adjust as you climb the mountain. Just slow it right down. Take this pill, it will help,' Ed said, handing out tablets.

'What are these?' Mikie asked.

'My friend invented these a few years ago, speeds up acclimatisation. Amazing things. Tammy, you seem okay,' Ed said.

'I'm used to the pressure underwater. Maybe that has helped. I feel fine.' She smiled, declining a tablet.

'Good for you,' Mina said, who felt uncomfortable at being constantly out of breath – it scared her.

'In a couple of days, we'll hike towards the Palcoyo Rainbow Mountain, along the Red River,' Ed explained.

'The Red River?' Mikie asked. 'As in blood?'

'Nothing quite so dramatic. I'll explain when we're there. We will then climb up to Machu Picchu. That is where

I think they are. It's on top of a mountain, in the middle of nowhere,' said Ed.

'Why are the Incas so keen to remain hidden?' Tammy asked.

'Well, the Incas used to rule this area once, and then they were almost wiped out.'

'How?' asked Jax.

'Give me chance to catch my breath.' Ed paused. 'In civil wars with each other, and with the Spanish Invasion, viruses from foreign invaders spread and wiped them out. This was long ago in history. More recently, of course, was Pisces. After merely a few hundred Inca descendants survived the virus, they decided to recapture their ancestral roots and honour their age-old traditions, returning much to the basic Inca ways and often refusing to liaise with the rest of the world.' He paused again, breathing slowly. 'Machu Picchu had been a tourist spot for many years and they reclaimed it and turned it back into a working farm. They live there and followed the English monarchy ways. China did the same. Returned to having an emperor and democracy and dropped the Communist political party set up that they had in place at the time of Pisces. People went back to their old ways a lot all over the world. Aboriginal Australians are now highly sought after for their spiritual wisdom and powers. Native Indians are now thriving and returning back to their former ways of life. In fact, they have a massive issue now of too many tourists wanting to live with them. Pisces changed the world. The Incas really do not like to welcome visitors either,' Ed explained breathlessly.

'How can they hide?' Jax asked.

'Oh, wait till you see Machu Picchu.' Ed laughed and

reached over to pat Jax on the back. 'You have no idea how big the world really is, do you?'

'I don't and yet you have no idea how big the galaxy really is, do you?' Jax smiled smugly as he patted Ed on the back in return.

'Touché.' Ed laughed again.

'Earth is a tiny little speck that aliens somehow managed to find in the whole galaxy. I so want to see more of space,' Jax said with a sigh.

'How do they communicate with anyone else?' Mikie asked.

'Probably with runners,' Ed replied.

'Runners?'

'Yes, Mikie, in the olden days, the villages were connected by Inca trails, very small pathways which weaved through the mountains from one village to another. The Incas valued runners – men who were fit and could run at great speeds across those trails. They carried messages back and forth when needed. That is how they communicated.'

'I could live there,' Mina said. 'You would feel on top of the world.'

'They're covered in thick jungle, making even a large village at the top of a mountain almost impossible to find, even from the air.'

'Why does Diego have red paint on his face?' Mikie asked.

'The Incas use a particular type of beetle to make red paint. The beetle is black until it dies then its body dries out and turns red. The Incas grind up the beetles to make a dye. They have used it for centuries to colour their clothes, paint ceramics and even their faces. That would be the red paint you saw on Diego's face,' Ed explained. 'Pisces wiped out almost all of the beetles, and only a few remained in my park until I bred them and brought them back to be reintroduced into the wild. There is only one area I introduced them, as per the king's wishes, along with the wild boar he requested. That, along with the Red River and waterfall that the bird showed Tammy, tells me where they are. They would have to remain close to the beetles and boar,' Ed said, smiling.

'So, you really do know where he is?' Mina sat up, excited.

'Pretty sure.'

*

It took just overnight for their breathing to settle down and then Ed insisted they be off as quickly as possible. They hired the farmer's truck again and he took them to where Ed wanted them to start the hike. They came to an open area near a river. A bright red river. Tammy looked at it suspiciously and scanned for crocodiles. Fortunately, there were none.

'On foot?' Mina moaned.

'Yes, the only way is on foot, sorry,' Ed said.

'Wow, look at that river!' Mikie said. 'It's amazing. Are you sure it's not blood?'

'It's stunning,' Tammy said, sighing.

'It looks like blood,' Mina said.

The Red River wound around the forest floor. They had never seen anything like it.

'It isn't blood,' Ed said with a smile. 'The Red River of Palcoyo flows from the Rainbow Mountains. Named due to the multiple colours of its clay grounds, snaking its way through the emerald-green hills only at this time of year, in the monsoon season. So, expect plenty of rain while we're here. Ironically enough, the brick-red river looks so otherworldly that it gives the impression of landing on another planet in the universe. That we are the aliens on a different planet, not Thalen or Marcellus. Funny that. Mineral deposits present in the different layers of clay form due to soil erosion, and the iron oxide coming off the red region of the mountains gives the river its colour. During the rest of the year, the flow of water is slower, and the colour of the river is a muddy brown. How you see it now is truly magnificent.'

'It's still quite hard to breathe,' Mikie said, taking a deep breath.

'Yes, we're still high up. Let me know if you want another pill, as we will be going up and down a bit, which will be hard on the lungs,' Ed cautioned as he looked around. Miles of trees and mountains stretching in every direction.

'Where, exactly, are we going to find them?' Mina asked.

'Somewhere in that direction,' Ed said, pointing north.

'And roughly how long on foot?' Mina gasped for air. 'I don't know, depends how slow you lot are. Come on, we need to get to a safe place to camp before it gets dark,' Ed replied.

'Camp?' asked Mina.

'Yes, as in sleeping outside. You don't want to be walking about in a rainforest at night. Predators out here are like Jet, remember, or worse,' Jax warned.

'We're going to sleep out here?' Mina asked.

'Yes, every night until we find him,' Ed said.

'Come on, Mina, this could be fun.' Mikie nudged her. 'Lighten up a little.'

Mina glared at him, unconvinced, and watched despondently as Ed set off along the river. Everyone else followed. Jet stayed at the back, with Mina, who was grateful for his company. Tammy had asked him to.

'Well, Diego, you had better be worth finding,' she mumbled, lagging behind.

Tammy watched Jet with a heavy heart. She sighed and couldn't hide her melancholy.

'What's up?' Jax asked.

'This is Jet's real home. He belongs here, and he knows it too. I'm scared I'm going to lose him.'

Jax put his arm around her shoulders and smiled, pulling her close to him. Tammy tilted her head, resting it on his shoulder.

'One of the hardest things about love is letting those you love be free. You can't possess them. It's not exactly hard to come back and visit him if he gets to live the life of freedom that he craves, is it?' Jax said.

'True. I'm just having to process the possibility,' Tammy said with a sigh.

'I know and I'm here to be your sounding board.' Jax smiled.

Mina watched, frowning, her heart sinking more with every step. This place was so vast. She missed her posh house in Notting Hill and all the nice things she had, until now, taken for granted. Suddenly a loud, terrifying growl rumbled through the trees and made everyone freeze. Except for Mina who rapidly picked up pace, suddenly aware that she was alone at the back, and caught up with the others. Wasn't it always the ones at the back picked off first? She couldn't remember. She quickly passed Mikie and placed herself in the middle of everyone, closer to Tammy and Jax.

'What the hell was that?' she demanded.

'Just stay close and you'll be okay,' Tammy replied, and laid her hand softly on Jet's head. He was purring profusely. It was a female jaguar following them. Jet had caught her scent and she had caught his. She was already trying to catch them up.

ELEVEN

JUNGLE DANGERS

PERU

The Andean Cock-of-the-rock bird landed on Tammy's outstretched hand and told her what it knew. Tammy nodded and fed the bird some Peruvian fruit – aguaymanto and camu camu – that she had saved for him. She was sitting down, underneath Sirocco, who was leaning against a large tree for support. He was also tired and neighed gently.

'Thank you, little tunki,' she said. 'We're still heading in the right direction.'

'Your spy is brilliant. How far away are we?' Ed asked.

'Probably a day or two at the pace we're going,' she replied.

'I don't think I have another day, let alone two, left in me,' Mina complained.

The forest was dense and on foot was the only way to travel undetected. They had stopped under the shelter of some trees where they were able to hook their hammocks and sleep hanging in mid-air throughout the night. This

was safe from most animal attacks and allowed Tammy to sleep. It had been the seventh night they had slept in the forest, and they were feeling the exhaustion now. They walked all day, every day, and relied on the birds to feed back information on how well they were doing. It felt more like a month. No plane nor helicopter could easily land. The Incas were successful in their desire to be difficult to reach. 'You should feel lucky one of the birds found him otherwise we could have been crawling all over this place for years living carefree and native,' Ed told Mina.

'What a wonderful thought,' Mina replied, sarcastically. 'Baths and washing are outdated anyway.'

'Is Diego on the move?' Ed asked, ignoring Mina's reply. 'No, he isn't going anywhere. He's still around the village, playing with the lightning apparently. So, we should be able to catch him up,' Tammy said.

'That's good to know, and he still won't speak with you?' 'No, I'm afraid not, Ed. He still ignores all our attempts to communicate,' Mikie said, coming to sit alongside Tammy and stroke the little bird. 'What a lovely colour.'

'Can I feed him?' Jax asked. Jax was leaning against a tree and came over to sit close to Tammy too. His hammock was alongside hers, as it was every night. He smiled at her. She returned his smile, handing him the last piece of the camu camu and encouraged the bird to hop over onto his hand. Jax focused on the bird as he ate, thrilled at his peculiar face as it hungrily finished off the fruit.

Mina sighed heavily. Mikie, if there was room, hung his hammock the other side of Tammy so they could all chat and talk. No one wanted to talk to her. She couldn't wait to meet Diego and hoped he was someone she could bond better with. She felt sure she could. It never occurred to Mina that her constant whining deterred the others from talking with her. Even Ed was fed up with it.

'Am I the only one not enjoying this?' she asked.

'Yes,' everyone said, at the same time. They laughed, and even Mina couldn't help smiling. She pulled out her water bottle and went to take a drink. It was empty. She threw it onto the ground and huffed, irritated that even the simple task of having a drink of water was difficult here.

'Would you like some of mine, I have some left?' Mikie said, offering her his flask.

'No, it's fine! I know how to find some,' she said. The truth was she wanted some space and needed to get away from everyone. She had been stuck with them every day so far and it was suffocating her. She was different from everyone else. She had always felt this way and even with her siblings, those most like her, that hadn't changed. She was not like anyone else and there was something in her that was untamed and dark. It crept throughout her cells like a disease every chance it was given.

'Just be careful, it's dangerous here,' Ed warned.

'As if I hadn't figured that part out already.' She forced a smile. 'Would anyone like me to fill their flask whilst I'm out and about?'

'That would be nice,' Jax said, handing over his flask.

'Me too, please,' said Ed.

'May as well top mine up then,' Mikie added.

Tammy was the only one who shook her head; she still had a full flask from earlier, and she could find water very easily. When they slept she made the water come to her and fill their flasks. She and Jax would sit up late laughing and watching it happen in the starlight. However, she knew not to interfere with everyone else. During the day they wanted to do it themselves and she respected their independence, especially where Mina was concerned. Offering help to her was like slapping her around the face, something Tammy found difficult to understand. She watched Mina as she stuffed all the flasks into her rucksack then wandered off into the forest. Tammy secretly told Jet to follow her.

'I'm hungry,' Jax said. The bird jumped onto his shoulder, the food now gone, and started to clean its feathers.

'Well, what shall we have tonight?' Ed rubbed his hands together with mock excitement. 'Fruit or more fruit?'

'Can't we have something more substantial?' Mikie moaned. He felt his stomach rumbling at the thought of food.

'We're out of anything I bought with us and completely reliant on our surroundings now,' Ed replied.

'Well what about if we go and catch some meat?' Mikie asked.

'We can't do that, what about Tammy?' Jax said.

'It's my choice not to eat meat because of my relationship with animals. How could I?' she said. 'But I'm not ignorant to the fact that animals eating each other is a big part of life. It's my choice to be vegetarian, not any of yours.'

'That's very big of you, Tammy,' Ed replied.

'I won't help you catch anything though, and if it's something adorable I'll help it escape you.' She smiled sweetly.

'That's fair enough,' said Ed. 'Mikie, shall we go and have a look at what our options are? Something not adorable and willing to be caught.'

'Oh yes.' Mikie smiled, and got up to join Ed.

'Jax?' Ed prompted.

'I'm a vegetarian too,' he said. 'So obviously no.'

'It will be fun bonding,' Mikie replied then saw their faces and regretted speaking. 'Sorry, that was thoughtless of me. I promise I will cut right back on meat.'

'We have all had to, Mikie,' Ed replied. 'But for now, let's go and seek some protein. Like you, a fruit only diet is something I'm struggling with and it's killing me.'

*

Mina was not aware that Jet was following her as she moodily stomped through the trees looking for water. She would go invisible if she had to, although Tammy had warned her that animals could still smell and sense her. Ed had shown her a type of leaf to look for, a very large plant, that held water. It wasn't long before she found one. She tipped the large leaves, in a funnel type fashion Ed had demonstrated, and carefully poured the water into her flask. She repeated the process with everyone else's flask until they were all full. Then she took a large gulp of hers, wiping her lips as she looked around, before topping it back up.

Upon hearing a strange noise, she turned and looked in the direction it had come from. It was hard to see anything in the trees so she crouched down and went looking for the sound. She came across a small clearing in the forest, a patch of long grass and no trees, the first she had found. She smiled with relief and walked out into the open space. The forest made her feel claustrophobic and confined.

'Oh, this feels good,' she said, spinning around and

looking up at the sky.

It felt great to see the sky above her, with nothing in the way, and to have all this space on either side. It was wonderful. It was muggy but not as hot as it had been the last few days. It was a refreshing change. Mina spun around and danced across the grass, enjoying the freedom. She came to an abrupt stop when one of her turns left her facing a puma. She froze, speechless, gulping in fear. The puma stared back, changing position to an attack stance, ready to launch. It began what could only be described as a roar but, being a smaller cat breed, it was more of a deep purr that ended in a snarl. Then it gave a high-pitched yowl. Mina turned in a blind panic and started to run, letting out a long-strangled scream as she went, which she didn't even know she had made. The speed of the puma surprised her and she knew immediately that she couldn't outrun it. She turned her earrings and activated her invisibility, which did nothing to deter the puma, hot on her heels. Jet appeared and ran in between Mina and the puma, banging into the puma's shoulder and forcing her into another direction, away from Mina. Jet terrified the puma who ran away as fast as she could with him now hot on her tail. Mina did not stop to look back and raced all the way back to camp. Before long, Jet ran to her side and joined her.

'Thanks Jet.' She gasped breathlessly as they both slowed to a jog and headed back towards the others. She turned her earrings off, feeling safe now Jet was with her. Mina had no intention of walking. Her whole body shook with fright. She was numb at the thought that she had felt almost non-stop fear ever since being trapped in the scrap yard. Or was it when Kieran had disappeared? How had she become such a disgruntled, fearful person all of a sudden? Her safe and comfortable life had completely vanished overnight. And yet Mikie and Tammy didn't seem anywhere near as unsettled about it as she did. Was it because they had each other? She did have Lei but they had the support of Jax, Ed, Jude and Stephen. Was that why she was more lost than the others?

'Oh Diego, I do hope you're more like me,' she muttered under her breath. He was her only hope.

Jet left Mina's side and vanished into the trees as they reached camp. He had ensured she was safely returned yet he was waiting for something. Mina didn't stop to look. She knew the puma had been a close call and no longer felt the desire to have alone time. Jet sat alone in the trees, calmly licking his paws and cleaning himself up when he heard a rustle in the bushes. He looked up, knowingly, as a female jaguar came towards him, hesitantly. This was not the first time they had met. Jet watched her. She cautiously circled around him.

Tammy and Jax had made a fire and were positioning some big stones over the wood in a hole when Mina jogged in.

'Where are Ed and Mikie?' she asked.

'Hunting,' Jax replied.

'Oh excellent, I'm starving for something more than fruit,' Mina replied. 'They should be careful though, there are things out there. Jet saved me from a puma.'

'Good for Jet, I'm sure he's watching out for the others too.' Tammy smiled.

Mina took off her rucksack and handed Jax his flask, nodded at his thanks and placed the other flasks in everyone's hammocks.

'Are we really safe in these hammocks?' she asked, sitting against a tree. It seemed highly likely that the puma could reach her in her sleep if she wanted to.

'Safer than on the floor, but no, not completely safe,' Tammy replied.

'Well, that's good to know.' Mina sighed, rolling her eyes.

'Don't worry, I have animals looking out as we sleep and they will wake me if I need to manage any predator. I stopped a Brazilian wandering spider – a huge fatal thing – from crawling on you last night so you're safe, Mina. Did Jet go off again?'

'Yes. Did you send him after me?' Mina said, gulping at the thought of the spider.

'Does it matter if I did?' Tammy looked at her. She desperately wanted to have the friendship they sometimes had all the time, but hostility was the most common response Mina gave her. Tammy couldn't figure out why or what triggered it. She blew hot and cold all the time; one moment Mina was friendly and nice and the next Tammy was sure that Mina was plotting her murder.

Mina shrugged. 'He saved my rear end either way so I really can't complain.'

'And yet you will.' Jax sniggered and promptly received a dig in the ribs from Tammy.

'I'm worried about him,' said Tammy.

'Why? He is wild, free and seems happy out here.' Mina shrugged.

'I know, that's why I'm worried.'

'He craves a sense of freedom, doesn't he? It's getting

stronger now he's out in the wild, isn't it?' Mina said.

'You can feel his desire too?' Tammy tried to hide the frown creeping up on her forehead.

'Tammy, an idiot could sense his desire. Although I can also relate to his wild nature. Do you think you'll be able to let him go if that's what he wants?'

'It's not up to me.'

Jax gave Mina a look that indicated she should drop the subject, which she did. Instead, she watched what they were doing and decided to help. They were preparing a ground oven. Suddenly, a beeping sound came from the pocket of Jax's coat.

'Uh oh,' Jax said, pulling out the *seeker* and a small drone.

'What is that?' Mina asked.

'Remember the *seeker* I re-coded to alert us of any other *seekers* in the vicinity? Well, I upgraded it,' Jax explained.

'They've found us?' Mina gasped.

'Maybe or maybe not. Either way they are here scanning the area. Don't panic,' Jax said. 'It detects and draws in the *seekers*. It was beeping because there is one here, very close, just like last time. It uses a magnetic pulse to draw the *seeker* in. Watch this.'

Jax let his *seeker* go and it darted through the trees. Squinting, they could make the flash of silver as two other *seekers* found it and began chasing it through the trees. They held their breaths as the *seeker* came into sight. Mina and Tammy were frozen stiff and silent. Jax was smiling confidently. The *seeker* headed towards Tammy, then Mina, and then disappeared into the trees, the other two *seekers* close behind it. Jax released the small drone and it headed after them. He indicated that they should look at the video screen hovering in mid-air above his watch as they followed the chase from the drone's camera. It went after them on a seek and destroy mission. The drone followed them over a mile away to the river when the first *seeker* suddenly stopped, turned and faced the *seekers* chasing it. The two *seekers* abruptly stopped and hovered in front of it. The drone crept up behind them, unseen and undetected. They watched as the drone released a high pitched sound, undetectable to human and alien ears, that made the seekers shake and vibrate until they exploded in the air. Now merely pieces of metal, they dropped into the river. Lost forever.

Mina smiled. 'That's such a clever trick.'

'Thanks. I upgraded the solution after last time at Nan's cottage. Destroying them near us alerted the aliens to our whereabouts. This way they can be lured away and destroyed far from us. Their path and final positions will be logged and tracked. This is why I made them come by us and pass through. This area will be on their route and classed as cleared, so it's unlikely new ones sent out will cover old territory. They have no reason to cover this patch again. My coded *seeker* keeps them focused and locked in. They only have eyes for that. They never even acknowledged us, not that it matters as they can only track the route remotely, not obtain the full details without the chip inside them. So, that is one less thing we need to worry about. It works well.' Jax smiled broadly, taking a seat next to the ground oven.

'Well done, Jax, that is truly genius.' Tammy smiled up at him. He had grown even taller after a recent growth spurt and was more muscular. His intelligence never ceased to astound her. She blushed when she saw Mina staring at her with a huge smile.

Mina shook her head and watched as her sister drooled all over Jax. It was too funny and obvious and yet Mina had to admit Jax was looking good lately. His muscles, height and looks were reason enough to make the girls fancy him, but his skills seemed to know no bounds. Mikie had taught him to fight, there wasn't a wound he couldn't heal – with Tammy's help – and he was fit on top of all that too. Mina couldn't understand why she didn't find him attractive herself. She had every reason to, despite how clear it was that he was utterly besotted with Tammy. But he was off limits. They did make a cute couple, she had to admit. She couldn't recall ever fancying anyone.

Just then, Jax let out a loud girlish scream and jumped up into the air. Mina stared in horror as a small colony of black bullet ants marched past. Jax had been stung on his hand and was red in the face with pain as he limped away from them. Mina was about to laugh when she felt an excruciating pain in her leg and screamed with all her might. It was a sharp, blinding, electric pain and they were now both rubbing their wounds with tears in their eyes. Tammy instantly told the bullet ants to march swiftly away and they obeyed easily. Then, she placed a hand on Jax's bite and another on Mina's leg and began to heal their pain and calm the areas.

'Don't touch me!' Mina moaned before she realised that the pain was going.

'I can stop if you like?' Tammy smiled.

'No, n-no, don't you dare, please just make it stop, it's so painful!' she whined.

'Make up your mind.' Jax burst out laughing

uncontrollably.

'What's so funny?' Mina asked, laughing too. 'I w-was just looking at you before this h-happened, thinking how fit and s-strong you've become recently and then you went and screamed high pitched like a little girl.' After struggling to speak with the tears and almost hysterical laughter, tears from laughing and pain now streamed down her cheeks.

They all howled with laughter as the pain subsided. Then, Ed and Mikie returned wearing proud smiles on their faces until they saw them all.

'What are you doing?' Ed asked.

'We got bitten by black ants!' Mina declared. 'It was the worst pain ever.'

'Ah, that would be the black bullet ant.' Ed chuckled. 'That had to hurt! Its sting is so painful it's like being shot. You should be proud and take the pain, Jax, it's actually a coming-of-age ritual of the Sateré-Mawé tribe in the Amazon. I think the Incas do it now too.'

'You have to be kidding me?' Jax moaned.

'Honestly, they make their children take the pain of it to test how strong they will be as a man?' Mikie gasped.

'Well, you failed that one then, Jax.' Mina howled.

Mikie shook his head, smiling. 'I heard you back there and thought it was Mina. I've never heard you scream before, Jax. I think perhaps you should hide that in future.'

Jax blushed and looked at Tammy who was smiling sweetly at him.

'Tell me more, Uncle Ed,' Jax said, trying to change the focus from himself.

'In preparation for the initiation ceremony, bullet ants are harvested from the jungle and then sedated. While unconscious, the ants are woven into a pair of gloves made from leaves, with their stingers facing inward,' Ed explained. Tammy gasped. 'That is twisted.'

'To be considered a man of the tribe, boys as young as twelve will thrust their hands into the gloves for at least five minutes, being repeatedly stung the entire time. The tribe leads the initiates in song and dance during the ordeal, but this distraction is their only relief.'

'You have to be kidding me? I only had one bite and my hand was on fire! I don't think I could have taken two bites let alone several and over minutes!' Jax declared.

'That's probably why it's a boys' thing and not a girls' because we're too strong to need testing. I took it better than you did!' Mina taunted him.

'You so did not!' Jax scoffed.

'Did too! Mind you, I wouldn't sew them into gloves. I'd sew them into your underpants!' Mina declared, and stuck her chin out in defiance.

'Ouch, oh no no no. Sooo wrong,' Mikie said shuddering. Jax had gone quite white at the thought, all blood now drained from his face.

'Bras.' Jax spat at Mina.

Mina grabbed her breasts in her hands and covered them protectively. 'Oh no, that is cruel, too cruel,' she whispered.

'Pack it in, you pair,' said Ed. 'When the gloves are removed, the ants' venom continues acting for hours. It hurts like hell but it can also cause muscle paralysis, disorientation and hallucinations for hours.' He nodded, matter-of-factly.

'That is sick.' Jax blew out a slow breath. 'Man, that

really hurt but I'm not feeling anything else.'

'I can't imagine having to do that,' Mikie said, shaking his head.

'I've used energy to flush it all out and since it was only one bite, it wasn't too hard,' Tammy explained.

'That's not all,' Ed continued. 'While completing the ceremony earns the young men respect, they must wear the gloves a total of twenty times before being considered fully initiated as tribal warriors.'

'Twenty times? That is so not right,' Mikie said. 'I'd happily claim to not be a man; I don't need any ceremony to prove myself. I'd avoid the entire thing. But I can at least cheer you up – well, Mina at least, not Jax.'

'Oh goody, you caught something for dinner? What did you get?' Mina asked, excitedly.

'Meat. Now, close your eyes and hold out your hands,' Mikie said.

Mina, starving and enthusiastic, did just that. She felt the weight of something land in her palms and opened her eyes.

'Oh my God, argh!' she screamed, jumping to her feet and throwing the snake down on to the ground.

Mikie laughed. 'What is it again, Ed?'

'It's a bushmaster, a long one too, must be almost three meters long.'

Mina backed away and watched as they went over to the fire and gloated over their prize. Tammy and Jax moved away, not wanting to watch, a sense of sadness coming over them. Mina saw this and rolled her eyes in annoyance.

'It's just dinner, Tammy. We have to eat, you know. Although I'm not eating that! Can today actually get any worse?' Mina retorted.

'Don't criticise it until you've tried it,' Ed replied.

'It's supposed to be very tasty,' Mikie added. 'Plus, it's the best we could do with what we had. Everything else was cute.'

'Is it venomous?' Mina asked.

'Very,' said Ed.

'If we eat it, won't the venom poison us?'

'No, we will only be eating the good bits and avoiding the venom sacs.' Ed smiled.

Mina pulled a face and grimaced at the length of the long body.

'Why don't you guys go and take a walk while I show Mikie and Mina how to prepare a snake to eat?' Ed suggested. Tammy and Jax didn't need telling twice and promptly walked away into the jungle.

'I'm not looking,' Mina declared.

'Oh yes you are, young lady,' Ed said sternly. 'You don't eat with us unless you help prepare the meal. This isn't a hotel, you know.'

'Don't I know it!' Mina replied sulkily. She looked around, desperately trying to find a way to get out of what was about to happen.

TWELVE

DECEPTION

PERU

'Let's work over here on this fallen tree branch.' Ed laid the snake out on the wood. 'You hold the tail end, Mina. That's right, just there. Now, it's important to avoid the venom sacs so it's best to cut the head off just about here.' He pointed at the snake. 'Mikie, would you like to do the honours?'

'Sure,' he said taking the knife and cutting off the head.

'Oh gross,' Mina retched.

'Now, start at the tail and slice the body up the middle. It's not gonna be pretty that's for sure. Oh dear, that's unfortunate... Hmm, maybe if I... Sorry guys, this is bad...'

Mina screamed and retched, covering her mouth and looking away as guts spilled out on to the wood. Even Mikie gagged and had to take a step back.

'Sorry, Mina, this is gross, be very careful. OK, there are a lot of entrails in here so we need to get that away from the meat.'

'Oh my God, it's still alive,' Mina cried as it wriggled and moved.

'No, it isn't, that's just as I cut it. Don't worry, its very dead, Mina.'

'It really stinks,' Mikie added.

'Yeah, meat eating snakes do stink. There is an abundance of venomous snakes here and less is better as it stands.' Ed exhaled heavily and moved away to take a breath of air that didn't stink. 'Good grief, I haven't done this since I was a child. It's really disgusting. You have to be desperate to scavenge for food like this. Now, Mikie come here. You can get the skin off.'

'It keeps crawling, are you sure its dead?' Mikie asked wearing a look of absolute disgust.

'Yes, it's just reflexes and anatomy, don't worry. Interestingly, a venomous snake can still bite and kill you even after it is dead – that's due to a reflexive action of the nervous system. That's why we cut its head off at the start and bury it. Now pull the skin back. Yes, just like that. You can dry the skin out and keep it as a memento because unless you're desperate and starving, I doubt you'll ever do this again.' Ed chuckled. 'Now, we need to separate all the organs and faeces out and wash the body before we chop it up. Here Mina, take these entrails and chuck them in the bushes. Bury the head deep in the ground.'

'No flipping way!'

'Mina, come on now. You need to harden up and get used to guts. You're going to be fighting in a war, remember, not donning fancy dresses and attending balls,' Ed stated.

'You are sick making me do this.' She retched again as she tried to pick up the slimy body parts with large leaves, chasing them as they slipped and avoided her. Eventually, she managed to get them into the bushes. Ed and Mikie were trying not to laugh at her.

Mikie chopped the bushmaster into smaller pieces and Ed helped him to carry the tree branch away from camp, removing the blood and smells from their area. They were just finishing up when Tammy and Jax returned.

'I have a surprise for you,' Tammy said.

'What?' asked Ed.

'Look.' She smiled and pointed up to the sky.

Several Andean condor birds flew towards them, each dropping something on the floor next to Ed.

'What is that?' Mina asked, moving closer to the fire.

'Vegetables!' Mikie gasped. 'Oh, Tammy, you're fantastic!'

'Where did they come from?' Ed asked.

'I asked the birds to pinch them from the Inca village. They have worked quite hard flying with them and taking turns carrying them. Jax and I will make a vegetable stew.'

'Look, Ed, we've got spinach, corn, carrots and what is this one?' Mikie said, collecting the fallen vegetables.

'That is a sweet potato,' Ed said, upon examining it. 'And Jax, you remembered the ground oven trick really well.'

Jax nodded, smiling. 'The fire has almost fizzled out and is now ready to use some big leaves to cover the food on the heat of the rocks. Then, we'll cover it with earth and slowly cook it. The stones on the fire are placed in a certain way so that they heat up, like an oven. We can put the snake on one half, covered in soil, and stew the other side. Tammy has the closed metal pan for that. We have also prepared an open fire for later,' Jax smiled as he pulled a package from out of his rucksack.

'What is that?' Mina asked excitedly, sensing it was good news.

'Marshmallows, digestive biscuits and dark chocolate.' Jax winked at her and handed her the package.

'I take back everything mean I have ever said to you, Jax. You are my hero.' Mina smiled at him happily.

'Now we'll have a nice hot feast instead of fruit for this evening.' Ed smiled, and rubbed his hands together heartily. 'Jax and I used to do this when we went camping together. Nice job, Jax. You did everything perfectly.'

Mina was impressed. They prepared all the food, finding small bits of wood to act as skewers for the snake, and covered it with leaves and dirt to cook. Then they sat around the other fire. They had added some other items that they had foraged from the surrounding area, including mushrooms and ferns, the safe and edible ones, and yucca roots. As soon as the smells started to float over towards Mina, she felt her stomach rumble, and began to care less that it was a snake cooking. When the time came to open up the pit and reveal the delicious sight and smell of everything cooked, she realised just how hungry she was. Nonstop fruit and berries was hard with all the walking they were doing.

'You still refusing the meat?' Mikie asked, knowingly.

'I felt you in my head, Mikie, so just shut up and give me some food. I'm hangry and you don't want to mess with me right now,' Mina warned.

'Now, I warn you, guys, snake and tasty don't really go together,' Ed said.

'You told me earlier it was nice.' Mina gasped.

'Nice as in filling and protein, tasty it's not. And you

need to eat carefully because of all the bones.'

Mikie laughed and handed Mina a bowl of stew with a skewer of meat on the top. She smiled gratefully and tucked in while Tammy and Jax enjoyed the stew and fruit.

'Hmm, tastes like a roasted bike inner tube,' Mikie mused.

'Yeah, that about sums it up,' Mina replied. She didn't care; she was starving and needed something heavy in her belly.

'Snake meat is rising in the food industry,' Ed announced. 'It's low in fat and calories and high in protein. The only reason it doesn't take off is because you have to prepare it carefully or you'll get an infection or food poisoning.'

'And because it keeps moving even after it's dead, I bet!' Mina remarked.

'What?' Tammy gasped.

'Reflexes and nervous system, Tammy. Not suffering or anything. A venomous snake can still bite and kill you when it's dead just by the reflex action,' Mikie explained.

'That's why the very first thing you do with a venomous snake is cut off the head below the venom sacs,' Ed added.

'I'd rather starve,' Jax said.

'You can go weeks without food really, water is the essential thing. We could have done this entire journey without eating,' Ed said cheerily.

'Now imagine Mina without food for a week. Not sure hangry covers that.' Mikie laughed and the others joined in. Mina kicked him in the leg.

As the night grew darker, the crowd of animals gathered around Tammy grew. Birds, chimps, frogs, butterflies, six spider monkeys determined to sit on Sirocco's back, and even a sloth that wrapped himself lovingly around Tammy's neck. They were protected near her from the evening predators and in return, they warned her of any predators arriving. Jet was near, but no one could see him. Tammy knew he was resting with the female jaguar just out of sight.

'This is really nice, actually,' Mina said, as she chewed another piece of snake.

'Yes, not too bad considering the circumstances, eh?' Ed laughed.

'For the first time since we got here, I feel like my belly is finally full,' she added.

'Tell us another story, Ed?' Tammy asked.

'Oh, yes, what will it be tonight?' Mina added.

'Gore and sacrifice?' Jax laughed.

'Well, if I must, but we have heard enough about the Gods so how about a love story that doesn't go, shall we say, according to plan?' Ed raised his eyebrows, questioningly. Everyone nodded then gathered in closer to the fire and waited for Ed to begin, as he had done every night since they had camped out. It took their minds off the noises and prepared them to meet the Incas.

'This is a true story based upon the shepherd and the daughter of the sun,' Ed began. 'It was winter, the weather was cold and snow peaked on the mountain tops. A shepherd, named Acoya-napa – the Incas always used double barrel names back then – sat guarding his flock of white llamas. Traditionally, llama wool was used to make clothing, but these ones were to be sacrificed to their sun God, Inti. Acoya-napa looked up to the moon goddess, Mama Quilla, resting in the sky and sighed. She looked beautiful and bright this night.' Ed took a break to eat a marshmallow and licked his lips. For a moment, he could pretend this was a fun camping trip and everyone would be happy and live a long peaceful life. He continued, 'As he did each night, the shepherd picked up his flute and very softly and sweetly began to play to his flock. He knew nothing of the amorous desires of youth and felt no longing for true love. Until suddenly, two daughters of the sun God startled him as they appeared from out of nowhere. He did not see them until they spoke...'

For an hour they all slowly yawned and settled as Ed told the whole story. Then he came to the end.

'... They were awoken by a loud noise and stood up to see where the sound had come from. The princess held one shoe in her hand and kept the other on her foot. Then, as they faced the town they had come from, they were both turned into stone. To this day, the two statues can be seen looking at the palace, high up in the mountains.' Ed smiled at their sleepy faces as he added more wood to the fire.

'That's not a nice story really,' Tammy said, yawning and holding Jax's hand.

'I don't know, they were able to be together forever, and she wasn't sacrificed,' Jax added. 'I quite like it.'

'I warned you, it's not always a Cinderella story, even with the slipper added in,' Ed said. 'Now, try to get some sleep.'

'Easier said than done,' Mina grumbled as she remembered the puma and the black bullet ants. What else lurked in their vicinity?

*

The music stopped and the dancers sat down, exhausted and radiant after such a fun evening. Diego, Manco and Quilla headed in the direction of the king and Charles, laughing and holding hands as they went. Quilla was in the middle and looked happily from side to side at her two favourite boys. Diego watched her and saw how happy she was but he still felt an underlying sense of unease in her.

The king and Charles got to their feet, smiling, when Charles suddenly groaned in pain and fell to his knees.

'Uncle!' Diego shouted, letting go of Quilla's hand and running to his side.

Charles knelt, groaning and grabbing his head in pain.

'What is it?' asked the king.

'Headache, really bad...' Charles gasped, the pain making it hard for him to speak.

'Do you suffer from headaches normally?' the king asked, looking around the village with narrowed eyes.

'Never, I...' Charles couldn't speak; he groaned and fell back onto the ground.

'I've never known him to have a headache,' Diego said.

Diego knelt over his uncle, worried to see him in such agony, and he looked up at the king and Quilla. He saw their faces and knew they suspected something bad, something more than a headache.

'My instincts tell me this is not a normal headache and brought on by some kind of witchcraft. I do not dare to administer any medicines for fear of creating more danger for Charles. Manco, help get him into bed, there is something amiss here tonight.'

They started to help Charles to his feet when the headache stopped and he looked up at them all, bewildered.

'It's gone,' he said, confused.

The king frowned, and then he too fell to his knees, the same headache torturing him.

'Evil…' He gasped, holding his head against the pain.

'Father!' Manco screamed.

Manco fell to his father's side. Diego looked at Quilla who was surprisingly quiet. She did not see Diego watching her. She bit her bottom lip, looked at her father and then turned and looked over her shoulder, as if expecting something to be there.

'What is it?' Diego asked.

Manco looked up at them and he too realised his sister knew something.

'It's the vision you were going to talk about earlier, isn't it, Quilla?' Manco said.

'Yes, but there is no time to explain now,' she said. 'They are here.'

The king's headache ceased as quickly as it had started and he got to his feet. All eyes were on the hut that Quilla was mesmerized with. Everyone was holding their breath. Someone – or rather some*thing* – stepped out from behind the hut.

Diego's mouth dropped open as he saw the alien walking slowly towards them. His prestigious kaftan gave him a quiet and calm sense of peace, as did the gentle way he held his hands lightly across his stomach. Non-threatening. His large grey head bent forward slightly, in a nonaggressive manner, as he approached them. It was his large black eyes that held Diego's gaze; there was something about them that seemed vaguely familiar.

'Demons from the sky,' the king whispered.

'He is alone and seems peaceful enough,' Charles replied, naively.

Quilla looked at the alien and then at Diego, noticing how his eyes were of the same blackness. The contrast with his golden hair had been the first thing she liked about him. Her gaze returned to the alien; she was unaware that Diego had noticed her look. He was also wondering how his eyes seemed like no other human he'd ever met.

While Ed told stories in another part of the jungle, Lieutenant Kodo stopped by the fire and raised his hand in peace. He knew Ed was near and time was running out. He spoke for the first time, using the poshest English he could remember. His old billionaire friends had always encouraged him to speak what they termed the "Queen's English". Little did he know that they were mocking him because of old Mr Blaire. He was one of the many teachers kidnapped from Earth years ago and forced to teach English to the aliens. Mr Blaire insisted that he would die before he taught "common" English other teachers did and instead would teach the "Queen's English" only. What was yet to be realised was that he taught it poorly deliberately. It was his way of seeking revenge on his abductors. He taught them malapropisms; using the incorrect word in place of another, rendering the speaker as silly. Any alien who had been taught by Mr Blaire spoke in this manner. Lieutenant Kodo considered himself the master of both the "common" and the "Queen's English". None of his friends had ever corrected him.

'I illicit you in peace. Please may I come and conversation with you?' he asked.

The king and Charles exchanged looks. The king

nodded and held out his hand, indicating the alien should take a seat next to them. They all sat down.

'My name is Thalen,' Lieutenant Kodo lied. 'I have travelled far to come here and find Diego.'

'Why?' asked Charles.

'You must be his accordion?' Lieutenant Kodo smiled.

'His what?'

'I think he means guardian,' Quilla suggested.

'Yes, I am his guardian,' Charles answered.

'Then I must thank you for keeping him safe all this time. I am his father.'

No one spoke. They looked at each other and then at the alien.

'Charles?' Diego spoke, looking curiously at Charles.

'We had our suspicions.' Charles shrugged.

'I bet you thought I had disappeared into Bolivian, but no I am here. I know I'm early; I was not supposed to come and find you yet,' Lieutenant Kodo said.

'What do you mean?' asked Diego, looking between the alien and Charles.

'He was supposed to come when you reached the age of…' Charles began, but was silenced by the king's hand.

'Do not speak, let Diego's father, if that is truly who he is, tell us,' said the king. 'I am concerned that we both suddenly got headaches just moments before you appeared.'

'Of course,' replied Lieutenant Kodo. 'I was exposed to come on Diego's thirteenth birthday. I am a little early.'

Charles smiled; how could anyone but his father know that? Charles had not told anyone, not even Diego.

'Is this true?' Diego asked.

'Yes, it is,' Charles replied.

'Show him the note; I assume you haven't shown it him yet?' Lieutenant Kodo said, reassured that his plan was working and glad for the information he had read from Charles's mind.

'What note?' said Diego.

'I wasn't going to tell you yet, but your mother left you a note,' said Charles, and he went into their hut to find the note and promptly returned with it, handing it to Diego.

Diego read the note aloud:

> *Dearest Charles*
>
> *Time has passed so quickly and it seems an age since we last met. I have heard all about your recent escapades, but they have not made me change my mind about you. I'm dying and barely have enough time to ensure my child is safe. I therefore beg you to look after my son, Diego. I decided he would calm you down not to mention you owe me a favour!*
>
> *I know you will come to love him as your own. Only you have the skills to understand and develop his needs, to support him and keep him safe as he discovers his talents. Tell him I love him and will always regret not being there to support him throughout life. He is a wonderful child and should always respect himself for his own individuality.*
>
> *On his 13th birthday, his father will find him and all will be explained. Charles, it is important that you let him know he is loved and not alone – no matter what he does. He will face great challenges. Keep him safe and strong for me.*
>
> *Thank you. All my love, Sarah.*

Diego looked up at Charles.

'Why did you not show me this before?'

'There was never the right time.' Charles sighed.

'Why have you come now and not when he is thirteen?' the king asked.

'Well, as you have seen, Diego has some problems precipitating his own power and that makes it easy for the enemy to find him. Yes, the enemy is hunting him', he added as he noted their expressions. 'They want his powers and so I had to come early, they are but days behind me. I must take him somewhere safer.'

'It's safe here,' the king replied, uncertainly.

'I found you easily and therefore so can they.'

'That's a good point,' Charles said.

'We must leave medially,' Lieutenant Kodo pressed.

'I'm really glad you found us.' Charles smiled. 'I was getting scared of being able to keep him safe for much longer. You're right, his power is so strong, and he needs someone who understands it. I'm so relieved you are here.'

'I too am glad,' said Lieutenant Kodo, bowing his head in gratitude and understanding.

'How did you find us?' asked the king, suspiciously.

'The unnatural storms, lightning and the burnt trees. I tracked footmarks from the waterfall and heard the music in your village. It was not very hard, which is why we must leave now. We know another ship has been sent this way from the enemy. I have a spaceship waiting for us by the waterfall.'

'It's not safe to go through the jungle at night,' the king said.

'I have twenty soldiers waiting for us. I thought it safer

that only I approached you, so as not to alarm you in any way. They will guide us safely back.'

'And I am not scared of the dark, I went out alone last night, remember?' Diego added.

'It is not for me to decide. My heart tells me you should wait but I understand the danger you speak of. I have seen it in my dreams. I do not want the enemy to find us here. Will they know he has left with you?' the king asked.

'I give you my word that once he leaves with me, the enemy will have no further reason to look for your village, and they will leave you alone. They will know that I have found him and that it's jointless coming here. I will make sure of that.'

'I am thinking of those random headaches and I do not like this. Charles, what is your desire?' the king asked.

'I reprehend you perfectly and your concerns are valid,' said Lieutenant Kodo. 'I promise you, I just want my son safe. My soldiers could have charged in and taken him and yet I arrived alone.'

'I think we should listen to his father. I knew Sarah and she was trustworthy. Therefore, we can also trust the word of Thalen. Diego?' Charles asked.

'I'm happy to leave now, with my father,' he said. 'I don't want anyone here hurt because of me.'

'I shall come too,' Charles said, getting to his feet.

For an instant, Lieutenant Kodo looked annoyed but then he hid it carefully. Not before Quilla had noticed.

Diego heard Quilla gasp and turned to look at her. He assumed she was just upset at the thought of him leaving, as he too would have preferred to stay.

Everyone stood up and looked at each other.

'I don't think you should go,' she said, after seeing the alien's sharp look.

'Quilla, when all this is over, when everything is safe, I shall return to you,' Diego said.

He took her hand and smiled into her sorrowful face.

'I have so much to tell you,' she said.

'Then I shall return soon and you can tell me everything.'

'Quilla, leave the boy alone, it's his time and choice to leave us for now.' The king said before turning to Diego and Charles. 'I, too, will look forward to your safe return – both of you. We will always welcome you into this village'.

Charles smiled and shook hands with the king, as did Diego. The king patted Diego hard on the back and smiled affectionately. Quilla was quietly fuming. She could clearly see the trap – her visions made sense now, and both her father and Charles were far too keen to wash their hands of Diego. Yes, he was immensely powerful and neither of them really wanted to be his guardian, but all the same, there was no excuse for dumping him the first chance they had. She glared, nostrils flaring, at her father. He paid her no attention, incorrectly assuming her infatuation with Diego was the cause. Manco, on the other hand, was taking everything in and knew Quilla had reason to be concerned.

They said their goodbyes. Quilla felt it was all happening in slow motion and beyond her control to save Diego from this fate. Manco approached and hugged Diego in friendship. He didn't say anything, and Diego felt he couldn't speak either. He suddenly felt very sad. Things had changed so rapidly. He kissed Quilla on the cheek and felt confused as to why she wasn't responding. She seemed frozen in time. Lieutenant Kodo seized the moment and was keen to bring it to an end.

'Come, I feel danger blooms close,' he said, dramatically.

Quilla looked at him, eyes narrowed and fists clenched as they turned to leave. Charles packed and grabbed their bags quickly – they hadn't arrived with much – and gave Diego his bag. He slung it over his shoulder reluctantly then glanced over at Quilla and Manco and waved. Neither of them responded, just stood there. Diego couldn't help but feel disappointed. Charles and Diego followed Lieutenant Kodo into the forest, out of sight.

The other two aliens, dressed in less glamorous kaftans, stepped out in front of them. They saluted respectfully to Charles and Diego and did their best attempt at a sweet smile. It looked more like a grimace crossed with trying to go to the toilet. Diego frowned at them and how weird their facial expressions were. Charles smiled and saluted back, digging Diego in the ribs until he did the same. Charles was happy and relieved that the responsibility of Diego had been taken away from him. He blindly followed the aliens into the forest, his shoulders already lighter. Diego, however, felt sad and miserable at the thought of leaving the village. He followed with his shoulders sagging and his head bowed low. He did not notice the Andean Cock-of-the-rock bird watching from the tree.

*

'Come my children, let us sleep,' said the king.

'You go ahead, Father, we shall be there soon,' Quilla replied.

'Do not be long.'

'We won't. I just want to sit and stare at the moon for a while.'

'Manco, keep an eye on your sister. She will be wanting to cry silver tears.' The king smiled sweetly and stroked her hair affectionately.

'I'll make sure she's OK,' Manco replied.

They waited until their father was out of earshot and the other villagers were slowly making their way to their huts. Then walked towards the fire, where they could be alone.

'Something is wrong, isn't it?' Manco said.

'Yes, something is terribly wrong. Father said he saw demons from the sky but so did I, only when I saw them, they came here, just like they did tonight. I saw them in my dreams hiding behind that exact hut. They are the evil ones.'

'I know, I saw you looking at the forest, from where he appeared, before anyone else knew he was there.'

'I am certain, Manco, with all my heart, that the one in white is the most evil,' Quilla whispered. 'I do not know if he's Diego's father but he is not good at all. We must do something.'

'What can we do? He said there were others in the forest waiting for him.'

'I don't know. Father will never believe me – he patronises me. I wish I had told him I have visions before now.'

'Shush, Quilla. If you tell him now, he will think it is because you love Diego and don't want to see him go.'

'What?' she looked at him with surprise.

'Oh, come on, it's obvious! You love him. Fancy falling for someone younger than you! Nevertheless, it's true – Father will never believe us and therefore no one else will either. We can take weapons and go after them. We can follow them and see what we can do to help them along the way,' Manco said.

'Oh, thank you, Manco. You are the best brother in the world!' She smiled.

'Come, we know where they are heading, we can shortcut them to the waterfall. We will easily catch them up.'

Quilla nodded and quietly followed him into their house to get their spears.

THIRTEEN

MOUNTING SUSPICION

PERU

Diego looked up at the moon, remembering the story Quilla had told him about the goddess, and sighed at the thought of not seeing her again. They had not long left the village and it was a brilliant silvery moonlight this evening. When they left the cover of the tree canopies, the full moon illuminated everything so brightly they could see almost as well as they could in the day. Already the loss of his new friends weighed heavily upon him. It seemed unfair that just as he had started to feel as if he belonged somewhere and was happy, it had to end.

Charles felt the same. The village had been the nicest place they had ever lived and he had wanted to remain there. However, he really wanted Diego's father to take over the responsibility of this immensely powerful boy who, truth be known, terrified Charles more often than not. The first thing he planned to do when Diego left was to have an entire week of non-stop gaming. He would get enough food and beer in to last the week. He smiled at the thought of it.

'I promise you that we will go back there one day,' Charles told him. 'But you should make an effort with your father now, get to know him.'

'I guess you're right.' Diego sighed.

'Are you not excited to finally meet your father?'

'Not really. He talks like an idiot and I don't feel anything for him. Don't you think that's strange? I'd have thought I'd feel some sort of a connection or something.'

'Perhaps it's because you haven't spoken to him properly yet and maybe he only just learned English? He's also the first alien you've ever met; I guess that makes it a little weird.'

'A little?' Diego smiled.

'Ah, there is a smile or two left in you yet, Diego.' Charles laughed and jabbed him in the ribs.

'Ouch, stop doing that!'

'Go and speak with him.'

'Alright then.'

Diego picked up his pace until he was alongside the alien and fell into step with him. He looked up at his father and smiled, awkwardly.

'Tell me about my mother?' Diego asked.

'Oh, well, of course I should have erected you would want to know,' Lieutenant Kodo said. 'Well, let me think. She was pretty, clever and very strong.'

'How did you meet?'

'Err, by accident really. She bumped into me on a training enterprise in the army; we did a lot of work with the army back then. Yes, that was it, at the army.'

Diego carried on looking at him, expecting more. Lieutenant Kodo rubbed his forehead, trying to think what to say. His mind went blank.

'So, what made her like you? Did you go out on a date or anything?' Diego prompted.

'Not at first. She was the pineapple of politeness. I trained her to fight so we became friends at first. She was a bit shy and didn't know her own strength but I eventually taught her to realise her potential.'

'That doesn't sound like Sarah, she didn't do shy,' Charles said, coming up beside them.

'Maybe not, but with me as her preacher I guess she acted different than with you,' Lieutenant Kodo said, defensively.

'So how did you happen to get together, you know, to become my parents?'

Lieutenant Kodo looked away as he tried to think what might have happened. He had no idea about these things; he didn't do family – the army was his life.

'We just fell in love, and did artificial elimination at a clinic, that was all there was to it really,' he said, with a slight tone of annoyance in his voice.

Charles and Diego looked at each other, both sharing a feeling of uncertainty.

'Did you know any of my mother's family?'

'I met her sister and her parents,' Lieutenant Kodo lied.

'I didn't know she had a sister, what about her brother?'

'Oh no, it was her brother I met, not her sister. I render now. This old brain of mine isn't as good as it used to be, you know.'

'I thought her parents died when she was little?' Charles said.

'No, you must be bacon.'

'Bacon?'

'Yes, your English isn't very good is it. I had the best teacher.'

Diego frowned and guessed that he meant mistaken. It was strange how confident he was with his language skills. There was no point correcting him. His arrogance was clear.

'Am I the only child?' Diego held his breath as he asked.

'We will talk about that frater, now is not the time.'

'Why not?' Diego frowned.

'Because we do not have much time. We will be at the spaceship soon and then we will have all the time in the world to stalk about these things.'

'Is my uncle still alive?'

'Yes, he is.'

Diego was not oblivious to the tone in his father's voice and it sounded disappointed, or somewhat bitter.

'Did you not like my uncle?'

'He was not a nice man and did not treat your mother well,' he lied, realising his impatient tone had betrayed him.

'That's funny, I could have sworn I remember Sarah saying how well they got on,' Charles said, folding his arms across his chest and looking intensely at the alien.

'Perhaps at one time but not when I brew him.'

'What happened to my mother?'

'She died in childbirth.'

'She couldn't have…' Charles began.

'Why didn't she leave me with you?' Diego asked the alien.

'It wasn't safe.'

'Why?'

'So many questions! I can hardly blink fast enough to

answer them.'

'Well, he is bound to be curious given the circumstances,' Charles said. 'And she couldn't have died in childbirth.'

Lieutenant Kodo looked at him sharply, then recovered himself and smiled. This was proving to be harder than he would have liked and he could see the suspicion rising in Charles. The walk to the waterfall suddenly seemed a very long way. There was only one thing he could think of doing and that was to read Charles' mind to try to learn more. He had not wanted to because the man's brain was delicate and the sudden headaches would equally raise suspicion. But it was a risk he had to take. Charles was going to figure out he was lying soon anyway.

'My headache is back.' Charles groaned and fell to his knees.

'Oh dear, do you suffer badly from them?' Lieutenant Kodo asked.

'Argh!'

'Uncle?' Diego crouched next to him. 'He never has headaches; they started tonight at the village, just before you arrived.' Diego frowned as he said it, and looked at Charles, wondering why this might be happening. Something wasn't right.

'One thing about my people is that we focus heavily on entrancing our natural abilities. I know how to use energy to heal and I could perhaps try to cure you if you'll let me?' Lieutenant Kodo offered.

'By all means,' Charles said, through gritted teeth.

Lieutenant Kodo took hold of his head and pretended to try to heal him. In reality he did a full-on mind read, knowing it would lead to his eventual death, but not before giving him the answers he needed to all these questions. Diego watched as Charles fell, unconscious, to the ground.

'Charles!'

'Oh dear, they seemed to be too strong for me to heal. Never mind, we can snort him out on the ship. We'll carry him until we get there.'

Lieutenant Kodo clicked his fingers and called over his two soldiers to carry Charles between them. They moodily picked him up, knowing he wouldn't last long and that they had to suffer this burden just to keep this boy happy.

'Don't worry, my son, this is easily transfixed when we get to the ship. He will be as good as new in no time.'

Diego looked at his father, unconvinced by his flippant and cold words, and feeling that something was very wrong. He watched as one alien took Charles' arms, the other his legs, and marched behind with him. Diego looked over his shoulder at his uncle, a sense of fear starting to grip at his stomach. Charles didn't look good.

'Come, my son, let us do more of this father and son stalking, I like it. But this time, tell me something about you?'

'Like what?'

'Tell me about that crystal around your wrist and what you can do with it.'

'It's something my mother left me; didn't you know about it?'

'Of course I know, I just wondered how much you had wormed about it. Let me have a look at it and I'll tell you all that I know.'

Diego held up his wrist.

'Not like that. Take it off, let me look at it monopoly. I

can't see it like that.'

'I never take it off,' Diego said, pulling back his wrist when his father went to reach for it.

'Don't be silly, I'll show you how to work it monopoly,' Lieutenant Kodo said.

'No, and I'm not being silly.'

'Of course, you are. I could show you all sorts of tricks with it, give it to me!'

Diego stepped back, again shocked by his father's sharp tone, and instinctively put his arm behind his back.

'I know about the fire at school and the man who died; you cannot wield the flour of the cube. If you let me hold it, for just one minute, I shall show you how to wield it. Trust me, Diego, my son.'

Lieutenant Kodo was too close to Diego and looked creepy even though he tried to fake a friendly demeanour. Diego looked into his eyes and considered what he had said. He started to bring his arm around and was almost about to offer him the cube when he saw something in his eyes. It was a very brief shimmer of greed or desperation, something Diego couldn't quite put his finger on, but it was enough to make him hesitate. Their eyes locked and Diego pulled his wrist back again, in defiance, having decided that he did not like the look in his father's eyes. Lieutenant Kodo took a deep breath and carried on walking, deep in thought. Diego watched him, now feeling slightly scared of his own father.

*

They kept walking and Diego looked at his cube, watching

the light within glow. It never rested. He thought back to what Quilla had told him when they had again discussed his dream. She had told him to talk with the otter and he had. Diego was floating in space with elephant trunk shaped pillars of interstellar gas and dust in front of him, with blue and purple gases surrounding the white stars. It was beautiful and full of colour. The otter appeared next to him, as it usually did, no higher than his lower thigh. The otter had a moustache which sat between his whiskers and twitched as he talked. He wore a red kaftan with metallic gold embroidery around every edge. He seemed very spiritual and important somehow in how he held himself. This time Diego spoke to him.

'Are you real?' he asked.

'I AM,' replied the otter calmly.

'Who are you?'

'I AM.'

Diego frowned. 'Do you s-p-e-a-k E-n-g-l-i-s-h?'

'Of course I do, you silly fool, what else would you call it? Do I say Qui or Si or YA?' The YA he pronounced as *eeah*. Diego suspected it was Russian. He had learned a little of that from Charles. 'Bardo is the name. You may call me Master Bardo.'

'Master? As in a schoolteacher?'

'No, you fool!' Master Bardo huffed with frustration. 'I'm a spiritual master, a guide, if you like. I have mastered many things.'

'Except how not to invade someone's space! Why do you keep appearing in my dreams?'

'Because I'm your father's guide. I'm trying to connect with you and guide you too. Not that any of you listen to me. I get more interaction from a brick wall than I do with you guys. So, finally you speak to me. Notice how, unlike you, I'm not rude and stare silently back at you. I respond. And yes, in E-n-g-l-i-s-h!' Master Bardo declared with somewhat more emotion than Diego was expecting.

'Not mastered inner calm either, by the sounds of it.' Diego huffed. For a moment, he thought perhaps this master would explode as his moustache twitched back and forth. His temper was surely getting the better of him. 'Right, OK then. What do you want to guide me with?'

'I am here to tell you about this,' Master Bardo said, waving his arm at the stars and pillars in front of them.

'What about it?'

'Listen to me this time! This is the Eagle nebula. Space is dark and there are only two ways of seeing anything; when light is emitted from something, like the sun, or reflected by an object, such as the moon. The composition of all baryonic matter in the universe is 75% hydrogen and 24% helium. That is because these are the two most basic and simple elements generated in large quantities by the big bang and scattered across the entirety of space,' he explained. 'On Earth you call these types of elements gases. These gases are not distributed evenly in space so when enough gas collects it becomes a cloud. Most gaseous clouds sit in complete darkness – not easy to see. If an interstellar gas cloud grows big enough, its cumulative gravity can compound some of the gas into a single concentrated point. Here is the tremendous pressure of a cloud bigger than an entire solar system, with the varying hydrogen atoms that make up the mass, which can collide and combine in a process known as fusion.'

'Why are you telling me all of this? I didn't come here for a science lesson, you know,' Diego said.

The otter rolled his eyes impatiently. 'I knew you wouldn't just listen. Respectfully, I am not a primary school teacher either, but your father insisted that I come and tell you.'

'I'm not primary school age,' Diego replied, folding his arms in annoyance, feeling aggravated.

'Really? You act it.' They glared at each other. 'This process accelerates until the cloud collapses into itself, creating a mass of fusing gas held together by the strength of its own gravity – a star. In this way, nebulas can basically be seen as star factories. The main by-product of this is the generation of light. When you have a light source a true nebula is born.'

'A cloud of gas lit up by the stars, basically?' Diego interrupted.

'Are you sure you are not in primary school? You have the concentration and focus of a much younger child,' Master Bardo remarked. 'Each star's life depends on its mass and is limited, so a new process of nebulaic construction takes place when the stars die. Star death changes the nebula. Their forms create some amazing displays. What you see were known as the pillars of creation. They were named such because the gas and dust that create these finger-like protrusions were in the process of creating new stars. They look a little like the shape of an elephant's trunk. This is where baby stars make their way up to the status of a full-blown star. They're larger than the solar system and are made visible by the shadows of EGGs, which–'

'EGGs?' Diego interrupted.

'Evaporating Gaseous Globules, which shield the gas behind them from intense UV flux. EGGs are themselves incubators of new stars. The stars then emerge from the EGGs, which then evaporate. A supernova shockwave destroyed the pillars of creation 6,000 years ago. No one on Earth realises this yet. Given the distance of roughly 7,000 light-years to the pillars of creation, this would mean that because light travels at a finite speed, this destruction should be visible from Earth in about 1,000 years. Beautiful, isn't it?' Master Bardo stroked his moustache and looked at the view.

'Yes, it's beautiful,' agreed Diego. 'Why are you telling me all of this?'

'Look carefully into your crystal, Diego. Really look. Can you see the pillars of creation? Can you see the starlight?'

Diego squinted his eyes and looked at his crystal then gasped as he saw the view in front of him contained within his cube. Mouth wide open, he glanced at the otter.

'Yes, incredible, is it not? I helped your father to harvest the power within the nebula and place it into your cube before the supernova completely destroyed it. It lives in your crystal. This is why you accidentally electrocute people when they so much as lay a hand on it. Even contained it is powerful. Only you can unleash and protect that power. If you let me, I will start teaching you.'

Diego had looked at Master Bardo, stunned. Then he had vanished.

Diego told Quilla everything that Master Bardo said and she had confirmed that she had seen visions confirming this when she asked for guidance. There was speculation among academics as to whether the pillars of creation had been destroyed by a supernova or were in the process of being destroyed. It all confirmed that what the otter said was correct and made sense. There was an Eagle nebula. Quilla agreed it did look exactly like the pillars of creation in his cube.

'Does this mean that you have the power to make and destroy stars?' she asked.

'I hope not.' He gulped. 'I'm a little scared of it to be honest.'

*

Diego now looked inside the cube again and glanced at his so-called father who had wanted it so keenly. He needed to remember that he was the one with the cube and the power and not to allow this alien to intimidate him. He looked to his left and saw a vision of Master Bardo watching him, arms folded, shaking his head in annoyance. Then he vanished.

'What is the name of the assistant you sent to me?' Diego asked, after a long silence.

Lieutenant Kodo turned to face him with a blank expression on his face. They stopped walking and looked at each other. Diego felt a rush of fear run through him and backed away. His father almost smiled, but the smile wouldn't quite come. He had no idea about an assistant because Diego had only told Quilla.

'It has been a long day and perhaps now is not the best time to talk about these things. We shall have a nice long discussion when we finally get to the ship, as I have said before. Until then, let us put all our energy into getting there faster, shall we? For the sake of Charles. He needs urgent medical attention.'

Diego looked deep into his eyes and knew then that this was not a person he could trust, father or no father. He slowed down his pace as they headed forwards, slowly lagging behind. He looked over at Charles and wondered how he could run away and leave him alone with them. Just then, he noticed something move in the trees and paused to look. Lieutenant Kodo stopped and looked at him.

'What is it?' he asked.

'Nothing, just a bird no doubt,' Diego said.

Lieutenant Kodo turned away and walked on. Diego began to follow when his eye caught something else move in the trees. He squinted and strained his eyes, looking closer. Whatever it was, he couldn't see it, and it was too fast. Yet, he felt that something or someone was watching them. However, he had felt this for days now as his paranoia was increasing. He felt the hairs stand up on the back of his neck and shivered. He looked quickly at his father, noticed he was still walking ahead, disinterested, and returned his gaze to the trees.

'Keep up,' Lieutenant Kodo shouted over his shoulder.

'There's something in there,' Diego said, pointing into the trees.

Lieutenant Kodo turned around and walked to Diego's side. He peered into the trees and then turned to one of the other aliens.

'Take a look,' he said.

The alien put Charles down and went into the bush and moved around; half-heartedly looking for something he was sure was just a figment of Diego's imagination. He walked back, shaking his head and shrugging his shoulders.

'Stop displaying games with me, Diego. Come, we are wasting time,' Lieutenant Kodo said, impatiently.

'What's the hurry? I need to sit and rest a while,' Diego said.

'I have told you that the enemy is close at hand, there is time rebuff to rest later.'

'Tell me about the enemy, Father, whilst I catch my breath,' Diego insisted, putting emphasis on the word 'father'.

He now really doubted this person was his father after all. He wanted to buy some time, somehow, until either Charles woke up, and they could make a run for it, or he could think of another way out of this situation.

'We do not have time,' Lieutenant Kodo said.

'I'm sorry, Father, I must sit. I'm exhausted. Do you know I was up all night, hunting on my own? Shall I tell you all about it whilst we rest?'

Lieutenant Kodo tried to conceal his irritation, releasing his breath in a long, steady flow and taking control of his temper. He needed to remember that this boy had the cube and could cause destruction that he and his aliens could not outrun. He must keep up the facade until they got to the spaceship where he had technology that should be able to neutralise the crystal cube's power. He must remember his life depended upon the success of this mission.

'Of course, son,' he said, forcing a smile, albeit a cold one. He reluctantly sat beside Diego. 'I'd love to hear all about it.'

FOURTEEN

THE FALLEN

PERU

Tammy was in a deep sleep and didn't notice the small Koepcke's screech owl gently pecking at her nostril and lip, trying to wake her up. She dreamily waved her hand over her face to stop the tickling and pinching, knocking the owl away. The owl leaned over and started to pull at her hair. Tammy merely flicked the owl away again. The owl, undeterred, bit her nostril again, pulling it harder this time.

'Ouch!' Tammy winced, rubbing her eyes and slowly waking up. 'What are you doing?'

The owl spoke to her, chirping away to normal ears, but telling the whole story to Tammy.

'Oh no! Quick, everyone, wake up!' she yelled, jumping out of her hammock, the owl flying to a nearby branch.

'What's the matter?' Ed asked, sleepily.

'They have Diego, they got to him before us,' she said.

She had packed her hammock away and loaded Sirocco with her items before the others had even managed to crawl out of bed.

'Hurry; there is no time to lose. If we don't get to the spaceship before them, we might never see Diego.'

'Oh no,' Ed said.

He pulled his hammock down and packed it away, ushering Jax, Mikie and Mina to do the same.

'But it's pitch black and we haven't had any sleep,' Mina said, rubbing her eyes. 'How can we catch them up?'

'Where is the spaceship?' Mikie asked.

'At the waterfall. We must get to it before them, it's our only chance. You're right, Mina, we won't make it on foot,' Tammy said.

'Oh no, what now?' Mina moaned.

'Camas!' Mikie said, reading Tammy's thoughts.

'Yes, from the Incas' farm. I've already called them and they're on their way. Mina, will you ride Sirocco with me? We'll get there ahead of everyone; it will give us time to act if we have to. I need your help.'

'Why me?' Mina asked, looking horrified at the thought of getting on Sirocco.

'Because only we can sink the spaceship. Please, Mina, I know Sirocco is big but he won't hurt you. I really need your help.'

'Come on, Mina, you liked riding the jeep fast, I'd have thought the idea of going fast on Sirocco would excite you?' Jax teased.

'Oh, all right.' She sighed. 'I don't want to ride a cama either, whatever that is.'

'It's a hybrid camel and llama. Most uncomfortable to ride, I imagine,' Ed mumbled. 'More so for them than me perhaps. I'm far too big for one of the poor things.'

They were just about ready when the camas arrived, three of them, large creamy-coloured ones. Ed, Jax and Mikie looked at them, the boys having never seen one before.

Mina laughed. 'I'm glad I get Sirocco now.'

'They look even smaller now they're here; do you think it will carry me?' Ed did not sound pleased, either.

'They are stronger than they look, trust me, and hurry. It will be uncomfortable for them and for you, but they can travel fast through the forest and will know short cuts,' Tammy said.

They climbed onto the camas. Mina joined Tammy on Sirocco.

'Actually, it's not too bad once you're up here, Sirocco is quite comfy,' Mina said.

'You're going to love this ride.' Tammy smiled at her.

'I'm looking forward to it now,' Mina said, excitedly.

'Well, good for you. I can confirm by the looks on our faces that we men aren't looking forward to this.' Ed laughed.

Tammy spoke to the camas and watched them trot away, with the men bouncing awkwardly on their backs.

'Oh, this really hurts!' Mikie moaned.

'I want to ride Sirocco,' Jax shouted.

'You should try being my age!' Ed groaned.

'Thanks, Tammy, this is one I won't forget,' Mikie said.

Tammy and Mina laughed.

'Jet?' Tammy called.

They looked around; he was nowhere to be seen.

'Where is he?' Tammy asked.

'I don't know, I haven't seen him since I filled up my

water bottles,' Mina replied.

Just then, he came running from the bushes and raced ahead to the camas.

'He won't leave me yet,' Tammy said.

She didn't notice the female jaguar watching them from a tree and yet she suspected she was near. She felt jealous of her. This female that was trying to steal Jet away from her. There was no time for such thoughts now. She must focus.

'Go, Sirocco, faster than the wind,' Tammy leaned forward and whispered.

Sirocco neighed and reared up in the air, causing Mina to grab tighter onto Tammy's waist, then darted after the camas.

'Whoa,' Mina yelled.

'Wait until he gets going,' Tammy shouted over her shoulder.

'You mean this is slow?' Mina gasped.

As she asked, Sirocco changed rhythm and they rocked as they sped through the forest, overtaking the camas and ducking to avoid low hanging branches. Tammy and Mina sat as low as they could on Sirocco's back, keeping their heads below the level of his. Tammy clung to his mane as Mina clung to her waist and the wind rushed past them.

'Oh yeah!' Mina screamed.

Tammy giggled, telling Sirocco to go faster still. They couldn't see Jet in front of them but Tammy knew he was there. He was too black and the night was too dark to see him, and yet every now and again she caught his yellow eyes lit up in the moonlight, as he looked over his shoulder to check on her. It was the perfect camouflage for him here. She sighed.

Owls prowled the skies and reported to Tammy on the progress of the aliens. It wasn't looking good at all. She took a path far enough away that they wouldn't be able to hear Sirocco's hooves, and used the owls to make a lot of hooting when they were alongside the aliens to mask their presence. They could hear the waterfall ahead of them and stopped when it came into sight. Tammy and Mina jumped off Sirocco. The owl flew to Tammy and landed on her outstretched hand.

'Tell me what you see,' Tammy said.

The owl flew away towards the river.

'My legs hurt,' Mina grumbled, rubbing her thighs and calves.

'You get used to it. You're using muscles you haven't used before. As they strengthen, the pain and aches go.'

'I'd like to get used to it. That was the most wonderful thing I've ever experienced. Sirocco, you are magnificent!' She landed a kiss on his nose.

'So, you aren't scared of him any longer?'

'Scared? I was never scared.'

'Oh, come on, I saw the way you looked at him.'

'Well, he's so big! But no, I'm not scared anymore. I'm in love.' She laughed.

'Good.' Tammy smiled. 'I know Sirocco is pleased about that.'

The owl returned and landed on Sirocco's head, much to his annoyance. He told Tammy what he had seen.

'Good, now find out where the others are,' Tammy said.

Again, the owl flew away, this time in the opposite direction.

'Well?' Mina asked.

'The spaceship is there and the aliens are still inside. He is just going to see how far Ed and the boys are in comparison to Diego. Then we'll know how much time we have.'

'So how does it work when you talk with the animals? Sometimes I hear you and sometimes it's silent.'

'They hear my thoughts. I talk aloud sometimes but I don't have to. I guess that is more for my benefit than theirs,' Tammy replied.

'I wish I could do that.'

'Well, I wouldn't mind being able to walk through things and not even Mikie can help me learn that from you.'

'I guess that's what makes us unique, even as brothers and sisters, we are so different. Let's have a look at the ship.'

Sirocco and Jet stayed behind whilst Tammy and Mina crawled up the bank of the river until they could just about see the spaceship. They saw the burnt tree that had fallen and Mina noticed Tammy's sad expression. It surprised her.

'Does it upset you when plants and trees die too?' Mina asked.

'Not all the time, but if it's unnecessary then yes. With the trees I find it really sad. They are highly intelligent, you know.'

'They are?'

'Yes. Trees are smarter and more connected to nature since they have been around much longer than us. They're so lovely. Their energy is pure. When I see a fallen tree, if it is an ancient one, it can hurt more than seeing a small dead animal.'

'Then I am glad I don't have your skills; they sound too painful.'

Tammy smiled but Mina realised the truth of her words and stared at her sister in a new way; until now she hadn't realised just how emotional her powers were and how much they affected her.

'Oh Tammy, does anyone realise how closely these things affect you? How do you manage to stay so happy?'

'Jax gets it. Mikie does since he can read my thoughts and then he also feels it. I have good friends, don't I, with them and the animals? It's life, Mina, everything has a beginning and everything has an end. I learned a lot in Africa and had to control my emotions – it's hard when animals feed. Hunting and killing their prey. I find it all hard but I have to accept it. I know that one day I will ask the animals to fight for me and as a result, many will die. Part of my way with animals is to accept all this, especially when a cat kills something to eat, something I would perhaps call a pet. I have a unique understanding of the circle of life but I also know the sorrow that comes with my gift. I feel every death and carry it as a burden.'

'I'm sorry, Tammy, I never realised.'

'Thank you for caring. Do you know who else feels the same?'

Mina thought about it for a moment and almost suggested Mikie when she realised and smiled. 'Jax.'

'Yes, he and Ed share a similar bond with animals but Jax has a very strong connection.'

Tammy looked back at the spaceship; there was still no movement as far as she could see. They crawled as close as they could get without being seen and then hid behind the dead tree.

'What is that?' Tammy asked.

Mina looked at the stone tlachtli ring on the tree and shrugged. It was obviously there for a reason but what that was she couldn't guess. She could see footprints in the dirt, from humans and aliens.

'Probably something to do with a sacrifice ceremony.' Mina sighed. 'Well, this is how they tracked them.'

'Yes, the village is up there,' Tammy replied.

'I hope we get to see it.'

'Hopefully,' Tammy said, looking up at the mountain.

The owl returned and Mina watched as it landed on Tammy's outstretched hand and twittered away.

'There is a fight – something to hold the aliens up. Ed, Jax and Mikie should catch up with them shortly. We will not have much time to prepare but we can tell Mikie from here what we plan to do so they're ready,' Tammy told Mina.

Mina nodded and rubbed her hands together; she was more than ready for a fight. She wasn't worried about Diego being hurt in the fight as she knew the aliens wanted him alive.

*

Diego watched his father as he spoke quietly with the other aliens, the ones carrying Charles. He didn't look happy. He had barely let Diego finish his story about his hunting trip before mumbling some excuse and running off. Diego knew he was no expert on father and sons, but he was certain that his own father was bound to be interested in what he did. Whether this was his father or not, it was blatantly clear that he didn't like Diego and had no interest in him whatsoever.

However, the thought of his own father not liking him

hurt so much that he tried to bury his doubts and trust him. The truth was, he felt rejected by both the king and Charles. Both of them were clearly intimidated by his powers and keen to wash their hands of him. Perhaps his father was just really worried and the enemy was really close on their heels? Perhaps he was merely frustrated that Diego felt he had time to sit and discuss something trivial whilst he was fearing for all of their lives? No matter how Diego tried to look at it, whatever he told himself, he returned to the one single belief he had; this alien could not be his father. He had no one he could turn to and trust.

'You have five more minutes, that's all,' Lieutenant Kodo told him.

'What are you all talking about?' Diego asked.

'Never you mind.'

'Thanks,' he mumbled under his breath. 'Nice to know you care.'

He was sitting on a fallen tree, almost rotted away over the years now, as he watched the aliens talking in the open field. He couldn't make out what they were saying but he found their movements fascinating. This was the first time he'd been able to clearly watch them in the moonlight. He heard a noise behind him but just as he was about to turn and see what it was, his father looked over. Somehow, not knowing why, Diego knew to be quiet.

No one was watching now and he could hear the rustling behind him. It was getting closer and he wanted to turn and look – what if it was a puma or something? He knew that if he turned around, the movement would draw the attention of his father, and he didn't know why that should bother him. He just knew to follow his instinct on this occasion.

'Diego.' He heard a whisper. 'Do not turn around.'

'Quilla!' he whispered.

'Yes, and Manco is with me, we have been following you, we didn't trust him.'

'I don't either. Charles will not wake up. I don't know what to do.'

'We will help you,' Manco said.

'Do you have people with you?' Diego asked.

'No, it's just us, but don't worry,' Manco said.

'It's not safe, stay away. I don't want to see you get hurt,' Diego told them.

His father looked over briefly and Diego looked down at the floor, avoiding his eyes. When he looked up, he was no longer watching.

'When you leave the clearing and get closer to the edge of the forest, you must fall, hurt yourself, draw attention,' Manco said.

'How?'

'I don't care, just make a scene.'

'What are you going to do?'

'Leave that to us, you just do what we said,' Manco said. 'Don't worry, my friend, we will get you out of this and then you can do that thing you like to do with the storm. OK?'

'OK,' said Diego.

'Be careful, Diego,' Quilla told him.

'And you!'

Diego took a deep breath, stretched and stood up, then started to walk. His father seemed relieved to see him getting up and marched on ahead. Diego watched him carefully, and scanned the trees when no one was looking at him. Quilla and Manco were excellent trackers; even knowing they were there he couldn't detect them. He was impressed and would later tell them how good they were. The small open clearing was coming to an end and soon there would be nothing but trees all around them. Diego howled in pain and fell to the ground, holding his leg and screaming as he rolled around.

'What is it? What have you done?' His father raced over.

The other aliens stood and watched, eyes narrowed, as they scanned the area. They only knew how to distrust and suspicion was their survival tactic.

'I've been bitten,' Diego whined.

'Quick, show me the wound,' Lieutenant Kodo ordered.

'Ah, it hurts so bad.' Diego rolled away, holding his leg tighter, not letting him see.

'Show me the wound! I need to suck out the venom, you suited boy!' Lieutenant Kodo spat. He must take this boy alive or Marcellus would kill him for sure.

Just then, Manco came running out of the forest, his spear raised high in the air as he lunged forward. He threw his spear and it went through chest of one of the aliens. He fell to his knees and Charles landed with a thump on the floor. Quilla appeared beside him, her spear held high too. She threw it. The aliens were now aware they were under attack and took evasive action. The spear missed.

'Don't kill them, I want them alive,' Lieutenant Kodo ordered.

The other alien went after Manco and Quilla who were now running towards the forest. Their plan was to lead the aliens back into the forest, where they would take them out one by one with the poison dart blow gun, when they were close enough to hit. Before they reached the trees, the alien had cut them off. He turned and faced Manco with his laser gun. Manco panicked. He was worried about Quilla now and all he could think was to try to distract them whilst she made an escape. He knew he was done for. He stopped and stared at the alien.

'You both get back here or I'll shoot him,' Lieutenant Kodo commanded.

Turning, Manco's eyes opened wide as he saw Diego with a laser held against his temple.

'Run, Quilla!' Diego shouted.

Diego watched as the injured alien snapped the spear in half and limped towards Manco and pulled his hands roughly behind his back. He tied them together. The same alien then limped over to Diego and tied his wrists, jumping back in shock as he accidentally touched the cube.

'Argh,' the alien gasped, as he struggled to handle the pain and only his ability to heal himself helped him to overcome the agony.

Diego didn't care. His anger was activating the cube and he doubted any of them could survive touching it in another minute now that it was heating up. Let them try and take it.

'Both of you come here or I will shoot him,' Lieutenant Kodo warned, dropping his so-called Queen's English.

'He won't, run now,' Diego shouted.

'Do you want to test me?' Lieutenant Kodo sneered.

Quilla looked at Diego. She was not willing to take the chance. With her head held high, Quilla walked over to Diego.

'Is there anyone else following us?' Lieutenant Kodo asked.

They remained silent. Lieutenant Kodo held his laser to Quilla's forehead and looked at Manco, repeating the question. Manco looked at Quilla, scared for her life and not knowing what was the best thing to say. They might be killed if the aliens thought they were alone or they might be safer if they thought there were more following them. Manco was confused.

Lieutenant Kodo was about to pull the trigger on the laser when Diego spoke, 'There is no one else. Don't harm them.'

Lieutenant Kodo looked at Diego, certain he was telling the truth. There was no point pretending any longer; it was obvious Diego knew he wasn't his real father. The plan had changed. He looked at Diego and smiled. A chilling, cold smile.

'Ensure everyone is tied up securely,' he told the others.

Diego thought about his cube and looked up at the sky. He had summoned the storm from nothing before, and he could do it again. His breathing got faster as he started to get ready. He didn't really have a plan as to what he was going to do. He rarely did. He didn't know how to get Manco or Quilla away from the aliens and was scared that they would get killed before he could do anything.

'Let them go, you do not need them,' Diego begged.

Lieutenant Kodo grabbed Diego's wrist sharply, and looked at the cube.

'Don't even think of activating this or they will be instantly killed!' he growled.

'Then let them go.'

'If I let them go there is nothing stopping you from activating the crystal. They will be safe as long as you come with me, quietly. I will release them when we are at the ship. You have my word.'

'I wouldn't activate the cube and risk my uncle's life, would I? Otherwise I'd have done that before now,' Diego said, nodding towards Charles.

'Yes, but this time, Diego, we are not going to have him with us.' Lieutenant Kodo smiled.

'What?' Diego's mouth dropped open. 'What are you going to do with him?'

'Leave him. It is not worth our effort to carry him with us any longer and we don't have anyone to carry him now, you fools.'

'You can't leave him out here. He's unconscious, he'll be eaten by something!'

'He's already dead, my boy, didn't you realise?' Lieutenant Kodo laughed, and patted Diego's head, patronisingly.

Diego pulled his head sharply away and stared in horror at Charles as he lay, face down, in the field. He was still breathing, he was sure of it.

'Please don't leave him,' Diego begged.

Lieutenant Kodo ignored him. The other alien grabbed Diego and pushed him forward. He marched onwards, watching the back of the alien that was supposed to be his father.

'Who are you really?' Diego asked.

'I'm Lieutenant Kodo. Your father's enemy. You are too easily fooled to be considered anything special. You don't deserve that cube!'

FIFTEEN

DISH SERVED COLD

PERU

Tammy and Mina closed their eyes and tried hard to contact Mikie; he answered but was not as clear as usual. It was hard to telepathically communicate far away while he was running. He told them they had found the body of someone comatose and assumed it was Charles. They had put him on a cama rather than risk him being eaten by something. Therefore, Jax and Mikie were taking turns in running and riding the only other cama. That was why Mikie wasn't coming through as strong as normal and couldn't concentrate on speaking with them; he was breathless and exhausted. Tammy explained the situation with the spaceship and said that she and Mina would take action since they were almost here and they were out of time. The fight had not ended in success, the owls had said, and they needed a bigger delay.

'*Mikie, contact Diego, speak with him. Maybe this time, now he needs help, he will listen?*' Tammy suggested.

'*I'll try,*' Mikie said.

'It's time, let's do it,' Tammy said, turning to Mina.

'Oh yes, let's teach these losers a lesson.' Mina smiled.

Tammy admired Mina's bravery and boldness. She was always so enthusiastic to get out there and prove what she was capable of. Tammy, however, just wanted a quiet and peaceful life; she had nothing to prove. She just wanted to spend time with the animals, do simple things with them, and avoid any hassle. She didn't want to fight. She felt people's suffering – even her enemies.

'What are you looking at me like that for?' Mina asked.

'I was just thinking how I admire your boldness and how different we are, considering we are sisters. In fact, I am so different to all of you. Even Mikie likes a good fight. How can I be so different and yet we're all so similar?'

Mina thought for a moment. 'Tammy, we talked before about how you feel the pain that other animals, even trees, go through. You communicate at all levels with different forms of life. How could you do that and then get excited over a fight, when you know and feel the pain and loss so acutely? You couldn't be how you are if you were more like me.'

'I guess you're right, I never thought about it like that. Well then, now I understand why I admire your attitude even more; I would love the peace of mind to be able to kill aliens and not feel any consequence.'

'Well, this is going to be ugly so perhaps best not to dwell on the matter, huh? Time to sink a ship, don't you think?' Mina smiled and pulled Tammy along by the arm.

*

'I'll catch you up, I'm going to try and contact Diego again,' Mikie said.

'All right, Mikie, but be careful,' Ed replied.

'I will.'

'So, shall I continue to ride the cama or would you prefer me to run? I'm fine with either,' Jax said.

'Do you mind if I have the cama then? That way I could still ride slowly rather than having to run harder to make up the distance. It will be easier for me.'

'No problem, he's all yours.' Jax smiled. 'I do loads of running after Jet and Sirocco. It's more comfortable to run anyhow.'

'Isn't that the truth? I hurt everywhere. Thanks Jax, I owe you one,' said Mikie.

'I'll remember and hold you to it.'

Mikie watched Ed and Jax vanish with the body of Charles and sighed. Whatever Diego's problem was, he hoped it wasn't going to get in the way today, of all days. He climbed up on the back of the cama, knowing it would steadily follow the others and he wouldn't have to worry about direction and could just focus on contacting Diego's mind. It was bumpy but he could focus better than when he was running.

'Diego, don't ignore me, I must talk to you, you are in great danger. Diego, I know you can hear me, we are near... Diego...'

*

Diego felt a slight ache in his head and could hear Mikie trying to talk to him. He looked around to see if any of the aliens could tell what was happening, worried in case they could tune into this mind-reading conversation at all. Could they also hear Mikie – was it on a wavelength they could detect? The alien walked behind him, his eyes glued to the crystal on his wrist, no different to how he had been doing for the last ten minutes. He appeared to hear nothing.

Lieutenant Kodo walked alongside Quilla, knowing she was the one he would hide behind if Diego lost it. Manco, on the other hand, was just in front of them, deliberately aggravating Lieutenant Kodo by repeatedly stopping randomly and unexpectedly. It made Diego smile – he was keeping him alert, trying to make him angry so he was more likely to make a mistake. It seemed to be working. Lieutenant Kodo was exhausted and fuming. Manco would be looking for an opportunity to make his move and expect Diego to be ready.

'*Now is not a good time, brother,*' Diego replied.

'*I beg to differ, now is the perfect time. You are in danger,*' Mikie said.

'*Tell me something I don't know.*'

'*How about that we are all right here?*'

'*Here?*'

'*Yes, we are very close to you, planning an attack, but we need your help,*' Mikie told him.

'*Who else is with you?*'

'*Our sisters – Tammy and Mina. And a couple of others.*'

'*Sisters? Are those the girls who were trying to contact me with you before?*'

'*Yes.*'

'*So, there are four of us?*' Diego wasn't convinced.

'*Yes, we are quadruplets,*' Mikie said.

'That's ridiculous, my note from my mother didn't mention–'

'No, it wouldn't. We all had a note, which implied we were the only child born. It isn't true and was done for our own protection. We are quads.'

'Well, I'm apparently walking along in the woods, having a nice stroll with my father, and I'll tell you what – I don't believe that either!' Diego said.

'Well, that's understandable, I guess. So, they conned you into going with them?'

'Yes, now leave me alone.'

'Wait a minute. If you know you're in danger, then why not accept our help and get yourself out of it? You can choose to ignore me afterwards.'

Diego sighed. He had to admit it made sense and there was little else he could do right now. If Manco did have a plan, it would probably be as useless as the last one, when he got himself and Quilla captured so easily. He didn't want to see them hurt.

'What's on your mind?' Diego asked.

*

'They don't have much variety in the type of spaceships they fly, do they?' Tammy said. 'Looks the same as all the others, except the cargo ships.'

'Easier for us,' Mina replied.

They were in the water, holding onto the fallen tree, the rapids pulling at their clothing. It was the closest they could get without being seen. There was still some life left in the poor, fallen tree; Tammy had helped it grow some small branches so it could wrap them around her and Mina, keeping them secure, and around the tree trunks near the bank so they wouldn't get pulled away. The water was cold in a refreshing sort of way and there was no sign of activity on the spaceship.

'Ready?' asked Mina.

'Not yet, just a few more minutes, they're almost here,' Tammy replied.

'Are you sure we are safe with them?' Mina asked, glancing at the water.

Tammy looked down at her pendant; a slight green glow had begun. 'Fairly certain.' She smiled.

'They're supposed to be quite big, aren't they?'

'Huge.'

'And very aggressive?'

'Oh yes. They eat each other too, especially after mating; the female will swallow the male whole.'

'That is gross! No long term relationship there then,' Mina joked.

'They aren't after long term relationships; it's just food, and they don't even look after their own babies. They will eat one or more of the males from the breeding ball to sustain them throughout gestation, which is about half a year. It's pretty sick really, isn't it? But good common sense. Not like the male is needed after that!' Tammy grinned.

'I'll tell Jax you said that!' They laughed. 'And you're sure we're safe around them, in the water?'

'I certainly wouldn't be in here if that wasn't the case. You shouldn't misunderstand animals, Mina, they do what they must to survive. In this case, the dad just does a lot more to support his children than he expected when he joined in the breeding ball! Their purpose has been served. Anyway, they have arrived.'

'Where?' Mina strained her eyes, searching the water.

'If you look behind the rear of the spaceship, you will see their tiny eyes looming just above the water.' Tammy pointed at the tiny dark brown beady eyes peering eerily above the water's surface.

'Oh yeah, wow, there's quite a few out there.'

'Not really, probably only about ten. I couldn't safely control more than that and there aren't many big enough to eat an alien close by. I have to be able to control them because once their aggression kicks in, they'll go for whatever is more convenient and that, most likely, will be us or even each other.'

'Hardly fair considering they are doing us a favour,' Mina said.

'Exactly, so we must ensure they don't eat each other. They wouldn't normally get this close to each other if left to their own instincts.'

'It's so creepy and something really big has just moved past my leg, Tammy!' Mina squealed.

'Well, they are huge, Mina.' Tammy smiled. 'The head and eyes of the green anaconda are tiny but its body is wide and long, making it the heaviest and biggest snake in the whole world. Some of them here are as big as ten meters, although most aren't. They kill by asphyxiation and are semiaquatic. That's why they are great for this fight because they can help in and out of the water. As long as they swim by, don't worry about being touched, it's when they wrap around you that you need to worry.'

A large anaconda swam right in the middle of Mina's

legs and she froze. She trembled in fear and tried to stay as still as possible until it had moved past her. It seemed like the snakes body would never end.

'It's freaking me out, Tammy. You just keep them from eating me and I'll sort out the ship,' Mina said, trying not to let the fear engulf her again. 'Why are you always so calm?'

'I must be. The animals react to my energy, so I need to be calm and in control,' Tammy replied. The eerie little dark eyes slowly drew nearer, the rest of the form hidden beneath the surface. Mina concentrated on the ship's doors, barely visible due to the smooth design of the ship. Fortunately, she remembered where they were, and slowly the doors started to open.

'You could go invisible and get closer if you like?' Tammy suggested.

'No thanks, I bet those things would still know where I was.'

'Yes, they don't use their eyesight to hunt, but I'll keep them away from you, don't worry.'

'It's not a problem, I can do what I need from here, and I have no intention of going anywhere near those things!'

The spaceship started to take in water and Tammy and Mina heard loud shouts from inside. The aliens started to panic, crying out, not knowing why it was happening. One by one, the aliens started to abandon the ship as it sank slowly. Two of them crawled up onto the top of it, carefully balancing. They were not far from the bank, intending to jump for their lives. The greys weren't the best of swimmers, and some had never learned. One of the aliens on top of the ship froze as he sensed he was not alone. Hesitantly, he turned his head to look over his shoulder and peer at the water. The water began to move. His eyes were full of terror.

A huge female anaconda was the first to appear. She was an olive-green ground colour with black blotches all over her long, wide body. Her head had distinctive orange and yellow stripes on either side and seemed small compared to the rest of her. Her eyes, beady and almost black, sat on top of her head, allowing them to be the only thing visible when in the water. She rose slowly out of the water. The alien never took his eyes off her face, his head tilting back as he followed her rising higher and higher. Her monstrous form rose out of the water and swayed slightly as he watched, trembling, rooted to the spot. It was not until she opened her mouth wide that the alien was able to move, and his feet slipped and flailed as he scrambled to get away from the ship and reach the riverbank. He released a high-pitched hysterical scream and that was when she sprang forth.

Her sharp, rear-facing teeth – that once embedded prevent the prey from wriggling free – sank deeply into the alien's bulging forehead and then, in a split second, she wrapped her coils around him tightly until asphyxiation occurred. He wriggled momentarily as she moved over the space ship and around his body. She then walked her jaws over her prey, working the the alien down her oesophagus.

Mina watched what was happening on the spaceship and began to dry heave. As the snake crawled down the alien's body she kept trying to look away but found her eyes glued to the vile scene in front of her. Now and then the alien's legs twitched as if he was still alive. It seemed to take forever. Then, just as the snake seemed finished and looked over the water and at the scene around her, she moved towards the bank. She started to move her body muscles again, mild waves of contraction moving backwards up her body, until she expelled the alien in all the digestive enzymes and gastric juices from her gut. His body flopped onto the bank as he was regurgitated out.

This finished Mina off. She gasped and promptly vomited into the water. 'Oh dear lord, that's just disgusting,' she said once she had finished.

Tammy, eyes-wide, splashed at the puke as it drifted towards her and shook her head in dread. 'Oh no no no! Please don't let it get in my hair. Get a grip, Mina.'

'You of all people, who won't eat meat, surely must see how repulsive that was?' Mina couldn't contain the disgust and shock on her face.

Tammy shrugged. 'The digestive juices in a snakes gut helps to break down and digest their prey but it has another use too. It will keep the regurgitated dinner preserved until they are able to get round to eating it later on. Even in the heat. Snakes often do this when they are lucky to find lots of prey at one time and save the rest until later.'

'What are you telling me? That this is them saving up for a picnic in the jungle later on?' Mina shuddered and dry retched once more. She paused, hand over mouth, debating whether she needed to puke again.

'Do I need to swim away from you? Are you done yet?' Tammy asked.

'Don't you dare leave me alone with these things!'

'Then stop hurling your puke my way. They can't move after swallowing an alien so they'll regurgitate them out until the battle is done and then feast afterwards. Are you done or do you need to do a bit more of your own regurgitating? Which, by the way, is no less gross than the

anacondas doing it.'

The female green anaconda then returned to the water, leaving the stinking body on the bank as a deterrent to other aliens. The alien left standing was frozen in shock, his mouth agape. Another alien tentatively peeped around the door and looked at the corpse. The waters were still and he took the opportunity to climb out of the sinking door and up on to the top. Again, the anaconda rose out of the water with elegance and grace and struck fast. She grabbed the startled alien's head in her wide-open jaw, pulled him off the ship, up into the air, and wrapped her body tightly around him as they both plunged into the water. It happened so fast that several other aliens didn't see what had taken him, just the swirling, disturbed surface of the water as he was plunged beneath the depths. Mina was as horrified as the aliens. As more aliens were forced to abandon ship, more anacondas appeared. Another anaconda snuck up behind the ship, on the bank, and latched onto one alien who stared at it in silent terror before he was dragged under the water. Another alien started screaming at the water and pointing after his friend. They had obviously never seen anything like this before. It was a new creature to them, and the speed at which it struck left them helpless and terrified.

Some scrambled to the top of the ship, others swam as fast as they could to the riverbank, avoiding the dead alien. Others swam into the depths of the river utterly confused. But wherever they went, an anaconda was waiting. It was chaos. Of course, Tammy suspected this level of fear, which was why she chose the anaconda. A much undervalued assassin. The element of surprise was an added bonus. Very few people got to see anacondas of this immense size; they were far too shy for that under normal conditions. The few humans that did come across such a large anaconda often merely vanished from existence and never lived to tell the story. They wouldn't normally come out to blatantly hunt humans, or aliens, as was now the case.

Mina and Tammy watched as some aliens managed to escape onto the banks, or swim to the other side while an anaconda had its mouth full and couldn't grab them, but they were followed by small beady eyes in the water. Then, there was a flash of olive green and black skin, a whish of water and, one by one, they'd disappear too. Very few made it to safety, and the bank was no safer than the water with semiaquatic predators on the loose.

The aliens left clinging to the sinking spaceship didn't know what to do. Everything that the others had tried so far, except for staying where they were in or on the ship, had resulted in death. They clung to the ship, as it slowly sank, as if it were their last resort. It was a desperate and lame belief. An anaconda popped its head out of the sinking ship's door, looked at three aliens clinging on for dear life and hissed. The closest alien let out a strangled scream and swam backwards. He was promptly swooped up in to the air and then dragged under the water by another one waiting behind him.

'That is really disgusting,' Mina said, as she watched the attack. 'You should have got crocodiles!'

'Do you think you'd have coped with that any better? They don't have the speed, agility and ability to work in and out of water in the same way. With the anaconda, the aliens don't stand a chance. Look, they can't even fight back, it's a losing battle.'

'They're monsters!'

'No, they're not, they're huge, efficient predators. Remember, Mina, you were intimidated by Sirocco until you rode him.'

'He doesn't swallow and regurgitate people,' Mina spat back. 'I'm traumatised for life now!'

'What scares you is that you're suddenly at the bottom of the food chain.' Tammy laughed.

'What's wrong with that? And what happened to you being affected by all this death? You're as calm as a Buddhist monk! Who wants to be at the bottom of the food chain? No one says, "Oh God, please can you create me to be at the bottom of the food chain because I'd hate to dominate over evil predators on the planet. Thanks God, much appreciated." I like being at the top of the food chain for good reason, thank you very much.'

'You need to calm down. Jude taught me to be calm. Well, how to pretend to be. You should try it sometime. Only in our own cities are we top of the food chain. As soon as you put us with nature, it's all fair game. The hunter becomes the hunted. In a place like this, there are snakes, pumas, crocodiles, all sorts of beasts waiting to eat you for breakfast. Even the bushmaster that Ed bought back for dinner could have gone both ways, you know. It was probably hunting them at first. Go for a swim in the ocean and you are a tiny speck of dust and shark bait. Go into space and you're even smaller. It's all relative, Mina.'

'Thanks a lot, Tammy, now I'll sleep much better at night. Look, I know you're right but at this moment I'm struggling with what just happened. I can never unsee that!'

'At least it might prevent you from wandering off alone

all the time in a jungle, as you like to do. It isn't safe.'

'Shush, I hear something and the ship hasn't finished sinking yet!'

They heard conversation coming from the bushes and breathed a sigh of relief when they saw the camas come forward. They got out of the water and ran towards Ed, Mikie and Jax.

'You have just missed the most disgusting thing ever,' Mina declared.

'No time to explain things now, Mina, help us hide him,' Ed said, getting Charles off the cama with Jax's help.

'Yes, hurry, in the bushes over there, we have only minutes before they get here,' Tammy said, as she nodded to the owl. Then, she told all the owls that now it was daylight the Andean Cock-of-the-rock birds could take over and they must sleep. She informed the owls where to go and ensured a vast array of insects ran out and into their direct line of vision so they could feast after having lost an entire day of eating by helping her. Then they could sleep on a full stomach. The circle of life was as it should be and Tammy felt no guilt feeding them for their hard work. She chose to be vegetarian but she couldn't make carnivores and owls eat fruit.

'The ship is almost gone?' Mikie asked.

'Yes, and what about Diego?' Tammy replied.

'He's in.'

'Good.' Tammy was relieved.

'You OK, Mina?' Mikie asked. 'You look pale.'

'No, I am not, thanks for asking. I've seen things I can never unsee,' she declared dramatically.

'Ah, OK then. You shall live.' Mikie giggled.

'I can't walk,' Jax moaned. 'I can't ever ride a cama again. I'm not sure I'll ever grow up to be a man now, I've done irreparable damage!'

'Tell me about it. I think I now have undescended testicles,' Mikie complained.

'Don't be such wet blankets,' Mina said as she burst out laughing.

'I'm not kidding!' Mikie said.

'He's right, it will take me a week to be able to walk normally again,' Jax added.

Mina and Tammy tried hard to stifle their giggles as they watched Ed, Jax and Mikie walk in a funny way. It had obviously not been a comfortable journey, which is why camas were only used when absolutely necessary. Ed and Jax carried Charles into the bushes and hid him, carefully and safely, whilst they prepared for the attack.

'Is everything ready?' Mikie asked.

'Yes. A few have ran into the trees on the bank but they aren't safe there. They just don't know it yet. Team anaconda is ready and waiting to launch,' Tammy said.

'Team anaconda, I like that,' Jax said.

'You wouldn't have liked what I just saw,' Mina said tartly. 'Not even you, Jax.'

Jax looked at her and registered the upset on her face. He was about to say something funny and then thought better of it. 'One thing you learn as a trainee vet, Mina, is that as much as you love animals, you have to accept that their world is brutal too. You cannot truly love them unless you accept the brutality. It's the circle of life.'

Mina sighed. He was right of course. She had seen the guts of a snake as it was cut open and now she had seen the guts of a snake as it regurgitated an alien. There was a certain poetry to it, really. How many people could say they had seen what she had seen and lived to tell the tale? Mina was starting to think that if she could embrace the animal kingdom in the same way that Tammy and Jax could, then her fears would diminish.

'The aliens hiding along the riverbanks will probably run out to join the others as they come close,' Ed suggested.

'Yes, and I can read their minds. They think that the anacondas are only water-based,' Mikie added. 'None have attacked on land yet. Not fully.'

'So, let's pretend we are leaving then double back and hide. We will leave a space wide open for when the others arrive and they can come rushing out all together,' Ed said.

Mina smiled, turned her earrings, and disappeared. Ed, Mikie, Jax and Tammy pretended to walk away then doubled back and hid, taking their positions in the trees. Sirocco and Jet followed. Tammy told the anacondas to hide well. They did – under leaves, in the water, and high in the trees.

*

'Where the hell is it?' Lieutenant Kodo yelled. 'Where's the darn ship?'

Diego smiled. Lieutenant Kodo went ballistic and grabbed his head in frustration.

'No, no, no, no, no!' He groaned.

'Something wrong?' Diego asked smugly.

Lieutenant Kodo glared at him. 'Do you know something?'

'I'm an idiotic boy with no brain and I know nothing.' Diego chuckled.

Quilla looked at Diego, surprised by his cockiness, just as the other aliens came running out of the trees towards them. They were screaming hysterically and shaking their heads in terror. Lieutenant Kodo didn't see them at first and was trying a crystal broadcaster unit, shouting into the speaker of his wrist watch. It crackled loudly, hiding the noise of the hysterical aliens charging towards them. It didn't help with the buzzing Lieutenant Kodo had ringing in his ears. That and the bitter taste of metal in his mouth as fear overwhelmed him and he felt sure he would be killed for his failure. The pressure was breaking him. He had failed too often. Diego laughed out loud.

'Where are you guys, where is my darn ship? Come in, come in...' Lieutenant Kodo bellowed down the speaker.

Nothing, nothing but static. He turned to face Diego, and saw the smile on his face, and felt the anger rise within him, replacing his fear. Then he followed Diego's gaze and spotted the aliens running frantically towards them.

'What has happened? You think this is funny?' he said.

He grabbed Quilla by her upper arm, spinning her around to face Diego, and held a laser to her face.

'How funny is it now?' Lieutenant Kodo asked.

'We're ready. Now, Diego,' he heard Mikie say. 'Remember, Mina is there, Quilla is perfectly safe.'

Mina, invisible still, snuck behind Diego and cut the ties on his wrists. Diego took a deep breath and activated the cube. He held his wrist high and summoned a storm cloud. The alien who held him tried to grab his wrist, but Diego just about managed to keep him from reaching the cube.

'Stop! Stop! Or I'll kill her, I mean it!' Lieutenant Kodo shouted, panicking.

Diego ignored him, trusting in Mina intuitively, and that she had the laser weapon under her control as Mikie had promised. Lieutenant Kodo watched in horror as the cloud began to form above them. Mina watched in amazement. Quilla smiled. She knew she would not die this day. Her visions had been clear. She had seen herself much older with Diego. She was calm and confident and smiling encouragingly at Diego who lacked her faith. Diego concentrated with all his might and aimed the cube upwards as sharp crackles of thunder and lightning raged within the one cloud in a bright sunny sky.

'This is your last warning,' Lieutenant Kodo growled.

'No, you fool,' Diego said and glared menacingly at Lieutenant Kodo. Quilla stared at Diego in surprise. He was suddenly terrifying. 'This is *your* last warning. Let her go or die.'

SIXTEEN

UNITED

PERU

Lieutenant Kodo gulped and pulled Quilla in closer to him. All the other aliens gathered behind Lieutenant Kodo and Quilla. Diego looked up at the cloud and the lightning crackled angrily above them. Lieutenant Kodo was about to squeeze the trigger of his laser but screamed when his arm was bent backwards and the laser fell to the floor. In that moment, Diego drew a circle around the group, and made it burn. They were now encircled by a ring of fire, which kept them all inside.

'What is the point in that? Is that the best you can do? Did you screw up again, Diego?' Lieutenant Kodo sneered as he tried to locate Mina. He knew it was her. 'I will only ask you one last time, Mina–'

Before he could finish, Lieutenant Kodo felt a sharp pain in his throat as Mina karate chopped him. He choked and grabbed his throat, his eyes watering, as Quilla fell to the ground. Mina punched him repeatedly in the face, forcing him to stumble backwards to the edge of the ring of fire. The other aliens quickly jumped out of his way. He gagged, struggled to pull himself together then attempted to strike Mina, using his ability to sense her energy. He struck thin air as she danced easily out of his reach. He tried and failed again. Mina spun up and around in the air and kicked him in the face. He reeled further backwards, narrowly avoiding falling into the fire.

Through the fire, Mina could see the green and orange head of an anaconda as it came closer to them. She felt the hairs prick at the back of her neck and goosebumps raise on her arms. These things were by far the creepiest things she had ever seen.

'But at least you're on my side,' she muttered.

And then something happened that surprised Mina. She locked eyes with the anaconda and something passed between them. An understanding, a connection, and Mina felt the corners of her mouth twitching into a smile. She nodded at the anaconda. Just then, Lieutenant Kodo growled, lunged towards her with all his might, intent on attacking her. Mina moved just as he was about to strike, went into a set of backward flips, spun around in a circle, cartwheeled back towards him, and delivered an impressive ground kick right up into his chest, lifting him off the ground and into the air. At the exact same time, Diego pointed his cube towards him and struck him with lightning. Lieutenant Kodo felt the force so hard that he flew through the air. His eyes, wide open in shock, surprised at Mina's speed and power, watched her as he went high over the wall of fire and straight into the mouth of the awaiting anaconda.

Only the anaconda had seen and connected with Mina.

To everyone else, she was still invisible and all that was seen was Lieutenant Kodo flying through the air. The anaconda released him from her mouth, wrapped her strong body around him and held him there, at the end of her tail, gazing down at him. Lieutenant Kodo stared back in shock, horror and disbelief. Then she did something very strange. Through the flames, Mina watched as the anaconda leaned forward and puked up another alien. Lieutenant Kodo released a strangled scream and wriggled in disgust and terror, almost managing to get away from the anaconda whilst she was in such a difficult position.

'He's going to get away again!' Mikie gasped.

'No, he isn't,' Tammy said calmly.

The anaconda's tail held firm, and as the last of the alien came up, she had full flexibility of her body again and squeezed Lieutenant Kodo until his eyes bulged. She moved closer and looked at him threateningly. He suddenly stopped wriggling as she opened her wide mouth, revealing her sharp, curved teeth, confidently taking her time as she drew him closer to her. All the while, she wrapped herself slowly and carefully around his body. He was just about to scream once more when she grabbed his head in her jaw, embedding her teeth into his head and held him tight as she squeezed. Lieutenant Kodo barely made a sound and couldn't even struggle.

Master Bardo appeared in front of Diego once more, with a smile almost daring to appear beneath his moustache. Diego looked around to see if anyone else could see him. It appeared not.

'That was very nicely done, Diego,' he said. 'You have potential yet.'

Then he vanished again.

Diego helped Quilla up from the floor. 'Are you OK?'

'Yes, Diego, I am, but I'm just trying to understand why that alien was bobbing about like that.'

'My sister is here and she is invisible.'

'Oh!'

'Did you see that little otter creature?' Diego asked.

'No, was he here again?'

'Yes, very briefly. He keeps coming and going.'

Master Bardo appeared again, only to Diego, and elevated himself from the ground until he had floated level with Diego's face.

'That little otter creature? You call me that again, boy, and you'll lose an eye!' Master Bardo hissed.

'Well, thanks, very helpful, I do say,' Diego replied.

'Watch your attitude,' Master Bardo insisted. 'I planned to visit you for a short time every day to teach you to fight better. I won't bother if you talk to me like that.'

'I'm good, thanks. I don't need your help,' Diego retorted.

'You don't have any choice in the matter. Your father insists. I shall see you soon and you will fight with me.' Master Bardo then vanished once more.

Diego looked at Quilla and shook his head.

Manco sprang into action. With his hands still tied behind his back, he headbutted the alien nearest to him, spun around, then kicked him in the face. Mina ran to his side and cut his hands loose. Manco gasped, feeling her, but not seeing her.

'I'm here to help you,' she said.

The other aliens had been startled by Lieutenant Kodo being taken by the anaconda on land and now stood terrified, wondering what they should do and where they should go. They knew that they did not want to end up on the other side of the fire with those creatures. Quilla gasped, eyes wide, as Jet appeared, jumping impressively high over the flames. He landed in front of her, looking menacing and ready to kill. Manco and Diego instinctively stepped in between Quilla and Jet. Jet turned his back to them and faced the approaching aliens. He jumped and threw himself at one of them, pinning him to the floor and biting his shoulder. The alien screamed in agony.

Quilla, Manco and Diego watched, mouths open wide, as they saw this happening and then turned to see something even more unexpected. There was a loud neigh as Sirocco ran and jumped over the flames, landing between the children and the aliens. In a display of sheer agility and strength, he reared and kicked, as he had never done before. Whilst Jet chewed on one alien, Sirocco kicked and knocked another high into the air and up over the flames.

'Leave one for me,' said Tammy. 'I need some practice.'

'Me too,' said Jax.

There were just four aliens left. Tammy, Jax, Manco and Diego lined up ready to take one each. The aliens were far more comfortable fighting the children than the panther, horse or snakes and fell into ninja style poses of defence. Tammy and Jax started circling two of the aliens and slowly closed the gap between them.

'I'll just stand here and look useless then.' Ed huffed.

'I'll keep you company,' Mikie laughed.

'Well, if you think I'm going to play the part of some silly damsel in distress, you have another thought coming!' Quilla said, fuming, as she shoved Manco and Diego out of her way.

They watched, stunned, as she fought using her spear, taking on the two aliens alone and moving faster than they thought possible. She turned and twisted with grace and ease, crouching low one moment and then spinning in the air. The aliens never stood a chance. Her spear was a blur of movement. Diego watched her, overwhelmed with respect, as she avoided every single strike either alien made. Manco was in shock, stunned that this was his fragile ladylike sister, and stood transfixed as she made short work of both aliens.

Tammy and Jax practiced their fighting skills too. They were fast, for beginners, and got a couple of hits in for each hit they took. One alien punched Jax in the face and his nose started to bleed.

'Hey, that wasn't nice!' Tammy yelled and charged at the alien.

They fell on the floor and rolled about as she hit him. Jax moved on to the other alien and practiced some of the kung fu Mikie had taught him. They moved fast and proficiently as Tammy and the other alien scrambled on the floor. Jax kicked the alien backwards, out of his way, and picked Tammy up. Then, he swung her around in a circle, as she kicked both aliens in the head. As they stumbled towards the fire, clutching their heads, Sirocco appeared and reared up, kicking them one by one over the fire towards the anacondas, who moved swiftly to catch them.

Tammy started to direct water from the river to put out Diego's fire. The smoke and steam was everywhere, stinging their eyes. Mina wiped her face, smearing black smoke all over her and yet remained invisible to the others. Quilla had knocked both aliens down and they lay unconscious

on the floor. Quilla turned to glare in defiance at Manco and Diego, still furious that they had both deemed her some useless fragile girl who needed protecting. One of the aliens groggily got up and made a run for it. He was on his feet before Mina realised and had run towards the forest. Manco grabbed his spear and held it above his head, ready to throw it, when Mina grabbed his hand and stopped him. Manco struggled with her, not understanding what had grabbed his spear.

'Just watch,' Mina whispered.

Manco frowned and looked at the alien just as a large anaconda swooped down from a tree and lifted him out of sight, into the canopy. It happened so fast he had almost missed it. Manco gaped in horror.

'Pretty grim, isn't it?' Mina said.

'Why can't I see you?' Manco asked.

'You will soon.'

'I want a pet one of those,' Manco said, looking at Tammy, who he had seen controlling them somehow. 'Can I please have one?'

Tammy smiled.

The fire smouldered, slowly dying away, doused by the water Tammy kept moving over from the river. It was quiet and everyone was staring at each other. Manco couldn't take his eyes off Tammy. He was bewitched by her. Quilla hugged Diego, relieved he was safe, then ran and hugged Manco.

'Who are all these people and where did they come from?' Manco asked, looking from one to the other.

'Let me do the introductions,' Ed said, walking forward.

Quilla stared transfixed by the absolute whiteness of

Ed's hair. Ed noticed her look and paused, used to surprising people with his stature and hair.

'Your hair is so very white…' Quilla pointed at his head.

Jax burst out laughing, as did Mikie.

'Sorry.' Jax laughed. 'It's just that we've all watched anacondas eat and vomit up aliens, which you've probably never seen before in your life, and it's his hair colour that you mention as unusual.'

Quilla smiled brightly. 'Yes, I suppose that does sound rather funny. To be fair, I had seen a lot of this happen in my visions already. I thought Diego's golden hair was interesting but yours is like snow. It's beautiful, as bright as the moonlight. May I?'

'Err, of course,' Ed agreed awkwardly and leaned down to allow Quilla to touch his hair.

'Your hair is just like my wife's,' he said.

'It is? Is she from here?'

'No, and yet she is as raven-haired as you. Let me introduce everyone,' he said.

'I'm Ed Brunswick. I'm helping the children find each other. This is my nephew, Jax. These are Diego's siblings; Mikie, Tammy and Mina. Mina is here somewhere.'

'I heard her,' Manco said.

'And you are?' Ed asked.

'This is Manco, prince of the last Inca tribe,' Diego said coming forward. 'This is his sister, Princess Quilla and I guess you all know that I'm Diego.'

'Diego, it is good to meet at last,' Ed said, shaking his hand. 'My wife and I adopted Tammy and just want you to know that we are fully here for you too, through thick and thin. We have our own isolated and secure island with many hybrid children and I can promise you that we will keep you safe there. I'm here for you.'

Diego was speechless. Ed came across as a strong and confident man who would always have his back. He immediately felt Ed was someone he could trust and depend on. Completely different from Charles. Could this be the guardian he had needed for so long?

'Finally, you let us speak with you,' Mikie said.

'We have been looking for you for ages,' Tammy added.

Diego acknowledged them with a brief nod and then he saw Mina appear in front of him as she turned her crystals and became visible. He stared at her, transfixed, since she resembled him so closely. Manco and Quilla noticed it too and also stared at her. In one way it was like looking at himself; their hair, eyes, and shapes of their faces were identical. She looked like his sister, whereas Mikie and Tammy did not. Mina was also staring at him, feeling awkward, nervous and unsure what to say. There seemed to be an invisible connection, which only they could see and understand, as if it had always been there but only now could they realise it.

'Mina…' he whispered.

'Diego,' she replied, nodding.

They stood, slightly smiling at each other, amazed at the connection they were feeling. Mikie and Tammy looked at each other and smiled too. They knew what was happening and it was a good thing; the same feeling had crossed between them. It was as if the other half of themselves had been found, a feeling of completion, an understanding that they were one.

'What is it?' Ed whispered to Tammy.

'Mikie and I felt the same connection, Ed, like we had finally been put back together. I think we are two sets of sesquizygotic twins,' she said.

'I'm positive about it,' Jax added.

'What are sesquizygotic twins?' Ed asked.

'Jax researched this, so I'll let him explain,' Tammy said.

'Identical twins are monozygotic and start as one egg fertilised by one sperm that then splits into two, creating the twins. They share 100% of their DNA. Fraternal twins are dizygotic and are basically two eggs fertilised at the same time by two different sperm – basically two pregnancies occurring simultaneously. Non identical. They share 50% of their DNA and is normally the only way you can have mixed gender twins,' he explained. 'Now, sesquizygotic twins are incredibly rare, so rare they almost hardly ever occur. This is when nature goes against everything it stands for and two sperm fertilise the same egg, later splitting to create semi-identical twins, which can be different sexes. They will share 50-100% of their DNA depending upon how much DNA from both sperm is held in each half.'

Ed nodded his understanding.

Jax continued, 'When Tammy started telling me about her strange connection to Mikie, I ran blood tests and analysis on them and researched twins. Sesquizygotic twins are rare and incredible. Only a handful of cases have ever happened in human history, just within the last century. That's just twins. The chances of it happening twice in one pregnancy and creating quads should be impossible,' Jax finished.

'Good work, Jax. Who would have thought?' Ed said, amazed, before turning to Diego. 'We should perhaps guide the prince and the princess back to the village, Diego. I would very much like to meet their father again; we met once a long time ago. And then we would be very grateful if you would come with us to the island.'

'Come with you, why? An alien has just pretended to be my father, my uncle is lost out there somewhere and is probably dead or close to dying, and you want me to leave with you? I'm not going anywhere. I'm going to find my uncle and stay here,' Diego replied.

'I understand how you feel, but I can at least set your mind at ease on one level – I believe we have found your uncle.' Ed pointed to the side of the river, under a tree.

Diego followed Mikie until they came to the pale, drained body of Charles, covered with a blanket, safely lying by the side of the tree. He was still unconscious but alive. Mikie, Tammy and Mina walked over to him.

'They did the same to our uncle,' Mikie said.

'Our real uncle, mum's sister,' Tammy added.

'Will he get better?' Diego asked, looking up.

'We hope so. We used healing energy on our uncle, it was slow but it worked. We can do the same with him,' Mikie said.

'Charles?' Diego whispered.

'The aliens scan and read minds. A human mind can't take it. They get extreme headaches, and if it's read too much and too fast then they go into a comatose state,' Mikie explained.

'That's how they knew everything they lied to me about! Charles started getting headaches just before they arrived. Deep down I knew it!' Diego muttered, clenching his fists angrily.

'He'll be all right, we'll get him safely back to the village and make him better,' Quilla said, taking hold of his hand.

'Come, let us all head towards the village, we can talk more there,' Ed said.

'I'll carry my uncle,' Diego said.

'There is no need,' said Tammy. 'Sirocco, my horse, will carry him.'

'Oh yes, that magnificent horse, he is yours?' Quilla asked.

Tammy nodded as Sirocco came over and neighed. Diego and Quilla stroked him and admired his beauty. They lifted Charles up onto Sirocco's back then headed towards the camp. Mina looked around to see if there were any anacondas still lurking about, but the forest was now still and silent. No dead bodies remained on the ground. It was wiped clean.

'They're still here,' Tammy told her.

'Really? I have to say I quite like them now. Fascinating assassins,' Mina admitted.

'Good I'm glad you feel that way. Better to admire than fear nature. Did you notice that the body the anaconda puked up earlier has gone? They've dragged it into hiding to digest safely. They can't travel on full stomachs so will need to stay put for a couple of weeks or so as their stomach acid digests the food. They'll leave once they've eaten everyone. Manco, Quilla, please tell your people not to disturb this area for a month – give them time to eat and move on?'

'Of course.' Manco nodded.

'Oh please, let's not talk about it anymore!' Mina said.

'Let's not talk about what?' Jax asked. 'Normally that means something is worth talking about.'

'Well, I can't stomach thinking of it any longer, I've had all I can take,' Mina said and picked up her pace, joining Diego.

Diego was leading Sirocco, Manco was out in front and Quilla was at Diego's side. Mina joined them and looked at Quilla sternly, willing her to leave them alone, and Quilla gracefully walked away. She went and joined her brother up front, looking back over her shoulder at Mina. She was letting Mina know this was her choice, not that she was intimidated, and trying to convey, in one long look, that her behaviour was rude and unacceptable. Mina shrugged; she didn't care. Quilla meant nothing to her and she wouldn't let her get in the way of them taking Diego back to Vivacity Island. She knew that they were close and that Quilla was why Diego wanted to stay. It was obvious to anyone.

'Hi,' she said.

'Hi,' Diego replied. 'So, you are my sister?'

'Yes, one of them. The best one, of course.'

'Of course.' Diego smiled. 'They don't look like we do.'

'No, we are far better looking.' She smiled sweetly. 'And smarter too, I believe.'

'Ha! Too funny. I doubt that; Mikie seems really switched on,' Diego said, looking over at his brother.

'Careful what you say, he reads our minds and knows everything,' Mina whispered.

'That's not true,' Mikie told them telepathically.

'Ha! Cute.' Diego smiled at him. 'Read my mind again and I'll sacrifice you to the sun.'

'Understood.' Mikie nodded respectfully.

Mina smiled. 'I can feel an instant understanding between us. I've watched this between Mikie and Tammy, and I feel that with you.'

'Yeah, me too, it's strange,' Diego said, looking down at the floor as he walked. He seemed deflated.

'Are you OK, Diego?' Mina asked quietly.

'No, not really, Mina. I knew nothing, absolutely nothing. I suspected Mikie was related to me, but Charles only gave me the note from my mother last night, then this alien pretends to be my father and I really believed him. I felt as if someone finally wanted to get to know me. No one wants me to live with them. I'm a health hazard. I blow things up and start fires accidentally. Now you are all here wanting to take me somewhere else, but once you realise what I am and what I do you won't want me around either. I just don't know what to think or believe anymore.'

'You know what, I feel the same way. As if I'm an outsider that no one gets and no one really wants. I understand what you mean. I did know quite a lot from my guardian though. Lei, she's called. She and our uncle have fallen in love. You'll really like them both. Lei was mum's best friend. I knew early on that I was not all human and nothing like other children. It must be hard not knowing anything. I will say that Ed and Jude are amazing, and so is their island, and they will never turn you away or make you feel unwanted. It will be nice now that we have each other. Do you want to know what I know?' she asked.

'Yes, that would be nice.' He smiled at her. 'I feel that I can trust you.'

'If you and I cannot trust each other, how can we ever trust anyone else? Our mother, Sarah, separated us all at birth to keep us safe. You will start to notice how our energy is increased, our powers too, when we are together.

So together we would have been much easier to find. Quads are unusual in humans, let alone quads that are half human and half alien. I've noticed that my power is stronger since being around Mikie and Tammy because of how we react together.'

'So, we are half aliens and that's where our power comes from?' asked Diego.

'The aliens don't have strong powers like ours, even those who have crystals. They have evolved their telekinetic abilities, yet we are unique it seems,' said Mina. 'We rescued thirty hybrid children from their ship. They were creating variants of the Pisces virus and experimenting on them to try to make them powerful like us. It wasn't working. It seems that our power comes from the Pisces virus, from a vaccine strand that was given to our mum prior to her pregnancy, which mutated into something different with her unusual blood type. Somehow, it manipulated our blood whilst our mother was pregnant with us and that is why we are so different. The aliens have been experimenting on children trying to figure out how to make it happen again. We rescued loads. It was horrible,' she explained.

'But why?'

Mina told him about the war and the aliens needing a new planet, and that some were good and some were bad. She told him more about Lei and how she had worked with their mother, and the things she knew about Sarah and what she worked towards. They discussed Tammy and Mikie's background, and Stephen and the Brunswicks.

As they neared the village, Diego started to understand everything and was surprised it all made sense. Neither of them cared that Manco and Quilla were listening. But Mina was conscious that Quilla kept peering over her shoulder at her, fully aware of the threat she posed to her. They both wanted Diego to be theirs and saw the other as someone who might jeopardise that. Mina pretended not to notice as she continued talking with Diego.

SEVENTEEN

JET

PERU

Manco and Quilla guided them through the shortcuts they knew, and they all used the time to get to know one another. They were all exhausted now that the adrenaline had subsided. No one had slept much. Diego and Quilla were really starting to feel the sleep deprivation. As the day progressed, the humidity increased and everyone was sweating profusely. The jungle was hot and muggy. They were also really hungry. Manco pointed out some fruits they could eat as they walked; Aguaymanto, camu camu and Chirimoya. Ed, Jax, Tammy and Mikie walked behind the others, chatting amongst themselves about the events of the past few days and how they might get back home faster than they had arrived here.

'You look relieved, Ed,' Mikie said.

'I am. Just very happy to finally have you all safe together.' He smiled.

'Yes, it is a relief. I thought we had lost Diego for a

moment,' Tammy agreed.

'Are you sure we don't have to worry about the villagers or any other aliens finding us?' Jax asked.

'We're all right, for now. It'll be a while before they realise the aliens are not returning. I can't sense any others and the villagers are good people, I know that from Diego,' Mikie replied.

'Good, then perhaps we have earned ourselves a little rest when we get to the village. I think we have a day, maybe two, before more aliens come looking for this missing ship, which, by the way, you could have not sunk so we could have flown out of here!'

'Sorry, Ed. I couldn't think of anything better,' Tammy replied.

'Neither could I. It was the best we could do,' Mikie said.

'I agree. Just saying how handy that ship would have been right now, that's all,' Ed told them.

'It would be nice to stay at the village for a little while,' Tammy said.

'Perhaps we will be welcomed there, even if just for a good night's sleep and some food. I met the king once and he is a great man. Plus, I'm starving. This fruit isn't filling anything up,' Ed complained as his belly rumbled loudly.

'I'm starving too,' Mikie said.

As if on cue, his stomach rumbled too. They all laughed.

'I'm fine. Guess being a vegetarian means my stomach doesn't need anything heavy. The anacondas were a wicked idea,' Jax said to Tammy. 'I loved the way you did that, aren't they just awesome?'

'Yes, they're incredible. Even Mina started to warm to them,' Tammy replied.

'If the truth be told, I wasn't overly keen myself,' Ed said. 'There was one point when I was sitting with Charles and one came far too close for my liking. Scared me to death. I was worried it would snatch Charles or me away. Cannibalism is rife among them in such close proximity – are you controlling that still, Tammy?'

'Yes, it's just something I remind them of every few hours, not a big job. I could manage the amount we had, that's why I didn't call any more.'

'I know but I have never, in all my years of managing animals, seen anacondas so large. I might have even set those ones, or their parents, free out here in the jungle,' Ed said.

'Actually, they told me they were older. One of the older females was almost thirty years old,' Tammy told him.

'No way! They normally only live a third of that in the wild.' Ed gasped.

'Not here. They told me they hadn't been affected by the virus except for the food shortage. They had to eat each other in order to survive. Some species, the anaconda being one, seem to have a natural immunity to Pisces,' Tammy explained.

'Or at least the ability to suppress it,' Jax added.

'I have never come across them,' Quilla said.

'The way they grabbed the aliens and wrapped around them – wow!' Mikie said.

'Or dragged them into the water to drown them. Surprisingly clever,' Jax added.

'It was amazing. I really do want one as a pet. I will give you anything, Tammy, to help me make a pet of one of them,' Manco pleaded.

'The moment Tammy left, it would eat you Manco,' Ed explained.

'Most certainly. They are not pet material,' Tammy agreed.

'Life can be so unfair,' Manco sighed.

'How can they eat something as big as the aliens? They just seem long and thin in comparison,' Mikie asked.

'Well…' Tammy started.

'What it is,' Jax interrupted, 'is that they can eat anything about one and a half times the width of their bodies. They can stretch that much. Those were the largest anacondas you will ever see. People have been trying to track them this size and prove they exist for years. Only Tammy can encourage them out. They, my friend, are the bees knees of the jungle.'

'Magnificent creatures.' Ed nodded his agreement.

'If anyone does manage to come across them out here, they won't live to tell the story.' Jax touched his nose, emphasising the fact.

'Well, they certainly did the job.' Mikie shivered.

'They do what they need to do to survive in a big scary world.' Tammy shrugged.

'Yes, but they are what's made this world big and scary.' Mikie said, laughing.

'And they'll be even bigger after the feast they've just had, best watch your back now.' Jax giggled.

'Stop it, Jax, you shouldn't wind people up like that,' Ed said, but he too couldn't help but smile.

Jax noticed that Tammy was looking somewhat sad and he came closer to her, so no one else could hear them.

'Where is Jet?' he asked.

'Not far away, in the trees.' Tammy sighed.

'What is it, there's something going on, isn't there?'

'Yes, he has a friend. She's with him now, shy and staying out of sight.'

'Does he want to stay with her?'

Tammy nodded as a feeling of sorrow washed over her. She choked back a sob. Jax took her hand in his and gave it a gentle squeeze. He didn't realise Mikie was watching and listening. They all knew, deep down, what was going on.

'Perhaps it's time you faced him?' Jax suggested.

Tammy stopped and stared at Jax for a moment, then she lowered her head and reluctantly nodded. He was right, she had just been avoiding this moment for a while.

'Let's all stop for a minute, give the horse some water, and rest up,' Mikie shouted to those in front.

They all took a moment to sit and rest, getting Sirocco some water. The camas were following behind them all and took this opportunity to graze and get themselves a drink too. Manco and Quilla helped them find the water from the large plants, knowing where it would be. They all rubbed blisters and aching muscles, still sore after fighting. They didn't have many injuries apart from a few scratches and bruises.

They all snacked on more fruit. Manco gingerly handed Tammy a Chirimoya, a heart-shaped, dark green apple that tasted like a combination of banana, pineapple, peach and strawberry. Jax glared at Manco who promptly ignored him and started making conversation with Tammy about her power with the animals. Quilla handed around some Aguaymanto; small, golden, cherry or gooseberry looking fruits, hidden under a non-edible paper like skin. When ripe, the fruit was a yellow-orange colour and had a sweet and sour taste and a pleasant flavour. Ravished, everyone eagerly ate whatever they could.

'I always loved foraging for my own food,' Ed murmured with a mouthful of Chirimoya. 'Peru has the most magnificent selection to forage from in the world.'

'Tammy, it's time,' Jax said, interrupting the conversation she was having with Manco.

'Yes, you're right,' she replied.

'Time for what?' Manco asked.

Jax ignored him. 'Do you want me to stay here or come with you?'

'I'd prefer it if you came with me,' Tammy said.

He nodded and followed Tammy into the trees. Manco watched, his brain working overtime on how he could get Tammy away from Jax. Everyone else was too busy focusing on the fruit to notice. It was muggy and the air was hard to breathe. Jet could not be seen at first but then he stepped out in front of them. His head hung low, as if he knew how bad this was. He wasn't happy. He looked torn and pulled apart. Tammy could feel his discomfort and she didn't want that. She desperately wanted him to be happy and not feel awkward.

'Jet.' Tammy sighed and bent down onto one knee.

He came up to her and let her stroke his head. Then, he looked behind him and the female jaguar stepped out; slowly, hesitantly, cautiously. Jet encouraged her to come closer and Tammy smiled.

'She's beautiful, Jet. I can see why you like her.'

Jet purred loudly and with pride. Tammy touched the jaguar's face and smiled at her, stroking her cheek. She had tawny-coloured fur with beautiful spots – like dark rosettes with dots in them – that covered her entire coat. Jet was the same colour underneath too, but due to the melanistic gene he was a black panther. His rosettes were hidden unless you looked closely in the light.

Jax knew to stay calmly at Tammy's side. This was the female jaguar's first encounter with humans and Tammy wasn't exactly what you'd call human. Whereas, Jax definitely was. He knew his head would fit perfectly in the jaws of this amazing creature and had a healthy knowledge of what she was capable of. He didn't need to be a vet to understand that. A tear slid down Tammy's cheek, which Jet licked away. Another tear fell, then another. Tammy sniffed and wiped them with the back of her hand. Jax produced a tissue from his pocket, which she accepted with a smile and blew her nose as she stood up.

'I know you want to go, Jet,' she said, in between sobs. 'I'm really happy for you. Truly, I am. I just don't want to lose you. This is where you belong, I know that. But I'm going to miss you so much! You were my first friend who taught me so much.'

She dropped to her knees in front of him, tears streaming down her cheeks as she hugged him close. Jet placed a paw on her shoulder and licked her cheek once more. The female came over and licked Tammy's other cheek.

'I know you'll look after him and teach him the ways of the wild. You have four, you know,' Tammy told the female.

'Four what?' Jax whispered.

Tammy looked up at him and smiled. 'Four babies growing inside of her.'

'Wow, Jet, you don't hang around do you,' Jax said,

shaking his head and smiling. 'Congratulations.'

'He's going to be a father.'

'You won't lose him,' Jax said. 'He will always be here, and we can come back and visit all the time. Diego will want to return and see the Incas too, so we could all come and then you can see Jet. He'll come whenever you call.'

Tammy nodded at what Jax said, knowing it was true. This wasn't the end of their friendship; it was just a change and he wouldn't be there every day anymore. She slowly and reluctantly stood up, took Jax's offered hand, and looked down at Jet and his newfound love.

'I love you enough to let you go,' she whispered. 'Don't feel torn anymore. Enjoy your much deserved freedom, my friend. I shall always love you.'

Jax stroked Jet's head and said goodbye.

'It's time,' he said softly.

Jet released a distressed, drawn out yowl as he skulked away, head hung low. He hadn't eaten for a while, being so sad at the thought of not seeing Tammy anymore. Tammy pulled herself up straight, being brave for his sake, and smiled. She sent her love and joy towards him, using her energy to lift his, and worked on his body to increase his energy more positively. Jax stood near her and watched her work, moving her hands gently as she raised her palms in his direction. She told him that he would be happy now, that being a father would bring him immense joy, and not to miss her as she would check in often. They could still talk each day. Jet cheered up at this thought and because of the energy boost she was giving him. Then he and the female jaguar were gone.

Tammy turned to Jax, buried her head in his shoulder,

and cried. Jax wrapped his arms around her and held her close. They stayed together for a while, Jax rocking her gently, until her crying had stopped. He held her firm, neither rushing nor moving, feeling sad himself. Then, taking her hand, Jax walked her back to where everyone was sitting. Everyone looked at them as Jax held Tammy's hand and guided her to a seat. Her eyes, red raw from crying, made it clear something had happened.

'Jet?' Ed asked, walking up to Tammy and embracing her.

'He's gone,' Jax explained. 'With his mate.'

'Oh Tammy, I'm so sorry,' Ed hugged her tighter.

'He's only gone and got her pregnant already,' Jax said. 'Four babies she's carrying.'

'Oh that is such wonderful news!' Ed exclaimed. He had tried and failed to breed Jet for years and this warmed his heart.

'He didn't say goodbye to me!' Mina said, shocked and hurt as tears sprang to her eyes.

Suddenly, Jet rushed out from the trees and ran in a circle around everyone. Mina gasped in delight as he ran over to her and jumped up, placing his large paws on her shoulders. She hugged him tightly, a sob breaking through her normally hard reserve. Jet purred and nuzzled in to Mina's neck. Mikie also walked over and hugged Jet, sharing in the feelings of his brother and sisters. Then, Jet moved away and walked slowly over to Ed.

'Look,' Jax said to Tammy.

Tammy, who had been blowing her nose again, looked up and watched as Jet strolled over to Ed, who also had tears in his eyes. After all, he had raised this black panther from a cub on his own safari park. Ed dropped to his knees, his heart aching with love and loss, tormented by his mixed emotions. Jet placed his paws on his shoulders and licked his cheek. Ed laughed, wiping away a tear as it fell, and hugged Jet tightly. Then he pulled away and nodded at him.

'You go and be free, my boy,' he said. 'You deserve it. I'm so proud of you.'

Jet looked over at Tammy one last time. Their eyes locked like magnets as the love they shared passed between them. After the longest time, he blinked, turned towards the trees and vanished. She knew she wouldn't see him again for a long time.

'Until we meet again,' Jax said, squeezing her hand.

Again, Tammy buried her head into his shoulder and let him hold her whilst she cried. A feeling of sadness passed amongst the group that only the loss of a really good friend could bring. There was silence as they all dealt with their own feelings at losing Jet. Even Manco and Quilla choked up at what had happened.

'I hate to break the mood but since he is staying here, I don't suppose he could become my pet? Would that help? Shall we ask?' Manco whispered to his sister.

'Be quiet and say nothing, brother, now is not the time. This is a big moment.'

'But is it? It's not that big a moment if they visit often and he lives with me, surely?' Manco persisted.

'Shush,' Quilla said, nudging him in the arm.

'Tammy.' Ed came to her side.

She turned away from Jax and fell into Ed's embrace.

'Oh Ed!' she cried. 'I feel a big hole inside of me, it's such a horrible feeling.'

'I know, Tammy, I know. It is both a sad and a very happy occasion. Jude and I did this repeatedly. You must think not of your loss but of Jet's gain. Every animal you love and lose takes a little part of you with them.'

'He was a great fighter,' Tammy said.

'He IS the best!' Jax said. 'He will fight with us again yet.'

'Yes, the war will reach Peru,' Ed agreed.

Manco, about to ask if Jet could be his pet now, received a sharp dig in the ribs from Quilla. He looked at her, rubbing his wound, open-mouthed. She shook her head and warned him with a glance not to open his mouth. Manco was gutted. He could just see himself standing with a black panther next to him in battle.

Quilla leaned in close and whispered. 'It will happen, Manco, I have seen it. You fight alongside him.'

Manco's eyes lit up as he smiled with glee. He would go down in history as the prince who fought with an otorongo.

*

It began to rain; a heavy, tropical downpour that often occurred in the jungle. With the sticky humidity, the rain was welcomed and cooling. They were climbing the mountain to the village and could hear the villagers in uproar about something, their voices echoing over the sound of the rain. It was a steep journey and their legs ached, especially for those who were still recovering from the pain of riding the camas. It was also hard to acclimatise to the altitude again and Ed had ran out of pills, giving only a small dosage to each and spreading them out as best he could.

Manco left his sister's side and joined Tammy, Jax,

Mikie and Ed.

'What is all the commotion?' Ed asked.

'They will be worried about my sister and me, wondering what to do, no doubt,' Manco replied. 'Are you alright, Tammy?'

'Yes, thank you,' she said.

'I think that was a really nice thing you did, letting Jet go off and be free like that.'

'Harder than I thought.'

'Yes, I can imagine. Well, I can't really, we don't tend to form close bonds with such animals, but I am starting to see how unique you all are, and I know what it's like to bond so closely with someone then lose them.' He looked over at Diego.

'You are good friends with my brother, aren't you?' Tammy asked.

'Yes, I would die for him, which is a very big privilege for a prince to say.' Manco smiled.

Mikie could tell immediately that the way Manco had emphasised the word 'prince' had annoyed Jax. Using his rank to his advantage. He felt Jax's posture go stiff and defensive, and saw the way he looked at Manco and then at Tammy. Yes, Mikie thought, smiling, he's very jealous. Jax had once told him he worried that Tammy only saw him as a brother. Mikie and Jax felt like brothers. It wasn't Mikie's place to share his sister's personal thoughts with Jax but he couldn't help but smile because he knew Jax didn't have anything to worry about. Tammy adored him and they shared a bond with animals that Manco, and probably no other person on the planet, could break. Mikie could see Jax and Tammy running Brunswick zoo one day, the perfect pair, in perfect unison.

It amazed him how oblivious to all the attention Tammy was; she had no idea what was happening around her. But then, Mikie thought, she was still upset about losing Jet.

'My father is the king,' Manco continued. 'He will welcome you into our village as he did with your brother, Diego. I hope you will stay and rest with us a while?'

Jax bit his tongue in annoyance. They all knew his father was the king – he didn't have to say it. Jax had already been dropped by a girl at school for not being rich enough. Ironic considering he was likely to inherit his uncle's island. And now a prince was trying to impress his girl.

'I think we would appreciate that,' Ed said.

'We must dance tonight, a victory celebration, you will all have so much fun. Do you dance?' Manco asked, looking sincerely at Tammy.

'Oh, well, not really, I guess. I've never tried,' Tammy replied.

'I will teach you. I am the best dancer,' Manco boasted.

'I can dance and will teach Tammy myself.' Jax glared at Manco.

His voice was defensive and challenging, letting Manco know, in no uncertain terms, that he was stepping on his toes. Ed and Mikie exchanged looks and had to hold back smiles. The jealousy was obvious to everyone but Tammy. Manco saw it too and decided he was more than up for the challenge; if this boy wanted a fight, he would certainly give him one. It wouldn't be the first time he had taken a girl away from someone else.

'I think Tammy should learn from the master,' Mikie said, trying not to look as amused as he felt. 'Manco should show her the proper way of the Incas.'

'Absolutely,' Ed agreed, slapping Jax playfully on the shoulder.

'Then it is sorted.' Manco smiled triumphantly, knowing exactly how Jax felt and letting him know he would not be scared away so easily.

'I'm really not a very good dancer,' Tammy said, shyly.

'Tonight, my fair lady, you will be the best!' Manco said and happily walked away, re-joining his sister and Diego in front of Sirocco.

This time Tammy did notice the sharp look that Jax gave Mikie and blushed, as she finally realised what was happening. Tammy slowed down, allowing them to move ahead as Jax fell in line with her.

'Don't mind them,' she said.

'I'm not, I just wish they'd mind their own business,' he replied, sulkily. 'I don't want you to dance with the 'prince', as if that counts for anything out here in a place like this!'

'I can't very well get out of it now, but don't worry, I'll come and dance with you as soon as I can politely get away.' Tammy smiled, taking hold of his hand.

'Promise?'

'Yes, promise.'

'I'm sorry, I'm being unfair, aren't I? I don't possess you and shouldn't stop you socialising with anyone else, even if I know they're after you.'

'After me? No, you're being sweet, but you have nothing to worry about, Jax. If I could choose anyone on the planet to be my dance partner, it would always be you.'

'You really mean that, don't you?'

She nodded and gave him a soft kiss on his cheek. She

was glad when he smiled back at her, his jealousy now gone. They continued to walk a little slower than the others, keeping their privacy, and Tammy was glad to see the added bounce in Jax's stride. Mikie looked back over his shoulder and saw them, walking sweetly side by side. They were perfect together.

'That was naughty of us.' Ed chuckled, noticing him looking.

'Yeah, I know, but I couldn't resist.'

'Me neither. Do you think there will be a problem?'

'I doubt it. We have bigger things to worry about. I just find it funny that Tammy is so slow to pick up how much Jax adores her.' Mikie shook his head.

'Well, I guess she is distracted with all the animals. She feels the animals, you know. The constant thoughts and emotions of all the animals in her head doesn't leave much room for her own. Or for other humans. Besides, they're still so young.'

'They get on well together, don't they?'

'Yes, they do,' Ed replied, giving Mikie a strange look as he did.

'What's that look for?'

'I've just realised that I'm talking to you as if you're an adult. You're so grown up and mature, I find it hard to remember you're only twelve.'

'Yeah, everyone says that.' Mikie smiled.

*

They reached the top of the mountain, breathless and tired, and stopped as they saw the village.

'Oh my…' Mina started to say then trailed off.

'It's beautiful!' Tammy gasped.

'Thank you.' Manco smiled, proudly.

Jax felt his heart sink. It was a most stunning home.

Ed saw that he looked as sick as a dog. He saw Mikie notice too and told him to telepathically pass his message on to Jax. Mikie nodded.

'Jax, Ed told me to tell you that as stunning as this place is, Tammy will always choose Vivacity Island and Africa. Stop worrying.'

Jax blushed and nodded. *'Easier said than done,'* he replied.

'We saw Machu Picchu from the HP but this is even more spectacular than I expected,' Ed said.

'Well, we have added a lot of modern knowledge and flair to our village,' Manco said, spreading his arms widely. 'My father has travelled the world and learned many things; we have used modern approaches as well as our traditional ways. I am proud of our village, it's peaceful and beautiful.'

'You have every reason to be proud,' Ed replied.

Mina was still staring at the village, amazed by the warm feeling that came over her. It was a feeling she couldn't understand and it felt good.

'You like it, don't you?' Diego smiled, looking sideways at her.

'Uh-huh.' She nodded.

'Do you feel it too?'

She looked at him then, surprised by his words, but also knowing that he knew.

'Yes, I think I do. It's as if I've been here before, as if it's… Well, as if it's…'

'Home?'

'Yes, home.' She sighed. 'That's just what it feels like.'

'That's how I felt too. Maybe we were here in a previous life,' Diego suggested.

'Maybe,' Mina whispered, still mesmerised and taking everything in. She did not notice Quilla give her a worried look and walk away.

As they approached the centre of the village, they could see a group of Incas gathered in front of the king, loudly discussing what they should do about finding the prince and princess.

'What are they saying?' Tammy asked.

'They are just deciding how many people to send looking for us, but we can help them out there. Father!' Quilla shouted and ran towards the king.

'Quilla!' He waved, relief flooding his face when he saw her. He opened his arms wide.

Manco walked slowly and manly towards his father, stopped in front of him, and bowed slightly. The king smiled and reached out to rub the top of his head and then thought better of it. Not in front of everyone; Manco was a young man now. Instead, the king placed his hand on his son's shoulder and smiled.

'You had me worried there, brave son.'

'I know, Father, I'm sorry. We have guests and so much to tell you.' Manco pointed to Ed and the children.

The king looked at them, one by one, nodding politely but searching for Charles. He had a bad feeling of foreboding. As soon as they had noticed that Manco and Quilla were missing, he realised he had made a mistake letting the aliens take them.

'Tell me, my son, why are our camas following you all like a pack of dogs and where might the alien and Charles be? Please tell me Charles is safe?'

Manco and Diego looked at each other, silently deciding who should tell the king the bad news.

EIGHTEEN

GREEN EYED MONSTER

PERU

'He's here, on the horse, Father. He's not well. The aliens did something to his mind.' Manco said, sadly, pointing to Charles' body.

'The headaches…' Diego said.

The king walked up to Charles, raised his head from the saddle and looked at him. He was still in a coma.

'Oh my friend, please stay with us. Take him in there,' the king ordered, pointing to his house, his eyes not leaving Charles. 'He's very unwell. What happened to him?'

'We will explain all later,' Diego said. 'It was a trap. He wasn't my father.'

The king sighed and watched as two villagers moved to lift Charles from the horse. They carried him into the king's house as instructed.

'How did they know so much? We have had enough visitors here lately, and been deceived, why should I trust anymore?' asked the king.

'Father, the headaches happened when they read minds and dug out the information. That is how they knew so much. These people saved us, Father,' Quilla said softly. 'And they are Diego's family.'

'You are definitely his family.' He pointed to Mina. 'Come here, my dear.'

Mina walked forwards and stopped in front of the king. He held her chin in his hands and looked deeply into her eyes, moved her head side to side, and smiled.

'I have heard about twins,' he said.

'We are more than twins.' Diego smiled and stepped forward, taking hold of Mina's hand. 'We are quadruplets!'

The king looked at Tammy, Mikie and Jax.

'This is my brother, Mikie, and my sister, Tammy, and the one who looks like me is Mina.'

'Well, I must therefore welcome you into my humble home.' The king smiled.

'This is Ed Brunswick, who looks after Tammy, and his nephew Jax,' Diego continued the introductions.

'Ed of Brunswick zoo? I know you, we met once a while back, I believe?'

'Yes,' Ed replied, holding out his hand.

The king looked down at Ed's hand, paused, and then slowly shook it.

'It has been many years since I saw this gesture, I almost forgot about handshaking! Many of us stopped greeting people with handshakes after the pandemic. I shall make an exception for you, my dear friend. You did a great many things with the animals, Ed. It broke my heart to see no animals around these parts, but with your help we soon fixed that.'

'You were heavily involved, if I remember correctly? You were responsible for helping to repopulate all of South America,' said Ed.

'Yes, but you wouldn't have seen me much, I was in the background doing the organisation out here. I placed many of the animals you sent over to us. I thank you for that.'

'I do remember something about a boar breeding program that was requested and I argued that it wasn't native to these parts,' Ed said, raising his eyebrows questioningly.

The king laughed aloud. 'I admit, I argued the case for that and signed off the papers. They make good hunting and good food for our festivals. We traditionally have cuyes – guinea pigs – living on the floor of our huts, but they are small and we now need many to feed the whole group. It is unsustainable and gets somewhat unhygienic. It was a small deviance that I blame fully on Oxford and the amazing hog roasts that Charles invited me to when I was at university. I'm not proud of myself and yet I am proud of my festivals. Boar can be free and we don't have to farm or feed them. It's very convenient.'

'Yes, I do understand. I'm a little naughty with the occasional meat treat myself now and then when I have the chance, which is why we sent so many over.' Ed smiled. 'They have bred well then, I take it?'

'Very well indeed and I don't allow any hunt on young males or females. They have a good life that is free in return for serving us later in life.'

'You shouldn't eat meat,' Tammy stated. 'You don't need meat in your diet. You should be vegetarian or, better still, vegan.'

'And yet it's a very personal choice and we do like to

live and let live without lecturing people, don't we?' Ed said tactfully, with a warning look.

'Well, it's true, to be fair, and we do not have meat regularly. It's a rare treat and only used for celebrations. We eat insects more – a very sustainable source of protein. We are lucky because most built up areas in the world just don't have the choice anymore. If they want meat protein they can only get insects,' the king said.

'Well, we shouldn't even need to eat meat. Our nails and teeth are not sharp like a natural carnivore and meat damages our digestive system,' Jax added.

'Well, that is true, and it causes heart disease. This was a leading factor in reducing meat production even before the pandemic, actually.' Ed nodded. 'Not just because of the shortage of meat or climate change. After the pandemic, we actively refused to start breeding herds of cattle again for meat production and switched to insects. We learned how fast people died from the virus because of their ill-health. Heavy drinkers or meat eaters went hard and fast. I can't argue with that.'

'Not enough though,' Jax added. 'Humans only traditionally ate meat because of limited farming, or that in winter fruit and veg weren't around so meat was all they could eat. We had short lifestyles as cavemen and evolved to living now, as we do, for over ninety years on average. Just because of a better diet; less meat. It amazes me how we know this and yet still people persist in eating meat.'

'It's our choice,' Manco said firmly. The thought of stopping boar hunting was unbearable. It was a sport as much as it was a way of feeding the village at special times.

'And that, my dear friend, is why he will never be a threat

to you and Tammy,' Mikie told Jax telepathically.

'Come, it is wet and we have many things to discuss. I want to hear about the alien and where he has got to and if we are safe.' The king indicated for them to go ahead of him in to his hut.

He stopped Quilla and Manco and pulled them aside. Mikie eavesdropped. He could not bring himself to trust these people as readily as the others seemed to – just in case. Not to mention that he was nosy and loved eavesdropping.

'Quilla, how long have you had the sight?' the king asked.

'Oh, Father…'

'How long?'

'As long as I remember but I thought they were just dreams until recently. They have been getting stronger. I meant to tell you.'

'It's my fault, Father, I should have–'

'Quiet, Manco,' the king interrupted. 'It's not your fault. I should have somehow made you want to tell me, to feel that you could tell me.' He smiled at his daughter and stroked her cheek. 'Come, no more secrets now. Let's discuss what has happened. Quilla, please ask someone to bring refreshments.'

'Yes, Father.'

'Please, sit,' the king waved his hand, indicating that they should sit on the hay placed in the centre of the floor. Manco quickly made more small piles of hay to create more seating for everyone. He was put out when Tammy sat on Jax's lap and tried to get her to move to another seat.

'I'm fine here,' she said.

'There are plenty of seats, please take one,' Manco

insisted.

'She said she's fine here,' Jax said sternly.

Manco smiled and accepted defeat. For now. It was cosy with them all in there and they sat on the hay in a circle, legs crossed, faces tired. A man and a woman appeared carrying trays of food and chicha. They gratefully accepted the drinks of chicha and when the man's tray was empty he helped prepare some hay as a table for his wife to place the plates of appetisers down. They looked colourful and beautifully arranged. Quilla pointed at each one in turn, describing what they were: ceviche, a raw seafood platter with lime juice, cheesy Peruvian tequeños with avocado dip, stuffed Peruvian empanadas, starchy tamales and meaty anticuchos. She hadn't finished talking before they tucked in and sighed with pleasure at the assortment of tastes.

Mina was devouring one of the meat skewer looking appetisers – the meaty anticuchos – when Mikie leaned in and whispered in her ear.

'You know that's guinea pig, right?'

Mina froze, the chunk of meat still in her mouth, as she looked at the skewer and then at Mikie. He was smiling. Defiantly, Mina started chomping and gulped down the meat.

'I'm hangry. I've been forced to eat bugs. I've helped gut a snake. I've eaten snake. Then, I've made friends with snakes. If you think this is going to upset me you don't realise how hardy I have become,' she hissed then took another chunk of meat and chewed it heartily.

'Fair enough, I'm impressed with your growth,' Mikie said, chuckling as he reached for one himself. 'Have to admit, it's a lot better than the snake.'

'A bike's innertube is a lot better than a snake,' Mina retorted.

'This drink is delicious,' Ed said.

'Thank you. We take great pride in our food and drink,' Manco replied.

'I'm concerned about Charles and don't know how best to treat him. He is unable to take any liquid or herbs, although we won't give in. What did they do to him?' the king asked.

'The headaches happen when the aliens read your mind from a distance. If they read the mind close up then a human brain cannot take it and collapses into a comatose state, which could eventually be fatal,' Mikie said, matter-of-factly, as he stuffed a piece of meat into his mouth.

'That is why his headaches began before they arrived,' Diego added. 'They were probing for information to use to deceive us with.'

'It happened to their uncle but it's all right, they know how to cure him,' Ed added.

'Well, I'm not so sure we can. I am worried. We just need to rest a moment then we shall go and help him,' Tammy said. 'However, his brain is not like something we have seen before.'

'What do you mean?' Ed asked.

'His mind is far more damaged than Stephen's was.' Mikie sighed. 'I don't know why, but it's really bad. There was serious damage to his brain cells from long before this.'

'I have no idea what to do to try and help him. And the alien – what of him?' the king asked.

'He was not my real father. Just a bad guy,' Diego said.

'So, I gathered,' said the king.

'He was fed to an anaconda,' Diego added. 'Rather dramatically, actually. There are ten giant green anacondas feasting on them down by the waterfall as we speak.'

'Yes, we must warn the villagers to avoid the area for a few weeks,' Manco said.

Two women arrived with more trays of food and drink, passing them around the circle, smiling at the grateful nods and thanks they received. They all gulped down the chicha and ate the food, trying hard not to wolf it down impolitely. Not everyone appreciated the chicha. It was pale yellow and slightly milky looking, but the sour aftertaste was surprising.

'What is this stuff?' Jax asked, failing to hide the disgusted look on his face.

'Jax!' Ed said sharply.

'It's all right, Ed, I know it isn't the tastiest of drinks, but it serves our farmers well after long, hard days. This is called chicha; it's a traditional Peruvian drink made from fermented sweet corn, which is easy to grow for us. Don't worry, fermented usually means it contains alcohol, but this one is alcohol free. It's full of energy and goodness and helps keep our people strong without needing to stop and eat food – it is a meal in itself,' the king said.

'Liquidised sweet corn?' Jax frowned. 'Food in a jug?'

'Yes, it was traditionally used to keep farmers working long hours. It will revive you. The bread and chicha will fill you up and the camucamu berries – the red and purple cherries – are full of vitamin C so will help restore your strength too,' Quilla added.

'I found and ate these out in the jungle, I wondered what they were.' Tammy smiled gratefully.

'You are lucky we have some special food right now because it's the time of our annual festival celebrations. The festival of the sun. So, we have some leftovers from yesterday. We must work with what is easy to farm up here and what grows in abundance. We work with nature,' the king said.

'I like that.' Tammy smiled.

'Shame we missed the festival,' Mina said.

'I have to thank you for getting my children safely home. They would have been gone by the time we went after them. I should have realised they wouldn't just go to bed. I was too keen to have the responsibility taken away from me – something I shall live to regret. Each year we have the festival Inti Raymi, which in our native language is Quechua.' He pronounced it *kechwa*. 'This means resurrection of the sun. We already celebrated this yesterday, but it ended early. As we have lots of leftovers, tonight we shall do it again, in honour of Inti's merciful return of my children and to honour our new – and very special – guests,' the king declared.

'That sounds like fun,' Mina said.

'That is most generous of you indeed,' Ed added.

'It's a big honour,' Diego said, leaning closer to Mina.

'It's huge fun,' Manco said. 'It will be great for you to see all our costumes. So, we shall just have an extra celebration. Right, Father?'

'Yes, my son, to show our new friends the Inca way and offer the promise of our support to them.'

'We can't thank you enough, I know this is a great honour,' Ed said.

'Tonight, we shall all eat, dance and be merry, whilst

Inti allows us to be. There is trouble coming – we all know that. It's time you explained what has happened and what this trouble is.'

Ed, Jax, Quilla and Manco sat with the king and explained what had happened and what Ed knew was coming. Meanwhile, Mikie silently told Tammy, Mina and Diego to follow him. They went to Charles and sat around him, whispering so as not to disturb the king. Upon occasion, the king and his children glanced over to see what they were doing, but each time it appeared that they were doing very little.

'*Diego, you have never done this with us before. We all have the ability to connect to source, a healing energy we can call upon when needed,*' Mikie told him.

'*Just do as we do, trust us.*' Mina smiled.

'OK.' Diego nodded.

'*No need to talk out loud, remember?*' said Mikie.

'Oh, right. *I mean yes, right, got it.*' Diego replied.

'*Everyone touch the palms of your hands and then warm them up by rubbing them together. Now place them, palms down, on Charles. Close your eyes and go with the feeling. Ready, Tammy?*'

'Yes, Mikie,' Tammy replied.

Diego looked at Tammy for a moment, wondering why Mikie had spoken only to her.

'*She is the only one who can heal on a cellular level and has the most powerful energy,*' Mina told him.

'*Oh,*' he said.

They sat around Charles and Diego could feel the heat rising in his body. He briefly opened his eyes and peered at everyone. No one moved. Mina opened one eye, looked at him and sighed, then closed her eye again. Diego did the same. The feeling was similar to when he used the cube. There was a light tingling sensation that ran through him, and a white light that seemed to come down inside him from his crown chakra and radiate around the room. His chest felt the immense energy as if it was pushing out of his heart and ribs, ready to explode. The heat was amazing; it felt hot enough to burn and scald him but it didn't even make him sweat – it was like some sort of magic heat.

As the white light passed between them and rose above them, at least that was how Diego was imagining it, he could feel it passing into Charles' body too, washing away his pain. The power was dramatically increased now Diego was here. Mikie and Tammy looked at each other, knowingly; only they remembered what it was like just the two of them. Mina increased it and now, with Diego, it was phenomenal. The white light then started to get brighter and a dark, electric violet colour formed around its periphery. The intensity increased as golden light started to come in. It was very hot in a blissful way. Diego started to see flashes of the inside of Charles' body and his brain, and saw a darkness, like patchy black clouds, wrapped around his brain tissue. The light was trying to dissolve the patches and Diego realised he was seeing what Tammy could see.

*

'The war is definitely coming…' Ed's voice trailed off and he stopped mid-sentence and stared over at the children sitting around Charles.

The king followed his stare. Ed had watched them

do energy healing before and he knew they had saved Stephen's life with it, but this was different. This was much more powerful than anything they had done in the past. The white light was highly visible, and the electric violet and gold light was new. The speed with which it travelled over Charles' body was amazing.

'What are they doing?' the king asked.

'Is that magic?' Manco gasped.

*

'That was strong,' Mina said, looking at Mikie and Tammy as they stopped.

'I have never felt anything as strong as that before,' Mikie said.

'We are together now, we are stronger together, we will feed off each other and get stronger still,' Tammy answered.

'How do you know?' asked Mina.

Tammy shrugged. She just did. They realised it was silent in the hut and looked over at the others, who stared at them in disbelief.

'Now there are four of us...' Mikie started to say, and then shrugged too.

He wasn't sure what to say or how to say it. Ed nodded. He seemed to understand. The king, Manco and Quilla didn't seem as surprised as he expected them to be. Then Mikie remembered the conversation he had overheard about visions. They were not without special gifts of their own.

'Did it work?' Diego asked.

Tammy looked at Mikie. No one spoke.

'Did it work?' Diego repeated.

'I don't think so,' Mikie said. 'His brain is just too damaged. I don't know why.'

'There were different kinds of damage,' Tammy said. 'It wasn't just the damage from the alien reading his mind. His brain cells were strange and damaged from much longer abuse – something that happened years ago. We shall just have to wait and see.'

'You know something?' Ed asked the king.

'Yes, unfortunately Charles had a very difficult past. He was brutally beaten by his alcoholic father as a boy and the repeated blows to his head caused severe injury,' he began. 'Charles was often in pain from these injuries when he was younger, but never headaches. He managed to get off the prescription pain killers many years ago after he became addicted to them and then other addictions began to take him over.'

Diego tenderly held his uncles hand and felt his heart sinking heavily.

The king continued. 'Drugs, alcohol, and gaming. All of which, just on their own, cause permanent and irreversible brain damage. His brain is not likely to be in a good way. Children, what are you known as?' asked the king.

'The Children of Pisces,' Mina answered.

'Ah, the Children of Pisces. I like it. Well, I have seen many amazing things in my lifetime and heard of many more. There have always been amazing people – men and women of remarkable abilities, some often inexplicable. I believe in magic, I believe wizards and dragons once lived, and I believe there are many other amazing people in the world today we do not yet know about.' The king smiled warmly.

'How do you know for sure?' Ed asked.

'I just do.' He sighed as he looked at Mikie.

Mina's eyes opened wide as she realised that the king could somehow see things, not hear them or read them in people's eyes, but just know about things he shouldn't know about. That must be where Quilla's ability came from.

'I once belonged to an organisation called Mensa,' he said. 'Have you heard of it?'

'Yes,' Ed and Jax said in unison.

Everyone else shook their heads.

'It's a group of highly intelligent and gifted people. They identify people with special talents and bring them together to do good for humanity. As a child, I knew I came from royal and Godly descendants and had special gifts. I thought I was unique. Then, when I was approached by a man from Mensa, during my time in Oxford, I learned a shocking truth. As I walked into their boardroom, I was no longer unique. I was average in that room. I was normal, nothing special. I had a hard time dealing with that realisation as a teenager, I can tell you!'

Manco looked away even though Quilla tried to give him a supportive smile. She knew he worried about going to Oxford when he was old enough, and whether or not Mensa would have any interest in him. He had no gifts at all. He was not as smart as his father nor had visions like they did. He wasn't even the tallest boy in the village. There was nothing special or stand out about Manco and it played on his mind, weighing heavily on him. Quilla wished she could give him her gift but she could not. It did not reflect well on Manco, within the village, to have his father, sister

and now Diego with powers while he had none.

'I thought Mensa was just high IQs?' Ed said.

The king looked at him and shook his head. 'It is far more than that.'

*

That evening the music played, the Incas danced around the fire, and they feasted on a variety of wonderful food and drink. Charles remained in a coma as they hoped and prayed he would slowly recover with time. There was nothing else that they could do.

'Now, this is lovely!' Jax said as he drank a yellow-gold drink he was given. 'It is sweet and tasty, better than the last one. What is it again?'

'Inca cola,' Quilla told him.

'Nice.' Jax licked his lips.

'It's good,' Tammy agreed.

'Come, Tammy, let me show you how to dance. You have finished eating, haven't you?' Manco asked.

Ed and Mikie saw a flash of Jax's simmering rage before he quickly concealed it. Mikie chewed his cheek to stop the smile he felt. He just couldn't help but find it funny, despite knowing it was eating Jax up inside. He felt sure Jax would jump on Manco any minute. Tammy stood up and accepted Manco's offer to dance, despite the reluctance she felt.

'I'll taunt you about this green eyed monster of yours all your life,' Mikie told Jax.

Jax glared at him, the warning clear in his eyes, as he avoided watching Tammy move away with Manco. He couldn't avoid looking for long. Almost as soon as they started to dance, he had to look and felt the jealousy rising inside him. He hated seeing Manco with his hand on her waist, more so because it was clear to him that Manco liked Tammy and was clearly out to win her over.

'Diego, this may be our last chance for a while,' Quilla said.

'Well then, let us make the most of it.' Diego smiled, getting up to dance with her.

Mina, annoyed by this, watched them with narrowed eyes, suspicious as to what sort of power Quilla had over Diego. As they danced, she became even more worried as their affection for each other became clear. She decided to let them dance for a while but soon grew impatient. Both Jax and Mina were getting worked up over the dancing.

'Come on, you guys,' Mikie said. 'Don't be killjoys, let us all dance together.'

It took some persuading, but eventually, Jax and Mina went with Mikie and danced alongside Quilla, Diego, Manco and Tammy. The king watched, pleased to see them having fun. Ed was talking to him, helping him understand what had been going on. They also talked about what needed to happen next.

Diego spun around with Quilla as the others stamped their feet and bounced around with the rest of the villagers. Jax and Mina felt their resentment disappearing as they laughed and joined in. Mina was surprised when Quilla jumped in front of her and grabbed her hands, swinging her around, laughing. For a brief moment, Mina felt awkward and wanted to stop but then she saw Quilla's kind face and understood the good gesture. She did not want them to be enemies; they both wanted what was best for Diego and should be friends. Suddenly, they realised they should be working together and not against each other. Mina and Quilla laughed and danced together, and then encircled Diego as they both danced with him too.

Tammy laughed as Manco spun her around; she felt his arm go protectively around her waist and noticed Jax staring at the arm with disgust. She hated seeing Jax so sad and angled herself so that after the next spin, she would be able to turn into him. As she bounced in front of Jax, she gently and smoothly shoved Mina into Manco. He had little choice but to carry on dancing with Mina. Jax smiled warmly and placed his arm around Tammy's waist, where Manco's had been only moments before. Manco watched Jax and Tammy dance for a moment before he sighed and turned back to Mina.

'You don't stand a chance,' Mina said kindly.

'Yes, I know, I can see that now. You would think that at my age it wouldn't be too late to get the girl of my dreams, hmm?'

'Yes, you'd think.'

'I am a prince; I should be able to choose the girl I want.'

'Titles mean nothing to my sister, Manco. You don't understand her and her connection to animals. You and my brother love hunting; can you not see that my sister would never be able to accept that? Tammy and Jax are on the same level. He understands her and he saves animals, whereas you hunt them. She is too gentle, caring and giving for you.'

'I can be all those things too.'

'And, most importantly, Manco, she's vegetarian.'

'So?'

'So, you can't kill animals if you hope to win my sister's heart! Could you quit hunting and go vegetarian?'

'Oh, I couldn't do that,' Manco said without hesitation.

'Exactly, which is one of the reasons you don't stand a chance. Now, don't take it to heart, teach me how to be as good a dancer as your sister.' Mina smiled.

'OK, I can do that, but it'll take a lot of work, Quilla is very graceful you know,' Manco said, feeling more cheerful now.

'Don't worry about my self-esteem, will you?' Mina replied tartly.

'Ha! Your self-esteem is like titanium! Perhaps I looked at the wrong sister?' Manco said, as he watched her dance.

Mina looked at him, the smile fading from her face.

'Forget it,' she said coldly. 'I don't do second best and I don't do boyfriends!'

Diego and Quilla swooped past and pulled her into them, dancing her away and saving her from the awkward moment, making her laugh again. They had been eavesdropping and could tell it was going to end badly.

'Idiot!' Quilla hissed at Manco as she whooshed past.

Manco starred after them, puzzled.

'What?' he asked.

They ignored him and carried on dancing.

NINETEEN
LIFE CHOICES

PERU

Mina sat eating her fruit from a small bowl and watched Diego walking with Quilla. They looked nice together, she thought, but were obviously dreading saying goodbye to each other again. Mina gave them their space, feeling kinder towards Quilla after the dance the previous evening. She wasn't happy that Diego was besotted with her. Nonetheless, she couldn't help liking her either. Quilla was classy, smart and beautiful. She walked with grace and dignity. Mina realised that you couldn't dislike a girl like her – you could only adore her, be jealous of her, or long to be her. Mina couldn't stop watching her.

'They will miss each other,' Tammy said, sitting beside her.

'Yes. Do you think they could come with us, Quilla and Manco?'

'No, it's too dangerous. Plus, it would probably be a big distraction Diego could do without.'

'What, like you with Jax?' Mina said, tongue in cheek.

'Good point! But no, they belong here and will be needed to protect their own people.'

'I guess you're right, Tammy.'

'It was fun last night wasn't it?'

'Yes, it was great fun. I wonder if we'll ever experience anything like that again,' said Mina.

'I'm sure we will. These are good friends of Diego's and I'm sure we will all come back. He will for certain.' Tammy nodded at Quilla and Diego.

'Well, I hope I do too. I cannot remember a time when I had so much fun. I slept so well.'

'Me too, I can't believe how comfortable hay is to sleep on! I think it helps not having slept for two nights too.' Tammy laughed gently.

'I hope everything works out well so that one day we can just lead more normal lives and come visit friends like this and have dances. Can you imagine that? Do you think we will all survive?' Mina asked.

'I can only hope so. I do just love the simple things in life. Like sleeping in these little huts high on a mountain, peacefully listening to the sounds of the night.'

'What are you two chatting about?' Ed asked, walking towards them.

Tammy noticed how relaxed and contented he looked. Mikie and Jax were at his side. Whether in Peru, Africa or Vivacity Island, Ed just always seemed comfortable and fitted in. He worked with nature and was at peace everywhere except London, like her. She hadn't realised it before.

'We were discussing how well we slept and would like

beds of hay at Brunswick please.' Tammy smiled.

'Yes, I was thinking the same myself. I'll talk to Jude about it. The hybrids are doing the same.' He chuckled.

'I haven't seen you for ages, where have you guys been?' Mina asked.

'We went for a walk, it was nice. I see Sirocco is busy entertaining the children,' Jax said.

They watched as Sirocco trotted around with a little giggling boy on his back. The Inca children adored him, laughing loudly and taking turns riding him. They didn't see a horse often, let alone be able to ride one. They loved the attention. As did Sirocco by the look of it. Tammy smiled at him.

'He's having so much fun right now,' she said. 'Hard to find a good place to run with all these trees.'

'He won't leave your side is more to the point.' Ed laughed. 'He's just using those children as an excuse to stay near you.'

'Can you blame him?' Jax asked, then blushed as he realised what he had said.

'When are we leaving?' said Mikie cheerfully, winking at Jax and distracting the attention.

'Are you keen to go?' Mina asked.

'No, not at all, I could stay here forever. However, I don't think we have much of a window before the aliens realise an entire ship and crew are missing.'

'We shall leave first thing tomorrow morning,' Ed said. 'That is plenty of time to refresh ourselves before we continue on our journey.'

'Good morning, my friends. I couldn't help but overhear. Will you be going back via Cusco?' asked the king, as he came up beside Ed.

'Yes, we will,' Ed replied.

'Good,' said the king. He watched Sirocco, tenderly. 'That is an amazing horse, exceptional in every way. I see the bond with you and him, Tammy.'

'He's amazing,' she said.

'A good name too – the Sirocco wind is fierce and very appropriate to his speed and nature. But, alas, there is something not quite right with the scene.'

They all looked at the king, puzzled. He had a slight smile on his face, so his tone was more teasing than worrying, but they couldn't make out what he was teasing them about. Then he looked and pointed at Mina.

'You.'

'Me?' She gasped self-consciously. 'What have I done, what about me?'

'Yeah, what's Mina done now?' Mikie smiled, as usual, knowing what was coming.

'You see it too?' Quilla mused.

'See what?' Mina asked.

'Yes, I see it. I have a friend in Cusco who will have something for Mina. Ed, you must take her to see him. Tammy and this horse have a very good bond but there is something missing in Mina's life. If you tell my friend that I sent you and tell him to look at Mina, he will know what to do.' The king smiled.

'I don't understand…' Mina began to say, and then trailed off as the king laughed, loudly, and patted her on the back.

'You're not supposed to understand until you see my friend, and then it will be clear!'

'What are you talking about?' The curiosity was almost killing her.

'Time will tell.' He smiled kindly at her. 'It will be life changing for you! Son, why don't you and Diego take our guests on a small hunt before they leave, show them the Inca way?'

'Do you fancy a hunt?' Manco asked.

'No,' Tammy said quickly, and lowered her head.

'I'll stay with Tammy,' Jax said sympathetically.

'No, you can go; you don't have to stay with me.'

'I want to and besides, you know I feel the same way as you.'

'OK, thanks. We can go for a swim then?'

Jax nodded.

'I'm up for it, if you don't mind?' Mikie said.

'You should go for a swim in the waterfall. Take the slide, it's lovely,' Quilla suggested.

'Slide? That would be nice.' Jax smiled, looking at Tammy.

'Perfect.' She smiled back.

'I'm in for the hunt,' said Mina.

Everyone's faces registered surprise. Even Quilla looked shocked at the idea.

'What?' Mina said, holding her glare, then looking from the king, to Manco, to Ed.

'Well, err, it's just…' Manco started to say.

'Save your breath.' Diego laughed. 'There is no way you can say what you're thinking and get away with it. Mina is coming, like it or not, she is more of a man than most of the people in this village – well, in some ways that is.'

'More of a …' The king sighed.

'I'm not sure that is much of a compliment but thanks for vouching for me anyway, Diego,' Mina said.

'Well, I want to come too, in that case,' Quilla said.

'No,' the king answered swiftly.

'But, Father—'

'Women aren't allowed. It's out of the question.'

'What century do you think this is?' asked Mina defiantly.

The king stared at her, openly annoyed and not ashamed at showing it. Mina was challenging him in public.

'If Mina can join us, I see no reason why Quilla cannot. You believe in modernisation, Father,' Manco said.

'Yes I do, son, but not by placing my daughter in danger.'

'She has been in more danger than a hunt would put her in, and is more than capable,' Manco said.

'Please, Father…' began Quilla again.

'Girls can be just as strong as boys, even though you have the desire to protect us more than you would a son,' Mina said, smiling sweetly. 'I saved your son and Diego, and no man has ever saved me. In fact, only Tammy – a girl – has saved me. So, a little outdated, don't we think?'

'Tell him,' Diego said, nudging Quilla.

'Tell me what?' asked the king.

Quilla took a deep breath and let it out slowly. She looked between Diego and Mina and then made eye contact with her father. 'I've been hunting for years in secret, Father. All us women have. We are really good and sneak our catch in with the boys. We are in no danger. I'm sorry, Father, we just don't like the traditional way of having to do the women's roles while men do all the fun things.'

Everyone stared at the king. He was trapped by beautiful

girls glaring at him. He remembered his poor wife, who died so young and pleaded with him for more equality. Had he failed her? Had he failed his daughter? It was hard trying to keep traditions and yet change with the times. His wife would not want him to treat the girls differently, tradition or not. It was clear the young boys were happy hunting with women too. The old traditions were no longer important in this way. He could see that.

'I'm fully aware that saying no will make me look unreasonable, especially in front of everyone. I am not happy about this,' the king admitted, 'but I know your mother would also want more equality in this world. Things must change. Fine. I allow it.'

'I understand how you feel completely; they often make me feel like that.' Ed laughed.

'Yes, I can imagine.' The king laughed too and walked away.

'Girl power!' Mina said, putting her arm around Quilla.

'Girl power.' Quilla smiled sheepishly.

'It's funny watching the two of you,' Diego said. 'Quilla is so ladylike and you, Mina, are just a complete tomboy, aren't you? You're so different.'

'You know, you'd look lovely if you had your hair down more and tried to be a bit more ladylike,' Quilla said to Mina. 'All this girl power and boyishness is fine but sometimes, just sometimes, it is nice to embrace being a woman. Own what you are.'

'Good luck with that one!' Mikie chuckled. 'She's got so much testosterone I'm expecting her to have stubble before me!'

'Mikie!' Mina gasped and punched him hard in the arm.

'Yeah, Mina dressed as a lady? Not a chance,' Jax added.

Mina glared at them defiantly. 'Have you quite finished?'

'I tell you what,' said Quilla. 'After the hunt, tonight, why don't I lend you a dress and do your hair?'

'I'm happy with that,' Mina said, still holding her chin up in defiance. 'I can do girly.'

Mina couldn't help but smile at the idea; it would have made Lei laugh to hear this. How many years had she tried to turn Mina into a girl? It was easier to accept the idea from Quilla than it had been from Lei, and perhaps now it was time to prove that she could be anything she chose: absolutely anything.

'Let's get ready for the hunt then, gentlemen, and, of course, ladies.' Manco smiled and gave an exaggerated bow to Mina and Quilla.

Quilla walked past him, haughtily, and pushed him off balance as she headed to the hut. Manco fell into Mikie and they both laughed.

'Mina, come with me. I'll find us something appropriate to wear,' she said.

Mina followed, smiling.

*

Tammy and Jax watched as everyone left for the hunt. Sighing, they walked over towards the slide.

'It's hard, isn't it?' Jax said.

'Yes. But it's life.'

'They could have not gone and joined us for a swim.' Jax was annoyed. 'Why do we have to be the ones keeping the open mind and accepting them all the time?'

'It wouldn't be fair to force our views on them. Jude told me people would just resent it anyway. This is the tradition and way of the Inca people, it's what they do, and they're very proud of it. I cannot stop people from living how they have lived for so many generations.'

'You didn't say that about whale hunting in Japan,' Jax replied.

'I know and look at the trouble that caused. We need to learn from our mistake in Japan. Jude explained to us how they have suffered since – the population is starving. We caused that Jax, despite all our good intentions. You and I will change this world and help animals more, and one day put an end to all hunting. We just need to do it slowly and smartly.'

'I know you're right, Tammy. At least they aren't sacrificing people nowadays.' Jax laughed.

'Exactly, and they have allowed the girls to join in the hunt, so with time things will improve. One day, Jax, I would like to stop all humans eating meat.'

'I know. Me too. I was reading about how they used to hang and kill pigs in the past, how chickens were crammed into tiny spaces in dark barns, and what they did for beef was even crueller. Calves screamed incessantly for their mothers and were left out in fields or crammed into barns far too young.'

'I had to stop reading about it,' Tammy said sadly.

'Well, Tammy, people used to eat loads of sheep, pigs and beef. Inject them with hormones and feed them with animal meat and bone, even though they are herbivores, to unnaturally force extreme growth and get more meat off each animal.'

'That's awful.' Tammy gasped in disgust.

'I know. Ironically, this behaviour even killed a few hundred humans just under a century ago. It started in British herds in the mid-1980s after they were fed the processed animal remains of sheep infected with scrapie, a closely related brain-wasting disease. This led to millions of cows being killed because they developed a disease – Creutzfeldt-Jakob Disease, known as CJD – a neurological disease which causes rapid brain decay. It's always fatal as there's no cure. The brain and spine deteriorate rapidly.'

'Oh, those poor cows.' Tammy sighed.

'Then a CJD variant spread from the cows to humans who ate them. It was a nightmare and was never really eradicated until beef farming fully stopped. Not to mention how all the meat farming, in this manner, was contributing to climate change. Humans can be so foolish.'

'I don't understand why people would do that.' Tammy sighed sadly.

'The bigger the animal, the more burgers, the more money. It's always about money, Tammy.'

'Oh, that breaks my heart. Those poor animals. Those poor humans who died.'

'Talking of broken hearts – have you been talking with Jet?'

'A little. He's happy.'

'He isn't too far away then?'

'No, not too far.'

'I'm sorry you're so sad, Tammy,' said Jax.

'Oh, I'm fine,' she replied.

'I am the one person you cannot lie to.' Jax touched her cheek then tenderly tilted her chin to look at him. 'I see you.

I know you.'

Tammy smiled and blinked away the tears in her eyes. 'Bad times are coming and sad things are happening. Even worse things will happen soon and I've lost a great friend. I'm not going to be in the mood for dancing much, am I?'

Jax took her face in his hands. 'Not all the time. I will hold you when you cry and I will hold you when you dance. Tammy, I won't lie to you. We both know how hard this is going to be. There will be a lot of blood spilled, a lot of death, and no doubt many animals, humans and aliens sacrificed in a pointless war because no one can just grow up and discuss things rationally. Greed, as always, rules the day. I won't patronise you by lying about how awful this is going to be, and as strong as we all think we are, we'd be fools to think this won't change us. Those of us who survive will be broken. I just want you to know that I will be the glue that pieces you back together. No matter how long that takes. I will be there with you to help you heal and recover. We will have a life and we will dance.'

Their eyes were locked and she squeezed his hand tighter. They were at the slide now and Jax sat down, helping her to fit between his legs as he sat behind her. He wrapped his arms around her as she leaned back into his chest. He tightened his arms and tucked his face into the side of her neck and sighed. Tammy smiled and closed her eyes, enjoying feeling the heat of his breath on her neck. She felt warm and safe. She always did with Jax. It was nice.

'And now, we are going to go down this slide and we are going to scream and relish every fun second of it,' Jax whispered into her ear.

Tammy smiled as he pushed them off and away they

went. Both of them screamed all the way down as birds fluttered around their heads excitedly and joined them.

*

Later that day, it was clear that Charles was not recovering and he was not going to wake up. Too much time had passed without improvement. They had repeatedly tried to heal him and Quilla had even tried all the potions she could think of. The king was devastated that he had not seen the deceit and been able to save Charles, a friend he had known a long time, and had left Diego with no one to look after him. They all stood around Charles as he slept. He had never stirred and was even paler and weaker now.

The king sighed, staring in pain at his friend's face. 'I fear he will not last the night.'

'I just don't understand the extreme damage to his brain,' Tammy said. 'How anything can cause even more damage than what the aliens do is bizarre.'

'Drugs and gaming are horrendous. Both change the way the brain is formed and cause irreparable damage,' Ed explained. 'The brain never recovers.'

'Yes, it is very tragic. He came here to detox more than once. We would help him purge the substances from his body and nurse him back to health. Each time I saw how drugs were affecting him and taking away just that little bit more of him each time,' said the king. 'He was paranoid, anxious and mumbling, even after the detox. Once drugs have done certain damage there is no going back. Diego helped him stop drugs years ago but the gaming and gambling he always kept as a crutch. Except for when he came here to recover. Diego was a good influence on him.'

'I made him more stressed in life and made it worse,' Diego said sadly.

'No, Diego. That stress gave him purpose. His addictions and depression were his own demons to battle with – never anything from you.' The king placed his hand on Diego's shoulder. 'He loved you and all your problems and stress distracted him from his own. Don't ever blame yourself. You were the best thing that ever happened to him and I know. I know.'

Diego held back the tears in his eyes and nodded.

'I guess the reading just finished everything off,' Ed said heavily. 'I'm so very sorry, Diego. I will always be there for you and my home is your home now. You're welcome to live with us. You must meet the hybrid children.'

'And with us,' Quilla said, taking his hand.

'You will always be welcome here,' the king agreed. 'I shall prepare for burial and suggest we each spend some time saying our goodbyes. I'm so sorry.'

'I'm really sorry I couldn't heal him,' Tammy muttered.

'It's not your fault,' Jax and Diego said at the same time.

'There are holes and dark blotches and lumps on too many parts and they won't react to the energy. Too many little parts of the brain have been dead for too long. I'm so sorry.' She gave Diego a kiss on his cheek and left the hut.

One by one, everyone said a brief goodbye to Charles. The king whispered something in his ear, patted his shoulder and walked sadly out, and the others followed until Diego and Quilla were the only ones by his bed. Diego gulped and sat holding one of Charles' hands. Quilla knelt beside him, one hand resting on his shoulder. They didn't speak for a long time. She had seen this death but hadn't wanted to tell Diego. It was hard having visions. Charles had been a troubled man, but he was a good man all the same.

'We had an odd relationship, you know,' Diego said so quietly Quilla had to inch closer to hear.

'He isn't really my uncle so I always felt weird calling him that. He's an ex-boyfriend of my mum's. She loved him once. But his addictions made it hard for them to have a relationship. Charles told me he always felt kind of raw about being left with a child from her and another man when he had asked her to marry him and she had turned him down. We never knew why she did that. He found it very hard. He did love me though, that much I knew, and he certainly tried to parent me. He was clean when I was with him and didn't take a single drug. He would game a lot though and sometimes disappeared for a weekend then come back looking rough. I saw how relieved he was when my so-called father arrived and to finally have that responsibility taken off his shoulders. I felt bad for him. Why did mum do that to him?'

'My father was relieved slightly too at the thought of your father taking you. You're so powerful, Diego, it intimidated them. They don't know how to handle that power. And yet, they don't stop to think that you, since you were a tiny little boy, have had to handle it all alone. You had no choice. Charles knew people that only addicts can know. He used those connections to cover up for you and hide you and get you new identities when needed. I saw this in my visions. Your mum trusted and loved him. Having you certainly kept him clean from drugs, right? He would have always been sore about something. Father said he was more depressed before he had you and was far happier having you in his life. You were a gift to each other and I think your mum knew that,' said Quilla.

'Yes, I guess we were when you look at it that way. I'm going to miss him. Thank you, Charles. Thank you for always being there no matter what I did.'

Quilla felt tears fall on her cheeks as Diego bit his lip to stop it trembling. He wouldn't cry. He had probably never cried, she decided. As he sat staring at Charles he moved, slightly, and inhaled a difficult breath. He squeezed Charles' hand. Charles squeezed back and slowly, with difficulty, opened his eyes and gasped for air.

'Charles!' Diego exclaimed, pulling his hand into his chest and holding it tightly. 'Charles!'

Charles struggled to breathe and slowly focused on Diego. He tried to speak but his lips were too dry. Diego grabbed some water and tapped it on to his lips, pouring a little into his mouth.

'Charles, stay with me please,' Diego begged as tears began to slide down his cheeks.

Charles slowly shook his head. He swallowed a couple of times and looked at Diego. He was too weak to talk. He squeezed Diego's hand, smiled faintly and then slowly released his last breath. Diego squeezed his eyes shut and fell forward onto Charles' body. Quilla moved closer and wrapped herself around him and, unable to hold back anymore, he fell into her and cried as she rocked him gently and stroked his hair.

The king held an honourable ceremony that afternoon, rushing the preparation of Charles' body for the funeral, and buried him in a nearby cave with the rest of the Incas.

That was a privilege for Charles.

*

The plan was to eat well, sleep another good night, and enjoy dancing. The king insisted they take his boat along the river the next morning, which would get them to Cusco faster. Then it would be a hike up the mountain. Diego had sat for ages by the cave, heartbroken to have lost Charles. Eventually, he had gone for a swim with Quilla and washed for the dance.

They were all seated around the fire, passing food around and helping themselves to various tapa style food and lots of fish. Tammy, Quilla and Mina still hadn't joined them and the king sent Manco to go and hurry them up. When he returned, it was still another half an hour before they appeared.

Quilla emerged from her hut first with a large smile on her face, then Tammy, and Mina appeared next to her. Everyone looked and froze in shock. Either side of Mina, Tammy and Quilla beamed, pleased with the lady they had turned Mina into. Her long, wavy, golden hair fell loose around her shoulders and reached all the way down her back. They had placed a ring of pretty pink orchids upon her head, like a gypsy crown, and she had a little touch of red upon her lips. She wore a cream, silk, off the shoulder, long dress decorated with golden acorns and leaves around the edges, and golden sandals that laced up her calves. She looked natural and beautiful. Mina blushed at their silence. She suddenly felt awkward, until Quilla came to her rescue.

'They are so stunned they don't even know what to say.'

She laughed and hugged Mina warmly. 'That is by far the best compliment a woman could ever ask for.'

'It's true – you look amazing,' Ed said.

'I told you, didn't I? Didn't I tell you that you were more beautiful as a girl than a boy?' Quilla whispered.

'It's nice to see you in something other than trousers although you do look great in anything,' Mikie said.

'Yes, you could stick a potato sack on Mina and she'd look stunning,' Ed added. 'I shall be beating men away with a stick.'

'Come and sit down, eat something, Mina,' Manco said, offering her a seat next to him.

'Thank you,' she said politely.

She had remained aloof with him after the previous night, but she held no grudges. She could see the genuine shock on his face as he looked at her. Perhaps if she had dressed more like a girl, he would never have even looked at Tammy in the first place, judging by his expression now. She sat, awkwardly, still feeling strange in a dress and with her hair down. It kept falling over her face and she quite liked how it hid her from people. She couldn't remember the last time it wasn't in a plait.

Jax took a photo and sent it to Lei. He never knew that it brought tears to her eyes.

*

The next morning they said goodbye to the Incas at the village and hiked to the river. The boat was hidden well and like two wooden banana-shaped canoes joined together by a raft. Sirocco was able to stand on the flat raft section in the middle; it seemed just about strong enough, whilst the others took places in the banana-shaped ends.

'I just hope it takes our weight, otherwise we'll be in trouble if we end up in the water,' said the king.

'Yes, keep well clear of the water,' Manco warned.

'Why? What's in the water?' Mina asked terrified.

'Piranha, and they'll snap the meat off your hands if you dangle them in,' Manco said.

'What?'

'Fish with tiny little teeth. They can devour flesh off big prey as they attack in large packs,' Diego added.

'What! Why do you live in such a place? Why do you have a boat here? Why didn't you tell me this when we came for a swim?' Mina exclaimed, almost hysterically.

'There are none where we swim but we are heading out into the open now,' Manco explained.

'Well, we don't have to worry about that really, not with Tammy with us,' Ed said reassuringly.

'You can tell me what you mean by that as we sail down the river,' the king replied.

'You already know,' Quilla said. 'You have the visions too.'

'Yes, my dear, but sometimes it is nice to have people tell you.'

'Know what?' asked Manco.

'Well, you'll hear soon enough about what the Children of Pisces can do,' Quilla said and smiled at Diego.

'Manco, untie the rope over there and push the boat from the bank, it's time to be on our way,' the king ordered.

'I'm not getting in!' Mina stood, arms folded, on the bank.

Diego swooped her up into his arms and jumped into the boat with her struggling and screaming. The boat rocked.

'Whoa!' Ed said loudly.

'Get off me!' Mina yelled, punching Diego on the arms.

Diego held her fast. Manco untied the boat, jumped back in, sat next to his father at the back and started the little engine. Diego carefully put Mina down as they headed along the river. She huffed and glared at him angrily. Mikie and Jax exchanged looks. They knew they wouldn't have gotten away with doing that. Diego could get away with murder as far as Mina was concerned. They found it highly entertaining and couldn't wipe the smiles from their faces.

'Dear Sis, I mean this with the greatest respect, but stop being a diva,' Diego said. 'You're hardier than you think.'

TWENTY

KASHVI

PERU

They had been gliding down the river all morning, eating the hefty packed lunch they had brought with them. Tammy was now fast asleep in front of Jax, her head resting back on his chest as he stroked her hair. Everyone else took in the view of the Amazon as they drifted along. The river meandered along the mountains and lush vegetation. They had tried to avoid rafting and stick to the calmer waters, which wasn't always possible, and at such times, when the rapids were bouncing the canoes, Sirocco chose to canter along the banks rather than balance on the raft-like centre of the boat during the rapids. Mina loved the rafting, the bouncing and bobbing, declaring it the best fun she had experienced in all her life. No one could argue with her; it was enjoyable.

'The river is calm for now and we will find more rapids later on. You will do a lot of this rafting with us when you return,' Quilla said. 'Manco and I will take you to even better rapids. We are both very skilled at this.'

'I can't wait,' Mina replied. Suddenly, something moved in the water next to her and she screamed. 'What is it? Is that a pack of piranha?'

Manco smiled menacingly at Diego and winked. 'I don't know, best check it out,' he said and promptly dived over the side of the boat.

'Manco!' Mina shouted and gaped after him.

Manco disappeared under the water. Ed, about to get up, received a nudge from the king, who smiled and shook his head. Ed nodded. Diego stood up, made a big deal about taking off his shirt and shoes, and scanned the water.

'Oh, this isn't good,' he muttered, shaking his head and acting scared.

'Why would he do that? Why would he just do that?' Mina squealed.

Diego jumped over the side and swam next to the boat. He duck dived, looking for Manco in the dark, murky waters.

'Diego, get out,' Mina insisted. 'Is everyone insane? Mikie, wake Tammy up!'

Mikie was in the same boat as Tammy and watching calmly. 'She's tired,' he said.

'What is wrong with you all?'

There was another splash next to Diego, and then another further away. Mina's eyes darted from one splash to another. And then she saw something not too far away.

'Is that... Is that a crocodile?' Mina gasped, pointing to the eyes and log-like form floating in the river.

'Yup, sure looks like it,' Diego said.

'Get out! Get out!'

Suddenly, Diego screamed as he was pulled under the water. Mina shouted his name and leaned over, trying to grab his arm, but she was too late. Diego vanished under the water. His shocked face was the last thing she saw. Mina scanned the water for signs of movement. Nothing.

'Mikie, wake Tammy up! Jax, wake her – what is wrong with you?'

Mina was too busy shouting orders and screaming to see the smiles creeping onto everyone's faces. Mikie and Jax shook their heads in disbelief. Suddenly, out of nowhere. Manco hauled himself up in front of Mina and made her jump. She fell back into the boat as he laughed loudly, joined by Diego as he surfaced too. They both hung onto the side of the boat.

'What is wrong with you? There is a crocodile over there! And things splashing,' Mina said.

'That is just a caiman,' Manco said, pointing. 'And he only eats little fish and lizards. Not interested in us.'

'What about the piranha?'

'Ah, well, they are a bit busy avoiding those at the moment,' Manco said and pointed. 'The botos are here.'

'The what?' Mina looked at where he pointed but could see nothing.

The water's surface was still. Then, a dolphin came out of nowhere and arched over the river before landing with a smooth dive back under the water. It was an unusual dolphin, with a strange protruding round head and an elongated snout full of tiny teeth. As Mina stared, Quilla removed her dress and in a t-shirt and underwear, joined Manco and Diego in the water. Mina watched as they all swam with the dolphins.

'Botos are fresh water pink river dolphins,' the king said to Mina, smiling. 'They feed on the piranha so they won't bother us.'

'Unless you're a man skinny dipping!' Quilla laughed and pretended to pull Manco's shorts down. They fought in the water and he pulled her under. The dolphins watched them curiously.

'They look funny for dolphins,' Mina said.

'Their bulging head is an organ used for sonar to find prey through the murky waters. They have whiskers on their noses too, which help them to pinpoint the location of piranha and other species of fish,' the king explained.

'And they're multicoloured too. Pink?' asked Mina.

'Yes, they're born greyish. Some are pink because their capillaries are close to their skin, some are blue, and there's even the occasional albino. They are known for being aggressive with each other and fighting a lot, so their skin turns pink as it heals, reducing other colours the more they fight. The darker pink males, more flamingo pink, are more aggressive than paler pinks, and this helps to attract its mate.'

'Wow, they're amazing. And huge,' Mikie said.

'Yes, they grow to almost three metres long, and weigh about 180 kilograms. Legend has it that the pink river dolphins transform into handsome men and seduce the women of the town. Other legends claim that if you go swimming alone, dolphins can take you to a magical underwater city. Many of the locals believe that it is bad luck to harm these dolphins, and especially to eat them. This semi-magical condition can help these lovely animals to be protected and treated with respect. It is a privilege to swim with them. Try it,' the king urged them all.

Jax nudged Tammy awake and they all enjoyed a fun swim. Even Mina had to admit it was an amazing experience. Mina remained nervous of the occasional caiman that swam by, even though they didn't seem at all interested in them. The king showed Ed how to swim alongside them and duck dive the Inca way, which was rather like a mermaid. Ed loved it. He imagined bringing Jude here one day to do this. Manco, Quilla and Diego remained in the water long after the others got out, and using their spears, they dived deep, caught fish and threw them on to the canoe.

'That's dinner sorted,' Manco said proudly.

Mina rolled her eyes in disgust as a piranha landed and flopped by her foot. 'You said they weren't around us! I hate you all,' she declared.

*

Ed and the king steered them through the river bends as the others napped after their swim. Mikie sat up from his sleep and turned sharply to look at Tammy. He had tuned into her dream and it had startled him. She was again sleeping, exhausted from all the healing she had tried on Charles, yet it was not a deep sleep. She tossed and turned, mumbling words only he could understand as she dreamt. Jax had been watching her, unable to sleep on the boat, but now his gaze was on Mikie.

'She often dreams like this,' Jax said. 'Perhaps I should wake her up.'

'No, she is getting information,' Mikie replied.

'Information?'

'Yes. Just wait.'

Having overheard the conversation, the others turned and looked at Tammy. Her words were too quiet to make out, except for Mikie reading her mind, and she was obviously bothered by something. She remained like this for several minutes and then suddenly sat up with a start.

'No, stay there!' she shouted into thin air.

'It's OK,' Jax said, putting a comforting arm around her.

Tammy looked around, slowly realising where she was, and took a slow, shaky breath. She rubbed her forehead, found it was wet with sweat, and then blushed when she realised everyone was watching her.

'Where is she?' Mikie asked.

'You know?' she said.

'Yes, I caught parts of it as you slept.'

'Where is who?' Jax asked.

'Kashvi,' Tammy said.

'Who?' Mina asked.

'A tiger,' Mikie replied.

'What are you going on about?' Jax frowned, looking from Tammy to Mikie.

'I saw a tiger, she is called Kashvi, and is dying. We need to help her,' Tammy said.

'There are no tigers here,' the king said.

'Yes, there is,' Tammy said. 'She isn't supposed to be, but she's here all right.'

'You were just thinking about where to pull over and camp for the night, weren't you?' Mikie said.

'Yes, as a matter of fact, I was,' said the king.

'Then go where Tammy suggests and we can find Kashvi while you all set up camp. Would that be OK?'

'Do you really think there is a tiger here?' Manco asked. 'I've always wanted to see one.'

'If Tammy says there's a tiger, then I guarantee there's a tiger,' Ed replied, matter of factly.

'Is there a large rock structure somewhere along this river?' Tammy asked.

'Yes,' the king replied. 'Not too far from here, just past a bend. A short walk from the riverbank.'

'Can we camp there? She is near the rock structure.'

'Yes, we shall camp there tonight, but why is there a tiger here?' the king asked.

'She was on a small aircraft, in a cage, taken from her own land. They were bringing her here, but they crashed in the rainforest. She crawled out and dragged herself away from the wreckage to hide. She is injured badly'

'Would poachers have a reason to bring tigers to South America?' Ed asked, stroking his chin in thought.

'Perhaps they might. There have been stories of rich families living in these parts and fancying pet tigers,' said the king. 'They're considered to be a pet of distinction and I have heard rumours that they will pay handsomely for them.'

'But they are endangered, under protection; we were only able to release a few after Pisces. How can people think like that?' Ed said with dismay.

'That may not be the case, it's only rumours I've heard.'

'Tammy, will you be able to take us to the aircraft that crashed?' Ed asked.

'Yes, once she's safe.' She sighed.

*

Shortly after the bend they pulled up on the riverbank and secured their canoes. Sirocco was overjoyed to be off the boat and pranced around in the shallow water. Tammy laughed and helped unload the camping gear. He would have to stay at camp; the rocks would not be safe for him to climb and there was no need for him to join them.

'Father, Quilla and I can set up camp and prepare food whilst you are away,' Manco said.

'Thank you, son. Come, Tammy, I'll lead the way.'

'Shall I stay here?' Mina asked.

'I'd prefer it if you came, I could do with our combined energy to help heal her,' Tammy said.

Mina nodded and walked with Diego. The king, Ed, Jax, Diego, Mikie and Mina followed Tammy up the hill and towards the rocks. Breathless and sweating profusely, they came across some blood on one of the rocks, and silently followed the trail. It led to a cave and Tammy stopped, raised her hand, and indicated that they should all wait. She crouched down and crawled into the cave.

'Is that safe?' asked the king.

'Yes, for her,' Mikie replied.

Tammy crawled on her hands and knees, the cave barely large enough, and soon came upon the tiger. She was lying down, breathing slowly, barely awake. Tammy touched her head and stroked her. Kashvi was relieved she had come.

'I need to get you out of here,' Tammy said, softly.

She ran her hands over the tiger, feeling her wounds and sighing at what she found.

'Jax, can you hear me?' she shouted.

'Just about, are you OK?' he answered.

'Yes, but she has a broken leg, I don't know how to move

her.'

Mikie looked at Jax, who frowned.

'Just don't move her leg in any way. There isn't much room in there, is there?' he shouted back to her.

'No, none at all really.'

'Is it a smooth surface, the floor I mean?'

'Yes, pretty much.'

'Do you think there's enough room to get a stretcher underneath her?'

'Probably, why, do you have a stretcher?' she replied.

'Err, no.'

Everyone looked around, searching for something they could use, and Jax sighed. He was about to say there was nothing they could use when he noticed Diego and Mina getting excited about something and went over to see what they had. Diego had made a stretcher for a dead boar he had carried and was telling Mina about it. Mina was really good at making things and had made her own skateboards from scratch all her life. Together, they were grabbing long pieces of wood, pulling off vine and large leaves and discussing how to combine them.

'That's genius,' Jax said as they worked together.

'Think it might not hold her weight though,' Mina mumbled.

'It will if you tie in some more sticks in a cross shape at the back. Tie them in the corners like this,' Diego said. 'If it can hold a boar, it can hold a cat.'

'Like this?' Mina asked, showing him her effort.

'No, a little more in the corner like this.' He demonstrated what he meant. 'Yes, that's it, Mina. Perfect.'

'Diego, where did you learn this?' Jax asked.

'Inca first aid,' he winked.

The king laughed out loud as he and Ed watched. They had taught Diego Inca survival skills and he had remembered a lot well. Diego and Mina wrapped the vine repeatedly along, creating a fairly solid bed to lie on. The wooden sticks were longer, allowing them to hold them while walking in between.

'That's just amazing. Well done, guys.' Ed smiled, shaking his head in disbelief.

'Tammy, we have something you can push under her and pull her out on,' Jax shouted. 'I'll slide it forward to you now.'

Jax pushed the stretcher in as far as he could, until it reached her feet. Tammy lay flat on her back and moved the stretcher above her until it was on the other side of her body. When the stretcher was in between her and the tiger, she rolled awkwardly back on to her belly. She tried to push it under Kashvi but it wasn't quite flat and smooth enough. She needed to lift her up slightly but there was not enough room to lift the tiger and push the stretcher under. She was very restricted with what she could do on her belly. Tammy huffed in annoyance. She tried to find part of the vine on the stretcher that was still alive – it was all dead, except one small area on the bottom. She focused on the vine, made it grow and move around the tiger, lifting her up slightly as she pushed the stretcher underneath. Kashvi moaned with the pain and Tammy sent healing energy as a pain relief to help. She'd done it. Then, she started to back out, pulling the stretcher as she did, a tiny distance at a time. Jax was there, grabbing her ankle and pulling on her. As she reached the cave entrance, Mikie joined in and they pulled her out effortlessly.

When Kashvi came into view, they gasped at the extent of her injuries. She was covered in blood and her white bone stuck out from her leg. Jax gulped, taking in excessive head and rib injuries and likely internal bleeding, and looked at Tammy.

'We'll do it,' she said.

'It's a really bad comminuted fracture, Tammy.' Jax looked at her.

'I know it's bad, Jax. Can you fix it?'

She watched Jax examine the back leg of the tiger. He sighed.

'With your energy healing – maybe. She should have surgery. I can but it will hurt her. You just make sure she doesn't attack me, OK?'

'I can make the bits of bone float out and away,' Mina said.

'Good, do it,' Tammy replied. 'Mikie, Diego, Mina, can you place your hands on the tiger with me please? We'll use energy to help with the pain,' Tammy said, taking Kashvi's head into her hands.

'OK,' Mina said. 'Here?'

Tammy nodded as Mina placed her hands on the tiger's shoulders, Jax took her back leg, Mikie took her stomach and hip area, and Diego placed his hands on her spine.

'This OK?' Diego asked.

'Yes.' Tammy nodded. 'Jax, wait for my signal. The rest of you must think of a bright white light with a light blue colour around the edges. I will lead, you follow the vision.'

Jax stared at Tammy, not sure what the signal would be, and watched her close her eyes and concentrate. The others did the same. The king and Ed watched as a white mist started to emerge around the body of the tiger. Without opening her eyes, Tammy nodded, and Jax knew this was the signal. He took a deep breath, focused on the bone sticking out from the tiger's back leg and then, with all his weight, he quickly snapped it back into place. There was a loud and horrible *crack* and everyone cringed. The tiger roared and moaned in agony briefly before passing out. A few more strands of bone broke away and dropped into the flesh and Mina floated them out.

'The energy is working,' Mikie said.

'Yes, keep going, follow my thoughts,' Tammy replied.

As Tammy moved throughout Kashvi's body, Mikie helped amplify what she was seeing to the others. They could see the cells, bone and tissue on a microscopic scale and the light moving through. Blue, green, orange, yellow, violet – different colours for different purposes. The blood began to clot and stop bleeding out, holes closed, tendons re-joined each other, and tissues repaired themselves. They could feel Tammy working her way through the body, focusing on one wound after another, and making it better. They found a bullet embedded in her rib cage, which must have been there a long time, never treated, always a little painful. They watched it slowly wedging itself free, working its way to the skin's surface as it exited and dropped to the ground. Then the hole slowly healed and closed up.

Tammy understood that cells grow in number through a process called mitosis, whereby replicas of chromosomes in parent cells duplicate to form daughter cells, and the prophase, metaphase, anaphase and telophase each happened in order to prepare for cell reproduction and healing. She could instruct, in intricate detail, each phase to happen rapidly. Healing at a cellular level. The others watched as the cells moved and changed.

She also knew the different tissue types in the human body; epithelial, nervous, muscular, connective, areolar, adipose, lymphoid, yellow elastic, white fibrous, cartilage, and so on. Tammy enhanced the speed of cell and bone production and new threads of bone began to forge and seal the crack from the break. Then, an area of healing tissue began to form around the break, called a callus, and seal the damaged area. Then the tendons, tissues, muscles and cells in that area began to heal rapidly. There was one very large, gaping wound that wouldn't heal though. It had been caused by a piece of metal from the cage gashing into Kashvi like a knife wound. Right in her abdomen.

'Jax, we can't...' Tammy began.

'I know,' he said. He was working fast with Tammy, stitching up the holes and cleaning up the mess. Digging into his bag, he retrieved his medical superglue. Tammy opened her eyes and smiled at him as he started to glue the wound together. She marvelled at the way he worked, careful and precise, sealing the wound with delicate hands. Their energy eased the tiger's pain and now she was becoming alert again.

'One more thing,' Jax whispered.

He took a needle from his bag and moved Mina out of the way as he injected Kashvi in the back of her neck.

'What's that?' Mina asked.

'It will stop any infections,' he said.

'We should get her back to the boat,' Tammy said.

'That was incredible,' said the king, in almost a whisper.

'Yes, well done, you guys, that was amazing teamwork. Now, Tammy, what about the plane?' said Ed.

'I'll take them to it if you think you can carry Kashvi?' Mikie told Tammy.

Tammy nodded. He could read her mind and know exactly what she knew. Diego and Mina took one end of the stretcher, while Tammy and Jax took the other. They carefully negotiated their way over the rock formation back to the boat. Ed, the king and Mikie watched them go before setting off for the crash.

*

'Over there,' Mikie said, pointing.

Ahead of them was a plane, or rather what used to be a plane, half hanging in the trees. The king looked up at it whilst Ed mooched around in the wreckage that lay on the ground. He found some papers, the cage the tiger had been in, and the body of the pilot. He looked at the papers and sighed.

'You were right, it was a special delivery to an American family living in Lima. A pet tiger, poached from India,' Ed said.

'I'd hoped I was wrong.' The king shook his head sadly.

'There is another body up in the plane,' Mikie said.

'Alive?' Ed asked.

Mikie shook his head.

'Then there is no reason to stay here longer.'

'On my way back, I shall investigate this, find out who the tiger was intended for, and ensure he is prosecuted,' the king promised.

'I would appreciate that,' Ed said.

'It's the least I can do. This is my home and we work with nature. I know what you did for the animals on this planet, Ed, and I can only do my best to continue with your good work.'

'I thank you. It is not your fault,' Ed said, placing his hand on his shoulder. 'You are a good man.'

*

Manco and Quilla had gathered some fruit and were cooking the piranha on the fire – the camp was ready for the night and looked cosy. Manco had skewered the fish on small branches of wood and had argued with Quilla about preparing it properly. She had wanted him to fillet and gut it properly. He had wanted to leave the eyes and teeth on for effect. Manco had won the argument. Hammocks hung from the trees and small pots of water sat ready for their guests. Kashvi was near to the fire, the heat warming her limbs, and Manco had caught some more fresh fish from the river for her to eat. They had done all the energy healing that they could do for now. Jax had closed and bandaged all the wounds and created a makeshift splint of wood, bandages and leaves. Just the one wound kept bleeding and failed to seal.

'This superglue just isn't holding and I'm out of pain killers,' Jax moaned.

Quilla took her healing pouch and gave him the herbal superglue that she had invented. 'Try this,' she said.

'What is it?' Jax asked.

'A herbal superglue I created. It has herbal properties to

speed healing and numb the area. And this will help with the pain,' she said pulling out a small flask of liquid.

'Thanks,' Jax replied and applied the superglue while Tammy dropped some liquid into the tigers mouth. 'Wow, this superglue is genius!'

Quilla smiled.

'I want more of this, it is the best medical glue I have ever seen Quilla. Will you teach me how to make this?' Jax asked.

'Yes, as long as you keep it secret,' she nodded.

'I'm going to stretch my legs and meditate, I'm tired. Can you give Jax the recipe for the pain killer too please, Quilla? I can get the seeds and grow them and help to make more for when we are at war and can't use the energy pain relief healing all the time.' Tammy asked.

'Of course. I'm happy to help. Herbs are stronger than anything synthetically created.' Quilla replied.

'Great, I'll leave you to it then. I'll meditate with Sirocco as we ride and clear my energy.'

'Enjoy your ride, Tammy,' Jax told her.

Then they sat whispering as Quilla shared her secrets with Jax and he took notes on the screen from his watch. When he had the secret ingredients Jax thanked her and she looked awkwardly at him.

'What is it?' Jax asked.

'Can I ask you something personal, it might make you feel uncomfortable,' Quilla whispered.

'Go for it.' Jax was all ears.

'Do you feel awkward about the age difference with you and Tammy? We are both older than them. I don't see Diego as the same age as my brother. In no way at all,' Quilla sighed and looked down at her hands. 'My father isn't too happy about it.'

'Quilla, age doesn't matter. There is a big age gap between Ed and Jude and my parents. My father is fifteen years younger than my mum!' Jax smiled.

'No way!' Quilla gasped.

'Yes! However, Tammy and Diego, all of them, are not like normal humans. Plus, they're almost thirteen. I don't worry about it and I don't think you should either.'

'Thank you, Jax. I appreciate that.'

'Your father will get used to it. It's more uncomfortable for Manco, I'd imagine,' Jax told her. 'Hard to be a prince with someone like Diego at your side.'

'Yes, it is a problem. Manco is shorter, he doesn't have the abilities that my father and I have, and it hits his self-esteem harder than people realise. Even all the women, and I confess myself too, see Diego as our future leader. I don't know how Manco can handle this,' Quilla sighed heavily. 'I love them both so much.'

'We will help them and find a way,' Jax said, patting her hand as she squeezed them anxiously. 'I sometimes feel intimidated by Mikie, and Diego is even more powerful in some way and yet I handle it. I will talk with Manco and help him.'

'Thank you Jax, that would be great, just not yet. It doesn't matter with Diego going away for now. Perhaps in the future when we all come back together and you can share with him how you handle it,' Quilla smiled and nodded at him. 'You have brought me much relief.'

'And you have created an incredible glue. We must both make more as I fear we shall need lots and lots of it,' Jax replied.

'I think you are right. I shall get the women on it immediately. Thank you again.'

'You're welcome, Quilla, and remember, they need us. I see how Diego hangs on every word you say. Your guidance is precious to him. I keep Tammy grounded. Manco is needed as a solid friend to Diego, so he isn't alone. They need us. I also think that their alien DNA gives them an enhanced wisdom far beyond their years. Sometimes I think Tammy is older than me,' Jax smiled.

'I know what you mean. I keep reminding myself that Diego is younger. He feels older than me sometimes.'

'Exactly, so don't worry about it or whatever anyone else thinks. The road ahead is going to be ugly and we all need to support each other. I'm always here for you if you want to talk. If you need anything.' Jax put his hand on her shoulder and nodded.

'Thank you. And the same right back at you. Always,' Quilla replied and breathed a sigh of relief.

They looked over at Mina who was starting to pace back and forth in agitation. Manco liked Mina now, and yet she was never going to like him back. It was obvious to everyone but Manco. He could have his choice of every girl in the village and he thought that applied to the whole world. Mina was going to teach him a hard truth and Quilla knew it. Yes, her brother was a lot younger than Diego in many ways. Quilla felt sorry for him and protective. It felt good knowing Jax would help her.

'Are we safe here, so close to the water's edge?' Mina asked.

'No,' Manco replied, looking down at the fish he was

filleting for the tiger, keeping his face hidden.

'Then why are we here?' Mina asked sternly.

Manco looked up at her and smiled sweetly.

'You are such a tease,' Quilla said. 'Of course it's safe, Mina.'

Tammy and Jax declined the fish and stayed with the fruit. Quilla had kindly salted and steamed some weeds and herbs for them. Mina reluctantly took the plate Manco had given her, staring down at the teeth and gaping mouth of the fish. Gingerly, she took a piece and nibbled it. It tasted salty. She tried some more.

'This isn't too bad,' she said.

'Piranha is OK,' Manco said. 'Eat up and you can have a bit more.'

'It's really salty,' Ed remarked.

'And has some sort of pungent aftertaste I can't quite make out,' Mikie said. 'I can't decide if I like it.'

'Once you get past the salt there is a seaweed and blood aftertaste, but the salt mostly covers that. It will fill you up anyway.' The king smiled.

Mina gagged at the description and swallowed the piece she was chewing reluctantly. She was so sick and tired of strange food.

'Well, Tammy, first Jet, then the lions in Africa and now a tiger in Peru. Is there ever a cat in need that won't find you?' Ed smiled.

They were sitting around the campfire, eating and settling down for the evening, Tammy once more leaning backwards on Jax's chest, her hand stroking Kashvi lying at her side. Pain relief and healing energy happened automatically with every stroke Tammy gave. Jax stroked

Tammy's hair as Tammy stroked Kashvi. More than anyone else, Mikie knew how his sister needed Jax, how his strength kept her grounded. Mikie decided that the pain and conflict Tammy felt constantly, the voices and noises she heard from all the surrounding animals non-stop, was far worse than he faced with humans. He could zone out but she could not. She was part of the animal kingdom in a way. Her pain and exhaustion was real. Mikie worried about her. Sometimes the animals awoke her wild side and she had the sense to kill as fiercely as a tiger. Jax had something unusual about him – a sense of calm and maturity and an uncanny sixth sense that told him what Tammy was going through. It was almost as if Jax could read Tammy as well as Mikie could. He was who Tammy turned to when she needed safety, escape and warmth. Nobody but Jax could give her that. Mikie hoped he could have a relationship like that one day.

'For all our powers combined, we couldn't have saved that tiger if it wasn't for you,' Mikie said to Jax.

'You're right, Mikie. You did good, Jax, I'm proud of you. I'm proud of all of you,' Ed said.

'What will you do with her?' Manco asked.

'We cannot leave her here,' Ed replied.

'She won't be strong enough to go free again, will she?' Jax said, looking at Tammy.

'No, she won't, and she has had too rough a time of it in the wild. She needs an easier life.' Tammy smiled. 'Jax, I was thinking of your tiger, at the zoo.'

'What a wonderful idea! Uncle, could we breed her with my tiger? She will be happy there,' he said.

'That sounds like a good idea. We could then make amends for what was wrongly done here and set their children free, try to build the numbers back up in India. How does that sound?' Ed smiled.

'That sounds just perfect,' Jax said.

'I have seen the events of today with my own eyes and still I don't believe what my own eyes tell me,' said the king.

'That's nothing. You should have seen the anacondas spitting out aliens,' Manco said, making them all laugh.

'Tell me, Tammy, you said the tiger is called Kashvi, but how did you know? Is that what you named her?' asked the king.

'I don't know, perhaps I did or she did. I just knew that was her name.'

'I wondered because the name Kashvi is a typical native Indian name. I wouldn't have thought you would have known where she was from, and since the tiger is from India, well…'

'Really? How bizarre.' Tammy raised her eyebrows. 'I don't know; it was determined in my dream somehow, by her or by me. I wonder what that means.'

'Well, the name itself, according to the ancient Sioux Indians, means *friend to everyone*,' the king said.

'Well, perhaps that is why she chose the name,' Tammy said.

'But, did she or did you?' the king asked.

'I really don't know.'

'Have you ever learned about the Sioux Indians or anything where you might have come across the name?' Ed asked.

'No,' she said honestly.

'Well, wonders never cease. Animals give themselves names.' Ed smiled.

'So how long will it take to get to Cusco?' Diego asked.

'Are you in a hurry to get there?' Quilla said, lowering her eyes to hide her feelings.

'Yes, in a way; I've heard so much about Vivacity Island I'd love to see it, but also no because…' He trailed off as they looked into each other's eyes.

'We'll be there tomorrow, won't we, Father?' Manco interrupted.

'Yes. We won't camp tomorrow night but shall start very early in the morning and continue down the river. We will arrive late.'

'Will we still stop to see your friend?' Mina asked.

'Definitely. I shall tell you exactly how to get there, it's on your way.' The king smiled at her, knowingly.

'What is he going to give me?'

'A lobotomy!' Diego laughed loudly.

'He knows how to put puzzles back together. You will see.' The king said with a knowing smile.

Quilla winked at Mina and smiled. Mina, frowning, couldn't guess what it might be. Everyone tried to manipulate the king into giving them a hint. Even Diego tried to get Mikie to read his mind. Mikie refused to say anything or help, and the king wouldn't give in at all.

TWENTY ONE
CUSCO

PERU

Navigating rapids, the river and its tributaries, and piranha territory, they finally arrived on the Red River. Where their journey had begun. A gathering of men hovered along the riverbank, calling out to them and offering their services, selling anything and everything: donkeys, minibuses, vans, ponies, food, water, wine. Another man was waiting for them on the bank. He had seen them coming down the river, and hoped for their custom.

'This man I can vouch for,' the king told Ed, pointing at the man. 'I have used him several times. He will take you up the mountain with his horse and cart.'

Whilst the king arranged the transport, everyone hugged and kissed Manco and Quilla, saying they would love to come back soon. Manco gripped Diego warmly by the shoulders and smiled at him.

'My good friend, return soon, I will not survive my

sister's misery at your loss for long,' he said.

'I will,' Diego replied.

'Quilla…' Diego walked over to Quilla and hugged her tightly. He felt lost for words.

'Make sure you come back,' she said, her voice sounding strained.

Diego realised she was trying hard not to cry, and his heart leapt with joy. He couldn't help it. It was confirmation that she wasn't just being kind and that she did indeed like him. He was glad. He kissed her on the cheek, still not knowing what to say, deciding nothing was probably the best he had. He didn't want anyone to hear how strained his own voice would be right now. He squeezed her hand then gave her another kiss on the cheek before reluctantly pulling away, leaving something in her palm. Frowning, she looked down at his gift – a retablo. Quilla gasped at the small wooden box he had hand carved himself. A retablo was a special gift in Peru; a sophisticated Peruvian folk art in the form of a small box broken down into different compartments and shaped like a little house with doors on the front. As she opened the front doors, painted beautifully with art that resembled the nebula Diego saw in his dream, she gasped at what she saw inside. Diego had carved, glued and painted tiny little figures inside the box. There was a shelf dividing the little house in half. On the walls and sides were stars and elephant trunk shapes from the nebula, and a spaceship. On the bottom shelf was anacondas, aliens, Jet, Sirocco, Manco, the king, Mina and Tammy – tiny figures resembling each of them. On the top shelf was Quilla and Diego dancing, the moon, the stars and a fox figurine in front of the moon. Next to Quilla was a little labrador puppy, fox red in colour, just like Mama Quilla's fox in the story she had told him.

'When I return, I will bring you that puppy, and we will train him together,' Diego whispered.

Quilla looked up at him, tears in her eyes. 'Her. A girl. I always wanted a puppy.'

'I know. I remember you telling me. Her, then.' Diego smiled and turned away. He approached the king. 'I owe you so much and I don't know what I can say to even show how grateful I am.'

'You owe me nothing, my boy, but the promise of your return visit. You will break my daughter's heart and my son's friendship if you don't.' He smiled, resting his hand on Diego's shoulder.

'Thank you, for everything.'

'You are welcome, and I am deeply sorry about Charles. My home will always be open to you, Diego, never forget that. I just hope that when we next see you it's for a good reason, but my heart tells me it will not be a pleasant visit.'

'No, perhaps not. Not with the war coming.'

'Exactly. Until we next meet, my friends.' The king nodded to them all as they said their final farewells and left.

They loaded the tiger and everyone on to the cart while Tammy and Jax rode Sirocco next to the horse pulling the cart. They looked over their shoulder, waving, as they disappeared along the road. Manco, Quilla and the king would have to sail back now, whilst they had a huge mountain to climb before they could get a HP home. Mina looked at Diego and his sad face. She realised that she had never liked anyone enough to miss them. Not even Lei really – they barely spent time together when they lived in

Notting Hill. Maybe Kieran, Josh and Dan. She did miss her friends a little and wondered how they were getting on in agent training. Life had been so busy she hadn't had time to think, but for the moment she smiled as she remembered them and the trouble they used to get in to. Would she see them again?

*

It took a day to get up the mountain and their breathing got harder as they went. The guide was taking them to the ranch, as directed by the king. It was after lunch when they arrived. They dismounted at the farm entrance.

'I don't feel very good,' Mina said.

'I know, altitude sickness is horrible, even just adjusting to it is unpleasant. It will pass soon enough,' Ed said, putting his arm around her shoulder.

She bent down, placed her hands on her knees, put her head between her legs and tried to breathe. Her head was spinning and she felt faint. After a couple of slow, deep breaths, she felt a little better. She looked up and saw Tammy walking around, guiding Sirocco, a huge smile on her face.

'You aren't affected at all, are you?' Mina asked.

'No,' Tammy said, distracted by noises elsewhere.

'That's just so unfair! You look alright as well, Jax.'

'I'm not too bad, obviously Tammy is better than me. I reckon we have good lungs because we swim and run a lot, so we have trained our lungs well and probably grab more oxygen than you guys.' Jax shrugged.

'I think you're probably right,' Ed smiled.

'I'm fine too. Think it's all the martial arts that I do.

Could be the energy we have too, healing our lungs fast. Tammy and I have been using energy all our life and heal faster than you, Mina. I think it's definitely the energy too,' Mikie said.

'I run a lot and have been running up and down the Inca place, so I'm OK also,' Diego added.

'How good for you lot!' Mina spat. 'I do gymnastics and skate boarding and I'm fit and healthy too.'

'I think you're unfit and need to sort that out, little Sis.' Diego laughed and poked her in the side.

'Don't assume you're older than me and call me little Sis just because you're a boy! Maybe I was born before you. How outrageous and sexist!'

'I wasn't assuming I was born first at all, Sis, don't be so touchy. I meant you're a midget and little compared to me, that's all. You are a sweet dinky little thing,' Diego replied.

'If I'm not laughing, it's not funny,' Mina said haughtily.

'I'm finding it funny,' Diego said, folding his arms over his chest and smiling down at her.

'Me too,' Mikie added as Mina huffed and stomped away.

'Greetings!' yelled a man coming towards them.

'Saved by the Peruvian!' Diego said, rolling his eyes.

'Hello there!' Ed said cheerily.

The Peruvian heading towards them had an old, weather-beaten, friendly face and wore jeans that were well worn and looked even older than he was. He smiled from ear to ear. He didn't look Peruvian; there was something different about him.

'You must be Diego,' Ed said, stepping forward, offering his hand.

The man took it gladly and excitedly shook it. Mina and Diego frowned and looked at each other. The king hadn't mentioned his friend's name to them before, only Ed, and he would have thought they'd have mentioned something about it being the same as his. Mina looked at him and pulled a face at the coincidence.

'Yes, I am indeed. Call me Shaman Diego. Welcome to my humble ranch and tell me what I can do for you today,' the man said joyfully.

'I'm not too sure, the Inca king sent us, it's rather strange actually,' Ed said. 'He told me to tell you to look at—'

'Wait, don't tell me, I shall see if I know,' he interrupted. 'But first, I must marvel at this exquisite beast! What a wonderful creature. You have found your soulmate here, haven't you?' He looked at each of them one by one, then back at Sirocco, and then to them all again. His eyes sparkled with joy and something else. His gaze was penetrating and looked deep inside all of them, but not how Mikie would read minds. It seemed to Mina that this man looked deep into their souls. Finally, he stopped and stared at Tammy directly.

'Ah, you!' he declared. 'He is your soulmate. How very interesting.'

'Yes,' Tammy answered, smiling as he examined Sirocco.

'Yes, perfect, lovely,' he said, rubbing his chin and staring deeply into her eyes. He reached out to pat Tammy on the top of her head and then paused, staring down at her. He blinked a couple of times and then took a step back.

'What's wrong?' she asked.

'How strange…' he began, but trailed off into silence.

'What is it, Shaman Diego?' Ed asked, frowning and

coming to his side.

'Nothing, really. I just see your power, your gift, it's very interesting. I have worked with the Shamans for many years and seen some amazing people, but nothing like this. I recognised you. How?' He hummed, stroked his chin and looked Tammy up and down again.

'This is Tammy, her sister Mina, and brothers Mikie and Diego,' Ed said.

'Diego?' The man suddenly looked up at him.

'Hi.' Diego smiled back awkwardly.

'All the same age?'

'Yes, quadruplets. And this is my nephew, Jax.'

Shaman Diego stared at Tammy again, then Mikie and back to Diego. He was puzzled but then his expression changed as a realisation passed over him. He laughed.

'She did it! Hermosa Sarah, madre de calidad, ella lo hizo,' he said.

He grabbed Tammy's cheeks in his hands and squeezed them. Mina looked away, smiling and shaking her head. She was glad it was Tammy he was doing this to and not her, but she was also getting a little annoyed; this was supposed to be about her and yet again it was all about Tammy.

'Your mother, God bless her, that's why I recognised you. You are the exact image of Sarah. Incredible! And you–' He grabbed Diego and did the same to his cheeks.

'You knew my mother?' Tammy asked.

'Knew her? Knew her! Ha!' He threw his head back and roared with laughter. 'Your mother took so many horses from me over the years, made me proud she did, with the use she put them to. She promised she would name her son after me, as a sign of respect for everything I did, and my

God she did it!'

Diego ducked to avoid the friendly smack around the head, but he couldn't help but smile.

'Horses?' Ed said.

'Yes, horses, she was horse mad. Used them for fun and jumping before Pisces, supplied her agents with horses only from me too. Lovely woman, great friend. She always kept her word, even with giving my name to her son. It's a good name, boy.'

'I wouldn't know,' Diego said.

'It's a good, strong Spanish name, my boy, I'm so pleased. Now, I must not get sidetracked – the king sent you and you are here for a reason. OK, so, let me see.'

He stroked his chin looking back and forth between them all. He looked one last time at Tammy and Diego, smiled and then waved them away. He looked at Jax, Mina, and Mikie and then came back to Mina. He stood in front of her, put his hands on his hips and tutted. Mina knotted her eyebrows, not finding it amusing and feeling awkward at the way he was staring.

'It's you, girl. Yes, the king would see this. All of you go and wait over there, by the entrance. What I have to say is for this girl's ears only,' he said, suddenly.

He waved them away, absentmindedly, not taking his eyes off Mina. Everyone felt a little awkward at being dismissed in such a manner.

'Come, let the man do his thing,' Ed said.

'He's a very strange man,' Diego said.

'Yeah, what did Mom see in him?' Tammy added.

'A vast intelligence,' Mikie said matter of factly.

'I really don't know what the king said you would get for

me,' Mina said, fidgeting on her feet, looking down.

'What was your name again, girl?'

'Mina.'

'Ah, Sarah chose another nice name. I liked her – your mom, that is. So, the king saw something missing in you, eh?'

'I guess so.'

'Well, hard to miss it, really. It's like a great big canyon.'

'What is?'

'The hole in you. You see, in my land, a man is not considered whole unless he finds the right horse. That is what I do. I find the right horse.'

'Horse?'

'Not very bright, are you?'

Mina felt her cheeks colour and looked down at the ground.

'Mina, you have a hole so big in you the king's grandmother would have seen it and she was as blind as a bat! Insecurity, jealousy, loneliness, low self-esteem – you name it, you've got it. All these things stem from a fear and darkness within you. Remember, Mina, the only thing you ever have to fear is fear itself. It will destroy you and everything around you. It's time to fill that hole of yours and make you whole. Give you something you do not want to lose. At the same time, I have someone who needs saving. You will be perfect for each other, I think. Let's see if you pass the test.'

Mina stared, open mouthed, not knowing what to say. She was annoyed that he would say such things to her, but she also believed him. She did feel a big, gaping hole inside her. Always had done. Not that she had ever verbalised it in such a way. She folded her arms silently and stared down at the floor, avoiding his eyes, not sure what to say or do. He laughed then, grabbed her arm, and pretty much dragged her towards the stables.

'I knew it, I knew it, I should have known there was a reason for it,' he was saying. 'It just all makes sense now, wouldn't have believed it yesterday though!'

'What are you going on about? Are you even aware of how rude you are?'

'The horse that will fill your heart, my darling, she is a wild one. She only came in a month ago, not what I'd normally accept. There was something in her eye, something that made me say yes, and I always listen to the eyes. You have the same thing in your eye, which is why it happened – fate, you see. Everything happens for a reason, Mina, and in this case, she is wild and untameable. Just like you. She cost three million for racing, but since they couldn't train her, it was money down the drain. They tried everything, then said I could have her and try to do something with her or she was going to be very expensive dog food.'

'Dog food!'

'Yes, dog food. Much like you – perfectly useless if we can't fix this attitude of yours! Well, now she's yours.'

'You want to give me an untamed horse that cost three million and still no one wants her? No way, what if she tries to kill me? I can't even ride unless I'm clinging on to Tammy!'

'You will.' He smiled. 'Follow me.'

He walked her into the stables, towards the back, where it was dark. There was a consistent banging coming from one of the stables; something big was very angry, kicking the door, wanting to get out. It banged over and over again, filling Mina with dread. He had to be joking; surely, he wouldn't put her near something that wild and dangerous? The banging echoed threateningly, and Mina was terrified. She didn't want a wild, angry, insane horse. Sirocco was intimidating enough and he was tame. This man must be mad. Then she thought that perhaps Tammy could tame her, but did she want to ask her that? Shaman Diego stopped, just before they reached her door, and turned to face Mina.

'Mina, I have found the right horse for the right person for many years. The skill is in my blood, passed from father to son throughout the generations. I am a Shaman and I see souls. You and I, we have one soul. Animals are not the same. One soul is attached to multiple animals and sometimes they lose the connection to their soul, which is very bad. They get sick, they get wild. Animals need connections and some souls just need to be connected deeply to another soul. This is what I do. I fix souls and I connect souls who need connecting. Trust me. Do as I say. You hold that proud head of yours up high, march right into that stable, and you look her in the eye. That is all you must do. Don't hesitate, don't mumble, don't be weak. You will know when the time is right to bring her out.'

Mina hesitated; there was something about him that was reassuring and knowledgeable. She wasn't sure why, but she did trust him. She did as he said. She approached the stable door and looked in. Large dark brown eyes, just like hers, stared back at her. Then they moved closer towards her and the head of the horse came into the light. She was as black as Jet and looked gorgeous. Mina gasped. She should have been scared, she should have hesitated – the horse was

almost as big as Sirocco – but she didn't. She felt something happen between her and the horse as soon as their dark eyes connected. With her head held high, she walked into the stables and faced the horse. Then she walked up to her and stroked her nose.

'Hello, beautiful,' Mina whispered. 'You aren't so wild, after all. Neither am I but let's not tell the men that!'

She took hold of the bridle and calmly walked the mare out of the stable. Shaman Diego was waiting for her, a big smile on his face, his hands clasped together with glee.

'Your mother would have been so pleased. You have such a great horse, but don't tell anyone what she cost as a racehorse as she might get stolen. She will not behave with you as she has done in the past. She will not act so untamed and wild with you because you fill each other's hearts and souls. Do you understand now, do you feel it?'

'Yes, I think I do, she's amazing. Are you really just going to give her to me?'

'Of course; it was meant to be, like I said. Actually, the king will pay me something and it is a gift from him, remember. She never cost me anything but time. Let's saddle her up, ride her,' he urged.

'Not just yet. I shall in five minutes,' she said.

Mina walked the large black horse over to everyone else, smiling proudly. Ed sighed and shook his head, which made her laugh. Diego and Mikie clapped. Tammy nodded, as if something suddenly made sense now.

'Mikie, Tammy, I need your help, please?' Mina asked, stopping in front of them.

'Sure,' Mikie said.

He had read her mind and Tammy understood

immediately. Tammy closed her eyes as Mikie placed his hands over her head and learned how to horse ride. Letting go of Tammy, he took Mina's head between his hands, passing the knowledge on. He stopped, took a step back and looked at her. Mina opened her eyes and smiled.

'Oh, yes!' she said.

Forgetting the saddle, Mina pulled herself up onto the back of the horse and galloped away. Tammy called Sirocco, jumped on him and followed. There was no way she was missing this. She didn't even give a second thought to Jax or Mikie wanting to come with her, as usual. This was just for her and Mina.

'You gave her a horse.' Ed sighed.

'No, it's more than that,' Shaman Diego replied. 'I gave her far more than a horse. You will see.'

Mikie caught Shaman Diego's eyes and nodded, a knowing and appreciative gesture, for what he had done. He understood and was grateful. Mikie put his arm around Jax and Diego's shoulders and sighed as they watched the girls gallop away. They were going fast and would likely be gone a while.

'So, this is what the king meant – get her a horse? What do I owe you?' Ed asked.

'No, please, it will be handled by the king. We cannot take that away from him. Since you are friends of the king and Sarah, please stay and let me feed you. If anyone wants to join the ladies on the ride, go and tell that lad over there at the stables that I said you can borrow a horse.'

Mikie taught Jax and Diego how to ride. In no time at all they were mounted and charging off after the girls. Ed and Shaman Diego smiled broadly.

'Ah, to be young again.' Shaman Diego sighed.

'I didn't realise you did this sort of thing. I should probably get them each a horse so they can ride together across my island.'

'This is a rare gift my father passed to me. It was supposed to happen, you know – that girl needed love and nothing fills the soul like a horse.'

'I have never thought of it that way,' Ed said. 'I'm not a huge horse person myself.'

'No, for you, your soul animal is a dog, am I right?' Shaman Diego asked.

'Yes, I suppose so, I hadn't thought of it like that.'

'Follow me, I shall get us a drink. They will be gone a while. Such beautiful views around here. They're quite safe.'

Shaman Diego and Ed were sat talking and drinking coffee when the others came charging towards them at high speed, five horses kicking up a path of red sand dirt. Both Tammy and Mina were riding like experts, heads back and laughing. It made everyone smile; how could they not? Breathless, they came to a stop in front of Ed and Shaman Diego.

'I can't thank you enough, she's beautiful,' Mina told Shaman Diego.

'The thank you is in your eyes, Mina, and to know that the hole is sealed forever.' He touched his nose and bowed.

'Thank you, with all my heart.'

'You are most welcome.' He smiled.

'What are you going to call her?' Tammy asked.

'Oh, I've called her Mandi. I decided that on the ride, don't ask me why as I don't know.'

'She who must be loved,' Shaman Diego told her.

'What?' Mina asked, blushing, thinking he was talking aloud about her again.

'That is what the name Mandi means, you know – she who must be loved. That applies to both of you now.'

'I wonder what Mina means?'

'Honest and faithful. So now you will both share those qualities: honesty, faithfulness and love.' Shaman Diego smiled at her.

'It feels so right, so natural, isn't that strange?' Mina said, stroking Mandi's mane.

'No, it doesn't sound strange at all.' Ed smiled.

'Feast with me briefly and then take my love to Sarah,' Shaman Diego said.

'Shaman Diego, when did you last see her?' Ed asked, concerned.

Shaman Diego could tell from Ed's tone of voice that Sarah was gone and lowered his head in disappointment, sorrow wiping away his smile for the first time since they had arrived. Then he stood up, remembering the children, and replaced his smile. He looked at Tammy, as if he wanted one last glance at Sarah.

'You are so much like your mother,' he said. 'But with extra special talents.'

Tammy swallowed, feeling sad at the thought of such a wonderful mother she was never allowed to know. Mikie, Diego and Mina felt the same and looked down at their feet, uncomfortably.

'Well, normally I would say the world has been deprived of a wonderful person, an irreplaceable mentor. However, I look at the four of you and I see the truth, and what your mother has left us all with. I again say God bless her, may she rest in peace. I'm sorry if I upset you, I didn't realise.'

'Come, you boys must pick yourselves a horse too. You will be needing one. You can't keep sitting behind the ladies, you know. You need to be men!' Shaman Diego declared and indicated that they should follow him.

'I'm more of a man than most men, why do people say such things?' Mina murmured to Tammy.

'They're old. Stuck in their old ways,' Tammy said, giggling.

Mikie looked at Ed who nodded at him. 'Boys, go pick yourselves a horse. You can all ride together at home then.'

'Really?' Jax raised his eyebrows. He knew how expensive this would be.

'I appreciate the offer but you have done too much for me already,' Diego said politely.

'Go and get yourselves a horse now or run after the girls on foot at the island,' Ed said. 'It's the last time I will say it.'

'Come on,' Mikie said, and ran after Shaman Diego. Jax and Diego followed.

Shaman Diego explained to them how to look the horses in the eyes and seek the connection. He explained the breed of each horse as they were chosen. Mina had chosen a pure black Arabian racehorse. Mikie found a beautiful dapple grey Andalusian stallion with a black mane and tail. Jax picked a golden Palomino thoroughbred mare with a white stripe on her nose, white socks and a white mane and tail. Diego fell in love with an Arabian cross appaloosa stallion who had a mostly white body with a few dark spots, and a white mane and tail. There were so many to choose from and yet it had been quick and easy for them to decide. The connections between them and their horses were intense and held a sense of fate. They were all overly excited at the thought of riding together every day at Vivacity Island.

After tapas, Shaman Diego waved them all goodbye. Ed sat in the cart with the tiger while the others rode their horses. Ed had organised for a cargo HP to come and collect them seeing as they had five horses and a tiger to get back, and it wouldn't be long before they got to it. They would fly overnight and take the ferry from Southampton in the dark. If they were lucky, they would be home in time to have breakfast with everyone else.

'Shaman Diego is a very clever man,' Mina said, riding next to Tammy.

'Yes, he is,' Tammy said.

'I feel she's a bit like Jet – so black. Do you miss him?'

'Yes, but he is happy and that's all that matters. I can see why he knew she was the one for you but they are all great horses. I don't think I ever really appreciated the soul connection with horses until today.'

'Thanks for teaching me to ride – via Mikie, I mean.'

'No problem. Shall we see what these guys can do?'

Mina didn't bother answering; she shot off, leaving Tammy and Sirocco staring after her. Tammy held Sirocco back a little, sensitive to the fact that Mina might enjoy being up in front, and not wanting to show off with Sirocco's speed.

'Sometimes, we don't have to be the fastest,' Tammy told him, stroking his mane. 'So we can, on occasion, say ladies before gentlemen.'

Sirocco neighed and then they charged forward, after Mina and Mandi, catching up with them in no time at all. Diego, Mikie and Jax reacted fast and went after them; no way were they being left out of any race. Ed smiled happily as they raced forwards towards the airport. It was a big expense but to see them all riding together was priceless. He knew these horses would bond them all closer together. He just hoped Jude wouldn't kill him when she found out how much he had spent.

TWENTY TWO

REN

VIVACITY ISLAND

The HP staff had to move cargo into the passenger area to make room for all the horses. Then trucks had to conceal them and get them to the secret ferry port where Dave was waiting for them. They hadn't slept much, travelling throughout the night, and were still half asleep and groggy. Kashvi was responding to the healing well and although weak, she was starting to be more alert. Jax couldn't wait to put her in with his tiger but Ed would keep her at the hospital until she had fully recovered.

'Why did we have to do the basking sharks last time but can use trucks and ferry now?' asked Mina, scowling.

'Because they aren't watching as closely now. They think we are in Peru and those aliens have us,' Ed replied.

'Shall we take the horses for a run along the beach whilst we have the chance?' Tammy asked.

'Sounds good to me,' Mina replied, jumping up on Mandi.

As the others mounted their horses too, Jax looked at Ed and said, 'Uncle, you know the children could do with ponies so they can join us.'

'That's a good idea,' Ed said. 'I'm just worried about the cost.'

'Aren't you a billionaire?' Mikie asked, smiling.

'I am, yes, but Jude doesn't let me think like that. Our money could be wiped out rapidly. She is very sensible.'

'Zebras would be great for the children – in the safari park for visitors in the day, and the children can ride them before and after,' Tammy said.

'Do you think zebras can be tamed like that?' Ed asked, and then immediately regretted it when she tilted her head at him and he recalled the time she rode them.

'That's a compromise. We can breed more, the children can share them, we don't have to buy any, and they can graze naturally,' Jax suggested.

'Well, looks like you have it all figured out. Let's raise it with Jude later,' Ed replied.

'I can't wait to get back to the safari park, I've missed everyone,' Tammy said, as she climbed up onto Sirocco.

'It sounds lovely, I can't wait to see it,' Diego said.

'Then follow me and I shall give you the tour,' Tammy said and they all set off, galloping across the beach and over towards the safari park. Tammy could feel the animals' excitement building as they sensed her and she wore a huge smile as she charged towards them.

*

Breakfast was chaotic. Jude, Dave, Crane, Ben, Stephen and

Lei were all trying to calm the hybrid children down. They were too excited about Tammy and Mina returning to sit and eat. They had made two lovely, long, wooden tables alongside each other, covered by a wooden canopy to shelter them from the sun or rain as they ate. The hybrid orphanage was looking good. Mina had to smile because it looked like Stephen and Lei were married and living wild with thirty children. They were clearly happy. Lei had squeezed her tightly when she saw her; both had tears in their eyes and choked on words neither of them could speak. Something had changed between them. They were no longer guardian and daughter but more like close friends who understood one another.

'It feels a bit weird, this does, as if we are receiving a heroes' welcome when we haven't done anything,' Mikie said.

'Well, I wouldn't say you haven't done anything exactly. They're just pleased we've come back,' Ed said.

'They have heard so much about you from the aliens – you are heroes to them,' Jude said. 'Diego, you must be feeling raw. Loss is an awful thing to have to handle, especially so young. I know we are strangers to you but that won't be for long. Know that we are here for you.'

'Thank you,' Diego said quietly.

'Diego has incredible power with that crystal cube of his. Look inside it, Aunt Jude,' Jax told her.

'Do you mind?' Jude asked Diego.

He shook his head and lifted his wrist to show her. 'Don't touch it or you'll get a shock.'

'OK. Wow, this is incredible.' Jude gasped. 'That looks like stars.' She watched the swirling movement of the gases and light within the cube.

'It's like a mini nebula within the cube and all the power that comes with that,' he said.

'That is quite a powerful weapon,' she said, releasing a whistle.

'I'm not very good at handling it. People don't tend to want me around because I'm not always in control of it.'

'Diego, that is not true,' Mina said, touching his arm affectionately. 'You have a great power with that cube and have shown how much control you have.'

'Yes, but I can't wield it. I'm out of control sometimes, aren't I? Every time I get close to someone I'm scared of hurting them. I'm really worried about being around all these children. It's far worse when there is a storm – it kind of takes over me. Do you get many storms here?'

'Not as many as Peru, Diego. Stop fretting over it. We will all help and support you,' Ed told him.

'And we have our own gifts that we can use to help you with any accidents,' Mikie said.

'Yes, I have water to counteract your fire,' Tammy said.

'I might be able to help make you do things,' Mikie suggested. 'I can make people do things they don't want to so I can help you to control it.'

'Great ideas,' Jude said. 'Tammy and Jax, come and sit by me. I've missed you so much.'

Lei passed some toast to Mina and smiled at her. 'I was worried about you and missed you.' Lei said.

'Believe it or not, I actually missed you too.' Mina smiled. 'And I wore a dress!'

'No way!'

'I so did!' Mina laughed.

'Jax did send me a picture. You look stunning no matter how you dress. So, the king gave you a horse? Your mum loved horses so much,' Lei told her.

'Yes, and you know what? When I am with her, when we are running fast, my shadow disappears and I feel love and happiness and peace,' Mina said.

'That is amazing. I'm so pleased for you. She is a stunning horse, that's for sure. They are all gorgeous. Tell me what you've named them.'

'Mine is Mandi,' Mina said.

Jax added, 'Artemis.'

'Dakota,' said Diego.

'Oreo, as in the cookie,' said Mikie, beaming with joy.

They all chuckled at that and Jax rolled his eyes and shook his head at Mikie.

'What?' Mikie exclaimed.

'They are lovely, all of them,' Jude said and took a deep breath as she looked at Tammy and saw her sadness.

Ed had called Jude, told her about Jet, and warned her to tell the others and not to raise the subject. No one mentioned Jet and a sadness lingered in the air. Jude watched everyone tuck into their breakfast and sighed as discreetly as she could. She had a sense of foreboding at the idea that much sadness was coming their way, and that these beautiful children would have to face and deal with so much more pain than she had ever endured. How could she support them? How could she possibly get them through it? The responsibility played heavily upon her.

'Tammy, we have been waiting for you to settle before we reveal your surprise,' Jude said.

'Oh yes? I have a surprise?' Tammy asked, looking up at

her with a smile.

Jude pointed to the kitchen. Just then, a young girl stepped out and started to walk towards them. Tammy's jaw dropped. She had completely forgotten that she had asked Jude and Ed to bring Sukie from the orphanage to help them. She looked more grown up than Tammy remembered. She raced over towards her friend and they hugged tightly.

'Sukie! You look amazing. You look so much older dressed like this and not in the orphan uniforms,' Tammy said.

'Oh Tammy, I always knew there was something special about you. I have so much to tell you. I have missed you so much,' Sukie said, kissing her cheeks and hugging her over and over. She was thrilled to be given a home on the island with Tammy. They had bonded like sisters from very early on at the orphanage.

Mina watched, her mouth slightly open and the piece of toast hanging there no longer being chewed. She could not take her eyes off Sukie. She wore an emerald green sari with brown sandals and gold bangles, and her hair was long and black down her back. She had delicate little pearl earrings and henna tattoos over her hands and forearms. Mina thought she was the most beautiful person she had ever seen and couldn't understand why her heart was racing and butterflies fluttered in her stomach.

'You should try to swallow that bread, you look like a muppet,' Diego whispered in her ear.

She snapped out of her trance and looked at him. 'What?'

'I looked at Quilla like that the first time I met her,' he said, smiling. 'You need to act cool, Sis. Not have food and dribble hanging out of your mouth.'

Mina elbowed him and blushed. She was awkward and still felt her face burning as Tammy introduced Sukie to everyone. She suddenly felt shy and when her eyes locked with Sukie's, who smiled at her, she felt a warmth wash over her.

'Smile back, you numpty,' Diego whispered, hiding his mouth behind his hand so no one but Mina could see or hear his words.

Mina smiled back and said a weak hello, her throat suddenly dry.

'Sukie, you can stroke a tiger later,' Jax said.

'That would be awesome,' Sukie replied.

'Yes, I hear we have an injured tiger. Since when could you find them in Peru?' Jude asked.

'Poached for vanity, it seems, but the plane crashed near Inca land. Only she survived, badly hurt, but she's healing slowly. Crane put her in the hospital,' Ed explained.

'Poor girl! Imagine if Tammy hadn't have connected with her. It doesn't bear thinking about.' Jude shook her head sadly.

Ed nodded in agreement. 'Very lucky girl indeed. How's the camp coming along?'

'Excellently! We have a really good routine going now; the children are getting a proper education at last and they look healthier and are eating properly. Stephen and Lei have done a great job,' Jude said.

'And I love cooking.' Dave smiled.

'I'm really glad to hear it, I'm really impressed with what you have all done,' Ed said.

'Diego, do you know much about your mum?' Stephen

asked.

'A little. Charles didn't know her that well. They only dated for a year and he had a drug issue at the time and didn't remember much.'

'How about after breakfast we go for a walk and I'll tell you about my sister? Be nice for me to get to know you a little too. I am your uncle and want you to know that I'm thrilled you're here. Anything you need, I'm your man.'

'Thank you, I appreciate that,' Diego said. He was feeling self-conscious as all the hybrids were staring at him.

'Jude's plan was to have breakfast here and then go back to the house and sleep. None of us have slept properly for days,' Ed told them all. 'Once we have had some sleep, we can come and meet everyone and spend time getting to know each other. Shall we go to Brunswick house now and come back for that walk later?'

'Yes, sure, I didn't think about the lack of sleep,' Stephen replied. 'Anytime works for me.'

'Then let's get you guys settled at the house. You can wash and rest,' Jude said.

They headed off towards the house: Tammy, Jax, Mina, Mikie and Diego galloping ahead of the Jeep that carried Ed, Jude and Sukie. Since the horses were faster than the Jeep, they took a couple of detours and enjoyed the scenery. Diego stared, incredulous, as they turned past some trees to find Brunswick house beaming in the sunlight. He had never seen such a massive mansion before. It was surrounded by beautiful gardens and a huge pond, and towered high above the massive trees around it. The morning sun reflected off the pale-yellow Elizabethan stone walls, making it shine brightly and energetically. The front driveway was pebbled and surrounded by beautifully shaped bushes and flowers. Wide and elegant marble steps led from the driveway to the extravagant pillars surrounding the front entrance.

'Wow.' Diego sighed.

'I know how you feel, I was breathless when I first saw it too,' Tammy said.

Tammy and Jax smiled. Neither of them fully believed that this was actually their home now. Since their previous lives had ended, they had been so busy and travelled a lot. It hadn't really sunk in until now.

'I already discussed this with Ed and, technically, since he has officially adopted Tammy, then we own this house too. Kind of.' Mina smiled wickedly.

'I'm sure Jax doesn't appreciate you trying to take his home away from him,' Mikie said.

'Yeah, like my nan's cottage wasn't enough for you,' Jax said, laughing.

'You aren't upset about that, are you?' Mina asked.

'Not at all. Nan knows I would only sell it. I couldn't live and work as a vet there – no clients. I always planned to live here as a vet.'

'You mean you wouldn't want to run this place? Would you have time to do that and be a vet?' Mina looked at Jax and for the first time realised how conflicted he must be. He'd had his heart set on one thing for so many years and now that might not even be possible. She didn't know what she wanted to be, but the thought of having something thrust upon her and not being able to choose seemed unfair.

'Ed and Jude want me to run this place when I'm older, but I can't run this island when my heart lies in being a vet now, can I?' Jax said.

Mikie placed his arm around Jax's shoulders and shook his head.

'What?' Jax asked when they all smiled at him.

'Well, it seems obvious to everyone but you,' Mina said.

'What?'

'I think you'll be able to run this island and be a vet, after all.' Tammy smiled.

'Absolutely, look how much help you'll have; do you really think anyone is going to want to leave this beautiful place when the war is over? Not to mention thirty hybrids. You will no doubt train them up as vets and helpers and have loads of cover,' Mina added.

'Oh, well, if that's the case, then I don't have anything to worry about, do I?' Jax smiled and nodded.

'No, I think the problem will be telling people there isn't enough room,' Mina said.

'I don't know, I do think this house is amazing and the island is beautiful but I still love the Inca's village, and the thought of spending the rest of my life on the top of that mountain...' Diego sighed.

'With a certain young princess, no doubt?' Mina teased.

'Perhaps.' Diego blushed and shrugged.

'Well, you aren't going anywhere without me,' Mina added, but there was a serious and unsettling note in her tone.

Tammy frowned. It was possessive and jealous sounding. Sometimes Mina's attitude seemed to be too strong, or the dark side of her would rear its ugly head every now and then. Tammy noticed it, everyone noticed it, even Diego on occasion; she could tell by the sudden frowns or quick glances he gave her. Then, as if realising that she had revealed a secret, Mina would smile her beautiful smile – the one that said butter could never melt in her mouth – and no darkness could be detected whatsoever.

Just then, the Labradors came running towards them as Jude, now ahead in the Jeep, had arrived and opened the front door. Diego dropped to his knees, rubbing their heads in excitement.

'Oh, fox red! Quilla and I always talked about wanting a puppy!' he exclaimed.

'Yes, they're adorable,' Tammy said.

'We may breed her yet and then you can have a puppy,' Jude said.

'I want first pick of the litter,' Jax declared.

'I can never say no to you,' Jude smiled and put her arm around his shoulder.

'I want a lion,' Mina said.

'Keep on dreaming,' Jax taunted.

Mina pouted at him.

*

The day passed quickly. Everyone had a few hours sleep, then ate a quick sandwich before making their way to the hybrid camp. Tammy spent time with Sukie. Mina and Diego went walking with Stephen and Lei and discussed Sarah and what she was like from their point of view. Jude wouldn't let Ed leave her side; she had missed him so much. Jax and Mikie did some jobs for Stephen and Lei around the camp and helped Dave with some dinner preparations. Jude wanted them to herself on the evening so insisted they ate with her and Ed at the house and not at the camp.

They were in the dining room, the table laid all fancy with a buffet on the side, and Jude said she had another surprise for them.

'What is it?' Mina asked.

'We have another guest to introduce you to. She arrived this afternoon,' Jude told them.

'Oh, who is that?' Tammy asked.

Ed appeared with a young lady beside him. As she entered the room, escorted by Ed, she commanded attention. She wore a black and gold kimono and sash, known as an obi, and sashayed in with the grace and sophistication of a movie star that left both Mikie and Mina staring at her in shock. She had a short stylish bob, a little make up, and golden dangly earrings. She wore no other jewellery. She was older than they were, at fifteen, and elegant and petite. The energy in the room changed dramatically. Tammy knew this was no ordinary human.

'*Is she human?*' Mikie asked.

'*I don't know what she is but she's awesome,*' Mina said.

The young lady looked at Mina, boldly in the eyes, and they all knew she understood that they were communicating telepathically.

'*She knows we are talking about her but does she know what we're saying?*' Mikie asked. '*I can't read her mind at all. It's really weird.*'

'*We can tell her she has a big bottom and see if she takes offence,*' Diego suggested, jokingly.

She looked at them, individually, depending on who was speaking and when, as if she could hear them. Mikie was tingling all over. Whatever she was, she was no ordinary human, that was for certain.

'This is Ren Mochizuki of the Mochizuki clan from Tokyo. She works for the head of state now and it was requested that she come here and oversee our efforts to rebalance the Japanese economy,' Jude said as she welcomed her into the room.

'Please, let me take your jacket,' Ed said.

'Kimono,' Jude whispered and rolled her eyes at him.

'Yes, sorry,' Ed muttered. Ren undid her sash and allowed her kimono to drop. Ed caught it and left the room to hang it up on the hooks in the hall.

Everyone stared at her dress – a short Japanese-Chinese style sheath dress. It was the same black and gold silk material as the kimono, yet more modern and chic with a standing collar made from a single piece of material wrapped around Ren's neck, with the two ends meeting in the middle at the front. It looked expensive.

'She looks like she's made of China and will break if you touch her,' Tammy said.

'Makes me just want to wrap her up in cotton wool and protect her,' Mikie said.

'I was thinking that exact same thing,' Mina replied.

'Hi, it's lovely to meet you,' Jax said, being the first to break the trance they were all in and offer her his hand.

She shook his hand and nodded at the others. 'Lovely to meet you all too.'

'Please take a seat.' Jude motioned towards the table and everyone reached for the nearest chair.

Ren walked past Mikie and took the seat next to him. As she leaned over to pull out her chair, she leaned in and whispered in his ear, 'It is I who will protect you. *If* I think you are worth it.'

Mikie froze. Not only could he not read her mind but she could hear his telepathic communication even when he had locked it down to just his siblings. He got goosebumps and felt the blood drain from his face. He kept his eyes on the table and remained silent. He had no idea how to reply. Ren didn't seem to need a reply. She was already getting comfortable, pouring a glass of water, and acting as if nothing had happened.

Jude continued, 'The emperor of Japan, the head of state, has tasked us with finding a solution to their food economy crisis. Lei and I have sent some ideas of ways to grow food on their mountains and protect them from the elements, high enough to survive tsunamis and warm enough to grow all year round. As we develop some protocols, Ren will oversee and supervise our progress. Now, there is a slight situation we need to deal with.'

'We don't need to beat around the bush, we should just come right out with it,' Ed said. 'Tammy, Mikie and Jax. Somehow, Ren knows what you guys did in Japan and that is why she is here. The emperor wants her to assess your characters and see whether we can be trusted or not.'

Mikie gulped and looked over at Tammy and then Jax. They were silent.

'How could she know?' Jax asked Mikie.

'Did Jude tell you?' Tammy asked.

'No one told me,' Ren said and looked at them intensely, one by one. 'I am not your average woman. I have skills too.'

'Is the emperor your father?' Mikie asked. He was trying to decide if she was human.

'He is not. He was best friends with my father, the former prime minister, who died during the Pisces outbreak with my mother, if you must know. The emperor took me under his wing. My family have special gifts that are passed down throughout each generation. You do not have to be an alien to have power, you know.'

'We don't really know, we are just learning,' Jax said, a little annoyed. Her superior tone was starting to annoy him. He didn't like that she knew what they had done, was judging them, and felt superior to them. He didn't think anyone was superior to the Brunswicks, regardless of what airs and graces they put on.

'I'm sorry to hear about your parents,' Mina said. She hadn't been able to talk until now. She locked eyes with Ren for a moment.

'How do you know all of this?' Mikie asked, turning to face her. 'And why are you really here? Can we trust you?'

'Mikie, really!' Jude exclaimed.

'It's fine,' Ren said, smiling demurely. 'I'm here because I know what is coming and I know what you all are. The immediate priority is to feed my people and make them safe. After that, I want my people to be prioritised for tank training. I know what your father can do. I want my people to be able to defend our land. Can you trust me? For now, yes. We have a common enemy and so, as they say, the enemy of my enemy is my friend.'

'Fair enough,' Ed said, somewhat deflated. He gave Jude an intense stare. She had not told him that Ren knew everything.

Jude mouthed the words '*I didn't know*' and shrugged.

'So, what are your powers?' Mina asked.

'Maybe, if you gain my respect, I will tell you. For now, I'm unsure if you are just foolish children who rush into things without thinking of the consequences,' Ren said. 'I have every right to be angry. My people have suffered because of you.'

'And my whales have suffered because of you!' Tammy spat angrily and slammed her fists down on the table.

'Yeah, I don't appreciate you coming here and acting all hoity-toity and belittling us. We didn't do anything wrong but respond to mass murder. If anyone at this table should feel bad about their actions, it should be you,' Jax added.

Ren looked them both in the eyes. The energy in the room was hot and volatile. Tammy stared her down. Her fury was rapidly growing, and Mina looked at her in a whole new way. She looked terrifying. Her eyes were glowing and intimidating. Even Mina was scared. Suddenly, there was a strange thump at the window. Ren looked over just as another thump happened. Wasps were thumping one by one on the window, then creeping through a small hole in the corner of the pane and entering the room. Soon there was a neat little army of wasps sitting on the windowsill focused intently on Ren. Watching her, silently, tense, and ready to go.

'Impressive,' Ren said, looking Tammy in the eyes, a smile twitching at her lips.

'Is it just me or is it getting hot in here?' Diego joked.

'Let's all calm down,' Ed said. 'Now, you all have no issues with each other. We all want the same – everyone fed and comfortable and to win the war that is coming. Understandably, given how close all of us are to animals, the whale hunting offended us. But they are just twelve years old and snuck off to do something about it. Yes, it had devastating results, but it is normal to make mistakes and we shall learn from them.'

'A lot of good has come from this mistake,' Jude added. 'Now there will be more variety of sustainable foods and kinder animal welfare in Japan. Which is what you want too, Ren.'

Ren finally broke the staring competition that she and Tammy had entered into and looked away. 'This is true. I am not a fan of whale hunting myself but it was the only way we had to feed everyone.'

'Well, what has happened is in the past and all is done. We cannot change that but we can work together to change the future. I suggest we drop all attitudes and instead take this opportunity to get to know one another. I don't care what all of you see when you look around this table, but I can tell you what I see: an amazing collection of abilities that together will win this war and help us keep Earth to ourselves.' Ed took the time to look at each of them in turn as he spoke. 'So, I insist right now that you all calm down, change the tone, and become friends. We have bigger enemies just around the corner.'

'I just want to say that I am in love with your clothes. I want to wear things like you do. I almost always wear shorts and trousers but I really like your outfits,' Mina said to Sukie and Ren.

'We should clothes swap, that will be fun,' Sukie suggested, smiling.

'I really like that idea,' Mina said, smiling back at Sukie.

'Not on your life.' Ren huffed. Then, breaking in to a softer tone, she added, 'I have plenty that you can borrow but you will never see me in boys' clothes.'

'Oh, this smells gorgeous,' Diego said, finding the delay

on eating was starting to get to him.

'Then let's tuck in and enjoy.' Jude smiled, relief flooding through her. Things had been getting a bit intense and it had come as quite a shock that Ren knew everything.

'How can I ever look the emperor in the eye again?' Jude whispered to Ed as they headed towards the buffet table.

Ren suddenly appeared at her side. 'Don't worry, I am the only one who knows.'

'Who is that girl?' Mikie asked Mina, both of them besotted with her.

'I intend to find out,' Mina replied.

'Going to be torn between the two of them now, aren't you?' Diego giggled quietly so only Mina and Mikie could hear.

'What do you mean?' Mina asked, blushing.

'Shush, just a heads up, but she knew what we were saying when we were silent,' Mikie interrupted.

'No way!' Diego grimaced.

'Yeah way,' Ren said, coming up behind them. 'No secrets between us lot.'

Then she started helping herself to some food.

'I can't decide if I love her or hate her,' Mikie said.

Diego smiled as he and Jax shrugged and began to lift the silver platters on the table, sniffing each one as the steam rose, and sighing with adoration. Diego's stomach rumbled and as Mina turned to smile at the noise, she found hers did the same.

'So, what is it?' Diego said, stepping closer.

'Ahhh, mushrooms,' Jax said, replacing the lid on one. 'Potatoes, peas, cabbage, carrots, pasta, black bean casserole… Now that's more like it, Aunt Jude.'

'This is awesome, far better than some of the things we had to eat in Peru,' Mina said.

'Yes, like pet guinea pigs,' Tammy retorted.

'They aren't pets,' Diego replied.

'Oh, it's so horrible,' Tammy muttered.

'And they made me eat snake and piranha.' Mina pouted.

'Oh, I see,' Jude said. 'Well, it sounds very colourful and interesting.'

'I almost died,' Mina said dramatically, making everyone laugh. She blushed as both Sukie and Ren kept looking at her and she realised she felt somewhat intimidated by them both. So gorgeous and yet dramatically different in the way that they carried themselves. Ren was sophisticated, modern and confident, whereas Sukie was elegant, traditional, subtle and humble. Things had just become more complicated for Mina.

TWENTY THREE

POWER BAN

VIVACITY ISLAND

'Ouch! That really hurt!' Diego moaned as he landed flat on his back.

Master Bardo stroked his moustache and stared down at him. They were surrounded by trees, hidden from everyone, although no one else was up yet. Every morning, Diego was woken up for his training. It was far too early at 5 o'clock. He was given no choice.

'Get up!' Master Bardo demanded.

'No way! You're a lunatic. You're supposed to be teaching me to fight but you're just beating me up. You have anger issues, you do, and need a therapist.' Diego got up sulkily.

'Come on, Diego, you're better than this!' Master Bardo held his arm out in front of him and indicated with his fingers that Diego should attack him.

Diego tightened his lips in anger and charged. He ran as fast as he could. Using Kung Fu, he attacked with his left arm, then right, then left. Master Bardo defended well, blocking every attempt. Diego failed to land a single strike. Master Bardo swung around and used his leg to sweep Diego's leg. Diego jumped, turned in the air high over Master Bardo's head, and landed behind him. Master Bardo turned fast, but was slightly unbalanced, as Diego attacked once more. Faster this time. Master Bardo stumbled and it gave Diego a slight moment to elevate into the air and land a kick on Master Bardo's chest. This time it was Master Bardo who went flying back into a tree and was winded.

He looked at Diego and smiled. 'Oh, you will be a fine warrior yet.'

Diego smiled.

'Again tomorrow,' Master Bardo said and vanished yet again.

Diego shook his head. Every day he had to train with this Master Bardo and yet he had to admit the guy could fight!

He headed for breakfast. Fighting certainly made you hungry.

*

Tai chi didn't last very long the following morning because it became too hot to handle. Ben and Crane watched from the other side of the large pond as everyone else took part. Ren and Sukie had to keep stopping to take a drink of water. Then, Jude fainted and Ed caught her just in time.

'Jude, Jude!' Ed said, shaking her shoulders gently.

'What's wrong with her?' Tammy asked.

'She fainted,' Ed said, breathing a sigh of relief as Jude opened her eyes. 'Oh, you gave me such a scare!'

'I'm alright, just got too hot,' she murmured, slowly sitting up with Ed's help.

'Yes, the heat was getting too intense,' Ed agreed. 'I should have said something sooner.'

'I was just as capable of saying something, I was enjoying it too. I must be menopausal,' she laughed.

'What heat?' Tammy asked, puzzled. It was still early morning and the sun wasn't that hot today.

'From the energy,' Mikie said, coming over.

'It's so much more powerful now – very cool but very hot.' Jax wiped the sweat from his brow.

'Oh,' said Tammy.

'I could get used to that,' Mina said.

'Me too, I'm so pumped,' Diego agreed.

'I haven't felt anything like that before. It's incredible,' Ren added.

'Me neither. I had to keep taking breaks,' said Jax.

'I think from now on either you guys do it alone, or do a much shorter spell with us and see if we normal humans can build up to take it,' Ed said.

'Oh yes, let's just do it for less time, I wouldn't like to stop. It's invigorating,' Jude said. 'I'm alright now, look – I'm standing up.'

'You're wobbling all over the place, Jude, sit down,' Ed scolded.

Jude laughed and sat in the chair that Ben and Crane had just ran over with.

'Oh, what a rush!' she laughed.

'You are funny.' Mina smiled.

'I will help you to adjust. It will get easier but will take time,' Tammy said, and began to do some energy work on

Jude.

'Well, I'm feeling better already, so let me catch my breath then we'll head down to the hybrid camp shall we?'

'Can we go and check on Kashvi first? We can take the horses and meet you at the camp – if you don't mind?' Jax asked.

'What a good idea. Take Ren and Sukie with you, they'll enjoy that.' Jude replied.

'I'm thinking what you're thinking.' Mina smiled at Tammy, nodding enthusiastically.

'Yes,' Tammy nodded. 'Two zebras are on their way and we'll take the Labradors. This will be a great ride. I'll show you the fast route Sirocco and I like to take.'

'Excellent, I can't wait.' Mina replied.

'Can you ride?' Mikie asked.

'Yes,' Ren replied.

'No,' Sukie said. Mikie gave her a reassuring smile and then placed his hands on her head. She closed her eyes as he transferred his knowledge to her. When he finished, she opened her eyes and was in awe.

'Oh my, that is a neat trick.' She gasped.

'Yes, that is very interesting,' Ren added.

They got their horses ready and Ren and Sukie took the zebras. The excitement was building, knowing that a good, fast gallop was ahead of them. Mina looked at Tammy and raised an eyebrow. Tammy nodded. They understood each other. It was a race and neither of them wanted to lose.

'Bring it on,' Mina jeered as she climbed up on Mandi.

'I'll give you a head start, it's only fair,' Tammy said, getting on Sirocco.

'Absolutely not!' Mina said angrily.

'I'll take it!' Diego screamed and raced ahead.

'No way!' Mina set off after him and everyone else followed suit.

Sirocco and Mandi bolted across the field, overtaking Diego on his horse Dakota and disappearing into the trees. It looked as if two bullets had been fired out of a gun. Jax, on Artemis, and Mikie, on Oreo, were close behind and joined up with Diego and Dakota as they chased the girls. The zebras were nowhere near as fast. Tammy and Mina seemed to be clinging on for dear life as they rode, despite the large smiles they wore, repeatedly ducking to try to avoid the lower branches. Mina cut her face on a couple of branches, but Tammy used her powers to move them out of her way. The branches went higher, left or right to avoid Tammy, who was riding more gracefully than her sister, whereas Mina grunted every time she had to duck.

'That's so not fair!' Mina muttered under her breath, falling slightly behind.

The dogs were keeping pace, for now, but they began to show signs of slowing down. The sisters exited the trees and raced across a field. There was a brick wall up ahead, sectioning off part of the park from the field, that was low enough for the horses to jump. They were heading straight towards it. Tammy looked over her shoulder at Mina, and smiled. She had a good head start and was certain Mina wouldn't catch them up now. Mina frowned, her mind racing with ways she could regain the distance she had lost in the trees. Then she smiled.

The wall was getting closer; Mina turned Mandi away from Sirocco, so that they were no longer on the same path, creating more distance between them. She focused on the brick wall and watched it change shape. Tammy gasped as the brick wall grew before her very eyes. More bricks appeared from other parts of the wall and made the section she was heading for too high to jump. Meanwhile, Mina's section was getting lower. She laughed as she and Mandi jumped over the brick wall and Tammy was forced to turn and follow Mina.

'You horrible cheat!' she shouted.

'That's cheating? And you moving the trees wasn't?' Mina giggled.

They arrived at the safari park, catching their breaths, waiting for the others to catch up. Tammy was glad to see the genuine look of happiness on Mina's face. Sinking the spaceship together and this race had been two of the best experiences they had had together. She was so glad the king had arranged for Mina to get a horse. It gave them something to share and bond over.

'I can't believe you were scared of Sirocco at first, and now you outsmart me on your own horse.' Tammy smiled.

'I know. Strange, isn't it? I don't think I could ever be without Mandi beside me now. I feel like I'm a different person.'

'I know exactly how you feel. I annoy Ed by insisting Sirocco travels with us.'

'Well, at least he can easily transport animals across the world, that certainly makes the task a lot easier,' Mina said.

'True. Especially now he'll have to do the same with all of us.'

They chuckled and patted the horses, dismounting when the others arrived. Ren and Sukie were the slowest on the zebras. They went to the hospital and Crane took them all to meet Kashvi, who was confined to a small cage to restrict her movements. She was frustrated and ready to move about now.

'Ah, here she is,' Crane said. 'Hello, Tammy. Someone has been very eager to see you again. Normally, she would have to be on cage rest for a while longer and yet her healing has been so rapid I think you may as well just keep her near you. Your ability to heal is phenomenal.'

Tammy helped Kashvi out of the cage and asked if she minded the others stroking her, it being such a rare privilege to be up close to a tiger. Kashvi was happy and she even licked Ren's hand and Sukie's cheek, which moved them both almost to tears. Eventually, she would be put in with the tiger that Crane had operated on, but for now she could be at Tammy's side and get healing top ups throughout each day.

'How is the other tiger?' Tammy asked.

'His cancer has not returned, and I still hope they might breed,' Crane replied.

'How can he procreate if he has had treatment for cancer?' Ren asked.

'Given the nature of our work here, and during the pandemic with repopulating animals globally, we always remove any sperm or eggs from animals when they need to undergo anaesthetic and freeze them. We have his last sperm on ice, especially because many of the male tigers that we found seemed to be infertile and he was one of the few virile. And the females that we have are sadly also infertile or can't carry to term. If we are lucky he could still be a dad.' Crane smiled proudly.

'AI if that's not clear. Artificial Insemination,' Jax

explained.

'Lucky him,' Ren replied, nodding.

Tammy and Jax then took Diego, Ren and Sukie around the safari park for their first time, as if they were tourists, getting them ice creams, slush puppies, silly hats and even T-shirts with a picture of an elephant, lion and monkey that said: *I heart Brunswick Safari Park*. The elephants were over the moon to see Tammy again and they took out the hose and had a water fight party. Dave was laughing his head off and acting the most childish. He was in his element. The tension with Ren vanished into thin air and as they toured the safari park, they became closer and more comfortable with each other. They all took turns swimming with the sea lions and had to laugh when they saw that Jude had left several sets of swim gear and towels in the feeding shed. Then, they headed back to the house to shower and change before joining the hybrids at the camp.

'It's Diego, it's Diego,' the children shouted as they all arrived on their horses and zebras.

'Why are you so special?' Mikie asked, giving him a nudge as he charged past.

And then there was silence as they watched the tiger walking alongside Tammy and Sirocco. Mesmerised, they froze and just stared. Before long, Tammy had reassured them and Kashvi was suddenly getting lots of strokes and hugs from the hybrids, nervously at first and then more enthusiastically as they became more confident. The little girl, Alice, was shaking with nerves as she stroked Kashvi, eyes wider than normal, fascinated by this giant cat. Kashvi licked Alice's cheek, as tenderly as she could, and Alice gasped with how strange and painful it felt. Tigers have huge barbs on their tongues, to help them scrape fur and feathers off their food, and thus after just a few licks they would be scraping off skin the same way that hard sandpaper would. Alice stared at her and then promptly licked her cheek back and flung her tiny arms around Kashvi's neck as she spat out the hair.

'Friends for life,' Mina said, just as Pedro rushed up and wrapped himself around her legs, almost sending her flying over.

'Number three! I mean Pedro!' She laughed, grabbing Diego's shoulder for balance.

'I've missed you,' Pedro said, smiling up at her.

'I've missed you too.' She swept down, taking him into her arms, and hugging him closely.

The other children rushed around them, hugging Tammy and Mikie, trying to get past Pedro and hug Mina, whilst staring at Diego. Once the initial excitement and greetings had calmed down, they started whispering about Diego and looking at him with wide eyes. He was the tallest and most muscular of them all and, as far as the children were concerned, he'd been living wild in the jungle.

'I'm sure we can get Diego to tell you a wonderful story about the Incas?' said Mina.

'Yeah!' They cheered again. 'Story, story, story.'

'Thanks for checking that with me first, Mina.' Diego frowned.

'It'll do your confidence good.' She smiled. 'Now, Pedro, you'll have to go down, you're getting too heavy.'

'I'm glad you think so. Everyone but me seems to know what my confidence needs,' Diego moaned. He moved close enough to whisper in her ear, 'So, let me get this straight…

You want me to tell them a bedside story before I send them all to heaven with my power demonstration? This is all on you, Mina.'

'Oh, you are so negative!' Mina gasped and pushed him away.

'We have already said that we'll look after you,' Tammy said.

'How did you know what I said then? You couldn't have heard. Mikie, did you listen and tell?' Diego was annoyed.

'No, I didn't,' Mikie replied calmly.

'I heard you,' Tammy said.

'How?'

'I don't know.'

'The telepathy is getting stronger and clearer whilst we are all together,' Mikie said.

'Really? Without needing your help?' Tammy asked.

'That's right. It's just occurring more frequently, as if we can read each other's thoughts all the time.'

'Oh, I really don't like that,' Mina stated.

'Why, do you have something to hide?' Mikie said.

Mina glared at him. The children were pulling them over towards their camp where Dave was waiting eagerly for them. He was standing by a massive black iron cauldron, which was steaming over a real fire that burned deep below in the earth. It smelled wonderful. The four long, wooden tables and plenty of chairs that Stephen had made – enough to seat everyone – surrounded the cooking area where Dave stood.

They lined up to take a bowl of vegetable stew from Dave then took a seat while they ate it. Stephen and Lei had put a giant water butt in the area, so all the children had to do was take a beaker and fill it themselves from the small tap. They took a roll of bread each too.

'Oh dear, two of your horses have just done a big poop, right by my kitchen,' Dave said. 'We need some sort of a stable area here don't we? Until then, can someone shovel it out of the way of my food please?'

Alice, the young hybrid, jumped up from her chair and raced over to get a shovel. With great difficulty, she heaved it over to the poop.

'I do the poo poo,' she said. 'I do the donkey poo poo. I'm strong and good at it.'

'Oh my goodness,' Ren said quietly. 'She's so cute she makes crap seem adorable.'

'Yes, she somehow does,' Mikie said and they all burst out laughing.

'I'll help you there, Alice,' Stephen said tenderly. 'And I'll build something to accommodate the horses. They'll need cover anyway in winter.'

'Now who wants to hear about the Incas?' Mina asked.

'Yeah!' they shouted.

Mina and Pedro were sharing a beanbag and Diego stood in the front. Mikie spotted a small hybrid waving at him and pointing to a cushion near him. He nodded, smiled, and sat next to the little grey hybrid. Then, as did everyone else, he settled back to enjoy the story. Diego had already begun.

'...I stood still, hearing the beast rush towards me, and feeling the fear run down my shaking legs. The beast was big, that much I could tell, because of the size of the trees and bushes it was making shake as it moved through the forest floor. The ground shook as if an earthquake was coming, struggling to take its weight, and I felt sure the ground would crack open under the pressure at any moment. I swallowed hard and raised my spear; shaking and sweating as the beast drew near.'

Diego paused for dramatic effect, imitating his stance with the invisible spear held above him, looking into the faces of the children. Mikie and Mina looked at each other and smiled. There were gasps, eyes being covered and heads shaking. The children were mesmerised with every word.

'He's good, Mina.'

'Yes, Mikie, I thought he might be.'

'And then it happened. The beast burst out of the bushes and jumped into the air, heading straight towards me. I screamed, Noooooooo…'

The hybrids gasped and screamed, and Diego jumped in the air, avoiding the invisible beast. He grabbed a tree and swung his muscular body around it. Pedro snuggled closer into Mina's lap.

Mikie smiled broadly and clapped. 'This is the best story I've ever heard.'

Eventually, the story was over and the beast had made it back to the village. Some of the children had fallen asleep but most were invigorated by the story and infatuated with Diego.

'Oh, my back is killing me,' Dave moaned, straightening up. 'I've been spellbound and stood in an awful position for far too long. That was a brilliant story.'

'Diego, you're a good storyteller,' Jude added.

'Yes, I have a feeling you've made a rod for your own back now,' Stephen said.

'Show us the cube, show us the cube,' the children began

shouting over and over.

'It's show time,' Mikie said.

'No...' Diego started.

'Let's do it at the shore, where there is a lot of water,' Tammy said, putting a reassuring hand on his shoulder.

'OK.' He gave in.

They all went to the nearest beach, a pebble beach not too far from the main camp. It was where the hybrids often swam and collected creatures for their learning; sea cucumbers, starfish and periwinkles. The waves gently lapped at the pebbled shore. The quads stood next to each other, along the water's edge. Ren and Suki stood with the adults, keen to see what they could do. The hybrids gathered in a group, bouncing up and down excitedly.

'I really don't think this is a good idea,' Diego said, fidgeting awkwardly from one foot to another.

'It's fine, I have plenty of water here to douse any fires,' Tammy said.

'You might not be quick enough.'

'I'll help control your thoughts too,' Mikie said. 'If I need to.'

'You know what, I find it really unnerving that you can do that.' Diego groaned.

'I'll start. Mikie will say when you can go. Just play along and you'll be fine,' Tammy said.

'They just want to enjoy the show so stop panicking.' Mina smiled.

'I just don't want to kill anyone!'

'You won't, now get a grip,' Mina said.

Tammy began. A whirlpool started and gradually grew until the water in the ocean had a large hole in it. Diego joined in, as prompted by Mikie, and raised his cube. A large storm cloud started to appear and grow above the whirlpool that Tammy had created. As the cloud grew and got darker, they could hear thunder and lightning, and everyone gasped. Then the water started to rise from the ocean, forming a waterspout, a tunnel of water that looked like a tornado. It reached from the water's surface to the cloud and then another one started to grow until there was a pair of tornadic waterspouts. It looked as if two tornadoes were travelling over the water's surface, dancing as they moved along. The lightning started to flash in between them, the sky becoming like a fireworks display.

Mikie looked over at Ed and saw him swallow hard, worried, and realised that it was a scary thing to be able to do. He smiled. He took over the minds of Dave, Ben, Stephen and Crane and made them sing and dance like apache Indians, completely unaware of what they were doing, as if they were hypnotised. Everyone howled with laughter and clapped. Mikie could see that only Ed and Jude remained straight-faced. He frowned.

Jax and Mina joined in. Jax activated his technology kit and the speakers echoed around the beach, exaggerating the storm noises and other sound elements that one might use in a movie. Mina took all the pebbles around the beach and made them move. They danced in the air and then started to form a shape. The children moved out of the way as a large pebbled snake slithered around their ankles. Jax played some creepy music to go with the snake pebbles. The pebbles grew and grew, the head of the snake rising from the ground, up into the air. As it rose, it formed a wall of pebbles beneath its head, creating a wall of stone. Mina stood in front of the wall as it rose, not stopping until it had reached her height. Then the pebbled snake swayed back and forth, looking at her menacingly, she pulled a face of fear at the children.

'No, save Mina!' they screamed.

The snake came down, opened its pebbled jaws and took Mina's head into its mouth. Mina used her camouflage to hide in the pebbles so only the lower part of her body, the part not swallowed by the snake, showed. The hybrids gasped and covered their mouths. Mikie released the dancing Indians, who suddenly became aware of what they were doing, and stopped moving. Stephen glared at Mikie, who only smiled.

Mikie did some fancy back flips and comedy karate moves on the snake, trying to free Mina. Suddenly, Kashvi flew high in the air, over the hybrids, making some of them drop to their knees and gape at her magnificence. She landed on the rock snake and tried to help Mikie. Her teeth couldn't break the rock but she walked proudly around the snake, growling threateningly. The hybrids cheered and roared with delight. Diego listened to Mikie and made a streak of lightning come down from the cloud, hit his cube and then strike the pebble snake. It shattered into a million little pebbles, back where it had started, and Mina fully appeared with Kashvi proudly at her side. Everyone cheered and laughed, and Mina held her arms wide open and bowed for effect.

Then it all went wrong.

The lightning started to bounce across the beach, barely missing the children. Diego went white, the blood draining from his face, not able to control it. Mina and Mikie jumped back, out of the way, and Ed stepped forward. The hybrids all thought this was still part of the act and laughed, not caring at all when the lightning struck close. They had no fear. One hybrid was about to get hit so Mikie took over the mind of the child nearest and got him to move them all backwards. Mina made loads of pebbles rise from the beach and created a bridge above the hybrids, which was too thick to break when the lightning struck. Ed was just about to usher everyone from the beach when Tammy used the waterspouts to suck in the lightning. The pair of waterspouts acted swiftly, swallowing the lightning like a tornado would a house, and vanished into the sea. It was over in a few moments.

The ocean was calm once more and the cloud disappeared. The children were cheering loudly and screaming for more. Ren was watching them keenly and Sukie was clinging on to Lei's arm. Diego breathed a sigh of relief and Mina laughed. Tammy whistled and shook her head, smiling at Diego.

'That was sick,' Mina said.

'I told you,' Diego replied.

'And we said it would be all right, didn't we? I said Tammy would stop it,' Mikie said.

'Well, I don't ever want to witness anything like that again,' Ed said crossly. 'That was dangerous.'

'I agree, I cannot believe what you can do,' Jude said.

'Diego, that is some seriously sick power you have there,' Stephen gushed. 'My goodness, how have you handled that all this time?'

'Rather badly, if you must know,' Diego retorted.

'Fair enough,' Stephen responded and laughed heartily.

'It's not funny,' Ed said.

'It is when no one dies,' Stephen said tartly.

Ed looked over at the excited hybrids talking about it and re-enacting the scene amongst themselves. They chatted excitedly, saying things like: 'no wonder they want to find them' and 'as if we could ever have such powers'. Ed saw the smiles on their faces and hid his anger.

'I'm not taking any risks; I'm banning you right here and right now from using any of your powers until your father comes!' Ed said simply.

'Fair enough,' Mikie said.

'What?' Ed asked, having expected an argument.

'We understand, Ed, and agree with you,' Tammy said.

'Oh, well, OK then.' Ed sighed, wondering if he could really trust them.

Kashvi looked at Tammy and winked at her. Tammy walked up to her and stroked her. It was a good way to avoid looking at Ed since he would surely know they had no intention of stopping their practice. They all knew Diego was dangerously powerful, and with the right mindset he could control his abilities better. They would have to be more secretive. It was for Ed's own sake, they had decided, since he may not handle the stress as well as they could. Only Diego considered his advice seriously and yet he knew none of them would listen to him either.

TWENTY FOUR

THALEN

THE SPACESHIP

'We should focus on your birthdays now and await your father's return,' Jude said. 'We should celebrate it in style. February the sixteenth isn't it?'

'Yes,' said Tammy.

'No,' said the others.

'What?' Jude said.

'My birthday is the thirty first of January,' Mikie said.

'Mine is December third,' said Mina.

'Twenty sixth of February,' Diego added.

'Those are the dates Sarah put on the envelopes; she must have made them up to ensure the quads celebrated their birthdays at different times,' Lei said.

'Of course – there is no point in them all having the same birthday, they would have been easier to trace,' Ed said.

'So, the question is, which birthday is the real one? Do you know, Mikie?' Stephen asked, rubbing his chin.

Mikie closed his eyes and concentrated as hard as he could, then he opened them again, and shook his head.

'December, January or February, your father could come looking for you over any of those months.' Ed sighed.

'Then when do we hold their thirteenth birthday party?' Jude asked, hands on hips.

'I guess we have to have four parties.' Jax smiled.

'No, we can just have one. We could put all of our birthdays in a hat and pull one out. That's when we celebrate,' Mikie said.

'But what if our father comes before that date and we don't get to have a party?' Mina asked.

'Since it's only late summer, we have plenty of time to decide that. Perhaps before Christmas and then we have all the Christmas celebrations on top of that. These hybrids have never had a party and none of them know when they were born,' Lei explained.

'I suggest we have a big summer party too – a formal welcome to the hybrids. Then we will need to make up their birthdays so they feel special.'

'Good idea, Stephen,' Ed agreed. 'Now, go and get an early night. I for one could do with some peace and quiet.'

They all said goodnight to Ed and Jude then walked over to their horses.

'I take it we are on the zebras again?' Ren asked.

'Yes, is that OK?' Tammy replied.

'For now, yes. But I would like something magnificent like the horses you have,' Ren admitted.

'Maybe next time.' Mina smiled kindly. Ren smiled back at her and Mina again felt her cheeks burn.

'We'll meet at the pond after they go to bed, and then

make our way to the sea lions,' Tammy said.

'Why not just tell them what we are doing? It's not a big deal to go swimming with them and it's more polite,' Mikie said.

'Yes, and no doubt they would say it's fine, but that isn't as much fun as sneaking out in the middle of the night in secrecy,' Mina giggled.

They all chuckled and ran up the stairs. Mina tripped and fell. Sukie grabbed her hand and pulled her up. Mina smiled and they all rushed off to bed.

*

They waited until they heard Ed and Jude go to bed and start snoring. Jude snored very lightly but Ed rattled like a storm. They crept out of their rooms and down the stairs, meeting outside by the pond. The horses were already there. They were at the sea lions in no time. Their swimsuits were underneath their pyjamas, which they threw to the ground, and dived in. The moon was full and bright and the sky was so clear that it was almost as bright as daylight.

They splashed around for what seemed like ages, playing with a ball – them versus the sea lions – and found that the sea lions could outsmart them all easily. Ren and Sukie were pulling each other under the water and Mina and Mikie joined in. Diego watched Jax and Tammy, seeing the occasional look they shared, and it reminded him of Quilla. He sighed and felt sad. Leaning back in the water, he floated on his back and stared up at the moon.

'Quilla,' he whispered.

'You'll see her again, soon,' Mina said.

Diego stopped floating, looked at her, and smiled.

'Meanwhile, we don't have much time to relax between now and when the first of us is thirteen, so we may as well make the most of it. Before too long there won't be much room for fun,' Mikie said.

'Stop filling us with doom and gloom,' Mina moaned.

'He's right though,' said Tammy. 'Once our father comes the war will become very real to all of us, and our combined powers will not be used to entertain children.'

'Every time I think of it I get worried and feel sick,' Mikie said.

'Understandably, dear brother,' Diego said. 'The way I see it, we will all have our thirteenth birthday and then our childhood will abruptly end and we'll be traumatised for life. If we get to have a life. We're probably just all going to die.'

'And on that cheery note, let's play some more ball,' Sukie said.

'Let's not think about it for now and enjoy the moment,' Jax agreed.

'Where's Tammy?' Mikie asked.

'She must be under the water,' Jax replied. 'She's going to get one of us!'

They all started to giggle and huddle together, waiting for Tammy to attack, but she didn't come.

'She couldn't have got out, we'd have noticed,' Mina said, frowning.

'She can hold her breath for a very long time,' Jax said, but he too was starting to sound concerned.

Then Jax screamed and disappeared under the water, soon resurfacing alongside Tammy, choking and laughing at the same time.

'That was the longest yet, even I started to get scared!' Jax said.

'I'm not so sure that's a good idea. What if it happened for real? It is like playing cry wolf,' Diego said.

'I knew where she was, I was just playing around, and you would have felt her presence too if I hadn't been blocking the telepathy,' Mikie said.

'You! Get him!' Diego shouted.

Diego and Jax jumped on Mikie and he vanished underneath the dark water. Tammy and Mina laughed and watched the struggle beneath the surface. The boys stopped, gasping for breath and laughing. Then they all floated on their backs, staring up at the moon, holding hands in a circle as the sea lions drifted around them. The stars twinkled above.

'Do you think we are being watched?' Diego asked.

'It feels like it, doesn't it?' Mina said.

'I was also getting a strange feeling. Surely no one can see us here?' Ren asked.

'Hope not,' Tammy muttered.

'I don't want to talk about it, it makes me edgy,' Jax said.

'The question would be *who* is watching us? Is it just that one spaceship or do more aliens have eyes on us?' Mikie asked.

They lay staring up at the sky as the sea lions splashed around them.

*

On the small spaceship, that hovered undetected above the

island, stood a large alien dressed in a black and red kaftan with metallic gold flecks throughout the silk material. He wore a matching head wrap that covered almost all of his head, his golden hair hidden underneath. At seven feet tall he towered over most of the other aliens, and his pale white skin stood out against the shade of his kaftan. He was an intimidating figure that made the new crew nervous. His family were tall and looked human more than alien. His head was slightly larger because his brain was bigger. His species used more of the overall brain power and capacity than the human species.

A new recruit, young and nervous, had been given the task of taking over their leader's meal. It was a plate of fruit and nuts with a glass of almond milk. His knees knocked together as he approached the back of the large figure.

'S-s-senator, your excellency, I have your d-dinner,' he stammered, hands shaking the tray he carried.

The senator turned and took the tray from the young alien and then bent down, leaning close to him. His ears, nose and mouth could have passed as human but his wide oval eyes could not. The young grey gasped as he saw the eyes, the extraordinary bright green eyes, with golden flecks in them, like a wild animal. The shock made him take a step backwards and his mouth dropped open. All aliens had dark eyes. Didn't they? His mind spun, not sure if his fear was making him imagine this or not, as he stared.

'Please, call me Thalen,' the large alien purred and smiled warmly at the grey.

Dumbfounded, the grey was rooted to the spot. The door banged open and in charged a rather strange alien. He was only four feet tall with a long, slim body covered in thick and glossy dark brown fur with white tipped hairs. His head was blunt, his ears barely visible, with tiny little eyes, and whiskers. He had webbed feet with sharp claws and his throat and chest were a creamy white colour. He rather resembled an otter. He walked fast and was irritated.

'Get out,' he shouted at the grey. 'And warn the others about his eyes so no one else has a stroke, will you? Be a good chap now, shoo shoo. Go!'

'Ah, Master Bardo, so good to see you again,' Thalen said.

'The pleasure is all mine, my dear friend.' They shook hands and took a seat facing each other over the white desk.

'Tell me, how much progress did you make?'

'None! The only one I could get through to was Diego and he thinks I'm some sort of a cartoon figure, I'm sure! He literally stood gawping at me like I was a freakish creature. Can you believe it? No respect for my culture and ancestry and how amazing my race is.' Master Bardo huffed moodily, and his whiskers twitched from side to side.

'Well, to be fair, he doesn't know anything about your ancestry, dear friend,' Thalen said, trying hard not to smile.

'My family were glorious in their day and yet I am subjected to ridicule.'

'You can't even remember your family, nor where you came from. Your planet burned up so long ago. No one remembers its name or location. So tell me, how is my son going to know? He is a young boy, too young and innocent to understand your magnificence,' Thalen soothed.

'Well, yes, perhaps you're right. He spoke to me eventually,' Master Bardo muttered.

'There you see, he did speak to you, after all.'

'Barely. He still made me feel like he was doing me a favour. ME! When I am the one doing HIM a favour. So I have just focused on training him for now. Here you are watching them so you do use a code to get past security,' Master Bardo said. He approached the computer screen hovering at the side of the desk showing several children floating in water.

'Of course I have a code. I built the protection. I'm sorry, I couldn't risk leaving it with you, just in case your mind was read. Forgive me, dear friend. I certainly make your work harder than it needs to be, don't I? Tell me about Tammy. Surely, given her connection with animals, she would have spoken with you?' Thalen clasped his hands patiently over his lap as he smiled at Master Bardo. He had known him all his life. For centuries. He was moody but highly effective.

'Her powers were dumbed down at the orphanage and I couldn't get through. On the island she is preoccupied with her horse and some boy – I can't ever get her alone.'

'And yet the report said she was not on the island at times, when she was in Africa and Japan. Could you not get to her then?'

'No. One minute she was swimming with crocodiles, another surrounded by lions or hunters – can't really stop and talk then! These children don't sit still for long, you know.' Master Bardo shook his head. 'I don't know how I can even teach them the basics. To get this lot to meditate, I'd have to sedate them. I'm not joking.'

'They'll be fine once the training program starts and they have focus. Right now they're all over the place and have no idea what's going on.'

'Well, I tried to warn Diego that he was being duped

into thinking a grey was his father and he blocked me completely. Or the grey did. I wasn't completely sure who did it.'

'It's OK, no harm was done. I watched how they handled the situation and have to say that even without training they're remarkable. Anacondas, now who would have thought!' Thalen stroked his chin.

'That was a little revolting for my liking, I have to say,' Master Bardo complained.

'I can understand that. I was close enough to watch from my screen but not close enough to get there in time. I returned as early as I could. I had not intended to come for them for a few more months, but now that they have found each other, now that their powers are creating energy waves and giving away their locations, I had to race back early. Everyone else is a couple of months behind me. I could go no faster.'

'What do we do now?' Master Bardo asked.

'Well, my dear friend, now we pop in, say hello and start their training. You should go first,' Thalen said.

'Me? Oh no, please not me.' Master Bardo's whiskers were twitching again.

'Calm down, Master Bardo. It won't be that bad. You are a spiritual guide, you must guide.'

'I don't do miniatures. I'm far too superior for that. You were the exception and besides, you are a more intelligent race.'

'Now come, that is not fair. You taught me as a boy and you must teach them.'

'They're like gorillas – cute little baby things. I don't do children. Yuck. It's unbearable. They roll their eyes, they don't wash enough, they don't even brush their teeth unless you blackmail them. I can't work under those conditions. I can't do teenagers.' Master Bardo was getting himself worked up now.

'Do you always brush your teeth and wash often?'

'Everyday without fail.' Master Bardo nodded.

'Well, you still stink of fish!'

Master Bardo gasped in horror. 'Now, you leave the fish out of this. I know what you're trying to do and it won't work. I cannot be coerced.'

'I have no intention of coercing you. I'm just telling you that as my spiritual guide, you will start work on my children now otherwise I will find someone who will and you'll be out of a job. Perhaps you can help Marcellus to embrace his spiritual side instead?' Thalen smiled kindly, knowing full well Master Bardo would never let him down. Even if he did dislike teenagers.

'This is abusive!' Master Bardo stood up and paced moodily across the room. 'Fine. Fine. I'll do it.'

'I thought you might. You know, for a spiritual guru you really are not quite as calm as I'd expect you to be. You should meditate more,' Thalen told him.

'I meditate every day, Thalen. And then I have to return to this unfortunate existence and play silly little war games with you lot.'

'I'm sure you will do a wonderful job with my children.'

'I'm telling you that the moment one of them rolls their eyes at me, they will lose an eye! That's how the great masters taught respect when I was a lad.'

Thalen watched him stomp out of the room and giggled. He had always been the same and was the best master he had ever known. Master Bardo had not wanted to teach for the last hundred years and wished to retire to a quiet place like the mountains and live alone in peace. Until then, Thalen needed his help to train his children and unleash the extent of their power. Only a true master had the energy power to do that. There were not many true masters left.

As Thalen stood up he noticed a book that had dropped on the floor. A book Master Bardo had accidentally dropped. He picked it up. The title read *How to Survive Training Human Teenagers*. It had comments and sections highlighted throughout. Thalen threw back his head and laughed heartily.

ACKNOWLEDGEMENTS

Glad to see you are still here! I learnt to read later than most children, aged about eight or nine, and once I could, there was no stopping me. I would stay awake overnight to finish a book and struggle to function in school the next day. I escaped into books every chance that I could. I acknowledge and am grateful to everyone who let me do so. To the teachers in school who grudgingly tolerated my lack of attention when I had to scribble some brilliant idea down before I forgot it. I'd like to acknowledge those adorable teachers who turned a blind eye to it and respected my creativity. Having a computer science background, I am the sort of person that needs to have science behind what I believe in. What I write is not always necessarily fantasy, and where the line is drawn is up to you to decide. Still don't think aliens are real? Let's see how you feel at the end of the series, shall we? Mwahahahahaha.

There is a brilliant video on YouTube called *209 Seconds That Will Make You Question Your Entire Existence.* I highly recommend that you watch it. I see something like that and cannot imagine that something as tiny as Earth can be the only planet with life. My biggest dream is to meet an alien in person before I die. A kind one. And intelligent would be nice, to avoid disappointment. I believe everything is possible.

I thank my children, Thomas and Olivia, for brilliant feedback and making this something we can all enjoy together. I may have written this series years ago, for my children to enjoy, yet little did I know how much they would contribute and take part in the publishing of them all. My daughter has narrated the audio books, and both have helped with digital marketing, adding scenes and characters, and gaining work experience along the way. It has been a beautiful journey and I'm super proud of them. Thank you, guys!

I would like to thank so many people, those who did the cover, type setting, audio editing, copy editing and all the extra reads and feedback from friends. To Rich Woodhouse from Electric Breeze audio, for saving the day with the audiobooks. To Vicki Hamilton for teaching me how to master typesetting in adobe indesign and becoming a valued friend. Wonderful people who helped in their spare time when they didn't have to. I thank my animals, especially Gracie, Quilla and Mishka, who have been my earth angels for longer than I know.

In addition to animals galore, each book is filled with spirituality and energy, as was *Star Wars*. With the Jedi knights in touch with "the force" around them and able to levitate and move objects, just like The Children of Pisces can. Being trained to use energy, I must thank the great teachers of this world for their precious secrets and

teaching me how we can all be superheroes in our own way if only we learn how. To all the great ones, past and present, keeping us real in this world and reminding us of who we are and what we can be.

A huge thanks to YOU for purchasing this book and reading this far. You reading and reviewing is how you help Tammy, Mikie, Mina, Diego and their family continue to grow and live in our hearts. You give them life. Thanks especially to my children's friends – for your enthusiastic feedback. I'm glad you're enjoying this. Thank you!

Don't forget – turn that page for a sneak preview of Part Four – The Return of Thalen…

THE CHILDREN OF PISCES

THE RETURN OF THALEN

PART 4

READ ON FOR A SNEAK PREVIEW
OF WHAT COMES NEXT

Mikie landed face down on the white floor and felt his nose break. Again. The pain shot through his face and he winced. As he lifted his head he could see the red blood all over the floor. Could he afford to lose this much blood again? He didn't think it was possible to re-create so much blood each day and he dreamed of having more time to recover between each session. It seemed relentless. In the tank training there was no way of knowing what time it was, whether it was morning or the middle of the night, let alone what day of the week it was. He had no idea how long this had been going on.

'Get up, Mikie, you're better than this,' Adrodus said, making an unusual whistle-like-growling noise that vibrated through every inch of Mikie's exhausted body.

Not for the first time, Mikie wondered how an orca could growl let alone move and deliver spinning wheel kicks with such speed he never seemed able to dodge them. Adrodus stood on two legs, much like a human, but still had a fluke hanging down from his lower spine. It grew out from what would be the equivalent of the human tail bone. This allowed him to function with ease both in water and on land. As far as Mikie was concerned, it defied physics for him to carry that fluke and still be able to move with such agility. No matter how much Mikie learned, this standing orca was knocking the stuffing out of him. Reluctantly, Mikie pushed himself up and limped forward, flinching every time his foot was placed on the floor.

'Your leg hurts?' Adrodus asked.

'Yes, really bad,' Mikie replied.

'How can that be? This is not real. That isn't even your leg,' Adrodus looked down his nose, or rather snout, at him.

Mikie frowned. Although he knew this, how could he feel his leg hurting? He closed his eyes and tried to visualise his leg cured. He told himself that he wasn't really there. He went into his mind and tried everything he could think of to make the pain go away. Eventually, he gave up. He balanced on one leg, ready for the next attack, and braced for impact as Adrodus made a clicking noise and raced towards him. They fought, Adrodus delivering kicks, punches and chops faster than Mikie could deflect them. Adrodus dropped and swung his body around, using his leg to sweep Mikie's feet off the ground, and Mikie went hard down on his back. His head banged with force on the floor and the wind was knocked out of him. He lay dazed and coughing.

Adrodus jumped into the air and landed on him, bringing his fist down towards his face, and stopping just before impact. 'This is pathetic. You cannot be the son of Thalen. You are far too weak.'

Mikie stared into his eyes, angry and frustrated. Pushing him away, he struggled to his feet. Fury coursed through his body and his breathing increased rapidly.

'That anger will only cause your defeat,' Master Bardo told him. 'That is not the kind of energy you need. Think, Mikie, what do you need to do?'

Mikie took a deep breath, worked hard to slow his breathing and emotions down, and clenched his fists as he focused on the air around him.

'That's not air,' Master Bardo said.

Mikie frowned. If this wasn't air then this wasn't breath. And yet somehow he was breathing like this in the tank and feeling this anger for real. As he practiced his breathing and connected to the fake world around him, Mikie started to feel the water around his real body submerged in the training tank. He focused on that. The water on his hands, his body floating and no longer resting on the board they slept on. They floated during training. Their bodies moved as they did in the virtual dojo. He felt his buoyancy. He felt his real body. He connected to the demand valve in his mouth and felt the air being drawn in via the small and silent device. He felt the pain in his leg disappearing.

Adrodus turned to look at Master Bardo and raised an impressed eyebrow. This had not happened before. Mikie was starting to adapt to his artificial environment. And then Mikie, calm and calculated, looked up at Adrodus and smiled. Mikie moved into a defence stance, held one hand out front, and moved his fingers twice, beckoning Adrodus to attack, all pain in his leg now gone. Adrodus half smiled, one side of his mouth turning upwards. This was more like it. They fought again, faster this time, Mikie blocking every move, not even trying, glaring into Adrodus's eyes. He almost managed to hit Adrodus once. And then Adrodus hit him hard in the chest, landing a flat palm right in the middle of his solar plexus, and Mikie fell back, winded again.

'Come on, you're faster than this,' Adrodus said.

Mikie flipped himself back up on his feet and started to attack Adrodus with even more determination. He moved so fast that Master Bardo could only see the blur of arms flashing between the bodies of Mikie and Adrodus. Thalen appeared next to Master Bardo. They watched intently, impressed with the speed with which Mikie was moving. Adrodus grabbed Mikie by the shoulders. Mikie used his forearms fast in an upward movement and forced both arms away. He grabbed hold of Adrodus's arms and ran up the front of his body, flipping over backwards when he reached the top of his chest, and pulled Adrodus head over heels with him. Adrodus landed, did the same to Mikie, who did the same again to Adrodus. Then they fell, both still holding onto each other's arms, rolling around on the floor, wrapping their legs around each other until neither of them could move anymore.

'Get up, this is no time to cuddle,' Master Bardo barked. 'Get up!'

They let each other go and faced each other again.

'Maybe you are Thalen's son after all,' Adrodus said, smiling. And then flew up into the air and kicked Mikie hard in the face.

Thalen turned and looked at Master Bardo. 'He's faster than anyone I have ever seen so early on in training.'

'Not fast enough,' Master Bardo said, checking his computer and bringing up a screen with a dial on the front. 'I'm activating him more. He is faster than this.'

'If you are sure, Master Bardo. He has lost a lot of blood.'

'He still has more to spare.' Master Bardo pressed a button that made the dial increase to the red range. A message flashed danger and Master Bardo ignored it.

Mikie froze. His body started to convulse as it adapted to the increased energetic activation level. Blood came out of his eyes, ears and nose. Adrodus couldn't watch anymore and he looked away until it was over. It reminded him of the time he was here for training many years ago but he never advanced to the red zone. Mikie was going to a level Adrodus had never been able to reach. It was hard to watch.

ABOUT THE AUTHOR

Rachael started writing short stories and poems at a young age and had a poem published in America. She wrote her first novel aged thirteen, entered a few competitions and was then distracted by almost thirty years of a successful IT career and motherhood. From admin support, technical author, trainer to technical project manager. She never stopped writing, completing seven books (five for *The Children of Pisces*) while she stayed home as a single mother raising her one-year-old twin son and daughter and working as a childminder. During the COVID-19 lockdown, she introduced her eleven-year-old twins to this series, who fell in love with it.

She is at her happiest making up adventures in a quiet room with the fire crackling and cats jumping on the keyboard. Rachael loves to have fun, jumping out of a perfectly good plane, diving deep beneath the ocean, swimming with dolphins and taking her children in a hot air balloon over the Valley of the Kings in Egypt. They barely survived! She believes life is best lived to the full. Over the years, she has broadened her experiences from computer science to energy healing by becoming a holistic well-being coach for people and animals, studying Energy,

Aromatherapy and Zoopharmacognosy, as well as helping nurture creativity in others, including her children.

West Midlands-born Rachael grew up surrounded by animals in North Devon, caring alone for over sixty rabbits when she was just thirteen and now having "not yet enough" pets, including five dogs and eight cats. Rachael lives in a rural area on the River Thames, on the border of Berkshire and Oxfordshire. Once her twins have finished education, she aims to have a remote retreat where people and their pets can come to heal and replenish while she and her children keep on writing. Say hello to her on Twitter: @RachaelRuthH, Youtube: @RachaelRuth, Facebook & Instagram: @rachaelruthholistic or TikTok @relewin.

Printed in Poland
by Amazon Fulfillment
Poland Sp. z o.o., Wrocław

25932903R10237